To Shine with Honor

Book One: Coming of Age

By Joseph Scott Amis

To Shine with Honor, Book One: Coming of Age
Copyright 2016 Joseph Scott Amis

Published by: Real Crusades History

Print Edition
ISBN-13: 978-0-9976668-2-3

This book is also available in e-book editions at major online retailers.

For Gayle

Table of Contents

ENGLAND

COLOGNE •

HOLY ROMAN EMPIRE

• ROUEN

REIMS •

PARIS •

TROYES •

LOIRE RIVER

TOURS •

• VEZELAY
• NEVERS

• D

LIMOGES •

• C

CLERMONT •

• B

A •

• LYON
• VIENNE

LE PUY •

KINGDOM OF FRANCE

KINGDOM OF BURGUNDY

CHRISTIAN SPAIN

ISLAMIC SPAIN

BARCELONA

FICTIONAL LOCATIONS
A. THE BARONY OF MIREFLUERS
B. THE COUNTY OF SAINT-LILLE
C. MONT-BRISON
D. THE ABBÉ DE SAINT-AMAND

FRANCE CA. 1095

JOSEPH SCOTT AMIS

Cast of Characters

Coudre Family

Henri de Coudre - *knight, b. 1041*
Gabriele de Coudre - *wife of Henri, b. 1042*
Thierré de Coudre - *first son, knight, b. 1067*
Martin de Coudre - *second son, knight, b. 1070*
Galien de Coudre - *third son, student & scribe, b. 1072*
Alisende de Coudre - *daughter, b. 1074*

Evreux Family

Bayard d'Evreux - *Count of Saint-Lille, b. 1040*
Rosemonde d'Evreux - *Countess of Saint-Lille, b. 1043*
Gautier d'Evreux - *first son, knight, b. 1065*
Evrard d'Evreux - *second son, knight, b. 1068*
Beatrice d'Evreux - *wife of Gautier, b. 1055*
Olivier d'Evreux - *brother of Bayard, knight, b. 1044*
Renauld d'Evreux - *son of Olivier, knight, b. 1058*

Other Significant Characters

The Barony of Mirefleurs and the County of Saint-Lille
Alphonse de Rives - *Baron of Mirefleurs, b. 1046*
Sybille de Rives - *niece of Baron Alphonse, b. 1074*
Père Barnard - *resident priest at Fortress Mirefleurs, b. 1025*

Walter d'Avesnes - *Marshal of the Barony of Mirefleurs, b. 1039*
Enguerrand de Betancourt - *Viscount of Nevers, b. 1039*
Baldwin de Betancourt - *son of Enguerrand, knight, b. 1065*
Odo - *Viscount of Saint-Lille, b. 1038*
Roger de Lyon - *knight, b. 1060*
Jean Loudon - *knight, b. 1067*
Lorens Saint-Georges - *guard captain at Coudre Estate, b. 1070*
Paul and Lucie - *Coudre family servants, b. 1021*
Clement de Sens - *nobleman, b. 1074*
Otto Huber - *sergeant & executioner, b. 1051*
Reinhard Huber - *sergeant & executioner, b. 1053*
Lienart - *battle surgeon, b. 1039*
Alain - *armorer, b. 1069*
Lisette - *wife of armorer Alain, b. 1073*
Michel - *armorer and brother of Alain, b. 1072*
Robert - *Coudre Estate peasant farmer and man-at-arms, b. 1048*
Etien - *Coudre Estate peasant farmer and man-at-arms, b. 1048*
Milon - *son of Etien, b. 1076*
Jules - *peasant, b. 1070*
Clovis - *peasant, b. 1071*

The Abbé de Saint-Amand
Leo - *Abbot of the Abbé de Saint-Amand, b. 1031*
Benedict - *monk, priest, and scholar, b. 1056*
Joseph of Reims - *architect and monk, b. 1056*
Charles Falcard - *postulant monk, b. 1074*
Anseau - *postulant monk, b. 1071*
Sylvestrus - *monk, b. 1031*
Ernoul - *monk, b. 1061*

Troyes
Ulrich - *Bishop of Troyes, b. 1023*
Ludovico Santovini - *wealthy Troyes merchant, b. 1031*
Pernelle - *Troyes noblewoman, b. 1075*
Claire - *daughter of Troyes inn owner, b. 1075*

Historical Persons

Urban II (Odo of Châtillon), *Pope 1088-1099. b. ca. 1042, d. 1099.*
Adhémar of Monteil, *Bishop of le Puy, ca. 1082-1098. b. ca. 1040, d. 1098*
Guy of Burgundy, *Archbishop of Vienne, 1088-1119; Pope Calixtus II, 1119-1124. b. ca. 1065, d. 1124*
Peter the Hermit, *mendicant preacher. b. ca. 1050, d. 1115*

JOSEPH SCOTT AMIS

Part I

JOSEPH SCOTT AMIS

Chapter 1

7 April 1086, the town of Grand-Forêt, southeastern France

Galien de Coudre drew a sharp breath. Beneath a shield-shaped sign painted with crossed swords, his father, his brother Martin, and his sister Alisende waited, but Thierré wasn't with them. Galien clenched his fists and gritted his teeth. His unspeakable eldest brother could have at least shown him the honor of joining the family for his day of coming of age.

As he walked over the cobbled lane winding among the cottages, Galien put aside his bitter thoughts. His family greeted him warmly. He pushed his long, sandy-brown hair back, straightened his gambeson, and stepped up into the armorer's workshop. The proprietor Jacques laid a bundle on the table and rolled away the deerskin, to reveal a superbly crafted belt and scabbard with a hilt showing. Galien reached out, uneasy, only touching the pommel. Henri de Coudre put a hand on his son's shoulder and said, "Go ahead, draw it."

Galien did as his father bade. The leather grip felt just right in his hand. He turned around to study the newly-forged weapon. No better sword was to be had, of singular purpose and fit for a knight of great prowess: thirty-eight inches from point to top of weighty domed pommel, broad thirty-two-inch blade with two cutting edges, of elegantly tapered proportion, not adorned save small crosses of inlaid silver. At two-and-a-half pounds in weight, a perfectly balanced sword that could strike off an arm with a keen edge and punch through a hauberk with the hardened steel point. Galien held it up before his face. With the plain nine-inch steel handguard set between blade and grip, it made for a distinctive reminder of the Cross of Christ.

He looked at his father. "It's wonderful, but I'll not need it at cathedral school. You surely spent three livres to get me a knight's blade."

Henri chuckled. "Galien, you know I make certain each of my sons has the best sword I can buy at his coming of age and knows how to wield it, become he knight, priest, or diplomat." With this, Henri reached into his belt purse, took out a heavy silver seal ring, and slid it onto the forefinger of Galien's right hand. "You're a man now, and fully fit to take your place beside your brothers."

Galien stood, red-faced, as his father buckled the sword belt around his waist and stepped back, smiling with pride at his third son. Martin de Coudre, at sixteen, two years Galien's senior and a young man bound for knighthood, shook his hand and embraced him; Alisende, already tall and pretty at twelve years, hugged his neck and kissed his cheeks.

A man-at-arms stepped up from the lane. "Sir Henri, Baron Alphonse would have you come to the fortress, right away."

"Is Bayard starting more trouble?"

"My lord, it's not Count Bayard this time. Peter de Villiers has blocked the road to Vézelay with a force of mercenaries, and Baron Alphonse needs your counsel."

Henri sighed. "I'd hoped to spend the day with you, but a knight's duties too often bear no regard for family."

"Father, I ought to come along," Martin said.

"No, son. I'd not deprive Galien and Alisende of your company. All of you enjoy this fine day together." Henri handed Galien a green leather bag bulging with coins, and turned to walk away with the man-at-arms.

Galien and Martin each held one of Alisende's hands in their own as they strolled at their ease. Alisende said "I'm hungry!" and Galien gave her a denier, bidding her buy herself a sweet. The brothers watched her trot toward the center of Grand-Forêt, circled with thatch-roofed buildings and cottages, crowded with people of the Barony of Mirefleurs come for the market fair held in the week after Easter. Galien took a seat on the grass, his back against the trunk of an old oak tree. With his new sword and scabbard over his knees, he absently toyed with the bronze chape at the end of the belt. After a quiet minute, he heard Martin say, "What troubles you?"

"I'm not so sure I want to go into the Church."

Martin looked at him, surprise on his face. "You've never told me that before, and you've always been so pious."

"With cathedral school near, I've been thinking more."

"Has that sword got you to thinking of the knight's life?"

Galien drew his sword a halfscore inches from the scabbard and lovingly ran a finger over the blade. "Perhaps it has."

"Maybe you ought to ask father if he'll let you become a knight instead."

"No, the soldier's life is for you and our wretched excuse for a brother. I'll go into the Church and become a bishop like father wants. Truly though, all I want is a quiet life of study and writing, with a wife who understands me. Right now, I'm making enough silver with my scribe work to think of marrying. Had father given me the coin he paid for this sword and scabbard, I could have a five-acre freehold and a sturdy cottage."

"Galien, Father and Mother didn't have you schooled in letters so you could live like a peasant. Besides, how could a charming and good-looking young nobleman like you not rise high in the Church?" Galien only grunted, and Martin nudged him with a grin. "High Church officials don't lack for women."

At that moment, Alisende returned, excited to see the sights of the market fair, and Galien said, "We'll talk more about it later."

The marketplace, crowded with people of all stations, smelled of freshly-baked bread and pastry, roasting meats, and human bodies. Galien and his brother and sister browsed tents and tables of food and drink, wares, and services of all varieties, tasting of the samples freely offered. With the coin his father had given him, Galien bought a deep-red cap embroidered with intricate golden designs for Alisende and a silver-mounted wine flask for Martin, but had not enough left for a dagger he fancied for himself.

A grimy hunched man in a ragged crimson robe approached them. "Good lords and lady, I've just returned from the Holy Land and with me, I carry relics of God's saints." He held up a tiny silver vial, whispering through snaggly teeth, "Indeed, the Blood of Our Lord Himself."

Alisende gasped with wonderment, but Galien said, "The Turks in the Holy Land not let any Christians pass in peace. Take your cat bones and sheep's blood elsewhere." Galien stared at the charlatan until he shuffled off to seek his next victim, and Alisende pulled him toward a trio of dogs doing clever tricks. She watched them clapping with delight, and Martin gave their trainer a denier.

Galien saw the stone church across the busy market and handed Alisende the green bag, which yet held twoscore silver deniers. "Sister, go to the priest and fetch the parchment and quills he had made for me."

"I'll go if we can draw and do letters tonight, and you'll give me some wine."

"We'll draw and do letters, but I won't give you wine until you're fourteen and old enough for Father to let you marry."

Alisende stuck her tongue out at him. "You only turned fourteen today, and I'll not marry until I can choose my own man, no matter what Father wants."

"Fourteen is old enough to serve duty at arms and get killed by Count Bayard's raiders. Now, go and do as I told you." Alisende stuck out her tongue again and dashed toward the church, long blond hair flying from beneath her fine new cap.

Martin mused, "Too bad Thierré is on patrol today and can't be with us." Galien didn't answer, and Martin elbowed him.

Galien snorted. "Can't you see I'm brokenhearted?" He ground his teeth at the thought of his bullying eldest brother and spoke no more.

Martin broke the tense quiet. "I wish you two could get along."

"The lout could have left patrol duty to be there when Father gave me my sword and ring. He's never thought of me as anything but a bookrat."

Martin smiled, stroking his short, dark beard, already heavy at his sixteen years. "You might be a bookrat, but you're as good at sword and horse as any knight. I've never understood why Thierré doesn't at least show you some respect for that. I've given up hope that the bad blood between you will end."

"It doesn't matter. He's a knight now, and I'll be in cathedral school. We'll soon be rid of each other until the Last Judgment, but I swear, if he calls me 'runt' one more time, I'm going to hit him. I don't care how big and tough he is."

"Forget about Thierré for today, Galien. Think of the fine supper that Mother has waiting in your honor."

"Mother should stay in bed. She's in no condition to be making a bother over me."

"Indeed," Martin said, nodding gravely. "But no one alive, not even Father, can tell her what to do."

As Galien and Martin waited for Alisende, friends and acquaintances spoke to them, and Galien graciously accepted the many well-wishes for his coming of age. Shortly, Alisende returned from the church. Galien took his cloth-wrapped writing supplies, smiling to himself. Already, his precocious command of written French and Latin and his neat, artistic Carolingian lettering were putting plenty of silver into his purse while Thierré dumbly hacked away at the pell with his sword.

Martin spoke up. "I'll buy us the best wine at the tavern."

"Might I have some unwatered wine, Martin?" Alisende said.

"Sister, today we'll let you have a taste, in celebration. I don't think Mother would mind."

They walked toward the tavern, Galien grateful to God for his good-natured brother Martin and his sweet, innocent sister. Two boys of their age, sons of peasant farmers on their father's lands, sat on a low stone wall at the edge of the market area, taking long swallows from an earthenware pitcher of strong ale; a younger boy sat beside them, not drinking.

"Look, Jules," one said, sniggering, "The holy man Galien de Coudre is wearing a sword. It's nearly as long as he is."

Jules flashed an insolent grin. "And he's swaggering around like a knight."

Galien gripped his sword hilt. He let go of Alisende's hand, walked to the boy, and held up his seal ring. "Yes, Jules, I now bear the authority of my father, and I've caught you and Clovis poaching in his forest one time too many."

Martin took Galien's arm and grabbed the pitcher from the older boys. He poured the ale onto the ground and said, "Take Galien's words to be a fair warning. My father's never had you flogged for your mischief, but you don't know what his youngest son might do."

Jules looked at Martin, hostile resentment in his eyes. "What about our ale?"

"You two troublemakers best not drink in public places. But if you want more ale, find yourselves some honest work for a change." Martin and Galien again took Alisende by her hands. As they walked toward the market, Clovis could be heard to say, "The Devil damn all noblemen to Hell."

Galien looked back, but the two older boys had vanished into the maze of alleys and lanes between the cottages and buildings. The younger boy, about ten years of age, yet remained. Galien said to him, "Milon, why do you keep following those two around? They'll only get into trouble and try to cast the blame on you."

Milon shrugged. "I'm not of a landed family, and I'll never get to be a knight, so who cares?"

"Milon, my father cares, and yours certainly does. Etien is the most respected man-at-arms in the barony, and you'll eventually gain the same respect."

"I know, Galien, but it's not the same as being a knight."

"Well, you know you're always welcome at the house to practice with my father and me." Milon nodded halfheartedly, Martin tousled his hair, and the Coudre brothers and sister continued their walk to the tavern.

At the tavern, Galien spotted a familiar black and grey stallion in the horse shelter. He turned to Martin and Alisende, scowling. "Thierré's inside, no doubt drinking more than he should."

Martin put a hand on Galien's shoulder. "Let's at least speak a word with him. Surely, he'll be decent to you on your coming-of-age day."

They didn't have to go inside. With his three men-at-arms behind, Thierré de Coudre came from the front door of the tavern and walked toward his horse. The nineteen-year-old knight's head was bare; his handsome clean-shaven face framed with blond hair falling past his shoulders; his helmet and the mail coif and padding under his left arm.

He looked Galien up and down. "Our little man looks so gallant today, with fine clothes and a sword. Have you finally found yourself a girl?"

"Thierré, you know this is Galien's day of coming of age," Martin said. "You need to give him the honor he's due."

Galien met Thierré's stare, smelling the wine on his brother's breath. Thierré sneered, "Truly, I'd forgotten. But now that the runt's old enough to serve as my squire, I'll give him the honor of lacing on my coif, and then he can run along and play with his sister."

Galien glared back, feeling the Norman blood of his mother come to full boiling fury. He snapped, "Any God-cursed filthy corpse robber would make a better knight than you are, *Brother*."

Alisende put her fingers to her mouth. With face red and eyes wide, she gasped, "Galien! How could you say such a thing?"

Thierré took a step forward. At six feet, he stood five inches taller than his youngest brother. He shoved Galien hard. "Mind your mouth, boy!" Galien staggered, but quickly regained his balance. He swung his right hand, punching Thierré squarely in the face. Thierré wiped away the blood running from his nose. Veins bulged at his temples as his blue eyes turned icy. He whipped out his razor-edged dagger, growling, "I'm going to save the Church the trouble of making a eunuch of you."

A crowd began to gather, drawn by the curses and commotion. Well-dressed nobles stood side-by-side with humbler folk to watch the sons of the honorable knight Henri de Coudre fight their feud before a good many people of the Barony of Mirefleurs; eager boys who would be warriors cheered them on. Thierré took a wide, taunting slash at Galien, and a noblewoman cried, "Guardsmen!"

Steel rang as Galien drew his sword. With his mail hauberk gleaming dully in the sunlight, Thierré took fighting stance, waited grinning, and suddenly lunged with the dagger. Galien deftly pivoted aside and stuck out a foot. Thierré stumbled on it but didn't lose his timing. In one swift motion, he drew his own sword and took position, saying, "So, you want a real fight, boy?"

Galien took the long guard and muttered, "Don't try me, you drunken fool."

Men-at-arms in guardsmen's colors grabbed Galien from behind and took his sword. Burly veteran sergeant Otto Huber punched Thierré, knocking him off his feet. He grabbed Thierré's arm and pulled him up. "I'm taking both of you to the dungeon. Make it easy or hard, at your choice."

Thierré snatched his arm from Otto's grasp. "I'll see you flogged, Huber," he spat.

Otto grabbed him by his hauberk and drew him close. "Take it up with Baron Alphonse and your father. You'll be getting the flogging, and I'll be more than happy to lay it on."

Thierré grew quiet at this fearsome prospect. He stood still beside Galien while the guardsmen manacled their wrists, and walked docilely as they were pushed toward the oak-barred prison wagon.

The wagon bumped and shook on unsprung wheels along the narrow trod-earth road leading through the dense forest between Grand-Forêt and Fortress Mirefleurs, Baron Alphonse's stronghold and the place of governance for the Barony of Mirefleurs. Galien and Thierré, at last bound as brothers in dread of their father's wrath and the sure and painful punishment that awaited them, stared at their feet, fearing to talk to one another. Thierré finally spoke above the groaning of wood and rattling of metal. He shook his head ruefully. "You showed a knight's courage and skill back there, and I must give you honor."

"To Hell with honor. Did you truly intend to take my manhood?"

"Of course not. I only wanted to scare you. But I must admit, you're rather quick on your feet and with that sword. Has Father been teaching you?"

"He has. You only come home from the fortress for Sunday supper. I practice with Father in the front court on weekdays, and with the men-at-arms who live on the estate when they come to the house."

"With all that behind you, you'll be the best priest-at-sword in the whole Church."

Galien raised an eyebrow and smiled. "Today, I'm not feeling so eager to take up my destiny in the Church, but 'priest-at-sword'... I like that idea." The wagon rounded a bend. Fortress Mirefleurs loomed, massive and grey, at the top of the low hill ahead. The brothers turned pale and fell into silence.

Chapter 2

8 April 1086, Coudre Manor, the Barony of Mirefleurs

Daylight was breaking as Galien and Thierré rode into the front court of their father's house and handed their horses off to the stableman. Elderly servant Paul opened the massive oaken front door for them, bowed, and said, "Sir Henri is waiting for you at the table."

The brothers shuffled into the great room that occupied the largest part of the first floor of the century-old estate house. Paul opened the shutters covering the windows, casting the space in morning light, revealing plain and sturdy construction: stone-flagged floor, plastered walls, and hewn beams bearing the ceiling above. Henri de Coudre sat waiting on a bench at the family table, the hardened soldier's face which could be so pleasant now dark with fury, close-cropped salt-and-pepper hair and beard standing on end. Martin sat beside him; their mother Gabriele and Alisende, conspicuously absent. The errant brothers took seats across from their father. Paul and his wife Lucie brought a pitcher of water and cups and quickly retreated.

Henri glowered at Galien and Thierré in turn, and first spoke to the elder. "*Sir* Thierré de Coudre, is it, eh? I thought, at long last, I had a fine young knight and a fit heir in my first son, and now I find he hasn't shed his drunken brawling ways."

He stared until Thierré lowered his eyes, and then turned to Galien. "And you, *Father* Galien? A man of God turns the other cheek, but you took the name of the Lord in vain before half the barony and drew your sword on your brother."

Henri leaned back, glaring at his sons. Thierré grew even paler, and Galien's right eyebrow twitched as they waited.

Henri drew himself up, fists clenched on the table. "Both of you have dishonored your father and your family in a way I thought not possible, and to make it even worse, while your mother is so ill. Thierré, were we not facing a long siege at Vézelay come midsummer, you'd be spending your training days in the fortress stables with Jules and Clovis, shoveling out horse shit for the next six months. Galien, I'm not so surprised at Thierré, but you? You're a lettered young man who's to serve the Church, and you're a worse disgrace than your drunkard of a brother."

Tense silence fell upon the room. Henri took a drink of water, then addressed Thierré and Galien. "Baron Alphonse wanted to keep you in the dungeon for a week and have Sergeant Huber flog you, but in consideration of our friendship and the honor of our house, he released you and remanded your punishment to me."

Henri turned to Martin. "You are to witness humbly. Show no pride in your innocence, lest you be included."

He stood. "Thierré and Galien, go to the tree behind the stable and wait for me. Martin, bid the guards and Paul come out. Alisende and Lucie are to stay inside and watch over your mother. This is no matter for women."

Ten minutes later, Galien and Thierré stood at the oak tree at the north end of the timber-and-plaster stable building. A door opened, and Martin, the two men-at-arms, and Paul stepped out into the morning sunshine. Henri came from the main house, carrying a thick, supple leather strap, two feet long and a thumb wide. He crossed the grassy half-acre court fronting the house and stables and faced his sons. "Take off your shirts. Thierré, you're first."

Thierré grasped the oak tree with both hands, bare back exposed. Henri took stance behind him, drew the strap back, and swung in a fast, hard arc. Galien jumped, and his throat clenched at the loud crack as it hit flesh. Thierré jerked but made no sound. A broad red welt swelled on his back as Henri said "One," and drew the strap back for a second blow.

Galien watched in fear and fascination, wincing at each sharp crack as Henri continued the flogging, taking care to cover Thierré's entire back. Sweat dripped from Thierré's face and blood ran down his chin as he bit his lower lip. Henri counted "Six," drew back, and struck Thierré across the shoulders with extra force. He called "Seven," and lowered the strap.

Thierré sagged against the tree, taking deep, gasping breaths. His back was crisscrossed with welts, but he had not cried out. After a minute, he stumbled over to the witnesses, and Martin handed him a cup of water.

At his father's nod, Galien took a like position at the tree, drew a deep breath, and gripped hard. He heard the strap hiss through the air, and his lower back exploded in violent pain. Tears flowed down his cheeks, and he clenched his teeth to near breaking as Henri continued the methodical blows. By "Six," his back and senses were numb, and he hardly felt the seventh lash. He held tight to the tree to keep from falling to his knees, and when he regained his breath, weaved over to Martin.

Galien felt his father's piercing eyes on him, and all came to attention at Henri's commanding voice. "Punishment is complete and this matter is closed."

Henri pointed a rigid finger at Thierré. "You will not insult or demean your brother again," and turning to Galien, "You will behave as befits a man of God, and keep your sword sheathed. He swept his glare over both of them. "You will make peace between yourselves today, and henceforth conduct yourselves as the sons of an honorable noble house should."

Henri strode toward the front door of the house, then turned and spoke once more. "I sincerely trust that the same offenses will not happen again. If they do, you'll get a taste of the bullwhip from Sergeant Huber and spend two weeks in the dungeon on bread and horse water."

The men-at-arms returned to their guard posts. Galien followed his brothers into the cool, dark stable and slumped onto a bench, next to Thierré. Paul came with cloths and a basin of water. When they had washed their faces, Paul began to carefully rub soothing liniment onto Thierré's back. Galien gulped water and Martin refilled the cup. He sipped slowly until Paul finished with Thierré and began to work on his back. He jumped at Paul's first touch, but soon the liniment felt as good as a draught of strong wine.

Thierré was looking at him. "You didn't make a sound."

"I didn't?"

"None at all."

"Truly, then? I lost my senses halfway through."

"The old man gave us what's called a soldiers' flogging at the fortress. A disgrace in front of your fellows and hurts like the torments of Hell, but doesn't tear the skin off your back, like a bullwhip does. Yet, I've seen ten-year veterans break down crying after the fifth lash."

Galien raised an eyebrow. "Hmm."

"I got one myself, during my service days," Paul said. "You both took it like knights."

Thierré snorted. "Your service days? Defending Gaul from Julius Caesar?"

The white-haired servant chuckled, shaking his head. "Not that long ago, Master Thierré, but still more than a few years past. Baron Alphonse's grandfather and yours didn't spare on discipline."

Thierré put a careful hand on his brother's raw shoulder. "You did take it like a knight, Galien. I'm proud to have you for a brother."

"I've always been proud to call him my brother, Thierré," Martin said, with a smug look.

Thierré glanced sheepishly from Martin to Galien. "I say better late than not. Agreed, Galien?"

"Give me one good reason I should trust you. I can't think of any."

Thierré bowed his head. "I can only give the knight's oath to show my best will."

"That's well and good, but you must make your full apologies, and henceforth treat me with the respect due a man of my station."

Thierré put his right hand out to Galien. "On my knight's oath, you have my apologies and my promise."

Galien looked hard at Thierré. "If you ever call me 'runt' again, Father will know before you can blink an eye. Only a bagful of Roman gold might buy my silence."

Thierré held up his hands. "You've cornered me for a death blow."

"Then I'll have to give you a chance." Galien took Thierré's hand and they shook.

Paul brought an earthenware pitcher of wine from the kitchen building. After all had taken a long swallow, Martin looked at Galien and said, "When do you leave for Paris?"

"The first day in December. I'll be far away from home for the Christmas season."

"That gives you plenty of time for your studies."

"No, I've already done what I need to be ready for cathedral school. Since Father doesn't want me to risk getting killed serving duty at arms, Alisende and I will keep managing the estate accounts for Mother and I'll do scribe work for the rest of the time."

Martin winked at Thierré. "I think a swordsman like Galien might be finding such a life boring."

Thierré stroked his chin. "I can't help but agree. Perhaps Father would permit him to ride some patrols well away from Bayard's raiders and practice at the fortress, with the men-at-arms. What do you think, Galien?"

Galien grinned eagerly. "If Father gives his consent, I'll be riding out with you and Martin on the morrow. My sore back doesn't matter."

Thierré went to the arming room and returned, carrying two wooden sparring swords. He tossed one to Galien.

"Are you sure? All the men practice under my eye. We've agreed to put our past behind us, but that doesn't mean I'll allow anyone to let you off easy."

Galien took another pull off the pitcher, stood, and took ready stance, sword up. "As Father's son and your brother, I need to be an example and take your abuse better than the next man."

Thierré raised his sword. "If that's what you want, so be it, but don't complain that I didn't warn you."

JOSEPH SCOTT AMIS

Chapter 3

17 September 1086, Fortress Mirefleurs

Alisende held tight to Galien's hand as they turned away from their mother's newly-dug grave in the chapel burial yard, hearing spadesful of earth rattling on her coffin. Stout, lushly bearded Alphonse de Rives, Baron of Mirefleurs, put a big hand on each of their shoulders, squeezing them gently. He said, "None know how long the siege at Vézelay will last. Galien, though you and Alisende grieve for your mother, you now have full charge as master and mistress of Coudre Estate, until, by God's grace, your father and brothers return."

Galien stood straight, left hand on the pommel of his sword. "Sire, you need not fear for us or Coudre Estate. What I fear most is my father learning of Mother's passing, but he needs to be told, right away."

"Of that, you can be certain, Galien. My fastest horseman will leave for Vézelay within the hour. But now, you need to be a man worthy of your ring and sword."

5 October 1086, Coudre Manor

After Paul and Lucie took away the remains of breakfast, Galien stood working at his writing desk beneath a window in the big second-floor chamber he'd shared with his brothers; Alisende beside him in a chair, embroidery on her lap. "Galien... do you hear horses?"

As he looked out the window, a knight with a lance flying an unfamiliar banner rode between the gateposts into the front court,

Thierré and Martin close behind him, carrying the banners of Mirefleurs and the Coudre family. Galien dropped his quill, splattering ink over his freshly-lettered parchment. "They're home, Alisende!"

Brother and sister rushed down the corridor and stair, and Galien swung the heavy oaken front door open. Thierré, Martin, and the knight got off their horses, but as Galien and Alisende ran out to greet them, an enclosed wagon rumbled past the gateposts. Thierré took Galien's arm. "Father's in the wagon, and he's hurt near to death. Get on your horse and fetch the physician in Le Puy, and give no care to the cost."

+ + +

The sun moved lower in the mid-afternoon sky, and Paul and Lucie closed the shutters to the colder air. Before the fire in the great room, Henri de Coudre lay on the bed carried from his second-floor chamber. The Coudre brothers and sister, Baron Alphonse, fortress priest Père Barnard, and the knight who had ridden with Martin and Thierré stood around as the physician cut away the bandages, hard and sticky with dried blood, covering the stump of Henri's right hand. Henri, drowsy with the physician's potion of wine, herbs, and extract of poppy, gritted his teeth and tears flowed from his eyes, but he made not a sound.

Only the crackling of the fire could be heard as the physician cleaned the bare stump with astringent wine, sniffed for odors of rot, felt the flesh, and examined the stitches made in the battlefield hospital tent. Placing what remained of Henri's forearm on clean cloths, he addressed the eldest son. "Sir Thierré, by all rights, your father should have died before you left Vézelay, but the man who tended to this ghastly wound was surely guided by the hand of God."

"That man was our own Sergeant Lienart," Thierré said.

"In shortening the bone and stitching the wound for the best chance of healing, a schooled physician could have done no better, and a man of less fortitude than Sir Henri might have died of a failed heart from the pain of the treatment."

"Will he live?"

"He has an even chance. Blood poisoning will certainly set in, but if the flesh not turn gangrenous, he will live. If it begins to smell foul and rancid and turn black, he will very likely die. Your Sergeant

Lienart sounds to be the best man to take care of Sir Henri. Summon him, have him stay at Sir Henri's bedside, and I'll come back on the day after the morrow."

Alphonse rose. "It shall be as you wish, physician. Père Bernard will say Mass for our dear Henri every day." Barnard stood over Henri and said the Pater Noster, and he and Alphonse left to join the men-at-arms from the fortress, waiting outside. Paul escorted Martin, Thierré, and their knightly guest to the arming room, to help the battle-weary warriors exchange their blood-caked mail for a bath and fresh clothes.

+ + +

Lienart arrived as dusk was turning to dark. He took a chair at Henri's bedside, opening his surgeon's kit while the others gathered at the family table. Paul and Lucie brought food and wine, and Thierré, seeing Alisende glancing with interest at their guest, said, "Our father's life is in the hands of God and the capable men attending him. Now, I'd make belated introductions. Sir Baldwin de Betancourt, my brother, Galien de Coudre, and my sister, Lady Alisende de Coudre."

Baldwin bowed his head. "Your father lost his hand saving my own from a sure death. For this, my family is forever in debt to Sir Henri."

Alisende, clearly smitten by the handsome, courtly knight, said, "And who might your father be, Sir Baldwin?"

"Lady Alisende, my father is Enguerrand de Betancourt, and he serves the Count of Nevers in the post of viscount."

Alisende grew bolder. "Sir Baldwin, will you favor me with your company in a ride over our lands on the morrow?"

Martin, Thierré, and Galien glanced at each other, shocked at their little sister's audacious advance, but she was now thirteen years, nearing the age of marriage, and they held their tongues.

"Lady Alisende," Baldwin said, "Such would be more than a mere pleasure, but I need defer to your brothers."

Thierré, now somewhat recovered, looked at Galien and Martin, who nodded their heads in agreement. He said, "Sir Baldwin, our permission is given, at our honor."

+ + +

12 November 1086, Coudre Manor

Henri de Coudre rested comfortably in a big armchair near the fire; pale, thin, and weak, yet very much alive. The battle with blood-poisoning had nearly killed him, but two weeks past, his fever had broken, and the angry, red pus-oozing flesh at the stump of his hand had quickly healed, leaving a long, jagged scar that his sons regarded with endless admiration. "Thierré, Martin, and Galien, have wine brought and sit beside me."

He drank a goblet and stared into the fire, musing, "Your mother's greatest wish was to once more visit her home in Normandy, but God willed to take her back to Himself." He looked at Galien. "With Mother gone and Alisende to enter into betrothal to Baldwin de Betancourt, you're the only person in the family who can keep up with the estate accounts. You'll need to put off cathedral school for another year."

"Father, I'll do whatever you wish, but it'll take plenty more than a year to raise Alisende's dowry."

"Viscount Betancourt promised me his first son for Alisende on debt of saving his life, but any less than a thousand livres would still be an affront to such a high nobleman."

Galien frowned. "In a good year, the estate might show a profit of three hundred, but the opportunity for Alisende to marry into high nobility is more important." He grinned at Thierré. "Brother, you're going to have to save back at least half the coin you spend on loose women and drink, and myself, a good part of what I make from scribe work."

Thierré punched Galien's shoulder. "Tell me, bookrat."

"At least you two make fair coin," Martin said. "On a man-at-arms' wage, I'm half starving."

"Hardly," Thierré guffawed. "You save every last denier, and still say you're poor so I'll pay for your wine."

Henri slapped the table. "Enough! You boys will each give me a quarter of your earnings every month, until we have Alisende's dowry. And after will come your own turn at marriage, Thierré. I'll make a decent Christian man of you yet."

Part II: Five Years Later

JOSEPH SCOTT AMIS

Chapter 4

18 May 1091, the town of Grand-Forêt, Barony of Mirefleurs

Trees beside the hard-trodden dirt path cast long shadows in the late afternoon sun, as the patrol rode into Grand-Forêt. Nineteen-year-old Galien de Coudre sweated in his mail hauberk and steel helmet. His brother Thierré, the leading knight for patrols for the eastern border of the Barony of Mirefleurs, raised his right hand to signal a halt. The relief patrol would soon arrive.

Galien turned to Thierré. "My right stirrup is coming loose. I want to have Jacques repair it before we head back."

"Jacques died six weeks ago. His eldest son Alain came home from Clermont and took over the armory shop."

"You should have told me, fool. Alphonse put me to work writing on my last two patrol days, and I heard nothing about Jacques."

"My apologies. Jacques was a good fellow and the best swordmaker in this part of France, and we'll miss him."

Hoofbeats and the clatter of equipment signaled the approach of the relief. Thierré dismissed his men-at-arms. They reined their horses around and set off for the fortress.

"Lead your horse to the armory shop," Thierré said. "You can meet Alain and his wife, and we'll have a drink at the tavern while he repairs your saddle."

"A fine idea."

The brothers dismounted. Thierré gave a peasant boy a denier to hold his horse, and they paused in the cool shade of the huge old oaks bordering the center of the small town. As they walked toward the wattle-and-plaster thatch-roofed buildings, townspeople returning from the fields or completing the day's business greeted them cordially, with respectful nods and "Sir Thierré, Sir Galien."

They nodded in return and led Galien's horse among the cottages, stopping at the sign with crossed swords. Thierré glanced at the sky. "It's getting dark. I'll see if I can bribe Alain to do a last small job before he closes."

Thierré opened the bright-blue door. In the front room, a pretty young woman sat behind the table, counting the coins received that day and making marks on a wax tablet. She smiled. "Sir Thierré. So nice to see you."

He bowed gallantly and said, "Lisette, this is my brother, Galien. He's had a stirrup come loose. Has your good husband quit for the day?"

Lisette dipped her head, then smiled at Galien. "My honor to meet you, Sir Galien. I think Alain can work it in. I'm finished here, and you can put your saddle on the table."

She put the coins into a green leather bag, closed the tablet, and carried them around the corner, into the workroom. After a minute, the twenty-two-year-old armorer Alain came in, and Thierré introduced him to Galien.

"I'll be seeing more of you soon, Sir Galien. I'm to report for service at arms, come next training day."

"You're a swordsman, I'll guess." Alain's tall, lean build bespoke his weapon of choice.

"He's a good man with his sword, Galien. You should practice with him," Thierré said.

"If he'll have a bookrat as a practice partner, I'm game."

Alain grinned. "With Sir Thierré for a brother, no doubt a fearsome bookrat."

They laughed, and Alain said, "I'll get some wine from Lisette, and my tools. Bring the saddle in and we'll have a drink while I fix it."

Alain began work on the saddle. Galien and Thierré sat on a bench, sipping at their cups.

"Any signs of trouble from Bayard?" Thierré said.

Alain looked up. "None yet. The ungodly bastard strikes when least expected, and that has me worried. Two weeks past, I called the town men together to discuss organizing a ready defense. Not one was interested. They've all grown content, and think Bayard's given up raiding in his old age."

"I can't believe that fool of a duke made such a nonsense of a ruling last June," Thierré said. "No surprise that Bayard and Alphonse couldn't come to terms. Bayard had him by the balls from the start."

"I've only heard people speak of what was in the ruling," Alain said.

"Galien can tell us. He read it out line by line to Alphonse and the others, and even explained the jurists' nonsense to them."

Galien shook his head slowly. "If a man of the law did write it, he was under threat of torture. The ruling states that the disputed lands are to remain under governance of the Barony of Mirefleurs, but only Bayard or his successors have the authority to dispose of them, by any means they deem fit. It's a complete contradiction. I think the Duke of Aquitaine is tired of hearing about fifty years of squabbling between our barony and the County of Saint-Lille. He's decided to wash his hands of the whole matter and let us fight it out. The last ones standing get the lands."

Thierré frowned. "Well, that means only one thing. Bayard bought the duke with silver. The ruling gives him a back door to mount a full-scale attack to take back the lands, and even conquer our barony."

"You're right, Brother. We're hogs waiting for the knife. Bayard's forces outnumber ours, six to one."

Alain finished the saddle and drained his cup of wine. "This is serious, much more so than I believed. I'll try again to roust the lazy swine here in Grand-Forêt."

"Alphonse's people are first in his thoughts, Alain," Thierré said. "We're signing on more men and stepping up patrols. I'll bring you up at the knights' meeting tomorrow. You're a leader, if I've ever met one."

After bidding Alain a good night, the brothers saddled Galien's horse. "Still ready for that drink?" Galien said.

"Of course. I don't have duty till noon tomorrow, and you're not stupid enough to ride home on Route de Voleurs at night."

Galien nudged Thierré. "That honor yet belongs to you, Brother."

"It does, indeed. Those carrion-maggots know Death himself rides with Thierré de Coudre."

"As do I. A nice, warm pallet in the barrack will suit me just fine." Galien, though well aware of Thierré's formidable prowess at arms, worried at his impulsive brother's readiness to dare the Devil at any hour and venture onto the six-foot-wide trodden dirt path, aptly called Route de Voleurs, that led north from the southern border of the barony and past Coudre Estate, to Fortress Mirefleurs. Large trees and rock outcroppings provided abundant hiding places and vantage points for robbers. Baron Alphonse kept mounted patrols on the roads, but even the threat of public execution without trial failed to deter the brigands. They still attacked, at times daring to accost even well-armed travelers.

Thierré frowned. "Father will stay up worrying, but better that than you riding home alone."

"We need to talk about Father."

They entered the inn and took a table in the dim, noisy common room. A serving girl came to take their order. "A pitcher of your best wine and some bread and cheese," Galien said.

She smiled. "Yes, my lord. I'll bring it right away."

Thierré watched her walk away and grinned at Galien. "A fine little piece."

"Is that all you think about? We've serious matters to discuss."

"Yes, it is, but talk away. I'm listening."

"You and Martin come home from the fortress only two or three times a month, and I'm there all the time. Father's drinking a lot more and doesn't seem to care about the estate at all anymore. Alisende and I are still keeping it going."

"How well I know. Losing his sword hand at Vézelay two weeks after Mother died took all he had left out of him."

"Thierré, he's gotten worse. I fear he hasn't much time left."

"You're letting your thoughts run away with you, like you always have."

Galien frowned. "True. My mind can carry me into the darkest places."

"I'm not so afflicted. The last time I visited at the house, Father was out chopping at the pell left-handed. The old man can still swing a sword with the best."

"Hmm. He has been in the arming room more of late. He's been busy polishing up his weapons and gear."

"That's a good sign. What does Alisende think?"

"I've hardly an idea. We've grown apart some over the last six months."

"You never told me. You two have always been so close."

"She introduced me to some noblemen's daughters at the feast of Saint Stephen last year, and I wasn't interested. I guess she took offense."

"There's no reason she should have. You've had your head in a book your whole life and we all know it. You turn me down every time I invite you to ride to Mont-Brison."

"Brother, I've many things to admire in you, but your taste in women isn't one of them. That one time you got me drunk and dragged me there was plenty enough."

"I admit that it's not the best, but it suits me fine. I do my business and leave without a care."

Galien shrugged. "For myself, all I can say is that I'll know the right lady when she comes along, and I hope Father will allow me some choice in the matter. Anyway, I prefer to spend my spare time earning silver with scribe work, and to save it rather than spend it at a whorehouse."

"To each his own, I suppose. But, by the Blood of God, don't talk to me about marriage."

The serving girl brought their wine and food. Thierré paid for the order and gave her two deniers, with an inviting grin. She blushed and walked away.

"Seriously, Galien, I do think of more than just drink and women. I wish you'd brought up your concerns about Father sooner. He's never been a hard drinker before, and that worries me."

"I have now. We need to get together with Martin for a family talk."

"Agreed. Father's troubles have been especially rough on you. You had to put off your study for the priesthood to look after him and matters at home. Don't think I haven't noticed."

Galien leaned over the table. "Brother, I want to confess something that's been troubling me for years."

Thierré winked. "I'm certainly no priest, but I'll do my best to keep it a secret."

"I was starting to have doubts about going into the Church, then Mother dying and Father losing his hand saved me from it. I feel horrible that I've been happy at home and on duty at arms."

"Galien, think. You couldn't help what happened to Mother and Father, and you and Alisende have saved the estate from ruin." Thierré leaned back, grinning. You're a nineteen-year-old nobleman, and can't stay just a scribe for hire. If you don't want to go into the Church, knighthood is your only other choice."

"Thierré, you know I'm much more of a scholar than a soldier."

27

"Horse balls. You're a son of Henri de Coudre and a demon with that sword. You've grown three inches taller, and all you'd need is more weight on you."

"Hmm… perhaps I ought to think about it more seriously. I can't lie and say I haven't grown fond of the soldier's life."

Thierré raised his eyebrows. "It would give Father more cause to take heart, and you'd be the only knight at the fortress able to read and write."

"Father never expected me to become a knight, but I suppose he'd be happy if I did."

"He would be. But, knight or not, you have a scar any man would envy to show for your service."

"With two of Bayard's men trying to ride me down, I thought I'd never get away and pull that arrow out of my shield before the head could take my arm off. I still feel like a coward for running away."

"There's no shame in retreat when it's the best option. You got away with your life, and you didn't make a sound while the surgeon cleaned the gash and stitched it."

"I was stupid not to buy a mail hauberk when you told me to. Trying to save my coin nearly got me killed."

"Even a poor knight doesn't skimp on the best gear he can afford, if he has half a brain."

"This old beat-up hauberk cost what I earned in a year of scribe work, and I'm still paying the balance I owe. I know now it was worth it, but I had to learn the hard way."

Thierré held up the pitcher. "More?"

"No. I'd fall asleep on my horse."

"I'll finish it off, and we'll head back. There are some empty pallets in the barrack."

"Thanks. Maybe I ought to get used to sleeping there."

19 May 1091, Coudre Manor

Galien rode into the front court at midmorning. He dismounted and led his horse through the open stable doorway to the stalls. His father called from the arming room, "Galien, you're home?"

Galien entered and took off his helmet. "Yes, Sire."

Henri slapped his back. "Thierré didn't drag you off to Mont-Brison after your patrol, did he?"

"We only had wine and food at the inn in Grand-Forêt. Night had fallen, and Thierré bade me stay at the fortress. I hope you weren't worried."

"But little. You've sense enough not to ride Route de Voleurs at night, even if your brother doesn't. Come look at this."

Henri turned to an open wooden crate on the floor and lifted a round wooden shield, freshly covered with thick painted leather and set with the newest style of steel fittings. He put it on the work table. "The farrier in Saint-Julien brought it yesterday. Think an old one-handed knight might fight again?"

Galien examined the shield. The straps had been refashioned to firmly hold both forearm and upper arm yet allow freedom of movement, and a heavy leather cup had been added to fit the stump of Henri's right hand.

"It's cleverly made, Father. If you can wield your sword with your left hand, I'll not worry."

"You doubt me, boy? Help me strap on this shield and fetch me a sword, and we'll have a little match in the court. Pray you live to see your breakfast!"

27 May 1091, Coudre Manor

The air outdoors was cool and quiet in the last hour before dawn, but Galien couldn't concentrate on his prayers. The beads slipped from his fingers, rattling onto the stone bench. He rose abruptly and looked north up Route de Voleurs, toward Fortress Mirefleurs. At the knights' meeting held the day after he had met the armorer Alain, his father and Baron Alphonse had put the barony forces on high alert for an attack from Bayard, and warned that in years past, the count had always struck just before daybreak.

Galien saw no lights and heard no sounds. He let out a breath of relief and stretched. The dewy grass of morning squished between his toes as he walked across the half-acre court. Warm candlelight flickered in the first-floor windows and open front door of the old country house, and dim light filtered between the cracks in the wood-plank stable door. The stableman was about his rounds, feeding and watering the horses. Galien caught the sweet aroma of honeyed oat porridge; Paul and Lucie had begun to make breakfast. He headed toward the front door, his thoughts on a large hot bowl and the letters waiting on his writing table.

Hooves thundered on the road, and his stomach jumped. In a din of clattering steel and squeaking leather, Thierré and a man-at-arms rode into the court and pulled their snorting horses to a halt. Both were armed and in full dress for battle.

"Wake Martin, and both of you get in your gear for a fight," Thierré said. "Walter's assembling the company on the road north of the fortress. Be there before the sun rises."

Before Galien could speak, Thierré and the man-at-arms reined their horses around and set off toward the fortress. Galien dashed across the broad court to the stable and swung the door open. Martin stood half-awake in the arming room, fumbling at a wall sconce. Galien took the flint and steel, struck a spark, and the sconce blazed.

"Thierré was here. Has Bayard made a move?" Martin said. He threw water on his face and brushed back his short hair and beard.

"Thierré only told me there's a fight coming and rode off back to the Fortress. We're to ready ourselves for battle and meet the company on the road to Grand-Forêt."

"It's surely Bayard, and he's blasted well starting trouble. Let's get going."

Galien stripped off his prayer habit and Martin removed his nightshirt. They donned head and upper-body padding and tight, heavy boiled-wool braies. Both pulled on short, stiff leather shoes and buckled on spurs as two men-at-arms who served as house guards saddled their horses. Galien and Martin helped each other lift on their heavy mail hauberks. They drew mail coifs over their heads, laced them, then put on conical steel helmets with long nose-guards and buckled the chin straps. Martin grabbed his sword belt.

The door to the yard creaked open, and Henri stepped into the arming room. "I heard Thierré from my window. You two, come help me with my hauberk."

"Father... are you sure?" Martin said.

"Shut up and busy yourself. I haven't had a go at Bayard for a long while, and it's past time I took one."

Martin went to fetch Henri's hauberk, and Galien asked, hesitantly, "Father, Thierré said you and Count Bayard were friends a long time ago, but he'd had a pitcher of wine."

"It's a part of my past I've kept much to myself, but I expected Thierré would get drunk and tell you, sooner or later. Bayard and I were close friends as boys, and as young knights, we rode north together to enlist with old William's forces. Bayard got his keen taste for blood in the Conquest, and after we came home, he joined his father in raiding our lands. Since, we've spoken only with our swords."

Martin and Galien helped Henri put his battle gear on while the men saddled his horse. The brothers lifted Henri's mail hauberk onto him and tried to hold back smiles at the bulging waist. Henri stared at them. "What in Hell are you looking at?" He took Galien's sword from the rack and thumbed the blade edges, scowling. "Hmm. Oiled and sharp, like it ought to be. Wield it well."

Henri and Martin mounted their warhorses. A man-at-arms lifted a steel-headed ashen lance and a heavy kite-shaped shield to Martin's grasp, and Galien helped Henri strap his shield to his right arm. He mounted his own dappled-grey gelding. The man-at-arms held his round shield up, and Galien slid his left arm into the straps and grasped the handle.

Henri nudged his horse to a fast canter across the court and between the tall entry posts to the road, Martin close behind him. Galien took a deep breath. If God willed that he die in battle this day, at least his father could remember him with honor and pride. He gave the gelding his head and hung on for his life. After a quarter mile, Henri and Martin reined back their horses to a walk. Galien, feeling bloodless, pulled up next to them.

Martin jostled his shoulder. "Chin up, Brother. A taste of battle will be good for you."

"Martin," Henri said, "Galien's had nearly as much battle experience as you have."

"He has, and a prize scar to show for it," Martin admitted. "Pray for us, Brother."

Fortress Mirefleurs loomed massive and grey before the fading stars in the northeastern sky. Horsemen, foot soldiers, and wagons moved in a torchlit procession down the winding trail from the fortress gate to the road. Father and sons bowed their heads, Galien said the Pater Noster, and they turned their horses toward their comrades.

31

Chapter 5

27 May 1091, the County of Saint-Lille

As the sun's first light broke in the eastern sky above forested hills, Bayard d'Evreux, Count of Saint-Lille, brought his thirty-man company to a quiet halt behind the forest tree line. Two black-clad crossbowmen jumped off a wagon, snaked through tall grass toward the sentry shelter at the crossroads ahead, and when in range, loosed their bolts. The two guards fell, and the bowmen raised their weapons high.

At this signal, Bayard led his men to the crossroads. He studied the hard-trodden, half-mile path that led west into the Barony of Mirefleurs. Lights flickered at the path's end as the town of Grand-Forêt awoke.

Satisfied, he turned to the knight beside him, his eldest son and second-in-lead, and asked, "Your report, Sir Gautier?"

"Scouts found both objectives unprepared for defense."

"Our men are ready?"

Gautier reined his horse around and quickly took inventory. Five knights and five mounted men-at-arms, six crossbowmen and twelve men-at-arms in two wagons, and the two drivers, one a battle surgeon, waited in ready formation. "Yes, Sire. All is in order."

Bayard lifted his antique Viking helmet, a prize from his time in Normandy, pulled it over his mail coif, and buckled the chin strap. The nose, eye, and cheek guards masked his hawk nose and upper face; the high ventail of the coif hid the lower. He said to Gautier, "Order the attack now, before the sun rises. You and I will ride behind."

Gautier drew his sword and raised it. "Forward to attack! Spare the church!" He reined back his eager horse. High grass at the sides of the path muffled pounding hoofbeats, rattling metal, and groaning wood as the men on horse led the wagons at a trot toward Grand-Forêt. Bayard and Gautier watched, and as the company neared the town, they nudged their own horses to a fast trot.

+ + +

Deep in her dream, Lisette heard pounding hooves and rumbling wheels. With stomach churning, she sat up, shook Alain awake, and whispered, "Listen!"

They needed no more warning. Lisette jumped from the bed and pulled a dress over her head. Alain tugged on his shirt, leather braies, and shoes, and pulled on his heavy mail haubergeon. They rushed to the door and jumped onto the narrow cobbled lane. She followed him as he ran, sword in hand, to a house corner. There she crouched and watched as he ran to the small stone church facing the center of the town, paused, and yelled "Attack! To arms! Attack!"

The town priest, his dawn Mass interrupted, stood blank-faced on the church steps. "Bayard's men draw near." Alain said. "Ring the bell and be quick at it!"

The priest dashed into the church. A score of armed townsmen poured onto the green as soon as the bell sounded, but the alarm had come too late for a defense to be organized. Bayard's horsemen thundered into the town, swinging swords, flails, and maces. In half a minute, three townsmen lay dead and others fled through narrow dirt lanes, horsemen in relentless pursuit. Men-at-arms boiled from the wagons. Storming from house to house, they kicked in doors, jerking women, children, and elders out by their hair and clothes, punching and shoving them toward the center of the town. Others flung torches onto thatched roofs and wagons loaded with hay. The plastered-wattle cottages of Grand-Forêt exploded into roaring infernos.

Lisette shrank back in terror at the ugly sights of chaotic violence, and coughed as thick, sooty smoke billowed from the burning buildings, yet her eyes followed Alain in unwilling fascination. She lost sight of him as he dodged from building to building, then spotted him as he climbed atop an enclosed wagon and pulled himself onto a low stable roof. A knight turned hard into the lane between the stable buildings, and she gasped as her husband jumped from her sight. In half a minute, Alain, mounted on the knight's horse, charged from between the stables toward three horsemen milling about. With a blur-quick right swing, he cut deeply into a knight's sword arm, and on the return swing, smashed his broad blade into a second horseman's helmet. As he closed on the third horseman, men-at-arms threw a rope net over him, pulling him from the saddle.

He struggled to rise and two men swung maces, dropping him to the ground. A third man straddled him, raised a sword high, and thrust it into his neck. Lisette stifled her cry with a hand. She ran back to their cottage, crawled under the bed, and pressed her body hard against the cool plaster wall, sobbing into her hands.

By the time Bayard and Gautier rode onto the square, the raid was nearly over and the buildings collapsing into smoldering red embers. They watched as their men selected comely women and dragged them into a stable, then listened impassively to the sounds of ripping cloth, screaming and begging, and boisterous laughter.

After a time, Gautier banged on the stable wall with his sword pommel, then called, "All assemble. After we finish with Saint-Denis, we'll be back at the chateau in time for food and wine."

The men drifted to the square and assumed formation. Bayard took stock of his casualties: one knight critically wounded and another badly stunned; two men-at-arms and one crossbowman dead. As the men loaded the bodies into a wagon, and the driver-surgeon worked desperately to save the knight from bleeding to death, a scoundrelly foot soldier dragged an old man with long white hair and beard from behind the corner of a nearby cottage.

He addressed Bayard. "Sire, I found this old bastard lying in wait with a knife. What shall I do with him?"

Bayard glanced at Gautier. "I leave it to you."

Gautier nudged his horse a step forward. "Show me the knife, Gobert."

Gobert raised a twelve-inch razor-edged dagger. Gautier took it, thumbed an edge and whistled, and handed it back. "Use it on him, but don't kill him."

Gobert punched the old man in the stomach, pushed him to the ground, and straddled his chest, dagger in hand. The old man screamed and clawed as Gobert cut off his ears and nose and tossed them before Gautier's horse. A half-dozen men turned away, sickened; others watched spellbound and cheered Gobert on. Finished with the cruel task, Gobert yanked the wretch to his knees by the hair and held him up on display.

He leered at Gautier. "Shall I take his lips and eyelids as well, Sire?"

"I said don't kill him, Gobert. What you've done will suffice."

Gobert shoved his blood-soaked victim back to the ground, kicked him in the stomach, and stuck the dagger hilt-up beside him. "Keep this in your belt, grandfather, or I will take your lips and eyelids next time."

"Move out," Bayard said. The company followed him onto a narrow dirt road that led into a quarter-mile-wide area of dense forest. Their second objective, the village of Saint-Denis, lay another quarter-mile beyond the forest. It would fall easily, as had Grand-Forêt.

+ + +

Lisette listened, shivering, to the sounds of rattling metal and laughing curses fading into the quiet forest as Bayard's men departed. She crawled from under the bed and stumbled to the center of the town. The townspeople had laid out the dead: six men, one woman, and two children, on the ground before the church, in full sight of all. She stared silently at Alain's broken body. The man she had loved all of her life was gone. She had escaped death in the flames and battle, and gang rape at the hands of Bayard's henchmen, but she was now a widow at eighteen years, and would soon be without a roof over her head.

Again, the rumbling beat of hooves and wagon wheels shook the ground, and Lisette's stomach wrenched. Marshal Walter d'Avesnes and elder knights Fulbert de Ronchamp and Henri de Coudre rode into the town at the head of the barony company. Lisette's renewed panic turned to relief, and she fell into the arms of a neighbor woman.

+ + +

Galien waited with the second cavalry, watching his father, Walter, and Fulbert. With Bayard and Gautier but a minute away, Walter couldn't delay the company to aid the townspeople, yet many lay wounded and others wandered aimlessly.

Walter reined around. "Sergeant Lienart, take Clement de Sens and one man-at-arms. You will stay here and give help to these people." He turned to Henri. "Sir Henri, ride with the second cavalry. Those young men need a steady hand."

The battle surgeon Lienart jumped off a wagon and gestured to a man-at-arms. They grabbed the surgeon's kit and lugged it to the green. The downy-faced seventeen-year-old nobleman Clement, deprived of a rare chance to prove his prowess, punched his saddle and cursed.

Henri reined up next to Galien and nodded his head. "Permission to join your men, Sir Galien?" he said, with a wink.

"At our honor, Sire."

Walter raised a hand and signaled. Thierré, knight in lead, directed the first cavalry onto the forest trail taken by Bayard's company, and the second cavalry followed. They paused behind the tree line, then rode in stealthy single file into the tall, waving grass covering the broad meadow. Three hundred yards ahead, in a clearing beyond the meadow, Bayard's men stood assembled, readying to attack Saint-Denis. Walter put a finger to his lips, gestured to signal a line formation, and pointed to the count and Gautier.

Thierré led the first cavalry lancers, and Galien and Henri moved cautiously behind with the second cavalry. With the rattle of their equipment quieted by the tall grass, the seven lancers and twelve crossbowmen formed a sixty-foot line; two crossbowmen crouched close together between each pair of lancers. As Thierré rode to center position, Galien caught his eye. Thierré cocked his chin up and grinned. Galien, courage bolstered by his father's presence and his brother's goodwill, drew his sword and faced the enemy. Henri took up a chain flail, drew the handle strap tight around his left wrist, and set his teeth.

Thierré raised his right hand high, paused, and swung it down. The crossbowmen stealthily advanced a hundred yards, and holding their cocked bows at a thirty-degree angle, loosed one volley, and fell back. Thierré half-lowered his lance, and the lancers advanced at a trot, converged into close formation, and swung their weapons down to attack position.

Thierré leveled his lance, and the lancers' mounts bolted forward at a full gallop. A second later, Henri signaled, and the six men of the second cavalry charged with weapons drawn and then split in two directions. The crowd of foot men followed at a run, brandishing axes and swords, roaring a battle cry. The crossbowmen trotted behind with bows re-cocked, ready to pick off vulnerable men as the battle progressed.

The arrogant Bayard had made no preparations to face a counterattack. As his horsemen struggled to form a defensive line, the barony's lancers broke through, scattering them.

Galien, riding at a fast canter behind his father, had not a moment for fear as mounted knights led Bayard's foot men in a rush toward the barony's second cavalry and foot forces. Archers loosed their missiles, and two sharp thumps jolted his shield. Ahead, an axe man charged Henri from his right, and a knight closed in to his left, sword raised high for an overhand blow. Henri swung his shield out and knocked the axe man's weapon aside, and as the knight swung his sword down, he whipped the flail forward in a blur. The bar struck the knight squarely in the face with a crack of bone and splattering blood. He went limp and dropped his sword, and Henri charged toward the next opponent.

A man-at-arms with a heavy falchion upraised ran to attack, and Galien swung at his head. He heard a gristly crunch, felt hard leather and skull give way, and the man twisted and fell into the mace man behind him. A lancer charged at full gallop, and Galien reined his gelding hard to evade him. The lance head scraped his shield, and he pulled the horse into a fast turnaround, closing on the lancer as he raised his weapon to hurl it as a spear. Galien's sword cut through leather and flesh, and the lancer screamed and cursed.

Galien couldn't look back. He spotted the Saint-Lille banner a hundred yards ahead, waving and dipping, as Martin led a group of barony men into a furious assault against Bayard's horsemen. Galien reined the gelding fast toward them, his sword raised for attack.

With no forewarning, Martin's warhorse raised his head in an agonized bellow, pitched and fell to his knees, and collapsed on his left side. As Martin hit the ground, his shield twisted, and his sword flew from his right hand. The anguished horse struggled as Martin pulled both feet free from the stirrups, grabbed a dead man's sword by the blade, and gained his knees.

A tall knight, also unhorsed, strode over to Martin and raised his spiked war axe for a death blow. Martin, still on his knees, swung the sword, slamming the heavy round pommel into the knight's temple, toppling him unconscious to the ground. Martin dropped his shield and held his left arm, grimacing, then got to his feet. Galien pulled his horse to a skidding halt, jumped off, and ran to his brother's side.

JOSEPH SCOTT AMIS

Chapter 6

The short battle had ended, and forty-odd barony men regrouped in the meadow. Martin's men-at-arms, Etien and Robert of Coudre Estate, ran to stand beside him and Galien over the fallen knight. Galien retrieved Martin's sword, handing it to him as Etien unbuckled the chin strap of the knight's Viking helmet and pulled it off. The richly outfitted man came to dazed awareness and sat up. Robert pricked him between mailed shoulders with a dagger, thus signaling his new status as a prisoner.

Martin's horse lay on his side, dying in quiet agony, a crossbow bolt sunk deep into his chest. Robert opened a vein in the animal's neck with a sure dagger cut. He found a full wine flask in Martin's saddlebag and raised it for a swig.

Martin rapped Robert's steel helmet with mailed knuckles. "Give me that!" He offered his prisoner the first drink. The man took a swallow, glared at Martin, and tossed the flask back at his feet. Martin acknowledged the insult with a level stare, picked up the flask, and took a short drink. Galien took a sip and handed it back to Robert, so that he and Etien might have well-earned refreshment.

Galien realized at once who Martin held captive and studied his face, fine mail edged with bronze links, and gold-embroidered light-blue surcoat. The man who had nearly sent his brother to meet God was no ordinary knight. Twenty-one-year-old knight Martin de Coudre held Count Bayard of Saint-Lille, the richest and most powerful nobleman in the region, as his prisoner.

Galien looked on in disbelief as Martin stood with his sword pressed to Bayard's neck. Walter, Henri, and Thierré rode up and dismounted. Martin slapped the count's chin up with his sword and made his declaration: "Here sits Bayard d'Evreux, Count of Saint-Lille, defeated and taken by my own hand in single combat. My brother, Galien de Coudre, and my men, Robert and Etien of Coudre Estate, witnessed and will attest to the truth of my account. I claim Count Bayard as my personal prisoner, with this claim subject to the authority of my lord, Baron Alphonse of Mirefleurs."

Walter nodded. "The prisoner is in barony custody and your claim is noted, Sir Martin, you and Sir Thierré will escort him to the fortress." To Etien and Robert, he said, "Put the good count on a horse and secure him well."

Thierré punched Galien in the shoulder. "A fine fight, brother!"

Saint-Denis townsmen brought water to the wounded as men-at-arms carried the barony's dead, a cavalier and two men-at-arms, to a wagon and shackled the four of Bayard's men taken prisoner. With these tasks accomplished, Count Bayard restrained and guarded, and Walter satisfied that Gautier and his men had left the vicinity, the company fell into formation and followed the same forest road back to Grand-Forêt.

The town center was clear and orderly, the dead townspeople lying under a large canvas in the shade of the church walls. Galien and a few townsmen helped the wounded barony men into the church. Sergeant Lienart, ably in charge, had seen to the dead and moved the injured into the cool sanctuary. He walked among his patients, supervising Clement de Sens, the man-at-arms, and a young townswoman, as the priest cut bandages and came to pray with those in dire need. Galien waited as Lienart told Walter of his needs for more cloth for bandages and extract of poppy to ease the pain of the dying.

They walked back to the town center and their horses, the young woman at Walter's side. Galien pulled two arrows from his shield and Walter grasped his shoulder. "Well done, Galien. Come and visit with Baron Alphonse and me. We can still make a knight of you."

Galien bowed his head. "Sir Walter, I'm yet unsure." He glanced at Henri. "Father needs me at home. I can only hope that I brought honor to him today."

Henri put his good hand on Galien's back. "You did indeed, Son. I'll proudly second Sir Walter."

Galien looked at the pale young woman. "This is Lisette," Walter said. "Bayard's men killed her husband, yet she volunteered to help with the wounded."

"I met Lisette and her husband Alain only recently, on my last patrol."

"My husband spoke well of you, Sir Galien," Lisette said.

"I thought well of him, good lady, and looked forward to serving with him. I'm so sorry."

"I've granted her shelter at the fortress," Walter said. "The town's dead are to be buried at an hour past noon. Find her a seat on a wagon, stay with her, and see her safely to the fortress after the Mass and burials are finished."

Galien said, "Yes, Sir Walter," and Walter turned back to the company.

"I've a horse," Lisette said quietly. "Alain's brown-and-white gelding should be in the town stable if Bayard's men didn't take him, and his mail and sword are still in the church."

"You can ride, Lisette?"

"My husband taught me, Sir Galien. Now, I need to fetch my belongings."

"You needn't mind carrying that heavy mail and sword. I'll be pleased to take care of them."

+ + +

Galien left for the church and stable; Lisette returned to her cottage. Thinking herself in a dream of Hell, she washed her face, combed her hair and tied it back, and put on her best dress and shoes. From a small steel chest under the bed, she poured the handful of silver, gold, and bronze coins into a green leather bag and hung it under the bodice of her dress, between her breasts. With as many of Alain's costly tools as she could carry in a stout cloth bag, she walked through the cottage and armory shop where she had lived and worked with her husband for but six short weeks. His vicious drunkard of a younger brother would soon return to Grand-Forêt, to claim what was now his by birthright and evict her, or worse, invite her to stay in return for sharing his bed. She stepped down onto the grass, gazed at the blue door and painted shield, and turned away to seek Galien.

+ + +

Lisette found Galien waiting before the church, holding the reins of his horse and Alain's. Despite her grief and confusion, at the sight of him, she put a hand to her lips. With his finely-drawn face, clear deep-green eyes, and sandy-brown hair, clad in his bloodied mail hauberk, sword belted around his waist and helmet and coif under his left arm, he seemed a hero out of legend, come to carry her to the safety of his great castle.

She came to stand beside him, and they watched as the company moved out, wagons creaking and bumping over the hard dirt road in the hot late-morning sun. Martin and Thierré, flanking the bound count, rode behind Walter, Henri, and the banner-bearers.

Walter left a knight with six men under him in charge of the town. Able townsmen stood with the men-at-arms as the knight briefed them on a defense against Gautier, should he attempt a second attack, and then all set to digging graves in the burial yard beside the church. Galien walked Lisette into the church and sat quietly with her as she wept. After an hour, the church had filled with townsfolk, and the priest said Mass for the dead. Galien stood beside her at Alain's grave as men shoveled earth over his freshly wrapped body. Lisette placed a bouquet of fresh-cut lavender onto the mound of earth. Galien counted out ten deniers and handed them to the priest. He helped Lisette secure her possessions and mount her horse, and they rode out of the town, onto the road to the fortress.

Lisette spoke first. "Thank you for helping me, Sir Galien."

"You merit the thanks. Walter could only spare three men for the wounded, and they weren't enough."

"I couldn't just stand there and look at my husband's body." She again began to quietly weep, and they rode another half mile in silence.

"If you care to talk, I'll gladly listen."

She shook her head, and they rode without saying a word, accompanied by the steady clopping of the horses' hooves and the squeaks and rattles of Galien's equipment. They topped the winding path from Route de Voleurs to the fortress and rode through the open

44

gateway into the wide, bustling forecourt. Galien handed their horses off to a stableman and sought out the steward. A man soon came to show Lisette to her quarters. At Galien's nod, he picked up her bags and waited.

A knight from the company waved to Galien. "Lisette, I must go. I need to celebrate the capture of Count Bayard with the other men. I told the steward to find you a room by yourself, and food and wine are on the way there. Père Barnard is coming to talk and pray with you."

Lisette stepped close to Galien and grasped his hands in hers. "Sir Galien, God surely sent you to help me bear this terrible day."

"I'll come to see you as soon as I can, before I leave for home."

"Please do."

Galien bowed his head and turned toward the arched stone gate to the armory yard, vexed at the feelings roused by her womanly figure and the clean fragrance of her unscented skin.

+ + +

In the armory yard, Galien found a raucous celebration well underway. The barony's men-at-arms, noblemen and commoners alike, crowded the stone-walled garrison, drinking toast after toast to the day's victory. Baron Alphonse stood beaming beside a huge barrel of strong ale, passing tankards to the men as fast as the servants filled them. The rich, thick aroma of roasting boar drifted from the armory hall. Alphonse raised his arms, guards opened the heavy oaken doors, and the men crowded inside. Galien stayed behind and stood beside Martin and his father, sipping at his ale as Walter recounted the details of the battle to Alphonse. At Walter's nod, Martin came forward and repeated his account of Bayard's capture.

Alphonse grasped Martin's shoulders, grinning through his beard. "By Holy God, Sir Martin de Coudre, you're truly a son of your good father!" he proclaimed. "You well proved yourself a knight today." Alphonse slapped Martin's back, topped off his tankard and Galien's, and bade them accompany him, Henri, and Walter across the court to where the count, still bound, stood under guard.

Alphonse stared down his old enemy. "Bayard, you are now the prisoner of Sir Martin de Coudre. Under my authority, you will be held at Fortress Mirefleurs until acceptable terms of ransom are fulfilled."

The tall, redheaded count nodded to Alphonse and glared at Martin. "I will first have this pup torn apart by horses, and will then hunt down and kill his father and sons. I vow this to him, Henri de Coudre, and to you, Alphonse."

Henri flushed dark and half-drew his sword, but Martin held his arm. Alphonse's face turned beef-red and his gleaming black eyes narrowed. "This courageous young knight did only his duty and happened to spoil your morning of murderous amusement." He grasped Bayard's surcoat, drew him close, and said between clenched teeth, "Make no threats, nor curse my knights, lest I call my hangmen and have them cut out your tongue and eyes."

Walter called for an escort guard. Galien and Martin followed two armed knights as they prodded Bayard up endless flights of winding stone steps to the top floor in the fortress' tallest tower. There, they watched as the knights shoved Bayard into Fortress Mirefleurs' quarters for prisoners of high birth, a large, well-furnished room with one barred slit window, then pushed the iron-bound oaken door shut and threw the heavy bolts. With Bayard locked away and under guard, they returned to the armory yard. There, Alphonse rubbed his hands in unrepressed delight and bade Martin and Galien take seats beside him, Henri, Fulbert, and Walter at the baron's table in the hall.

Galien joined in the rowdy feast. He ate his fill of roast boar, bread, and vegetables, and took unsparing swallows of Alphonse's best wine at every call to raise the goblets. After an hour, at the thinnest edge of sobriety, he excused himself to his seniors and Alphonse and sought out Lisette's quarters. He knocked gently, gave his name, and entered at her bidding.

Inside the tiny servant's room, Galien took the cup of wine Lisette offered him. He pulled up a stool, and she sat on the edge of the bed.

"Thank you for having the food and wine sent, Sir Galien. I'd had nothing to eat today."

"You look much better. Did Père Bernard come?"

"Yes. He was most kind."

"Good. You've met my brother, Thierré de Coudre. He's a ranking knight, and I'll make sure he knows that you're staying here. Go to him or Père Barnard if anyone troubles you."

"Alain liked Sir Thierré very much."

"And Thierré liked him. Gautier of Saint-Lille will pay dearly for your husband's murder. He'll grovel in his own blood and vomit and beg mercy before my brother cuts his hands and feet off."

Lisette turned greenish-pale and dabbed at her eyes. Galien refilled her cup with wine and handed it to her. She drank it in two long swallows.

Color came back to her face. "I heard Sir Walter ask if you wished to become a knight."

Galien raised an eyebrow, grinning. "Me, a knight? I only ride with the second cavalry. I was bound for cathedral school and the priesthood before my father lost his sword hand in the battle at Vézelay and my mother died. My sister and I manage our family's lands, and I write and translate for Alphonse when Père Barnard becomes over-burdened. I also earn a little silver writing letters and contracts."

Lisette looked down, without reply. Galien rose to leave. "I'm sure you want to be by yourself."

"No, Sir Galien. Stay if you can. I'm suddenly all alone in the world, and sorely need some company."

"I'll be more than happy to stay. But the name is Galien. I don't go by 'Sir' with my friends."

Lisette smiled through her tears, and Galien paused, studying her: Heavy dark brown hair, wide-set brown eyes, olive skin with a scattering of freckles; face gently rounded, with full lips and finely shaped nose; her speech refined, like that of a noblewoman. "Tell me more of your circumstances, Lisette."

"My father owned the mill in Grand-Forêt. It was burned down in a night raid three years past. I was in Clermont with my husband, and my parents and brother perished before anyone could save them."

"Yes, I knew of the tragedy. Alphonse held an investigation, but no culprits were identified."

"Galien, my husband and I suspected that the miller in Saint-Denis set the fire with purpose of taking my father's business, but Alphonse found no reason to question him further, and there was no coin left to rebuild. Besides, Alain's father was becoming short of memory, and we had to get on with plans to take over the armory shop."

Galien took her hand. "Lisette, you've suffered more loss than many do in a whole lifetime."

Tears again welled in her eyes. "I can only trust it was all God's will, and He yet has a purpose for me. Though Alain's brother will now inherit the armory shop, I still have my father's ten acres as a freehold, and perhaps I can rebuild his mill there at some time in the future."

"Think not of the future too much. For the present, you need rest, food, and prayers, and you'll be safe here at the fortress."

"Galien, I'm still afraid. I have some coin along with my husband's sword, mail, and tools, but fear to let any of it out of my sight."

"With rightful reason. We can go now to Père Barnard. He'll keep your coin in the treasury, recorded to your credit, and the tools, mail, and sword will be locked up safely there. I'll sign and seal the record as witness."

"Alain's drunken brother grudged him his patrimony to the last denier. He might seek to claim both the coin and the other possessions, should they be shown to be held in my name."

"If you feel you can trust me, I can have Père Barnard record them under my father's name, and you will have my sealed guarantee of free access. For your former brother-in-law, none of it will any longer exist."

Galien held up his right hand. The silver seal ring on the first finger gleamed in the candlelight. He took a drink of wine, grinning with tipsy bravado. "You are under the protection of my family. No man crosses Henri de Coudre or his sons."

Lisette hesitated, and then pulled the bag of coins from her bodice. "Galien, you've shown me nothing but kindness. Noblemen have privileges I might at times resent, but today I'm more than grateful for them."

Chapter 7

3 June 1091, Coudre Manor

At midmorning on the fifth day after the battle, Galien stood at his writing table in the second-floor bedchamber, nearly finished with his second copy of the ransom terms for Count Bayard. Six copies needed to be meticulously lettered on fine vellum, and Père Barnard had assigned three to him.

Galien finished a sentence, put down his quill, and rubbed his eyes. He reviewed the succinct proposal. Alphonse asked a payment of fourteen thousand livres and Bayard's agreement to release any claim on the long-disputed lands and to deed them permanently and indisputably to the Baron of Mirefleurs. Only upon conveyance of the lands and delivery of the coin would the count be freed. The penalties for failure were also concisely stated: Bayard would be held in the noble prisoners' quarters for one month, and then transferred to the dungeon beneath the armory, there to rot on criminals' rations. If six months passed and the count did not or could not comply, he would be beheaded.

The lands could be deeded by the count's signature, but fourteen thousand livres? Even King Philip or the Count of Toulouse would be hard pressed to produce such an amount in coin with just a few weeks' notice. Galien guessed that Alphonse was starting high and intended to negotiate.

He heard the sound of hooves and looked out the open window above his table. Martin turned his horse off Route de Voleurs and rode into the grassy court. Galien powdered the inked vellum, waited a minute, and carefully dusted it with a soft-haired brush. Martin came into the room, greeted Galien, and looked at the document, stroking his short, dark beard.

"If you'd like, I'll read it to you," Galien said.

"Brother, we haven't time. Walter is taking the prisoners back to Grand-Forêt. He wants to gather the townsfolk and have them point out any involved in the rapes and cutting up the old man."

"I'm to go with you?"

"He's requested that you come, so you can record the testimony."

"Duty or not, I'm happy to. I've been in here writing for the last three days."

"And you better a knight's pay at it. Thierré and I are in the wrong profession."

They stopped in the service pantry and picked up bread, cheese, and a skin of water. In the arming room, Galien put on light leather armor. He belted on his sword and buckled his spurs as a guard saddled his horse. With round shields slung over their backs and hard leather helmets on their heads, the brothers reined their horses onto Route de Voleurs. The sun was bright but not yet hot, and the road busy with barony people seeking to complete their business before the heat of afternoon.

"I got some good news from Alphonse yesterday," Martin said.

"He's sending you and Thierré for a night at Mont-Brison's best whorehouse in reward for your valor?"

"No, horse balls," Martin snorted. He drew up in his saddle, looking down his nose at his younger brother. "Alphonse's going to grant me lands greater than Coudre Estate, in exchange for halving Bayard's ransom silver with him."

Galien raised his eyebrows. "A fair arrangement, indeed. I wouldn't start counting the silver yet, though."

"Why not?"

"How will Bayard come up with fourteen thousand livres in coin? Alphonse will end up settling for two thousand and the disputed lands."

"Alphonse's asking what he's sure Bayard's family can pay. Bayard and all of his fathers before him have been the Counts of Saint-

Lille since the time of Charles Magnus, and Countess Rosemonde is a daughter of the highest and richest nobility."

"If you're right, Bayard won't have to beg his noblemen and milk his peasants for the coin. You'll be the richer in lands and coin than any knight in the barony."

"I will be." Martin rocked back in his saddle, clearly ecstatic.

"Then again, this is the perfect opportunity for the noblemen of Saint-Lille to be rid of him. Father's said a good half of them hate him as much as ours do."

"And the other half are staunch loyalists, but all are ready to concede the lands and be done with Bayard's private feud. Having Bayard's family pay the ransom and letting him keep power will preserve peace and order in their county. Settlement of the land dispute with a possible open border can bring new opportunity for friendship and commerce with us. It's the best civil solution for them, and one that promises future gains on both sides of the border."

"Martin, I'm writing the agreement but it seems I'm only a mindless copyist. You've thought it through more than well."

"For now, the counterattack was a great success on our part, and we got Bayard. Whether I've guessed right on the rest remains to be seen."

Galien and Martin rode through the fortress gateway and into the armory yard. Six men-at-arms waited by their horses while sergeant Reinhard Huber and Walter d'Avesnes checked the bolts that secured the steel gate to the oak-barred prison wagon. Three nervous, fresh-faced young men and an older man with long, wild hair and beard sat shackled within.

Martin looked at the older man. "Where did you catch the heathen?"

Huber threw the last bolt. "Sir Martin, his name's Gobert. We caught the greedy fool looting the corpse of one of his fellows."

Walter signaled, the men mounted, and Huber took the wagon reins, and Galien and Martin fell in behind Walter. At Grand-Forêt, the townspeople had been notified of the meeting. Some sat and others stood talking, in the shade of the old oaks around the center of the town. They gathered together as the company rode in and halted. Huber and the men-at-arms brought the shackled prisoners from the wagon, and Walter requested the villagers recount the events of

Bayard's raid and identify any of the prisoners involved in the rapes and mutilation. To a person, they pointed to Gobert as chief instigator of the rapes and the knife wielder who had maimed the old man, but couldn't place the young men.

Walter bade Huber bring Gobert forward to face him. "Armsman Gobert, for the crimes of rape and atrocity, you stand condemned to death. Sentence will be imposed without delay." He turned to Huber. "Sergeant, do your duty."

Huber took a long rope with a noose at the end from under the wagon seat. He slung the rope over a stout oak branch and put the noose around Gobert's neck. Men-at-arms forced Gobert to mount a barebacked horse. Huber bade him pray and, after a minute, slapped the horse hard on the rump. The horse bolted and Gobert dropped, jerking and twitching as he strangled to death. Walter turned to the townspeople, and said, "Let him hang as long as pleases you," and then handed the priest ten deniers. "Give him Christian burial."

With hard justice served, Walter offered the remaining Saint-Lille men a choice: return to the count's service missing their right hands or join the army of the Barony of Mirefleurs. The young men right away defected to the barony and climbed into the wagon, freed of their shackles and their grim existence as foot soldiers in Bayard's army. At the edge of the town, the company halted before the disfigured old man's cottage, and Walter, on behalf of Baron Alphonse, presented him with one hundred silver deniers as compensation for his injuries.

On the way back to the fortress, Walter motioned Galien to ride beside him. "Good that you came with us today, Galien. Your written record will serve as important evidence of Bayard's atrocities. His noblemen won't be able to argue against it."

"Thank you, Sir. I'm pleased to have been of service."

"Have you given more thought to taking your oath?"

Galien took a deep breath. "Sir Walter, I'm no longer drawn to the priesthood. But after today, I'm going to have to think more on becoming a knight."

Walter smiled. "That is the other reason I asked you to come. You saw and heard but a small sample of the ugly side of war, that which a knight must live with all the years of his service at arms."

"You knew what was to happen before today?"

"Yes. Huber beat the truth out of Gobert after we got him into the dungeon. We'd already planned his execution. The people needed to see that justice is done swiftly in our barony."

"You were wise to bring me, Sir Walter. I was greatly honored by your words after the battle, but must admit I need to consider with care before I take on the knight's life."

"You have no cause for concern on my part, Galien. Your father knows he must soon release you from your duties at home. He very much wants you to become a knight, but also knows well that such would be a hard change of path for you."

5 July 1091, Fortress Mirefleurs

Thierré and Martin de Coudre stood behind Henri, Baron Alphonse, and Walter d'Avesnes, all seated in their chairs at the baron's table in the great hall. Two high noblemen of the County of Saint-Lille, Viscount Odo and Count Bayard's brother, Sir Olivier d'Evreux, took chairs across from them, and all turned to the opened doors as a guard detail led Bayard, manacled and shackled, into the hall. The guards removed the manacles and he took the chair between Olivier and Odo.

Père Barnard looked at Alphonse. "Are we ready to begin, Sire?" Alphonse nodded, and he and the barony noblemen signed and affixed their seals to the six documents on the table before them. Barnard brought the documents around to Bayard and the Saint-Lille noblemen. Odo and Olivier signed and sealed them. Bayard's face turned purple with rage and his hands shook. He took the quill from Barnard, scrawled his signature, and impressed the documents with his seal. The guards came forward to return him to his quarters. He cast a long and hateful stare at each man as they snapped the manacles to his wrists and pulled him toward the door.

7 July 1091, at the Saint-Lille border

At daybreak, Thierré and Martin watched from their horses as Reinhard Huber unlocked the door to the prison wagon and Bayard stepped down to the road. Thirty yards away, beyond the border markers, twenty Saint-Lille knights and men-at-arms waited on their horses. A black stallion stood saddled and ready for its rider.

Bayard turned to Martin and Thierré. "I made my vow the day you took me prisoner, and I'll repeat it now. I'm going to kill the both of you, your father, and your brother. You'll not have easy deaths."

Thierré grew pale, and the blue veins at his temples bulged. "Count, were I you, I'd start walking toward my horse and not look back. I've killed men in fights over whores, and taking your head now would matter even less to me."

Bayard glanced at Thierré's thirty mounted men. His face darkened, but he didn't reply.

"I've a promise of my own," Thierré said. "If Gautier again sets foot in the Barony of Mirefleurs, he'll come back to you roasted up like a boar. I'll put his seal ring between his teeth so you can recognize him."

Martin looked at his brother. "Thierré, that's enough. The agreement is concluded, and he's a free man. Sergeant Huber, lead him to the markers and remove his restraints."

Huber and two men-at-arms complied. Bayard crossed the border, mounted the stallion, and glared long and hard at Thierré and Martin. Finally, his men parted for him, and he reined the horse around and rode off at a gallop.

Chapter 8

11 August 1091, the town of Grand-Forêt

The patrol men lounged in the sunset shade of a big oak and watched their relief ride into Grand-Forêt. Thierré, in a good mood, invited his four men-at-arms to have drinks and food at the rebuilt tavern and inn. The men took a table, Thierré and Galien their customary one. The serving girl brought their order and sidestepped Thierré's flirtations.

"I might as well give up on her, Brother."

"For once, you're thinking with your head instead of your cock." Galien looked around the large, pine-floored room and up at the hewn-timber trusses supporting the high-pitched roof. The air was heavy with the pleasant smells of newly sawn wood and fresh paint. "Truly amazing how fast this place went up."

"Silver speaks and men act," Thierré said. "Come a year, this won't be a sleepy little town anymore."

"Alphonse got all he wanted for now, with the lands and Bayard in a cold sweat at the fortress for a month. His plan to spend his part of the ransom silver on barony lands and villages will only make him richer and more popular."

"He has some foresight. Another big nobleman with such a windfall might spend it to conquer his neighbors or on a sixteen-year-old wife."

Night was falling, and the tavern quickly filling up. "To speak of rich men, Martin ought to be here soon," Galien said.

"We've no more wine. I'm going to the front for a fresh pitcher and a goblet for Lord Martin."

Thierré rose, and Galien leaned back in his chair, sipped wine, and watched the crowd of Grand-Forêt townsfolk and people from lands surrounding who had come to see the progress of Alphonse's reconstruction plans. Martin caught Galien's eye from the front door, and Galien waved him over. Thierré returned with a pitcher of fresh wine and set a silver goblet in front of Martin. He filled it with a flourish, bowed, and said meekly, "To your liking, my lord?"

Martin elbowed him. "Sit down, horse cock."

Thierré and Galien raised their cups to Martin. "You've been scarce lately, Brother," Galien said.

"Alphonse and Father have kept me busy. Thierré, it seems they have big plans for the two of us, and Galien as well, should he become priest or knight."

"Martin, I've given up on the priesthood. I'm caught between peace and war with knighthood and the life of a scholar and scribe. Help me make up my mind."

"If the scholar's life is your choice, Alphonse will want you to study the law and practice in the new town he foresees for the meadow west of the fortress."

"A new town? Even Bayard's silver would hardly begin to build it."

"Alphonse had purpose in his proposal to divide Bayard's ransom equally. He's using his part to do the most needful for the barony right now, and wishes for me to build a great fortune with my gains and use it toward the good of our lands and people. I'm afraid my days as a knight on duty at arms are to be over rather quickly."

Thierré took a long pull at his cup and wiped his mouth with his hand. "Galien, I'll not rest until you've taken your oath."

Galien smiled. "I'd expect nothing else of you."

"You shouldn't. The Normans are the best knights in France, and we have their blood."

"Indeed. You and Alisende could both pass for Vikings, right off a longship."

Thierré slapped the table. "And I'll not let you go to waste as a mumbling jurist, you can be sure."

"Brothers, save your own talk for later," Martin said. "With the victory over Bayard, the barony has become wealthier in coin and lands, and Baron Alphonse has important plans for the sons of Henri de Coudre."

Thierré refilled his cup. "So, tell us."

"Thierré, Alphonse sees you and me as the barony's leading noblemen in five years. Come a few years more, Galien as well, whatever his occupation."

"That's easy for a rich man like you to say. At present, I'm but a retainer on a wage, and Galien a simple scribe."

"Thierré, you know that Coudre Estate will be yours when Father dies."

"Better it go to you or Galien than me."

"I'm soon to have my own. Alphonse arranged for me to take over Lethold de Fouchier's holding. His widow is worn out looking after it and wants to move to Limoges, to be near her grandchildren."

"That's a magnificent holding, with a grand old house," Galien said.

"To be exact, nearly a thousand acres of farm and forest lands and three working villages. It brings a fair income."

"Martin, I just don't want the burden of Coudre Estate," Thierré said. Galien and Martin gaped speechless at their elder brother.

Thierré shrugged. "I'm a knight, and nothing else. The siege at Vézelay was the happiest time of my life."

Martin looked at him, palms flat on the table. "Thierré, you're the eldest son of Henri de Coudre. The estate will be yours and you need to think of marrying, like it or not."

Thierré took a long drink, looking sullen. "I'd nearly rather rot in Hell than become a farmer."

Galien couldn't help himself. "You're going to need all of the coin the estate brings. Right now, you spend out your knight's pay on whores and wine."

Thierré punched Galien's shoulder. "Who asked you, bookrat?" He half-drew his sword, thumbed an edge, and grinned maliciously. "Gautier of Saint-Lille yet owes a great debt for his deeds at Grand-Forêt. I hereby vow to cut his legs from under him before I'm chained down to the estate and a family."

"We all agree that Gautier needs to be killed, but he's not here, and we've serious matters at hand," Martin said. "Thierré, Father's a farmer and also the barony's most honored knight."

Thierré shook his head. "Father didn't run the lands. Mother did, and Alisende and Galien took right over after she died. Alisende's much better at managing the estate than I'll ever be. It's a shame she'll be marrying soon."

Galien nodded. "With Martin's silver, Father will finally have enough for her dowry."

"Yes, she can finally marry that dog's ass Baldwin de Betancourt. I've never trusted his show of finery."

Martin raised a hand. "Let's get back to the point of this conversation."

"You mean what you're going to do with all of that silver?"

"Yes, Thierré, that's what I mean. It's important for all of us."

"Let's hear it."

"I've already put a thousand livres in the treasury, under father's name. That'll give him plenty of coin for the estate and the last hundred livres of Alisende's dowry. He'll have enough left over for a comfortable life in his old age."

Galien raised an eyebrow. "That's more than generous of you, Brother."

"I can afford to be so. Alphonse bargained well with Fouchier's widow. She was satisfied with enough to live out her last years well, and have a nice measure of silver to leave her grandchildren."

Thierré guffawed. "A knight who's closer to being a count can't wear second-hand equipment, and you'll need to gather a company."

"Thierré, beside women and drink, all you think about is the next war."

Thierré shrugged and took a bite of roast fowl. "What else should a knight think of?"

"To answer your concern, I've ordered new gear... mail and the fittings, and helmets, shields, and swords."

"And a warhorse?"

"The best bred year-old stallion to be found, and I had to go to Clermont for him. Thirty-five livres for him and the best of horse fittings, but he's the finest animal any of us will ever see."

Thierré paused, cup halfway to his lips. "Shit, Martin, you're not a count yet. That much coin would equip half a dozen men-at-arms and buy them good horses."

"He's my own gift to myself. Other than a guard staff at my house, I don't intend to maintain a company."

"Father told me you that intend to be generous with Robert and Etien," Galien said.

"I've granted each of them fifty good farm acres each on my new holding, and put fifty livres each under their names in the treasury."

Galien stared, wordless. Thierré near choked on his wine. "You've gone crazy, Martin!"

"No, I haven't. With my gains, I can reward them and their families for four generations of loyalty and friendship to our own. They're also two of the best fighting men in the barony, and they'll lead behind me when the need comes that I form a company. To those ends, I'm going to raise them to well-off peasants and allies with a landholding stake in my estate."

"Martin, I must give you credit for your forethought," Thierré said. "They can continue to farm their acres on Coudre Estate and rent out the lands you've granted them. Their own fortunes will grow, and the lord's share of the tenants' produce will bring you more silver."

Martin tapped his temple with a finger and winked at Thierré.

Galien nodded. "Their great-grandfathers fought beside Alphonse's and our own to secure the lands that are now the Barony of Mirefleurs, and their families have been Coudre Estate's leading commoners through the century since. Your generosity is long and well deserved."

16 August 1091, Fortress Mirefleurs

"Galien."

Galien turned to see Henri across the entry court. He put his writing portfolio into his saddlebag and bowed his head to his father. "Sire."

"I just ate breakfast with Alphonse. Come with me while I walk it off."

"I'd be honored, Sire."

They passed beneath the great open gateway to the fortress onto the cobbled forecourt. Beyond the trail that wound gently down to Route de Voleurs, they could see the vast open meadow that lay west of the fortress, turning brown with the heat of August. Henri and Galien took the trail down, walking side by side, Galien leading his horse behind him.

"I need apologize to you, Son," Henri said. "I've been busy with Martin and haven't had much time to spend at home."

"Père Barnard gave me some letters to write. I'm glad you spotted me before I rode off."

"Galien, you're now free of your duties at home. If you still want to go to cathedral school in Paris, Alphonse and I will make provision for your tuition and board. Should you decide for the soldier's life, Alphonse will hear your oath of fealty, and we'll retire your gelding and get you a fitting stallion."

Galien bowed his head. "I'm grateful, Father. I must tell you that I'm no longer drawn to the priesthood."

"Son, I pledged you to the Church, but I feel that God would rather see you happy in your occupation than miserable as a priest. I certainly would."

"Martin said I ought to study the law instead, but I've been feeling a surer call to the knight's life."

"Forget what Martin says. With the knighthood you've well earned, the education you have now, and our name, you'll be well enough positioned for a high diplomat's post in the service of a mighty count or duke, perhaps even the king."

"I hadn't thought of that, Father. It's an exciting idea."

"Then think on it."

They reached Route de Voleurs, pausing before Galien mounted for his ride back to Coudre Estate. Henri said, "Ah, I forgot to tell you. Now that our family fortunes have improved, and Alisende is to marry the first son of a high nobleman, I've decided to engage a lady's servant for her."

"Do what you need, Father"

"Galien, she'll be coming to Coudre Manor to live. Alisende is happy with my choice, but I want to know your thoughts before I hire her."

"All right. Who is it?"

"You already know Lisette, the young woman whose husband was killed at Grand-Forêt. I've been spending much time at Alphonse's table lately, and we've become great friends. She's smart and charming and excels at her service work here at the fortress. Alphonse's having a hard time consenting to let her go, even to his closest friend."

Galien's pulse quickened, but he kept his demeanor. "Father, you have my full approval to bring Lisette to Coudre Manor. What do Martin and Thierré think?"

"I've not asked them directly, but I know they like her from dining at Alphonse's table."

"Her husband took over the armory shop in Grand-Forêt after his father died. Thierré knew Lisette and him before Bayard's raid. He's vowed to cut Gautier's legs off in reprisal."

"I have little doubt your brother will succeed in his vow, and I'll applaud him heartily when he does. But let's get back to Lisette. Shall I make her an offer today?"

"Do so without delay, Father, before Alphonse wakes up from his nap and changes his mind. And offer her a generous wage."

Henri nodded, "I've made up my mind, Son," then patted his bulging waistline, frowning. Galien got on his horse, sat watching as his father strode powerfully up the trail, and then tapped heels to flanks, feeling lighthearted.

+ + +

Lisette bowed her head to Henri de Coudre and hurried to her room, flustered in anticipation. She sat on the edge of the bed, calming herself. Lady's servant to the daughter of Henri de Coudre, the barony's most honored knight! She took a long drink of water, stretched out on the bed, and began to think of all that to come with her move to Coudre Manor on the morrow.

In thinking of her fortress acquaintanceship with Henri's sons and daughter, she concluded that they shared aspects of his best qualities: Alisende, a charming young woman of her own age, who conversed and laughed with her openly and without pretense; Martin, a knight of gentle manner, much like unto his father; Thierré, wild and roguish in his ways, but also a man of highest knightly honor, who would not make unwanted advances.

Few servants could boast of an offer to equal Henri's: a salary of fifteen deniers per month, a private area for dressing and sleeping, and a stable stall with care and feeding for her horse. Clothes for daily work and dress occasions came with the position. With the salary, she'd be able to buy a nicer dress and shoes for herself, as well as add to her precious coin held at the fortress treasury.

Her breath caught and she blushed to every extremity at the thought of Galien de Coudre, and then found herself ashamed. Her husband had died a brutal death in Bayard's raid, but she had been drawn to Galien that day and in the first weeks by way of appreciation of his kindness beyond the call of his duty, and not long after, with a passion she'd felt only for Alain. A great gulf separated them: Galien, a nobleman of education and best family, bound for high accomplishment, and she, a peasant girl dealt a deadly blow by the cruelest of men, but by the grace of God given a fresh start. She called on her resolve to remain well-mannered and friendly, yet reserved, in Galien's presence, but held little confidence in her ability to do so. She could only pray to God for His help.

23 August 1091, Coudre Manor

At the sound of horses at a slow walk and men's laughter, Galien put down his quill. As he looked out the window, two men-at-arms rode past the gateposts; Thierré behind them, leading a spotted-grey stallion... his horse!

He bounded into the corridor and launched himself around the left turn to the staircase, barely missing Lisette and her armload of Alisende's linens before he caught the newel post at the landing. He grinned at Lisette, but she lowered her eyes, saying, "I'm so sorry, Sir Galien."

Galien laughed. "Lisette, the apology is mine. I wasn't looking where I was going, and I told you not to call me 'Sir'."

She bowed her head, eyes still averted, and said, "Yes, my lord" before vanishing around the corner.

Galien threw up his hands and ran into the front court. There, he coaxed the big sleek stallion to approach him, then stroked the animal's neck with his right hand while feeding him oats from the left. He jumped at a jab to his right shoulder. "It's a horse, bookrat. Are you just going to stand there and look?" Thierré said dryly, and the men-at-arms laughed with him.

Galien sneered at his eldest brother, backed up fifteen paces, and bounded forward, at the last second jumping with all the strength in his legs, landing straddling the horse's back. He took the reins and deftly guided the volatile animal in wide circles around the front court. Thierré raised his wine-flask and cheered, "To *Sir* Galien de Coudre!"

After Galien dismounted, Thierré handed him the flask, giving him the honor of the first drink. As he half-emptied it with one swallow, he felt eyes upon him, looked up, and saw Lisette quickly move away from a chamber window.

29 August 1091, Coudre Manor

In the arming room, Galien hefted his hauberk onto the work table, next to his sword, helmet, shield, and other pieces of equipment. He stood back, stroking his chin. With a day's work of cleaning and polishing and fresh leather and paint on the shield, he'd look a respectable knight. The hauberk and coif were showing their age, but with some repairs and a good oiling-up, they'd do for a few more years.

He heard familiar footsteps. Lisette appeared in the doorway, and with eyes lowered, she asked, "My lord, have you anything that needs washing?"

Galien folded his arms. "Lisette, look at me."

She complied timidly, and he said, "Why do you speak to me as if I bear a dread plague?"

"My lord, I'm but Lady Alisende's servant."

"You're not answering my question. We were friendly while you were at the fortress. Now, tell me... what is your reason for avoiding me here?"

Lisette clenched her fists, staring at him directly. "I'm not going to become your mistress."

Galien looked at her, blank-faced, then snorted out a laugh. "My mistress!? Whatever gave you that thought?"

"I'm only a lady's servant. Why else would a nobleman want to talk to me?"

"Lisette, have you never thought that I might like you for your own self, and enjoy your company?"

She blushed deeply and said, "I have, Galien. But I want you to know I'm a chaste woman. If you want a mistress, go to Mont-Brison with Thierré, or find a willing girl in one of the villages."

"Lisette, I'm not like my brother."

"You surely are not. Sir Thierré is a man of honor, who fulfills his manly lusts without compromising innocent women."

Galien folded his arms and leaned on the wall, bemusement on his face. "So you think I've been lying in wait for the right moment, when your will is weak?"

Lisette's façade broke down. She collapsed on a bench by the table, burying her head in her arms, over Galien's mail. "Galien, my life has changed so quickly, and I'm still confused."

"Confused by me? I've never heard anything sillier."

"I don't know... perhaps it's the memory of Alain's brother."

"Michel? He was working at the armory shop while Jacques was still alive."

"After Jacques died and Alain and I came back from Clermont, Michel started putting his hands on me and saying the filthiest things."

Galien raised an eyebrow. "You didn't tell Alain?"

"I wanted no discord between my husband and his brother, so I fought Michel off until Alain caught him trying to rape me. Alain dragged him behind the shop and beat him till he could hardly stand, and then threw him out on the road. He was working for the farrier in Saint-Julien until the day of Bayard's raid."

"Lisette, you know I'd never harm any woman, far less you. I don't think you're telling me everything."

"I can't, Galien."

"Yes, you can... out with it!"

"I... it's this, Galien. I've more feelings for you than you can possibly imagine, and with Alain hardly three months gone, God can only see me as a fallen woman."

20 September 1091, Coudre Manor

"Before you leave, will you look at my horse? I think a shoe has come loose."

Thierré stood up. "I'll be happy to. Sister. But where's the stableman?"

"This is his free afternoon. He said he was going to visit his father."

Alisende and Thierré left the house by the front door and walked toward the stable. Across the court, Galien and Lisette were sitting on the stone bench by the gateposts, talking with no attention but for the other. Inside the stable, Thierré said, "They didn't even notice us."

"That's no surprise. They're together all the time when Father isn't here."

"And so? It's time Galien started taking an interest in women."

Alisende took Thierré by the arms. "Brother, it's more than a passing matter. Galien told me he intends to ask her to marry him, and I dread the day Father learns of it."

Thierré grimaced. "I'll be more than happy to be safe behind the walls at the fortress when that comes to pass."

JOSEPH SCOTT AMIS

Chapter 9

3 October 1091, Coudre Manor

Martin de Coudre rode past the gateposts, toward the front porch. Lisette, on her way to the house with a basket of clean linens, walked over to greet him.

"Good afternoon, Sir Martin. How do find your new lands?"

"A good day to you, Lisette. I took a long ride this morning and visited with farmers and in the villages. All's well."

"I'm happy to hear. Galien's inside. I'll tell him you've arrived."

"Do so. I'll be in the stable for a while."

Inside the house, she leaned into the great room and called, "Galien, Martin is here, in the stable."

Galien closed the doors to the armoire and walked over to her, quill pen, parchment, and ink in hand. "I need to write a letter to the Abbot at Saint-Amand. I'll see Martin when I'm finished. Know what's for supper?"

Lisette laughed. "All I can tell you is I'm helping Paul and Lucie get it all ready. Wait till tomorrow and be surprised."

"Be that way, then." Galien leaned his shoulder against the tall stair newel post. He looked at her, grinning. Lisette couldn't help but blush, and she cursed herself for it. Galien, wearing her favorite of his gambesons, tight leggings, and soft kidskin shoes, made for a fetching sight.

Lisette shooed him away. "You'd best write that letter before Martin comes in. Once the two of you start drinking wine, you're good for nothing."

Galien started up the stairs. Lisette watched him for a moment, and her chest clenched. He might soon be lost to her forever. She re-tied her hair and pulled on her cap, took a bag of coins from the household strongbox, and left for a ride to the two peasant villages on the estate. The Friday afternoon hunting parties would soon be returning with a good selection of game from which to choose the main course for the family supper, on the morrow.

An hour later, she rode into the front court with two full game bags hung behind the saddle, pleased with her purchase of eight large wild ducks. At twenty-four deniers for the lot, they'd come dearly, but a supper with Sir Henri, his three sons, and his daughter all present called for the best.

She walked her horse into the stable. Martin stood by his stallion, brushing him down and sipping from his flask, lost in his daydreams. She smiled in silent amusement and lugged the ducks into the service pantry.

Galien stood at the work table, readying his letter. He heated a stick of sealing wax in a candle flame, dropped a blob of hot, viscous red goo on the folded edges of the parchment, and impressed it with the family seal on his ring. He eyed the game bags.

"Tomorrow's supper, eh?"

"Yes, and it's still a surprise."

"Tell me. Before long, you won't be seeing me anymore."

"Galien, this is just as hard for me. You know that."

Galien sat silent, his expression drawn and grim. Lisette said, brightly, "Perhaps a little wine will make you feel better before you go out to see Martin."

"Why not, and fill a cup for each of us. He'll be out in the stable for a good while yet. I think he's reliving the battle at Saint-Denis for the hundredth time."

Lisette climbed down the steep stair to the cellar and returned with two metal cups of fresh, cool red wine. Both took a drink.

After a quiet moment, Galien spoke. "I was ready for Alphonse to hear my oath, but now I'm getting hauled off to a monastery instead.

After Thierré and Martin, I can't be anything but a disappointment for Father."

"Thierré and Martin have told me of your fine record at arms. You proved yourself as well as Martin did in the battle at Saint-Denis. Sir Henri and Baron Alphonse know that." Lisette topped up Galien's cup. He drained it in one swallow and laughed without humor.

"Galien, you haven't left yet," she said. "Tell your father you'll take up service at the fortress. You'll be away from me there."

"No, I'll be best off far away for a while. I suppose six months won't make a difference."

"Six months away will bring you back to your senses, and you'll come home in more of a steady mind."

"Come home to be just one more of Alphonse's retainers? I earn more silver now than Thierré, and he's a knight of rank."

"Galien, we've talked over this already. You'll not be a retainer for long. With knighthood and your name and education, you'll have the world open to you, and I'm not going to be the cause for you to lose your opportunities. Your place is as a knight, with the nobility and a noblewoman as your wife. I've my own future to consider, and I'll not betray your father's kindness. Any other nobleman would have thrown me out, finding one of his sons was in love with a common servant girl."

"You prefer to wait for a local bumpkin, then?"

"Alain was hardly a bumpkin, Galien."

He looked down at the table and stammered, "I... I'm sorry, Lisette. That was a mean thing for me to say."

She put a hand on his cheek. "Galien, it's all right. Don't forget that I've had to deal with my own feelings. My husband was hardly more than a month gone, and I fell in love again. I still feel I've betrayed him and God, and now I can't have you."

Galien grabbed her arm. "You can! You only need to consent to my proposal."

"Even if your father were to consent, I cannot marry you and have you ruin your life. Only God can will that we be together, and if so, He'll make our path clear. That's all I can say."

"You'll wait on God, and one day you'll wake up and find you've become an old spinster."

"Perhaps I will, but I'd rather end up an old spinster than see you destroy your bonds with your father."

"At least Father can stop worrying for his other children. Martin's a landed knight at twenty-one years, and since Thierré declared his own war on Gautier of Saint-Lille, he's never been so happy. And Alisende will soon be married to the first son of a viscount."

"Sir Henri needn't worry about you, either. Go to Saint-Amand and get over your feelings for me. I'm happy here with the Coudre family and don't want to be forced to leave."

Galien took her hand and squeezed it. "I've been thinking only of myself."

"I'm pleased you understand that. Most men wouldn't."

"I should take this letter upstairs to Father's room before I spill wine on it."

"Your father has given me leave for the morrow, and I need to finish making supper for Paul and Lucie to cook in the morning. When you come back down, I'll have a pitcher filled with fresh wine. Take it out to Martin and wake him up. You've plenty to talk about."

Galien put the letter on Henri's desk and returned downstairs to the service pantry. From the cellar doorway, he heard Lisette moving about. He shut the door behind him, climbed down the steep steps, and put an arm around her waist. She tilted her face toward his, wrapped her arms around his neck, and they kissed long and deeply. Galien put a hand on a breast. She gasped and hesitated, but drew away.

"Lisette, we're alone in the house. Can't we just have one time?"

She put her hands on his chest. "No, Galien. I've never sinned with a man, and I'll not tempt God more than I have already."

4 October 1091, Coudre Manor

Martin and Galien woke hung over late in the morning. They dragged themselves from their beds in the second-floor chamber. Galien looked out a front window and watched Henri, Alisende, and Thierré ride off of Route de Voleurs and between the gateposts to the stable. Galien and Martin quickly washed their faces and combed their hair, before the family could see evidence of their previous night of drinking.

Half an hour later, freshly washed and dressed, the brothers came down the stair for supper in the great room, and joined Thierré and Alisende at the family table. Paul and Lucie brought watered wine and a platter with bread, cheese, and fruit. Galien's stomach hadn't yet settled and a drink of the wine made him feel better. Henri sat, relaxing, on the high-backed bench next to the fire. Galien filled a goblet from the wine pitcher and brought it to his father. "Join us, Sire?"

Henri rose and took the chair at the head of the table. Thierré spoke right away. "Father, none of us knew that Galien's decided to become a monk."

"Galien can speak for himself."

"It's all quite simple," Galien said. "Father doesn't approve of what's come to pass between Lisette and me. He said I ought to think of going away for a few months, and I chose the Abbé de Saint-Amand. Though I don't like the idea of becoming a postulant, I'll receive the best instruction in manuscript illustration in the scriptorium there."

Thierré leaned back, grinning at Henri. "I think you made more than a gentle suggestion, Father."

"Yes, and he chose the monastery. He'll be under no pressure to take binding vows."

Alisende smiled at Galien. "I'm happy to see you've finally taken an interest in women, Brother. After last Christmas at the fortress, I gave up on trying to introduce you around."

Henri scowled. "We all know you had your head in your books until Lisette came along, Galien." He shook his head and looked at the table. "I just can't understand why you couldn't have found a pretty young noblewoman, but I suppose it's only my fair due for my drunkenness over the last few years. I just assumed you'd be going into the Church, and didn't bother to look for a suitable bride."

"Father, it's not your fault," Thierré said. "Galien doesn't care for custom, any more than I do. As far as I'm concerned, Lisette's a match for any noblewoman. Galien can marry her, and I'll stand beside him."

"You don't give a care for much of anything," Martin said. "Galien's a nobleman and needs to marry within his own station, become he a knight or not."

Thierré emptied his goblet and glared at his brother. "With all that damned land and coin, it's Sir Martin High-and-Mighty now, eh?"

Henri slapped the table. "Thierré! Your sister is present. Watch your words."

Alisende rolled her eyes. "Father, with three brothers, I'd heard every curse known to mankind before I turned ten years."

Henri grumbled and took a drink of wine, and Alisende said, "I agree with Thierré. Noblewomen are for the most part boring. I'm not surprised Galien finds Lisette so much to his liking. She's become my best friend, after all."

Paul announced the first course of supper. The Coudres regained their demeanor while he and Lucie cleared the table. They returned to the pantry and Henri took charge. "All is settled. Galien will spend six months as a postulant at the Abbé de Saint-Amand, this at his choosing. If Lisette chooses to remain here, she's welcome to continue in her present duties." He laughed. "Had I been in her shoes, I might well have fallen for Galien, too." He looked at his youngest son. "You're an exceptional young man, and I'm as proud of you as I am of your brothers." He pointed his table knife at Martin and Thierré. "I'll hear no more of your squabbling."

Thierré raised his goblet to Galien. "I'll be waiting for you in the training yard, and you'd best be ready."

"Don't get eager yet, Son. He's much thinking to do," Henri said.

"Will you be leaving soon, Brother?"

"Father and I are riding to Saint-Amand on the day after the morrow."

Henri put his hand on the table. "When I return, I'll have important matters to discuss with all of you."

+ + +

While the Coudre family was deep in discussion, Lisette guided Galien's gelding over the road through the dense forest between the fortress and Grand-Forêt. Riding his old horse made her feel close to him, but she had an important decision of her own: return to her home town and rebuild her father's mill, or remain in Sir Henri's service.

But for the huge old oaks, Lisette hardly recognized Grand-Forêt. The stone church had been freshly repaired, and a new inn and tavern stood facing it across freshly laid cobblestones. New timber-and-plaster structures, under construction in orderly rows, were fast replacing the shop buildings and the jumble of plaster-and-wattle cottages that had burned in Count Bayard's raid. Late morning Mass was over, and townspeople stood chatting outside. She pulled the horse to a halt. The older buildings that hadn't burned still stood. The sign above the blue door to Alain's armory shop hung askew; the painted crossed swords yet dirty with soot from the raid. Beyond, she could see her small yet valuable holding, cleared of the burnt remains of the mill and cottage.

She found familiar faces among the many new ones. Neighbors welcomed her and told her of the months passed since Bayard's attack. Baron Alphonse had wasted no time in making good on his promise to rebuild Grand-Forêt. He had brought new families as well as young, skilled single people to the town, and it was beginning to prosper again. After half an hour of talk, she found a place to sit by herself in the shade of an oak, brushing off attractive young men who attempted to strike up conversations.

The terror and heartbreak of that May morning returned to her in a rush of memories. Though six months had not passed since the dreadful day, she was no longer feeling a sense of place for herself in Grand-Forêt. Her past life and marriage to Alain were fast fading into memory, and her new life in the household of Henri de Coudre had proven a pleasant and fulfilling one. Her passionate feelings for Galien had only grown stronger, but in a troubled and violent world, she had been fortunate to find a secure home with Sir Henri's family and couldn't forsake it, even for a genuine love. Though her rejection of his proposal had wounded him terribly and her own heart was broken, she had to put herself first.

She had no need to tarry longer in her home town. After farewells to old friends, she walked back to Galien's gelding. As she reached for the reins, a hand grabbed her forearm roughly. Alain's brother Michel yanked her close, breathing stale wine fumes in her face. "You damned whore. You took the coin and tools that were rightfully mine, and I haven't been able to keep my business up."

Lisette jerked her arm free and drew back toward the horse. "The patrols no longer come to the shop because you're a drunkard and your work is shoddy. I'm not to blame for your troubles."

"Those fancy knights you sleep with lie for sport. Once old Henri catches one of his sons with a hand up your dress, he'll throw you onto the road on your ass. You'll come crawling back and beg to get in my bed for a roof and something to eat."

She slapped his right cheek hard, and he pushed her against the gelding. "I want my silver and my tools, bitch. If you don't give them back, I'll just help myself to this fine nobleman's ride."

He grasped at the bridle and the horse pulled away, snorting. Lisette mounted quickly and grabbed a riding crop. She hit him across the face with a right swing and struck the other cheek on the backswing. He dabbed at the blood and reached for the knife at his belt.

Lisette reined the horse around. "Go to the fortress and take up your problems with Thierré de Coudre, but have proof of your claims. He has no patience for fools."

"To Hell with you and Coudre. Those God-cursed noblemen will let a lying slut steal an honest man's silver and hang him if he complains."

"You're no honest man. Alain and I earned the coin we had together, and the tools were his alone."

Michel spat, pointing the knife at her. "I helped my father build up that shop and then Alain stole it from me, and you're the thief who took my coin and tools. You think you're something on that nobleman's horse, but I'll not let this pass, you can be sure."

"Best you crawl back into your hole and not come out. Thierré de Coudre might decide you're worth as much without your hands as with them." Lisette put her heels to the gelding's flanks, and as he settled into a gallop, she said goodbye to Grand-Forêt. Though Baron Alphonse would certainly grant her the coin she might still lack to rebuild her father's mill, it would have to wait for a better time.

Chapter 10

6 October 1091, Coudre Estate

Galien rose after sunup, dressed, and checked his travel bags. He crept down the stair, saw his family at breakfast at the great room table, and stayed out of their sight. In the stable, he brushed his horse down, saddled and bridled him, and sat on the stall bench, cleaning and polishing his sword and dagger as he waited.

Henri and Thierré presently came for their horses. "Martin and Alisende and the servants are waiting. Go and say your goodbyes," Henri said.

Galien, feeling like a pariah, walked to the front of the house. He shook hands with Paul, and Lucie kissed him on the cheek. Alisende hugged him and said, "God be with you, dear Galien." Martin shook his hand and embraced him hard, in silence.

Lisette stepped forward, put a hand on his shoulder, and brushed her lips on his cheek. In a voice that barely masked a sob, she whispered, "Write to me, Galien." He nodded stiffly and turned to join his father and brother for the ride to Fortress Mirefleurs.

They spoke little during the quarter-hour ride. Galien relaxed with the swaying motion of his horse and the rhythmic clopping of hooves. If robbers lay in wait, the bright daylight and the sight of Thierré's ready three-foot sword would suffice to keep them in hiding.

At the fortress, Henri and Baron Alphonse drifted off into conversation, and Thierré bade Galien visit the armory to make farewells. There, though feeling even more an outcast, he put up a cheerful face. A swallow of strong ale lifted his spirits, and he gratefully accepted the rounds of drinks and rowdy good wishes from his comrades-in-arms. After an hour with them, approaching drunkenness, he left to clear his head in the solitude of the fortress book room.

Hardly a soul in residence at the fortress could read and write, and but for Père Barnard's careful attention, the valuable contents of the large closet would have long ago rotted away. A score of books and scrolls lay under a heavy cloth on a long table beneath the tiny leaded-glass window; twoscore others, neatly arranged on shelves. Galien picked up an old Latin Bible and spent the next hours pleasantly, studying verses from the Gospels that intrigued him, admiring the calligraphic style and elaborate illustrations. By late afternoon, amid fading daylight, his senses had cleared, and he left to dress for the evening meal in the great hall.

The soaring great hall never failed to excite Galien's senses and imagination. A wide fireplace stood at each end of the hundred-foot room; high-pitched ornamented timber roof trusses resting on columns spanned the fifty feet between the thick stone side walls. Baron Alphonse's noblemen and women dined at a thirty-foot trestle table set before the fireplace at the south end; the north used for cooking and preparation for table service. The fireplaces, torches in wall brackets, and chandeliers constructed from antlers holding tallow candles, provided warm light and cast flickering shadows onto the huge multicolored tapestries on the walls. The weapons and shields displayed gleamed dully, lending an air of knightly masculinity.

Alphonse's jolly disposition set the mood, and the food and drink were excellent and abundant. Galien endured the few minutes of well-wishing offered him and excused himself, happy to wander off with a goblet of wine. He took a seat at a table in the center of the room and fell into his thoughts. He felt himself in disgrace with his father and was relieved to be going to the monastery, where he would become, for a while, a postulant monk, away from his family, no longer a part of the world of men and women and the complications of their affairs. Perhaps God would provide answers for him there.

7 October 1091, on the road to the Abbé de Saint-Amand

Henri, Galien, and three men-at-arms set off on horseback early in the morning. Henri chatted amiably with the young men, keeping them fascinated with his endless war stories. Galien spoke little and rode somnolently in the unfamiliar countryside, enjoying the cool air, warm sunshine, and the sights of rolling green meadows, farmlands at harvest, and castles in the hazy distances.

At midafternoon, they stopped in Mont-Brison, a large town close to the main road. Henri and Galien took a room at a fine inn for wealthy travelers; the men-at-arms went to a soldiers' hostel, downcast at Henri's orders to refrain from heavy drinking and visits to the well-known brothel district.

Father and son took their supper and wandered the streets of the town until dusk. On their return to the inn, Henri climbed the stairs to their room, and Galien tarried to drink two cups of spiced wine by the common room fire. He found his father asleep and snoring, put on his nightshirt, and crawled into bed beside him. He lay awake for an hour, listening to the wind, his mind at rest for the first time in many nights.

8 October 1091, on the road to the Abbé de Saint-Amand

In the morning, Henri and Galien rode together. Henri cleared his throat and offered his apology for the beating he had meted out five years earlier.

"Father, you needn't apologize. I have nothing for which to forgive you. The bad blood between Thierré and me ended on that day, and I realized I don't lack courage."

Henri chuckled, clearly pleased his unsparing discipline had gone to good effect. "I saw the knight's blood in you that day. Thierré's mischief while he was training at the fortress got him a like flogging at least once a year, and you took my blows every bit as well as he did."

"Thank you for your good words, Father. I've felt lower than a worm lately."

"Galien, you know my concerns. Lisette is a good young woman, but your particular friendship with her is not fitting for a man of your station."

Galien stared ahead, suddenly sullen. "You seem to care more for station more than for your children."

Henri reined back and called "Halt." He glared at his son. "You will spend your time at the monastery, then come home and take your oath of fealty. By then, I'll have chosen a noblewoman of good family to be your wife."

Galien sighed. "You're my father, and your wishes are law."

"And they will be until I'm dead or lose my mind. With you and Thierré to worry about, I'm surprised I'm still sane."

"At least Martin and Alisende have met your expectations."

"Martin and Alisende have always understood what it means to be members of the nobility. I gave up on Thierré long ago, and now you've surprised me."

"It's right that I go to Saint-Amand. I'll be out of your life for a while."

"Don't be so bloody dramatic. All I want is for you is to come to terms with your station as a nobleman."

"I can't deny that I became fond of the soldier's life during my service at arms, and all the time I've spent with Thierré. I'll be ready."

"Galien, your record at arms has made me naught but proud. Your show of courage and skill in the battle at Saint-Denis quieted any doubts I had as to your fitness for knighthood."

Galien mused. "I still can't neglect my education. Perhaps I'll apprentice with a jurist in Clermont or Le Puy for a while."

Henri laughed. "You haven't that much time, Son. You're already near to twenty years!"

"Thierré did say I'd be the only knight at the fortress able to read and write."

"That won't serve you when a six-foot axe man is swinging at your skull, but it will further your advancement off the battlefield. I've always been proud that you and Alisende learned your letters, and your mother was, as well."

"You're right, Father. I think that to take your advice of seeking a diplomat's post is my best course."

"It is, indeed. But in the highest places that course will take you, never forget that you share your family's blood, Galien."

"I won't forget."

They rode at their ease for another hour, conversing pleasantly and pausing at notable sights. As the sun dropped low in the sky, they reached a high crest in the road. Vineyards spread in orderly rows across the valley below, and the white stone buildings of the monastery complex sparkled in the fading light of early evening.

They followed the road down into the valley. As they rode between rows of vineyard plantings, Henri said, "I've made other decisions, Galien. Alphonse has offered me a home and pension at the fortress, and I'm going to take him up on it."

"I'm happy that you'll be at the fortress with Baron Alphonse, Father. He's your closest friend."

"Since I lost my sword hand and your mother died, life hasn't held much joy for me. I haven't the will for landholding and farming, but the battle at Saint-Denis proved I'm still good for something. Alphonse is going to put me to work training the men-at-arms. That's where I belong, and Thierré will take over the estate right away."

"I think that the best choice for you, but though the estate is Thierré's patrimony, he doesn't want to manage it, any more than you do."

Henri nodded with an air of resignation. "I'm afraid Thierré's lack of interest in our lands is a hard truth I must swallow. He'll neglect the estate and be the first knight to sign up for the next big campaign that comes along. By the time you've come home, Alisende will be ready to be married."

"Thierré doesn't like Baldwin de Betancourt."

"Thierré doesn't like any man who might best him at arms. Baldwin's character is unspotted, and the children of their union will be born to a station far above our own humble place in the nobility."

Galien grinned. "You lost your hand saving the life of the Viscount of Nevers at Vézelay, but you gained the pledge of his first son for Alisende."

Henri regarded his handless right arm with a frown, and then grinned back at Galien. "Yes, God can grant unexpected gifts along with the hardest of blows. My sword hand was taken, but I gained the best of marriages for Alisende, and a dear friend in Enguerrand de Betancourt."

Evening turned to night as they approached the gates of the Abbé de Saint-Amand. Henri said, with a chuckle, "Galien, perhaps here you will decide to go into the Church after all, and not have children, with the worries that they bring. If so, feel fortunate. After twenty-five years spent raising all of you, I must yet see you not make mistakes you'll regret."

Henri, Galien, and the men-at-arms rode through the open gates beside the last few monks straggling in after the day's work in the vineyards. A dignified elder monk walked across the cobblestone court to greet Henri and Galien and directed the armsmen to food and quarters.

He spoke. "Sir Henri, you and your son are expected, but our brothers go to bed soon after Compline. I'll take you to your lodgings. Late supper will be served to you there and you will meet with the abbot in the morning."

After Henri and Galien had settled in, a novice monk brought flagons of wine and water and a plain but tasty meal of fowl, spiced roast carrots with parsnips, and bread and cheese. He told them where to find the garderobe and bade them good night, with God's blessings. Henri was too tired to talk. They ate quietly, put on nightshirts, and crawled into bed.

Galien listened to his father's snores and thought of Lisette with an aching heart and a fresh perspective. To ask her to marry him, knowing his father would certainly disapprove, had been a foolish impulse on his part. She had shown the wisdom to recognize it and the strength to prevent both of them from making a grave mistake.

9 October 1091, the Abbé de Saint-Amand

At sunrise, soon after Prime, the novice came in to restart the fire and directed them to the communal washing fountain. Galien and Henri rose and washed at the round fountain set in the middle of a service court, as monks of all ages and descriptions came and went.

The elder monk knocked at their room door, and Galien followed him and Henri as they crossed the cloister. This eighty-foot-square courtyard, bordered on all four sides with rows of Roman-style columns supporting stone arches and tiled roofs, formed the center of the monastery complex. The roofs covered twelve-foot walkways, and at each corner of the cloister, an ornate arched doorway opened to a large, two-story building.

They climbed the stone stairs to the abbot's quarters. The monk led Henri and Galien into a large chamber with a high beamed ceiling. Abundant, cheerful light streamed in through glass windows set in lead at the north wall; the fireplace on the south wall cast a pleasant warmth. The table in front of the fireplace was set for a meal.

A carved oaken door opened, and the abbot entered. The monk announced, "Father Abbot Leo," and bowed. Leo, a slender, disciplined, grey-bearded man of sixty years, spoke in a courtly manner. "Sir Henri, it is a pleasure to see you. Galien, you are welcome here." He gestured toward the table, and they took seats. The elder monk bowed and silently left the room. Within a minute, two others appeared with breakfast.

Abbot Leo and Henri chatted pleasantly. Leo inquired about the ride to the monastery and other members of Henri's family. Lastly, he voiced concern over Baron Alphonse's appetite for wine and rich food, and the large increase in his weight over the previous years. Leo turned to Galien. "Your father tells me you can read and write well in both French and Latin, and have made some study of ancient Greek and Hebrew texts."

"Yes, Father Abbot. Father engaged a priest to tutor me when I was a boy, and at every visit to Fortress Mirefleurs, I've taken the opportunity to visit the library and study the books and manuscripts."

Henri snorted. "You can hardly call Alphonse's old book closet a library, Galien. You and Père Barnard are the only people who've opened the door to that room in the last twenty years."

Leo spoke kindly. "Sir Henri, Galien may well have learned as much in Baron Alphonse's storeroom as cathedral-schooled men do in Paris or Rome."

Henri couldn't conceal his pride. "Galien learned his lessons well. Our family spent many a winter evening by the fire in our cold old house, listening to him read the Bible and stories of adventure."

Leo smiled at Henri and addressed Galien. "Galien, you seem a good young man, and I sincerely hope you will want our monastery to be your home. Scant few men here, other than myself, can read and write at all, and your literary skills and scholarly knowledge should prove invaluable in the future. However, you must pass the six months of postulancy before you can be accepted as a full novice."

"I'd only thought to stay six months, Father Abbot."

"We do accept young men of good character and family who want a taste of the monk's life. What do you wish to gain from your stay?"

"Instruction in manuscript arts and to study languages, philosophy, and history from the texts to be found in the library here."

"Your previous education and your father's generous donation will make that possible for you, but you must wear the postulant's habit and tonsure. For four months, you'll work on the assignments given you. We accept all of our men as equals in God's sight, and for rich and poor alike, these first months are passed in manual labor and instruction in our daily spiritual life. With that completed, you will be assigned as you've requested. If you do find the monastic life to be suitable, you can choose to take vows as a full novice."

"Father Abbot, I'm grateful you've accepted me with my present wishes."

"God brought you to us as He brings all of our men, even those who choose not to stay. I'm merely His doorman here."

Leo concluded the meal and discussion. "Galien, Brother Benedict will be here shortly, to escort you to quarters and start your instruction in our daily life. Sir Henri, if you'd like, join me for a tour of the monastery and vineyards before you start out for home."

Henri bowed at Leo's invitation and turned to Galien. "Some hard outdoor work will build your body and wind, and I'll keep your sword oiled and your stallion exercised."

Galien looked at Abbot Leo. "Father Abbot, I don't think you need guess at my father's fondest wish for me."

"I only want for you to be of steady mind, Son," Henri said. "Should you decide to stay and take the monastic vows, I'll be no less proud of you."

Leo put a hand on Henri's arm. "I think God will overlook that claim, Sir Henri." They all laughed together. Brother Benedict entered the room, bowed, and Galien followed him out.

Benedict stopped at a bench under an apple tree in the center of the cloister. They sat and he pulled back the cowl of his habit. Galien saw a handsome man of thirty-five years, pale-skinned and clean-shaven, hair dark and straight. His eyes were grey-green and remarkably clear, and Galien felt a curious sense of peace in his presence.

"How do you feel after your talk with Abbot Leo?"

"Anxious, but he seemed kind, as have all the monks I've met."

"Leo is a saintly person and a true servant of God and man. But like many men in high positions, his responsibilities cause him to lose touch with the daily lives of his charges, and he often sees only the ideal."

"What do you mean, exactly?"

"I mean that some men here are not what they seem to be at first meeting. For some, a monastery is a place to draw nearer to God; for others, of sick soul and confused mind, it is a hospital for the spirit. You will find precious few saints within these walls. Most here are ordinary men: decent, pious, and hardworking souls, but there are also scoundrels here, some in positions of authority."

"Hmm."

"Galien, you'll be fine. Come to me any time you're in need of help or want to talk. I'm of a noble family as well, and have a notion of the anxieties you might be facing. Above all, keep your faith, and endeavor daily to deepen it."

"Thank you, Brother Benedict. I'm feeling homesick already."

Benedict rose. "You need to be tonsured, and then we'll go to the postulant quarters and get you settled in. Soon enough, you'll have no time for homesickness."

+ + +

Leo walked Henri through the monastery complex and described the renovation work in progress at the old stone church building. Henri was pleased with Leo's plan to use fifty livres he had donated to pay the balance due for the new leaded-glass windows. The two men sat at ease on a low stone wall and watched the masons hoist carved finials onto the newly built dressed-stone side buttresses.

"Sir Henri, I've heard the story of your son Martin's great courage, and of the honor he brought to the Barony of Mirefleurs."

"Martin's always been a strong boy with his wits close about him, but Galien is the reason I'm here today. He's strong of mind and spirit, but at present, weak of will and unsure of his intentions."

"Henri, God has put Galien in the right place with us. I've seen weak men regain their strength here, many times. When you're fully rested, ride home with a lighter heart."

"Father Abbot, I have yet one more burden."

"Tell me."

"At Galien's birth, I made a promise to God he would serve the Church in the priesthood, and now that promise will most likely not be fulfilled."

Leo put a hand on Henri's shoulder. "I think God has changed His mind for Galien. If he becomes the honorable knight that you are, our Lord will be eminently satisfied."

Henri stroked his chin in a moment of thought. "Your good words relieve my mind, Father Abbot. Now, I need join my men and be off if we're to make Mont-Brison by sunset."

"To visit with you has been a pleasure, Sir Henri. Accept our humble blessings and go with God."

Leo bowed his head, raised his right hand, and made the sign of the cross. Henri returned the bow and walked toward his quarters, his bearing erect, as befitted a knight.

10 October 1091, Coudre Manor

The sun was setting as Henri walked his horse into the stable. After he had napped, washed, and dressed, Alisende joined him for late supper in front of the fire. He tasted the good food, took a sip of his best wine, then leaned back and smiled at her. "My worries for Galien are at rest, and we can talk of happier things. When can we expect young Baldwin de Betancourt to visit?"

"A letter from him was delivered three days past. He's to arrive at the fortress in ten days, and I can hardly bear to wait."

"Good. I'll have this house put in order right away."

"Thank you, Father. I very much want for him to come here for supper."

"I'm pleased that you've found Baldwin to your liking."

"Father, you're kind. So many noblewomen are married to men they don't care for."

Henri took her hand. "Alisende, your mother and I were happy together, and I don't want anything less for you and your husband. Now, I need to tell you of my own plans."

11 October 1091, Fortress Mirefleurs

After breakfast with Baron Alphonse, Henri visited the room on the elder knights' floor in the armory tower. It was comfortable enough for his austere needs, suited a man of his station, and he could look out the tiny slit window to the broad meadow of lavender west of Route de Voleurs. Satisfied, he took a seat on the chair by the bed and reflected.

He smiled to himself. After this morning's hard lecture, unruly first son Thierré had reluctantly bowed to his obligations. He would be moving to the estate after Alisende's wedding and had accepted that Baron Alphonse would be seeking to match him with a suitable bride. Henri had done his best for his sons and daughter. Thierré and Martin were now on their own, and Alisende had, as husband-to-be, a good young knight of wealthy family and name far greater than the Coudres. He felt confident Galien would benefit from his time at the monastery, find himself, and come home done with romantic notions toward Lisette, ready to take up the responsibilities of a nobleman.

Henri felt drowsy from the heavy breakfast. He stretched out on the bed, chuckling to himself in eager anticipation of his duties to come. Though the green younger men might not at first take a grizzled old one-handed knight as their training master seriously, a hard surprise lay in wait for them with Henri de Coudre. With this pleasant thought, he drifted off into a light sleep.

Shortly, the creak of hinges and wood awakened him. Elder knight Fulbert de Ronchamp, clad in a long grey hooded pilgrim's cloak, stepped over and looked down, frowning. "I see you've already made yourself at home in my room, Henri," he said.

"Indeed, I have. You can leave for the Holy Land and let me go back to sleep." Fulbert laughed aloud as Henri stood. The two men put their arms around each other's shoulders in a long, silent embrace. Henri couldn't help the tears that rolled down his cheeks. They might never see one another again in this life.

Fulbert put his hands on Henri's shoulders. "Don't fear for me, old friend. This is what I've wanted for so many years. Now that my sons and daughters are grown and gone, and my wife passed, I've nothing more to do before I die than make penance before God for all the killing I've done."

Henri thought of the tales he'd heard of the Mohametan Turks' atrocious cruelty to Christian pilgrims seeking to visit the Holy Places in peace and piety. "Fulbert, you know you need be more than wary of the Turks that rule in Jerusalem."

Fulbert opened his long cloak and half-drew the sword concealed beneath it, smiling. "A pilgrim ought not to be carrying this, but I think it a greater sin for a knight to not be able to defend the weaker ones beside him."

Henri nodded in agreement. Were he going to Jerusalem, he certainly wouldn't be leaving his own sword behind. He walked beside Fulbert through the courts of the fortress and stood at the forecourt beyond the gate, watching his lifelong friend tread the trail down to Route de Voleurs, there to meet with a band of pilgrims journeying on foot to Italy and a ship bound for the Holy Land.

Chapter 11

20 October 1091, Coudre Manor

Henri stood by as Alisende and Baldwin de Betancourt mounted their horses in the grassy court before the house. He glanced at the sun. "Best you two return well before nightfall, Sir Baldwin. I'd have Alisende here and you safe at the fortress before the robbers come out."

Baldwin smiled at Alisende, patting the hilt of his sword. "Not to worry, Sir Henri."

"Well enough. Enjoy your ride." Henri watched the couple ride past the far corner of the house and on to the meadow beyond, then went inside and took a seat on the high-backed bench before the fire.

Lisette came from the service pantry. "Would you like anything, Sir Henri?"

"I would. Fetch me wine and sit with me."

"The honor is mine, my lord."

She returned in a minute and sat next to Henri. Henri sipped at the wine and said, "What do you think of young Baldwin?"

"He seems to be of good manners."

"You seem reticent, Lisette. Speak your mind."

"It's only this, Sir. He drank a large goblet of wine in a rather short time."

Henri chuckled. "I'd not be concerned, dear girl. He's but a young man smitten and seeking to calm his nerves."

"I didn't think of that, Sir. My husband knew me from childhood and never thought to need such a tonic. We did enjoy many a time over a pitcher of wine, though." She smiled and wiped a tear from an eye.

Henri put his hand on her shoulder. "My heart aches when I think of his cruel death. I only hope that you've found some solace here."

Lisette dabbed her cheeks and smiled. "I have, Sir Henri. I thank God every day for His blessings in leading me to you and your family."

"I thank Him for you also. It took courage and character for you to stand with me and let go of Galien. Don't think I'm not sympathetic to your feelings for him."

They sat in close silence for a minute. Henri's chin dropped to his chest. He began to snore, and Lisette got up, lightly kissed the top of his head, and added wood to the fire before she returned to the pantry. A loud pop from a fresh log woke Henri. He took a sip of wine and mused on Lisette's concerns. He'd been enchanted by Gabriele so many years ago and had taken a stiff drink when her formidable father offered wine, and surely, Baldwin had only done likewise. Henri smiled to himself and drifted back to sleep.

"Sir Henri! Wake up and listen!" Henri woke to Lisette jostling his shoulder, and heard distant cries from the meadow: "Father! Help me, Father!"

The captain of the house guard rushed into the house with sword drawn. Henri grabbed his own sword from the wall, and they ran through the back doorway and onto the meadow. Thirty yards away, Alisende was stumbling toward the house, hair in disarray, left hand clutching the torn bodice of her dress. Henri ran to her. Her left eye and face were turning greenish-purple, evidencing hard blows. She fell sobbing into his arms, and he looked at the guard captain and Lisette. "Let's get her into the house."

Henri carried Alisende up the staircase to his chamber and laid her on the bed. Lisette covered her with a blanket and lifted her head to a cup of wine. She drank deeply.

"What happened, Daughter?" Henri said.

"He got drunk while we were riding and tried to force himself on me."

"Did he succeed?"

"No. He hit me when I resisted, but I fought him off and he took horse."

"In which direction, Daughter?"

Alisende pointed east, and Henri reddened with fury. He turned to Lisette, and said, "Lisette, stay close beside Alisende," then turned to the guard captain. "Lorens, I'll ride to the fortress. Leave one man here at guard. You and the other man ride fast after Baldwin de Betancourt."

+ + +

Lorens Saint-Georges leapt into the saddle and set off at a gallop across the meadow, the man-at-arms riding close behind him. As they dashed toward the low stone wall separating Coudre Estate from Route de Voleurs, Lorens loosed the reins and leaned ahead, and his horse jumped the wall with a mighty bound. He looked over his shoulder, and seeing that the man-at-arms had cleared the wall, drew his sword and thundered past curious peasants gathering beside the road at the village of Saint-Julien.

+ + +

Baldwin de Betancourt could barely see the markers at the south barony border, but soon he'd be across. Suddenly, his tired horse stumbled and balked, and Baldwin jammed sharp prick spurs into flanks, drawing blood, but rather than charge ahead, the exhausted stallion reared up on powerful hind legs, throwing Baldwin onto the hard-packed dirt road. The bruised knight pulled himself to his feet, in time to see two horsemen with swords raised, closing on him fast. Baldwin drew his own sword and planted his feet.

Lorens' horse was drawing rasping breaths and quickly faltering. Lorens reined him to a halt ten yards from Baldwin, and dismounted. The man-at-arms came to stand beside him.

The knight snarled, "Come no closer, or I'll cut you and your man to pieces."

Lorens advanced, sword out. "Betancourt, you've no choice but surrender, to me now or Alphonse's knights in short time."

"*Sir* to you, boy. One step more, and you'll meet God knowing your place."

Lorens took another step toward Baldwin, and said, with a taunting grin, "Might *Sir Rapist* please you better, my lord?"

Baldwin turned purple and charged, swinging his sword at Lorens' head, but drunkenness had rendered him clumsy, and Lorens easily ducked the hissing blade. Before Baldwin could regain his stance, Lorens slammed a mail-clad fist into his face; at the same instant, the man-at-arms came from behind and knocked him senseless.

+ + +

Baron Alphonse, Martin, and a knight followed Henri to the well-appointed room for highborn guests and stood aside as he rapped at the door. A distinguished middle-aged nobleman opened it. He beamed. "Henri! What a pleasure to see you again."

Alphonse stepped forward. "We're not here for a pleasant talk, Enguerrand. Where is your son?"

"Why, I don't know, Alphonse. I thought he'd gone to visit with Henri's lovely daughter."

Henri bristled. "He damned well did visit, and nearly ripped the clothes from Alisende's body in the course of his attentions to her."

Enguerrand de Betancourt stepped back, fell into a chair, and put his head in his hands. "My son Baldwin? He could not have done such a thing."

Henri said, more calmly, "From all evidence, he did so, Enguerrand."

"Then let us find the truth," Alphonse said. "If evidence bears out Sir Henri's claims, justice will need take its course." He looked at the knight. "Gather all the men you need to find Baldwin de Betancourt. I want search parties out on every road."

"It will be done, Sire."

Thierré stepped from the doorway shadows and said to the knight, "You'd best find him fast. If I get to him first, only hunks of meat will be left to question."

"Sir Thierré, you'd best stand down, and now!" Henri said. Thierré glowered, but he held his words.

Alphonse addressed those present. "Viscount Betancourt, of necessity I must ask that you stay in your quarters. Henri de Coudre, of same necessity, I must interview your daughter. Père Barnard will stand by as a witness, and the Bishop of Le Puy will provide a second priest at my request."

Henri and Enguerrand nodded in resigned agreement. Alphonse spoke sharply to Thierré. "Sir Thierré de Coudre, you will keep your temper in check and your sword sheathed. Speak out of turn again, and I'll put you in the dungeon. Don't even think to interfere with my orders."

While Alphonse chastised Thierré, another man stepped from the shadows, stood respectfully as the baron finished, and said, "Sir Henri."

Henry turned to the voice. "Lorens! Did you find where we might track the scoundrel?"

"There will be no need for a search, Sir Henri. Come outside, if it please you."

All present rushed to the great hall doorway. In the court before the hall, Lorens' man-at-arms stood beside Baldwin's horse; the fugitive knight slung over the animal's bare back, his hands and feet securely tied.

Alphonse walked over, slapped Baldwin on the buttocks, and grinned at Lorens, eyeing him up and down. "Before me stands a man who's looking more like a knight with every passing moment. I expect to see you in the hall for supper this evening."

23 October 1091, the Abbé de Saint-Amand

After Vespers, Galien and Benedict walked from the chapel to the cloister and sat in the fading warm sun of the autumn afternoon. "I'm sorry to see you leave so soon, Brother Benedict," Galien said.

"'Tis all in the life of a scholar, Galien. When new knowledge of my subjects comes to light, I must meet the presenter and hear out his evidence, oft debated to great and exhaustive length."

"You've my gratitude for your friendship in my first weeks here. I feel more at home now."

Benedict smiled. "I'm happy to have been of service, and I won't be in Paris forever. In the meantime, Brother Alexandrus will take charge of your group of postulants."

"Brother Alexandrus is a good man." Galien caught a movement and turned to see his fellow postulant, Charles Falcard, waving from behind a column across the cloister.

Benedict winked at Galien. "You have my leave to join Charles. I need begin to prepare for my long journey, but we'll see each other again before I depart."

Galien took leave of Benedict and met Charles in the cloister walkway. A pudgy peasant boy of seventeen years, he had befriended Galien in his first days at Saint-Amand. Charles' unceasing good humor had bolstered Galien's low spirits, and the revelation of mutual literacy and shared tales of their paths to that status provided the beginnings for a lasting friendship. Galien ceased to notice Charles' plain features and bad complexion, and Charles soon disregarded Galien's place far above him in God's order.

"Join a humble peasant for a taste of wine before supper, Sir Galien?" Charles patted the flask concealed beneath his habit.

"You already know the answer. Let's find a place where we won't get caught."

They sat out of sight behind a storage building. Charles opened the flask and passed it to Galien. As they grinned at each other in conspiratorial glee and took swallows, the loose left sleeve of Galien's habit fell away from his forearm. Charles stared at the jagged four-inch arrowhead scar. His eyes widened as he whistled. "What happened to you, Galien?"

"A battle wound." Galien traced the scar with a finger. "I rode with my barony's cavalry, and took it in a fight with Count Bayard's men."

In a low voice, Charles said, "Have you ever killed a man?"

"During the last battle with Bayard, I dealt a man a hard sword blow to the head from my horse, but the next one charged me with a lance and I couldn't look back. Later, my brother told me the blow killed him."

"Galien, you speak as a man who knows his horse and sword. You could become a knight."

"I'll be swearing fealty to Baron Alphonse when I get home."

"Then why are you at Saint-Amand at all?"

"My father was furious when my sister's servant and I fell in love. He brought me here to get over her. I'll not dishonor him by leaving before I've passed six months."

"Every day here must seem like an eternity to you, Galien."

"Don't worry about me. For the present, we have only to survive our assignment to hard labor in the vineyards, with dreams of the scriptorium to sustain us."

"Do you truly think I'll make it to the scriptorium, Galien?"

"Of course you will. Your knowledge of letters earned you a postulant's place, and in the future, will unlock the world for a peasant as surely as a hundred livres in silver."

25 October 1091, Fortress Mirefleurs

"A verdict has been reached," Alphonse announced. He turned to the knight behind him. "Bring Baldwin de Betancourt to stand before me."

Henri de Coudre and Enguerrand de Betancourt waited in chairs before Alphonse's table in the great hall; Martin and Thierré stood behind Henri. Guards brought Baldwin forward. Alphonse addressed him. "Sir Baldwin de Betancourt, you have confessed, under no duress or torture, to the violent assault and attempted rape of Alisende de Coudre. Testimony and evidence, impartially examined, confirms your admission. You stand convicted of all charges."

Baldwin stood silent, and Alphonse continued. "Rape or that attempted is a most serious crime in my jurisdiction. Such an attempt toward the daughter of a nobleman carries the penalty of death, but in view of your own noble status and voluntary confession, I waive this. I sentence you to be given twenty lashes with bullwhip and to have your left nostril pierced through with fired iron."

Baldwin turned white and looked to his father. Enguerrand stared back impassively.

Alphonse rose. "Sentence will be imposed in one hour." He spoke to the knight. "Return the prisoner to the dungeon." Baldwin struggled and cursed as the burly guards yanked him toward a side door.

"Wait!" All heads turned to Thierré. He stepped before the table, bowed his head, and said, "Sire, with your permission, I'd have a word with the prisoner." Alphonse nodded and the guards dragged Baldwin round.

Thierré stared at Baldwin. His face grew pale, the blue veins bulging. "Betancourt, I'd like nothing more than to watch your punishment carried out, but you have dishonored my sister and my family in a way for which even such a sentence cannot atone. To restore full honor to them, I can do no less than offer my own life."

All in the great hall waited with breath held. Thierré looked to Alphonse, and the baron nodded. Thierré stepped back. With a full swing of his right arm, he backhanded Baldwin across the face. "You stand challenged to a contest of arms, with no quarter to be asked."

Baldwin looked at his father and back to Thierré. "Accepted."

Alphonse spoke. "Sir Thierré de Coudre has made a challenge, and Sir Baldwin de Betancourt has accepted." He looked to Henri and Enguerrand. "With the consent of both of you, I will commute the sentence of corporal punishment to a matter of honor, to be resolved in single combat."

Henri and Enguerrand glanced at each other and reluctantly said, "I consent."

The Baron said, "Then I grant my own approval. The contest will be held at first light on Monday, in the privacy of the armory court. The contestants will fight until one of them is killed or the victor chooses to show mercy. I'll not stand in bitter wind and watch two men heavily armored slowly hack each other into pieces. Therefore the combatants will be held to like light armor and shield; for weapons like dagger, and sword or mace."

Alphonse addressed all present. "This decision does not absolve Baldwin de Betancourt of his guilt. Thus, I order Henri de Coudre be paid one thousand livres in compensation, no matter the outcome of the contest."

Enguerrand stood and bowed his head to Henri. "I will pay Sir Henri de Coudre twice that amount. Had I ten thousand at hand, I would gladly give it to him, but even such a fortune and my son's life would not begin to ease the affront his actions have brought upon Sir Henri and his noble house, nor erase the stain of dishonor I and mine must now wear."

Alphonse looked at Henri. "Sir Henri, have you words to speak?"

Henri rose. "Though his son has indeed caused the gravest of harm, I can only commend Viscount Betancourt for his humility and exercise of the highest of knight's honor throughout this ordeal."

"Very well," Alphonse said. "These proceedings are finished. I only dread to watch the contest to be held on the day after the morrow."

+ + +

Men-at-arms admitted Enguerrand de Betancourt to the dungeon beneath the armory. Baldwin stood in the open interrogation area fronting the row of oaken-barred cells, examining weapons and hard leather armor laid out on a table. A full cup of wine sat beside the battle gear.

Enguerrand glanced at the wine and then stared at his son. "Where did you get that?"

"I gave a guard a few deniers."

"You think yourself ready?"

Baldwin took a swallow of wine and smirked. "I can take Coudre with ease."

Enguerrand grabbed Baldwin's shirt with powerful hands and shoved him against a column. "You foolish shit. Thierré de Coudre is a man of deadly reputation and he's out to take your head." He picked up the cup and poured the wine onto the floor. "Best busy yourself with that gear and be at ready to fight a real knight for what might be left of your miserable life."

"Y… you don't stand with me, Father?"

"I stand with justice and honor, but that means nothing now. The honor of our own house is forever lost."

October 27, 1091, Fortress Mirefleurs

Thierré took his communion from Père Barnard in the fortress chapel and walked with Henri and Martin to the armory yard. He felt grateful for the long hooded cloak that cut the chill wind gusting hard from the north. Flurries of light snow swirled in the light of torches mounted on the walls as the witnesses warmed their hands over charcoal braziers.

A door opened as the thick clouds glowed with first daylight. Men-at-arms escorted Baldwin de Betancourt to stand across from Thierré. Alphonse stepped from the line of witnesses. "Combatants, take shields and weapons."

Both knights took up two-foot round wooden shields. Thierré took his sword and dagger from the low stone wall; Baldwin picked up dagger and mace. They took stance. Thierré studied Baldwin, well built and nearly six feet tall. His expression evidenced keen concentration. This man would be no easy kill.

Alphonse raised his right hand, paused, and said, "Begin!"

Baldwin charged to attack with a fast swing aimed at Thierré's head. Wood cracked sharply as Thierré deflected the mace-head with his shield. Baldwin grunted in pain as Thierré bashed the ironbound shield edge into his chest, but faster than Thierré could follow through with a sword stroke, Baldwin rammed the mace-head into his solar plexus, swung his shield to hit Thierré with a full blow to the right side of the head, and on the backswing, hit him in the left face. Blood sprayed from the open gash.

Baldwin stepped back. Thierré gasped for breath, seeing double through a red haze of pain, feeling the warm blood running down his neck. Tottering on his feet, he raised his sword and shield to ready position. Baldwin shot him a taunting grin and in a fast blur, swung the mace, striking Thierré's left thigh. Thierré heard a crack and pain exploded. His right fingers loosed, his sword clattered on the pavestones, and he fell.

The victorious Baldwin stepped forward to stand over Thierré. He paused, took a breath, and turned his head, tarrying to raise his mace and grin at the witnesses. Thierré pushed himself through the agony, onto his side. He pulled his dagger from the sheath at his belt. As Baldwin turned his head back and raised the mace for a death blow, Thierré rammed the dagger through his left calf. Baldwin howled at the sudden stab and Thierré pulled back on the dagger, ripping through muscle. Baldwin stumbled and fell onto his back, clawing at the gaping, blood-spurting wound in agonized panic.

With a mighty effort, Thierré pulled himself to his feet. He picked up his sword, limped over to Baldwin, and kicked him in the stomach as he struggled to rise. Thierré drew his sword high for the coup de grâce, paused for a moment, and lowered it. With his vision blurring, struggling to speak, he said, "To honor Viscount Betancourt's friendship with my father, I'll let his son keep his life, but he'll carry my mark." As Sergeant Lienart hurried forward to tie off the veins gushing blood, Thierré put his dagger into Baldwin's left nostril and slashed it open, kicked him once more, and his leg again exploded in furious pain. Thierré swayed around to face the witnesses, saw them through a red mist, and collapsed onto the paving.

29 October 1091, Fortress Mirefleurs

Alisende and Lisette rose from their prayers at Thierré's bedside in the fortress hospital. Père Barnard entered, knelt by Thierré and said a prayer, and made the sign of the cross over the unconscious young knight. He turned to Alisende. "Lady Alisende, your father is waiting for you in the great hall. His heart is torn apart, so be easy with your words."

Alisende looked at the kindly red-faced priest, now nearly fifty years at the fortress. Her heart began to soften in remembrance of his long vigil at her mother's bedside while she died a lingering death of tumors, and beside Henri when he came home from Vézelay with a hand lost, at Death's door. And of his infinite patience with Alisende's halting learning of letters while Galien charged ahead with his lessons like the most formidable of knights on the finest of warhorses. Barnard was their own man of God, and he spoke the truth that she needed to hear.

Outside the hospital, Lisette said, "Lady, best take heed of Père Barnard. You can't stay angry with your father."

"I know. Père Barnard made me feel better, but I still can't understand why Father had no idea Baldwin was a scoundrel."

"Forgive him his oversight. Most noblemen would have told a daughter to go inside and stop crying, and then made her marry him."

Alisende nodded, smiling. "I'm his pet daughter, and he always spoiled me. He saved the heavy hand for my brothers."

"No doubt with good reason, but I still can't bear to think of poor Galien flogged."

They entered the great hall. Lisette took a seat on a bench at a wall, Alisende next to Henri at Alphonse's table. Henri raised his eyes to Alisende's and said, "Daughter, this evil has all come to pass on my account, but truly, I knew not that Baldwin hid such low character."

Alisende put a hand on his arm and kissed his cheek. "Father, I hold you to no blame, nor must you blame yourself. Let us all put our efforts to prayer for Thierré's life."

Henri kissed her cheek in return. "Thank you, dear Alisende. We shall join in earnest prayer to God for His mercy upon Thierré, but what might I do to ease your own plight?"

"The estate is now a tainted place for me, and I'm frightened to stay there. I want to move to the fortress and bring Lisette with me. Should by God's grace Thierré live, we'll be at ready hand to care for him."

"All shall be as you want. I'll speak to Alphonse and arrange quarters for the both of you. Etien and his wife can move into Coudre Manor and take up managing the estate until God wills that Thierré fully recover. Etien's son Milon is of sufficient age to look after Etien's own holdings."

"I'm grateful, Father. And another thing. I don't wish to meet any young men. After what happened with Baldwin, I hold strong doubt that I'll ever want to marry."

Henri bowed his head to her. "Daughter, your heart and soul must heal in their own time. I swear on any honor left to me, I will not talk of a marriage for you until you tell me you are ready to consider it again."

Chapter 12

30 October 1091, the Abbé de Saint-Amand

Galien bent over his work in the vineyard, thinking of the prayerful respite that Sext in the cool dark chapel would bring from the sun and backbreaking labor of the late fall vineyard harvest. He looked at his friend Charles, whistling a tune as he easily went about his own tasks, and for the first time in his life, felt true appreciation for the work of the peasants at Coudre Estate.

After the noon prayers and meal in the refectory, Galien returned to his work, feeling refreshed. As he began to cut through a tough vine stalk, a sharp jab to his ribs startled him. The vineyard master, Brother Sylvestrus, stood close, staring at him with watery, faded blue eyes set close above a tuberous blue-veined nose. His white, sweaty skin exuded rancid body odor. He bared yellowed teeth in a crooked grin and spoke, words coming in a cloud of foul breath. "What be your name, boy?"

"Galien de Coudre, Brother."

"A nobleman, we have! Where be you from, and who be your father?"

"My home is the Barony of Mirefleurs, and my father, the knight Henri de Coudre."

"Know, son of Henri de Coudre, that all men here are equal under God. I'll bend that straight back with honest work, you can be sure."

Galien looked him in the eye. "Brother Sylvestrus, no son of Henri de Coudre shirks the tasks given him."

Sylvestrus' mouth twisted into an evil smile. "We'll see about that. And remember, your noble Brother Benedict won't be returning to look out for you for some weeks yet."

Sylvestrus lumbered out of earshot, and Charles said, "I can already guess what you think of him, so I won't ask."

"Don't. My reply would be most unholy, and urgent cause for a visit to confession."

"He's singled you out to break, I'm afraid. I must thank God I was born a poor peasant. No one can tell me apart from my fellows."

14 November 1091, Fortress Mirefleurs

Thierré sat propped up in his hospital bed. He patiently endured while the physician from Le Puy tested his vision and examined his leg. Finished, the physician put a hand on Thierré's shoulder. "Sir Thierré, you're the hardiest of men. By all rights, the blows to your head should have killed you where you stood. Had they not, the blood trapped there was more than sufficient to cause death within an hour. For three days, I doubted your survival, and for a week afterward, feared for your faculties of reason and speech."

The Coudre family and Baron Alphonse stood around in wait, and the physician said, "Now, your survival is assured, but I must voice my concerns. I know not if you'll recover fully from the spells of dizziness and blurred vision. The blow to your leg did not cause a complete break, but the bone was deeply cracked and bruised. It will heal, and you'll again walk, but I fear that in healing the bone might draw up and shorten."

Thierré drew a deep breath. "I'll not be able to resume my knight's duties?"

"Sir Thierré, I intend to do all I can. Your leg will stay held in tension by means of the splints in place, and thereby the bone might heal with no shortening. The effects of the head blows should lessen in a short time, but a year will pass before the full consequences are certain. A year will likewise be required for healing of the leg bone to fully solidify and make the permanent condition known. You're to stay in your bed until I judge time ready for the splints to be removed, and after, not ride or engage in exertion until I judge you fit."

Thierré laughed without humor. "I can hardly think to be so confined."

The physician said, sharply, "The choice is yours. Comply with treatment, and you'll have a good chance to again take up the knight's profession. Disregard my instructions, and you might well be crippled for life."

The physician gave Thierré a potion to make him rest. Alisende and Lisette stayed with him until he drifted off to sleep, then returned to their room off the great hall balcony and sat on their beds. "I was so grateful to God to hear the physicians' words, but fear your brother might ignore his counsel," Lisette said.

"He'll have to decide that for himself. He decided to challenge Baldwin without first telling Father or me."

"You said you didn't regret that he made Baldwin a cripple and a marked man."

"I don't. Baldwin got what he bargained for."

"Yet, you seem angry."

"No, no more. My anger over Thierré's challenge faded when Father told me he was near death."

"Then, other than his condition, what bothers you?"

"It's the way men conduct themselves. By and large, they're brutal pigs and I'll not have one in my life. I should think you, of all women, can understand that."

"I can, but I don't hold the entire male sex at fault for Alain's death. Time will soften your heart."

"Perhaps so, perhaps not. I have the thousand livres that Father gave me from the viscount's payment, so I'll not need a husband. I can pay my own way and yours for the rest of our lives, but without the estate, I'll need to do something with myself. I certainly don't want to go to a convent."

"Allow yourself time, Lady. Thierré needs you so much now."

"He does need me, and you as well. Together, I think we can keep him in his bed. You've sent off the letter to Galien I wrote for you?"

"On the day the physician said Thierré would live, Sir Henri sent it off by fastest horseman. No reply has come, and I'm perplexed. I truly expected him to come home right away."

"Yes, on concern for Thierré he would have left for home the same day. I'm fearing something might have gone terribly wrong."

17 November 1091, the Abbe' de Saint-Amand

After the prayers of Sext, monks from the kitchen served the noon meal in the refectory. Galien wolfed his food and drained his cup of water. After he returned to the vineyard, he couldn't stay awake, and fell asleep under the branches of an old oak tree. He dreamed of a corridor, with doors to monks' cells lining the walls, stretching to infinity. His father stood fifty paces down the corridor and Galien ran toward him, but Henri receded as fast as Galien could run, then Henri became Thierré and receded even faster. Abruptly, the doors to the cells opened and huge snarling black mastiffs jumped out, chasing him, overpowering him and pinning him to the floor, tearing at his flesh as he screamed.

"Galien, you're dreaming. Wake up." Anseau, another postulant friend, shook him. Galien looked at him groggily and then drifted off. After a peaceful sleep of a quarter of an hour, Anseau shook him again, and he got up to trudge back to the vineyard.

Galien waited with an enormous carrying basket strapped over his shoulders. Monks filled the basket with dried bunches of grapes from the final days of the harvest. The weight nearly sent Galien to his knees, but he stayed on his feet, staggered to the donkey cart at the end of the planting row, and heaved the burden onto the cart bed. He turned and limped toward the next basket load.

Charles' prediction had proven true. Two weeks after the day Sylvestrus confronted him, Galien felt himself nearly broken from the unceasing hard labor for which Sylvestrus had singled him out. The cunning Sylvestrus had realized that Galien's pride would not allow him to make a complaint, but Charles might do so for him, and had discharged Charles from vineyard work at the end of the first day, sending him to a labor detail at the church building, far from the vineyards.

The day's work ended at the early sundown of late fall. Galien left his tools at the vineyard gates, nearly too exhausted to shuffle to the chapel for Compline. Near the edge of the cloister, he heard a whisper. "Galien."

Anseau stepped from behind a column, beckoned him into the shadows, and handed him a folded parchment letter. "I had to go to Sylvestrus' cell just now. He wasn't there, but this was on the floor, and I know your name by sight." Anseau slipped away, and Galien hurried to the postulant quarters.

Inside, he looked at the letter by candlelight. The writing on the outside was Alisende's, and the broken wax seal bore his father's imprint. He opened it, read quickly, and jumped up, fury churning in his gut. At the door to Sylvestrus' cell, he banged until the monk opened it. "What do you want, boy?"

Galien held up the letter. "An explanation for this. I should have gotten it a week ago."

Sylvestrus grabbed him by the front of his habit, pulled him into the tiny room, and pushed the door closed. Galien gasped at the fetid fumes of wine, garlic, and spoilt meat that filled his nose. Sylvestrus shoved him hard, backhanded him with a callused right hand, and punched him in the stomach with the left. Galien doubled over in pain, and Sylvestrus threw him face-down onto his pallet, yanked up the habit, and crawled onto him, cock hard and erect. He grabbed Galien's throat with both powerful hands. "Move, and you're dead."

Galien feigned fear. "Have mercy, good brother. You can do what you want, but get me something to drink first."

Sylvestrus slurred a drunken chuckle. "I forget my manners. A good hump is all the better with some wine." He swayed to his feet and began to pour a cup from a pitcher on the table.

Galien jumped up in an instant. He grabbed the front of Sylvestrus' habit, yanked him off balance, and drove his right knee into the monk's groin. Sylvestrus grunted and collapsed to all fours. A knife clattered onto the floor. Galien tossed it aside, put both hands on the back of Sylvestrus' greasy head, and drove his knee into his face. Nose and maxilla shattered in a crunch of gristle, and blood splattered onto the stone floor.

The knife lay near and Galien picked it up. He kicked Sylvestrus in the solar plexus, watching with arms crossed as the perverted monk rolled in his own blood, gasping for air. Galien walked around him, delivering well-placed kicks to his chest, kidneys, and groin, then took a stool, drained the cup of wine, and poured another. He sat at his ease as Sylvestrus writhed, spat yellow teeth, and caught his breath.

Sylvestrus regained his hands and knees. "I... I thought you a weak boy."

"No son of Henri de Coudre is weak. Rejoice that you crossed only his youngest. My eldest brother would cut your hands and head off at first sight, but I'll let you live long enough to explain why I didn't get this letter."

"I didn't know it had come, in truth."

"You are a God-cursed liar. The seal was broken, and the man who gave it to me said he found it on the floor of this room."

"That man will be punished."

Galien got up and kicked Sylvestrus in the stomach. "None will be punished, save you. You knew what was in this letter and held it from me. Who read it to you?"

"B... Brother Ernoul, at the vineyard office."

Galien pulled Sylvestrus to his feet and shoved him to the wall. He grabbed an ear and sliced the lobe off. Sylvestrus let out a gurgling cry, and Galien cut the lobe off the other. "I've decided not to kill you outright, but you'll not forget your place again."

Sylvestrus dropped to his knees, hands to his maimed ears. Galien took a swallow of wine and addressed the crushed predator. "If you live, should you come within ten paces of me, I'll cut off your nose and lips and what's left of your ears. If I find you have violated any man here, I'll take your cods off and cut you open, and let the guard dogs tear the bowels from your body."

Galien stuck the knife in his belt and drained the half-empty pitcher of wine. He washed the blood from his hands and face and walked back to the postulant quarters. The wine soon overcame him. He stumbled to his pallet and fell into a deep, dreamless sleep.

Before sunrise, an elderly monk walked between the rows of sleeping postulants with his customary call for Prime: "Arise joyfully, for a new day in the Lord's service awaits ye."

Galien ignored him and went back to sleep. At midmorning, he rose, stiff and sore. He hobbled into the corridor and to the laundry room, where he picked up a clean habit. At the washing fountain, he stripped off the filthy one and bathed.

Clean of person and easier at heart, he went to the kitchen. There a cook, Brother Nestor, eyed him with knowing suspicion but gave him work. After the noon meal, the bell rang and the monks rose, bound for the afternoon's tasks. Nestor caught Galien's eye. "Abbot Leo would see you in his quarters, right away."

Beside the door to Leo's quarters, a sergeant and two men-at-arms in Lord Falcard's colors waited. The sergeant glared at Galien as he knocked, then the Abbot opened the door and bade him enter. Inside, Leo made no small talk. "You nearly killed Sylvestrus last night, Galien. Before I release you into custody of Lord Falcard's sergeant, I'll allow you to make your explanation."

Galien dropped the letter onto Leo's desk. "Read this, Father Abbot. Sylvestrus withheld it from me, and I knew not the tragic news within until another man found it and gave it to me."

Leo read the letter and looked up. "Galien, your family has suffered greatly, but that grants no leave to nearly murder the man."

"He assaulted and tried to rape me on threat of death when I confronted him with it last night. He's worked me harder than any donkey in the vineyards for weeks."

Leo stroked his beard, thinking, and then said, "I can accept that you acted to defend yourself last night, but I suppose I couldn't have expected you to report his ill-treatment beforehand?"

Galien shrugged. "I'd rather have died first."

"So, you expected to just endure the abuse?"

"I am prepared to do what is required of me. A son of Henri de Coudre accepts hardship without complaint. A grave harm or insult to family, self, or blameless person, he does not."

"You demonstrated that more than adequately."

Galien looked Leo in the eye. "Merely adequately, Father Abbot. I should have gutted him on the spot. Sylvestrus has my promises of what will come to him, should he again disturb me or any man here."

"And what were your promises?"

Galien repeated his warnings to Sylvestrus, and Leo paled. "How do you feel about what you did to him?"

"I feel no compassion for him or remorse on my own account, and I take pride in my quick thought and skill."

"Galien, I can understand the reasons you beat him nearly to death, but why did you have to cut half of his ears off?"

"He's a criminal. I only gave him the mark he should have gotten long ago."

Leo, flustered, rubbed his forehead. "I can't help but agree. Perhaps the knight's profession does suit you best."

"I believe it does, Father Abbot. How did Sylvestrus even come to be here, and what do you plan to do with him?"

"He's a man who's made trouble for many years, but I regret to say that I always gave him another chance. If he lives, he'll stay in menial assignments until he's fully recovered, then be expelled for the final time." Leo put his head in his hands. "How could I not know that one of the souls under my charge was suffering such grave mistreatment? Can you forgive me, Galien?"

"I can, Father Abbot."

Leo raised his head. "I accept with gratitude, and pray God will also accept on my behalf." After a pause, Leo spoke again. "Though this district is under the jurisdiction of Lord Falcard, my word is law at Saint-Amand. I'll dismiss his men and won't hold my own inquest into the events of last night. Your record is clear, and if you wish to leave us, do so with my blessings and deepest apologies."

"I won't dishonor my father by leaving before I've passed my six months."

"Galien, I'm pleased that you're staying at Saint-Amand. God grant that you find healing of spirit here."

"Father Abbot, I'll be content to return home, ready to take up my duties."

12 December 1091, the Abbé de Saint-Amand

After breakfast, a monk handed Galien a letter. He saw Alisende's handwriting, quickly broke the seal, and began to read. Anseau, sitting beside him, said, "Come on, or you'll be late for work."

"I don't care. My family is more important." He read the letter.

"How are your brother and sister?" Anseau said.

"Thierré still suffers from blurred vision and dizzy spells. The physician said he'll be able to get up by Christmas, but only with a walking stick. Alisende has moved to Fortress Mirefleurs, but is thinking to take a house in Clermont for herself and Lisette. She wants them to do charity work in the convent hospital there."

In a hesitant whisper, Anseau said, "Lisette... the lady you're in love with. She's a commoner, is she not?"

"She is, and through her letters, I find her feelings for me have only grown stronger. I'll be going home to become a knight after my time here is finished. I fear the difficulties that lie ahead for us far more than any enemy I might face."

"Keep your mind on the day at hand, Galien, and leave the future to God."

"You're right. Let's go to work."

Galien and Anseau stepped slowly on the sanded ice in the court before the monastery church, careful not to tip the wooden litter and the heavy limestone column section it bore. They inched up the wooden ramp placed over the steps, and a monk opened the doors to the warm nave. There, they set the litter before the designated column and stood straight, resting their backs.

A notably stout, dark-bearded monk measured the section with curved steel dividers, fingered the carving, and talked for a moment with the stone masons. The monk walked on to the next column, and masons spread mortar on the previously laid section. Galien and Anseau heaved the litter high, holding it steady while the masons lifted off the next section.

"That's the last one they can set by hand. The next will take rope and tackle to lift it high enough," Galien said.

Anseau raised his gloved hands. "What does it matter? We're but hauling-donkeys."

Galien grinned and slapped his friend's shoulder. They picked up the litter and headed for the wooden carving shed and their next load. Galien took joy in the demanding physical labor and the dexterity required for the construction assignment, feeling each day's backbreaking work to be a step in his purification from the corruption of Sylvestrus. He ate much and slept peacefully, and now, ten weeks after the bloody incident, he had regained the weight lost in the vineyards and added a halfscore pounds of solid muscle.

The artistry of the stonemasons and the architectural ingenuity did not escape his eye as the alterations gradually lent a light and soaring grace to the centuries-old Roman-style church. He ended his assignment at the church fit of body, and with a keen appreciation for the vision and toil necessary to construct such a building.

Of the incident with Sylvestrus, the perverted monk had been taken to the monastery hospital and remained there for six weeks. His shattered nose had healed, but flattened and twisted; his ears drawn into odd positions with the growth of scar tissue. With these disfigurements and only gaps in place of six front teeth, his evil expression had become all the more grotesque. His new task, barrel assembly in a corner of a vineyard cellarium, kept him far from others. When Galien happened to spot him, he seemed only a wraith moving from shadow to shadow, a ghostly remnant of what he had been.

12 February 1092, the Abbé de Saint-Amand

Galien at long last awoke to his day of deliverance. He stood through Prime and took breakfast in eager anticipation, and at midmorning, opened carved oaken doors to the bright north light of the scriptorium. There, he joined the elite of the Abbé de Saint-Amand: the scribes, translators, and manuscript artists. Brother Ignatius, Master of Calligraphy, Illustration, and Bookbinding, greeted him, directed him to a writing table, and described the writing and drawing instruments placed there. At a calligrapher's question, Ignatius excused himself.

"Galien!" A familiar voice hissed from the row of tables behind him. Galien turned, and Charles held both fists high. "We made it!" Galien grinned broadly at his friend and raised his right fist in victory. Brother Ignatius returned to Galien's table, bade Charles join them, and asked the two eager postulants to demonstrate their proficiency in the basics of manuscript arts.

Satisfied with their skills and impressed with Galien's command of Latin, Ignatius pronounced them qualified to continue studies and gave them copying tasks. They finished well before Vespers, and Ignatius excused them for the day.

In the vineyard office, Galien snickered as Charles skillfully cajoled a flask of wine from the cellarer, Brother Ernoul. Ernoul looked at him. "What's funny, *Sir* Galien?"

"You."

"Watch yourself, smart boy. You've eyes on you."

Galien stared at the pale, pudgy monk. "Best you watch your own tongue."

"The Abbot will hear of your insolence."

"I know you stole my lady's letter and read it to Sylvestrus. Open your filthy mouth to anyone, and you'll look far worse than he does."

After Compline and before evening supper, the two postulants stole away to their usual place behind the storage building. Charles raised his flask to toast his escape from a short and wretched life of poverty as a peasant farmer bound to Lord Falcard's lands, and Galien took a swallow in his friend's honor.

"We've two months left as postulants, and all in the scriptorium," Charles said. "Do you still intend to go home and become a knight?"

"My determination has only grown stronger."

"That will make your father happy, and you're fit for it now."

Galien looked at Charles with scrutiny. "You're much slimmer of waist and broader of shoulder."

"Think I'd have a chance with a pretty girl?"

"I made good coin as a scribe for hire, and you could also. The girls would notice, believe me." They passed the flask again, and Charles said, "Did you know that Leo expelled Sylvestrus a week ago?"

"I didn't. The bastard has stayed well away from me."

"He pulled a knife on another man after the evening meal."

Galien took another sip. "Good riddance. Someone beyond these walls will finish what I started."

"You've gained wide repute here. With a son of the knight Henri de Coudre as a prospective brother, the men of this monastery are sleeping more peacefully."

Galien smirked. "Brother Ernoul won't be." He handed Charles the flask. "Drink up, old friend. For the rest of my time here, I'll be happy as a simple scribe."

JOSEPH SCOTT AMIS

Chapter 13

15 March 1092, near the town of Clermont

At daybreak, Roger de Lyon rode past stone entry posts and onto the road. He reined his horse to a halt, looking back at the house where he had lived for five years and the rolling green lands lying beyond it. A sad parting indeed with a place and a lord he had loved, but to try to stay where he was no longer wanted was a worse thought.

He glanced at his three faithful men-at-arms, packed and ready for their ride to the Barony of Mirefleurs, and thought of the silver in his saddlebags, a tidy fortune, more than enough to make a fresh start in a new place of promise. But enough of longing and sentiment for good days passed. Roger grinned at the man riding next to him, raised his hand to point east, and they nudged their horses to an easy walk.

After a quarter of an hour, Roger spotted the border markers half a mile ahead, and at the same time, heard the thundering of many hooves behind them. He and his men turned as one, to see the first son of recently-passed Lord Chartain riding at the head of a halfscore knights and men, all in battle gear. A man-at-arms said, "Sir Roger, we need ride away quickly, and now."

"No, stand fast and ready your weapons. I'll talk to the bastard and see what he wants."

The force of horsemen halted, and a young man in fine dress rode forward. "You can't leave just yet, Lyon. I've not been paid all of the lord's share I'm owed."

Roger stared at him. "I paid you what was owed on lands that are no longer mine, to the last denier. If you want more of my silver, you can come and take it." Grinning to look like the Devil, Roger drew his sword. "But unlike your good father, you are no knight to speak of, and a cowardly boy besides."

The young man glanced at the knight beside him. "Take them!"

As fast as the words came, thunks sounded, and two crossbowmen slumped over the necks of their horses, axes thrown by Roger's men buried in head and chest. Roger spurred his stallion to the startled young man, punched him in the face with his left hand, and with his right, killed the knight beside him with one fast sword cut to the head. The knight toppled off his horse; the young man and the five men left to him reined their horses round, spurring them into a desperate retreat. A man-at-arms said to Roger, "Shall we give chase and kill them, Sir?"

Roger looked around at the five men lying dead in the road and to his own, all unwounded. "No, we defended ourselves and aren't hurt. That's sufficient."

"What about the dead men's gear and weapons and horses. Might we have them?"

"Leave them. These were honorable men we all knew and fought beside. Their only mistake was riding out to attack us at the whim of a fool."

The man-at-arms looked downcast, but said, "As you wish, Sir Roger."

Roger added, "You'll all have reward for your good fight. This evening, a feast at the best inn and the women of your choice will be at my own expense, and your purses will be heavier."

16 March 1092, Fortress Mirefleurs

Henri de Coudre rose before sunrise and urinated into his chamber pot. He splashed water from the table basin onto his face and put on a loose tunic and light shoes. In the armory, a servant poured buckets of hot water into a copper tub. Henri washed well with soap and a coarse cloth, and after the man had scrubbed his back, the armory barber trimmed his hair and beard and shaved the stubble from his neck and cheeks.

On the return to his quarters, he took the four flights of stone stairs two steps at a time. He dressed in his training day gear and patted his flat stomach. The leather vest with protective brass plates sewn to the front and the thick leather sword belt fit as they had in years long past. He sheathed a blunt practice sword, pulled a long cloak over his shoulders, and picked up a light, hard leather helmet. Ready for a crisp morning in the training yard, he made for the armory hall and breakfast.

As he walked, Henri reflected. Though the tragic events that had beset Alisende and Thierré had broken his heart, he had followed through with his plans and moved to Fortress Mirefleurs, soldiered on, and made a transformation that surprised him. He'd followed the daily soldiers' schedule to the minute, conducted training, and led armed patrols. As a result, he'd shed a score of pounds and become light on his feet and quick with his sword for the first time since the loss of his right hand at Vézelay. The veteran men, from common man-at-arms to knight, accorded him the same respect and deference given to Baron Alphonse and Marshal Walter D'Avesnes, and Alphonse soon raised him to elder knight status at a fitting salary. As anticipated, the freshly recruited men-at-arms and noblemen's sons hadn't taken him seriously on the morning of their first day under his tutelage, but by noon they were terrified of him.

He entered the cavernous armory hall and spotted Thierré. His eldest son had insisted on returning to what duties he could perform, and Henri bade him a warm good morning and squeezed his shoulder. Henri sat next to his longtime friend Walter and across from the German brothers, sergeants Otto and Reinhard Huber. Men on serving duty brought the customary training-day breakfast. The hearty food and drink would provide fuel for a long morning of demanding exercises and mock combat.

Walter looked up from his porridge and took a swig of small ale. "Henri, the knight who's to take Fulbert's place is arriving today."

"That's good to hear, but we need three elders, and I'm only half a knight."

"Yes, Henri, though you regard yourself a crippled beggar, I myself think that you yet count as one full knight." The four men laughed. All had watched Henri's prowess with his sword return to nearly what it had been before he lost his hand.

"So, Walter, tell us about the new man," Henri said.

"His name is Roger de Lyon. He's thirty-one years old and the second son of Godfrey de Lyon. After meeting with him, I judged him to be of high and honorable character. He served Lord Chartain faithfully for seven years, but he and Chartain's eldest son never got along. After Chartain died in January, I suppose there wasn't room for both of them."

"I met the good Godfrey a year before he died, and Chartain was an honorable knight," Henri said. "Lyon's years of service speak highly of him, but I'd hear more of his dispute with Chartain's son."

"Henri, Alphonse and I have both met with Roger, and we're certain he's a man of best character. He has quite a reputation at sword, though he doesn't put it on display for every fool who might cross him."

Henri grumbled. "Hmmph. We'll see about that."

"You do remember you were fighting for your life in the hospital tent at Vézelay on the day Peter de Villiers led his breakout. Roger performed feats of arms far beyond those of any knight on the field."

"I remember the pain more than well. Also, that Thierré, Martin, and Gautier of Saint-Lille first proved themselves the same day, and I did hear the name Roger de Lyon. Bayard even came to see me and offer well wishes for my recovery."

"With no choice but to join forces with us after Villiers choked off the main trade road with his tariffs and army of mercenaries, the scoundrel had to mind his manners and behave with honor for once in his disgraceful life."

Henri chuckled. "How could I forget?"

Walter put a hand on Henri's shoulder. "Roger is yours for today, but should you choose to abuse him along with the other men, be wary of the consequences." They laughed again and returned to their breakfast. Training exercises would begin in the armory yard when the sun rose over the east fortress wall.

A quarter-hour later, sunshine spilled over the parapets, bringing light to the yard, where Walter had the men lined up in ranks. Henri strode in with a riding crop in hand. He walked the ranks, according each man, noble and common, the same scowling head-to-toe inspection. When all had been scrutinized, Henri addressed them. "Of necessity, I've learned to wield my sword with my left hand, and want

114

all of our men to be able to do the same. We'll begin lessons as our exercise for the day." He looked over the ranks. "Otto Huber and Clement de Sens, change weapon and shield hands and take position."

Otto and Clement stepped out from the rows of men. The master mace wielder Otto had killed twoscore of enemies and more, but Clement faced him gamely, and Henri smiled. "Sens, even a defeat at the hands of Sergeant Huber will bring you the honor you think lost at Grand-Forêt. Fight well!"

A wooden passage door opened with a sharp creak. The guard on duty hurried to Henri. "Sir Henri, Sir Roger de Lyon is here. Baron Alphonse ordered him to report directly to you."

"Very well."

Henri turned back to Otto and Clement. "Stand down, but hold your positions."

The door again creaked open. A nobleman of fit physique and confident bearing walked across the yard and came to stand respectfully before Henri. "I am Roger de Lyon, reporting for duty and at your service."

"Well taken, Sir Roger."

Henri appraised Roger. He stood five feet ten inches tall, straight of posture, medium of build, and flat of stomach. The silver-hilted dagger at his belt complemented his finely cut nobleman's travel clothes. His features gave him an air of amiability, being regular and good, bordering on handsome, eyes brown and clear, face defined by medium-length dark hair and a well-groomed short beard and moustache. A wide, white swordcut scar from his left ear to the corner of his mouth tinged the amiable aspect with danger and lent cause for caution with this man.

"Would you like a taste of our training, Sir Roger?" Henri said.

"Certainly, Sir Henri. I'm ready to begin."

Henri turned to the waiting combatants. "Sergeant Huber, stand at ease in your position. Sens, rejoin the ranks You'll get your chance at Sergeant Huber later. Sir Thierré de Coudre, take Sir Roger to the armory for practice gear and weapons."

Thierré limped toward the armory door with his walking stick, Roger walking beside him. In the arming room, Thierré gathered the practice gear.

"Sir Thierré, I'm honored to serve with you and your father," Roger said.

"The honor is ours, Sir Roger, but I'm afraid you're out of luck today. Henri was going to let Otto Mace-man knock the piss out of young Clement in front of the whole fortress, but you showed up just in time!" He smiled and held out a hand.

Roger paused dressing to shake with Thierré. "Again, my honor, Thierré. I'll have no problems with Otto."

They returned to the armory yard. Henri addressed Roger. "Sir Roger, we're training at left-handed fighting today. I trust you're prepared."

With no hesitation, Roger switched the shield to his right arm and drew the practice sword with his left. Henri raised an eyebrow, then recited the standard instructions: "Practice rules apply. No blows to head, neck, or groin, stop sword thrusts on contact. This is about footwork, not killing each other. Match over with first man down or when I call it. Begin."

Otto hunkered; padded practice mace poised high, stubbly head glistening, waiting warily for Roger's first move. Roger lunged forward with a tentative sword thrust aimed at Otto's right side. Otto countered with a diagonal downswing. The mace head grazed Roger's shield as he stepped back.

Otto drew his mace back to regain striking position, and Roger swung his sword left and outward. The blade caught the handle of the mace and knocked it aside. He stepped forward on his right foot and rammed his shield hard into Otto's. Otto stumbled backward, and Roger thrust with his left hand, striking Otto firmly in the right chest with the blunt tip of the practice sword. Both men stood down at the nominal death stroke.

Henri raised his left hand. "Match over. A fine fight, Sir Roger. You're quick with that left sword arm."

"I favor my right hand, but fight equally well with my left, and best with a sword in each."

"We'll have a match soon. I'm a left-handed swordsman, but not by choice." Henri jerked his head toward his right arm.

"I look forward to that, with some foreboding. Your reputation precedes you, Sir Henri."

"As does your own. Welcome to Fortress Mirefleurs." Henri looked at Thierré. "Get Sir Roger settled into his quarters and be certain he wants for nothing."

"Yes, Sire." Thierré nodded to his father and joined Roger.

Henri faced the assembled men. "Sir Roger de Lyon has completed an excellent demonstration of left-handed defense against a most formidable opponent. He will join Sir Walter d'Avesnes and me as an elder knight. Let us welcome him to Fortress Mirefleurs." Led by Henri, banging weapons against shields, the men cheered in unison, "Sir Roger de Lyon!"

Thierré and Roger took seats at a long table in the armory hall. A serving man came and nodded. "Sir Thierré?"

"Bring us a plate of the best and a pitcher of wine with two goblets."

The man walked away. Roger laughed quietly. "Thierré, your father is quite the showman."

"He loves every minute, and it's a grand surprise. A year ago, he thought himself a useless old man."

"Oh?"

"After he lost his right hand at Vézelay and nearly died there, he came home knowing that my mother had died of tumors while he was away. He became melancholic and started drinking hard."

"That must have been difficult, Thierré."

"It was, but I think all's going to turn out for him. The Henri de Coudre you met today will likely outlive me."

"He's a truly honorable knight, as are you and your brother Martin. Few families can match yours in reputation for prowess."

Thierré grew sad. "My days of prowess are over. I can only pray my past deeds in battle will gain me a place in Valhalla."

"Spoken like a Northman, and you look the part."

"My mother was pure Norman. My sister and I take after her."

"Then think like a Norman. I've seen men badly injured heal and fight again."

"As have I." Thierré shook his head, grinning. "But patience is a virtue lacking in my character."

The serving man brought their food and wine. Thierré filled the goblets, emptied his in one long swallow, and exhaled. "Ahh! That makes me feel better."

"Hard drinking won't get you back in the saddle."

"Nothing around here for a damned cripple to do save drink. It's been six months since I was at Mont-Brison. My tavern girls must surely think me dead."

"Thierré, you challenged a viscount's son for the sake of your sister's honor and defeated him in single combat. I rather think your reputation has spread farther than a whorehouse up the road."

"Perhaps it has, but honor upheld and fame won won't heal my sister's heart."

Roger nodded gravely. "Indeed. How is she now?"

"Well of body, but still troubled in spirit. After I got out of bed and back on my feet, she wanted to be away from here and took a house in Clermont. She and her servant are working there, in the hospital run by the convent."

"After the incident with Betancourt, your father let her go with no man to look after her?"

"Alisende has always known how to get her way with Father. Besides, she's come to hate men and wouldn't have one near her."

"Whatever her feelings be, she did right in taking up activity again. I'll say my own prayers that God deliver the both of you."

Thierré and Roger finished their meal. "Thank you for seeing to my needs, Thierré," Roger said. "I left the inn hours before dawn and was quite hungry."

Thierré shook his head slowly. "My father should have sent you here and let Clement fight Otto Mace-man."

"I don't fault your father at all. Any fighting knight still alive at my age has killed a halfscore men like Otto, and Henri made a well-considered guess that I could best him, even fresh off the road. I needed to earn respect right away and got it with that fight."

"You did indeed. Otto's a dread killer. He's more wild boar than man."

"He is formidable. Were I unhorsed in battle and saw him coming my way, I'd be praying."

Thierré pushed himself to his feet with his walking stick. "I need bid men bring your things up, and then I'll help you unpack and move in. Your room is on the floor with Walter and my father."

They worked until early afternoon. Roger settled into his comfortable room and stretched out for a nap on the big bed, and

Thierré made his way to his own tiny room in the armory quarters. The day's exertions and the wine drunk at midday had caught up with him. He fell onto his hard soldier's bed and dropped off into a deep sleep.

At twilight, he rose. He scrubbed his face and hands with soap and water from the table basin, combed his long, heavy blond hair, and tied it behind his head. He opened the small armoire, put on a smartly tailored linen shirt and a dark blue gambeson, completing the outfit with a silver-buckled belt, a finely made dagger in a silver-mounted sheath, and a worked-silver medallion hung at his chest.

Thierré hobbled to the great hall in the crisp evening air. A guard opened the carved oaken door. Upon entering, he caught the aromas of cooking and smiled to himself. Resident knights at the fortress enjoyed a fair share of comforts, Baron Alphonse's evening table the best of them. Alphonse, a man not given to austerity of body or disposition, freely shared his large appetites and generous spirit. A regular evening meal at Fortress Mirefleurs would be a special feast at castles of other noblemen, or a costly dinner at a luxurious inn.

Alphonse sat in the center chair at his long trestle table in front of the fireplace, the elder knights and visiting noblemen nearest to him. Roger sat among them, drinking from a silver goblet, laughing and joking with his new peers. Thierré took his customary seat with the younger knights, next to his friend Jean Loudon.

"You were with Roger de Lyon today, Thierré. What do you think of him?" Jean said.

"He's lethal at arms and crossed only at great peril, but he's also a right agreeable fellow. He'll get along with the men of our age, as well as the elder knights. Alphonse and Walter made a good choice in him."

"I've heard Alphonse brought him to get rid of the robbers."

"I know less than you, then. But if getting rid of those bloatflies is what Alphonse wants him to do, he looks to be more than sufficiently capable. We both watched him take Otto out in half a minute."

Alphonse rose to his feet. "I would like to offer Sir Roger de Lyon yet another welcome to Fortress Mirefleurs. He is a courageous knight and proven leader, with more than fifteen years of experience in times of war and peace. Let us offer best wishes that he will be successful here."

Thierré raised his goblet. "To Sir Roger!"

The others followed in the toast, took a deep drink, and looked to the sumptuous meal. Rows of congealed upside-down puddings molded with lion and boar heads atop them, platters of steamed fresh asparagus in garlic and butter sauce, bread and cheese, and flagons of wine and water were set along the center of the table. Serving men placed a wooden plate with a whole roast duck in butter sauce and choice cuts of roast boar before each nobleman.

Thierré studied his lord. At forty-five years, Baron Alphonse's undisciplined habits of heavy eating and drinking had begun to show in his person. Thierré guessed he carried fourscore unneeded pounds; he wheezed and gasped at the least physical exertion. His handsome features had grown marred by a thick network of varicose veins spreading over nose and cheeks; his olive skin appeared pallid, with a greenish-blue tinge.

Fifteen years previously, Alphonse's wife had miscarried their first child and herself died. He'd never remarried, and though a long succession of women had shared his bed, not one had borne him a bastard son or daughter. To Thierré's mind, the old gods of his own Norse ancestors had struck Alphonse infertile in punishment for his excesses.

Thierré regarded Alphonse as not long for life, and speculated on who might become the next Baron of Mirefleurs. The baron's only brother, younger and left a landless knight after the death of their father, had ridden away to seek his own fortune. Now, with twenty years since passed, of his whereabouts, nothing but vague rumors had been heard.

Jean nudged him. "Thierré, what are you thinking about? Look at this food."

Thierré's eyes fell on the roast duck, and the rich, smoky aroma triggered his outsized appetite. He started eating and didn't stop until he had picked the duck clean to the bones and finished a goodly portion of every other item in the huge meal.

The serving men brought wine. Thierré, still pensive, drank one small goblet and said his goodnights. On almost any night, he would be among the last drinkers to quit the great hall, but this evening, he was the first knight to leave. In his room, he undressed and got into bed.

Alphonse's shocking look of ill health and the sound of his wheeze haunted Thierré and kept him from sleep. He faced himself with truth. With the forced lack of exercise, and heavy eating and drinking, he had already put on unwanted weight. Should he continue to spend every evening as if it were his last, his injuries wouldn't heal properly, and he would fast come to the same condition as Alphonse.

He thought of years past with discomfort. Galien had shown real intelligence in learning letters, but Thierré had ridiculed his youngest brother's efforts as unmanly. Now, Thierré decided, he would learn this for himself. He had plenty of time on his hands, and Père Barnard was willing to teach for a small fee. He would ask the priest on the morrow.

Despite the long afternoon nap, the pain in his leg had again tired him. In another minute, he fell asleep and snored loudly.

Chapter 14

12 April 1092, the Abbé de Saint-Amand.

The scriptorium grew dim with coming evening as Galien carefully put final touches to a knight battling a demon, drawn within an intricate golden character. Charles leaned over the writing table, and Galien looked up, rubbing his eyes.

"Galien, only an artist gifted by God could draw with such skill. The character is of itself a work of art."

"It seems to come without effort. I drew much when a young boy."

Charles poked him. "Your rich noble father bought you all the parchment you asked for."

"Your sad life of deprivation surely wasn't as bad as you've made it out to be, my churlish friend. Neither of us lack for parchment here, and you can letter text at five times my speed, and nicely."

"It's been a grand surprise for me. Never before I came here did I have facility for long practice. I had to beg the village priest who taught me to save every scrap that might take letters."

"I've told you that your skill will put plenty of silver in your purse. Hold no doubt, you'd have your choice of the girls." Galien looked around the scriptorium, at the rows of monks busy at writing tables beneath the high-vaulted plastered ceiling. In two more weeks, his postulant time would be finished, and he free to return home.

Charles' voice brought his attention to the present. "Galien, what are you thinking about?"

"Do you want to take the next vows?"

"I'd not thought of anything else until you brought up pretty girls again. Truly though, a scribe's position in such a great monastery is far better than a poor peasant has a right to hope for, and I'll accept it with gratitude to God. Your own thoughts?"

"I'm eager to go home. With what I've gained here, I can earn better coin than ever in spare hours, and be more than ready to seek a high position in the service of a great count or duke."

Charles wagged his head. "You noblemen have it made."

"You lack only confidence, my friend. Don't underestimate yourself. I joke about silver and pretty girls, but the jokes hold truth."

"Hmm." Charles stroked his chin.

"Remember, you have made a friend for life in this well-placed nobleman. I'll make sure you don't lack for opportunities, should you decide to leave."

The scriptorium had grown dark with the setting sun, scribes busy straightening their tables before evening prayer services and supper in the refectory. Galien and Charles cleaned up their writing surfaces and followed the others out of the room.

"Much to consider, Sir Galien, but at the moment, I'm thinking only of food."

"As am I. Tonight, we can freely take of wine."

The next morning, Brother Ignatius summoned Galien and Charles to his high desk at the east end of the scriptorium. Before him lay pages of their best work. The scriptorium master addressed them. "Both of you have progressed very well. Your postulant time is nearly completed, and no gain is to be had in further training here. All the offices at Saint-Amand are in direst need of skilled scribes."

He looked at Charles. "Charles Falcard, with the completion of the new storage buildings, wine production will be greatly increased this year. The vineyard office needs a man who can record information quickly and do figures well. You've shown outstanding ability at both tasks, and I'm assigning you there."

Charles bowed his head. "Thank you for such an opportunity for service, Brother."

Ignatius nodded. "I'm confident you'll meet all expectations." He turned to Galien. "Galien de Coudre, the man who was assisting Joseph of Reims, the architect, has returned to Rome and training for the priesthood. Joseph is a man of great talent and exacting standards. I think you're the man to meet them."

"I saw Brother Joseph many times while working on the church building."

Ignatius chuckled. "He's quite a hard fellow to miss." At a likely fourteen-score pounds in weight, Joseph could not be mistaken.

Galien bowed his head. "Like my brother Charles, I accept your order with gratitude."

"Well enough," Ignatius said. "Gather your materials and report to your assignments. You're both needed at once. Galien, I'll need to show you the way to Brother Joseph's studio."

Charles left for the vineyard office. Galien followed Brother Ignatius through a long, torturous series of corridors and doors. Ignatius opened a finely carved oaken door at the end of the last corridor. They stepped into the light-filled studio, sixty feet long by twenty wide, and thirty-five high at the peak of the distinctive ceiling structure.

The sixty-foot north wall seemed at first glance to float without support. Three huge windows, fifteen feet high at the pointed peaks, stood between four stout twenty-foot pilasters supporting the unique ceiling. Intricately worked lead held clear and pale colored-glass panes, bordered with geometric designs in brilliant colors. The bubbled, handmade glass broke the north light, creating a shimmering mystical effect.

"Your father's donation helped complete the payment for these windows," Ignatius said. Galien gazed, speechless. The soaring effect of the room was akin to that of the newly remade church building.

Ignatius put a hand on Galien's shoulder. "I need take my leave. I'm sure Brother Joseph will soon appear from behind a pile of drawings or heap of stones. Put down your things, take a look around, and don't worry. He's a genial fellow."

Galien bowed his head to Ignatius. "Thank you for tolerating my ineptitude over the past weeks."

"You and Charles were both fine students. If you wish to return to the scriptorium for practice or more instruction, you'll be welcome at any time. God be with you, Galien."

"And with you, Brother Ignatius."

Ignatius turned to leave, and Galien looked around Brother Joseph's studio. Five minutes passed with no one appearing. He felt no apprehension and began to explore. Slanted drawing tables stood against the three windows, and a table as large as Alphonse's dominated the center of the room. Covered in calculated disarray, it bore drawings inked on parchment, large smooth slates for scribing, intricate architectural models, and bound-parchment books. Ruling and measuring instruments, quills and pens for drawing, and miniature tools for modeling lay scattered about.

A wide fireplace surrounded with stone carvings stood centered on the east wall of the room. Two high-backed armchairs covered in rich old tapestry fabric faced the fireplace; a round table between them held a silver decanter and goblets. Wooden bookcases, adorned with carvings and cluttered with books, scrolls, and curious objects, stood beside the fireplace.

In the northeast corner of the room, a twelve-foot square area of the floor was set with smooth slate, providing a surface on which to scribe full-sized building details and work out geometric problems. Samples of building materials leaned against the walls and lay about in stacks.

Galien set his materials on one of the drawing tables, stood at a window, and marveled at the wavy views through the handmade glass panes. The studio was fit to be a duke's receiving chamber. What monk could use such a room only for himself?

He felt another's presence and turned to face a heavy, dark-bearded monk. Galien recognized him right away. "The Lord's peace be with you. I am Joseph of Reims, and you must be Galien," the monk said.

"And with you, Brother Joseph. I'm Galien de Coudre, reporting for service."

"You've had some time to look around? I hope you're not thoroughly bewildered, but even if you are, that won't delay us from catching up on this pile of drawings I have to finish."

"I spent six weeks working on the construction crew at the church building, and have always had an appreciative eye for architecture."

"Hmm. I don't recall seeing you there, but it seems ten years I've been holed up in this studio, trying to finish the foundation design and drawings for fund-raising for the new church in Bourges. In any case, work on a building crew is always good experience. It gives the first-hand feel and sharpens the eye."

"I learned much there," Galien said.

Joseph walked to the big table. "No doubt you did. Now, it's time to get busy. I hope you don't mind some late evenings. We have three months of work to finish in two weeks."

"I don't mind at all. I sleep best after a long day's work." Shadows of Sylvestrus' evil touch yet clung to Galien and invaded his dreams, and he welcomed the promise of activity and diversion.

"Very good," Joseph said. "Set up your materials on one of the drawing tables and I'll bring an old parchment over for you to practice on for today. We'll start by going over some architectural terms, and then you'll letter them in the style I use."

Galien practiced until twilight and then examined his assignment. Though simple in content, it called for time and precision in execution. Thirty architectural drawings, meticulously inked on the best parchment, lacked written information to be complete, and a list of specifications needed to be neatly lettered on parchment from Joseph's notes, scattered about on wax tablets, discarded drawings, and scraps. For the drawings, Joseph needed no more than titles and simple notes designating building materials and dimensions, but their value and the architect's standards for the placement, style, and artistry of the notations left no room for inattention and errors.

In the days following, Joseph left Galien alone at the drawing table under the window and worked at his big table to complete a wood-and-plaster model of the new church. Galien interrupted Joseph's intense concentration only as he finished one drawing and began another. Joseph looked over the completed drawings, said, "Very good," and added them to the growing stack on his table.

For ten full days, Joseph and Galien spoke no more than needed. Galien left for prayer times and to eat in the Refectory, bringing a full platter back for Joseph to eat at the work table. After supper, Joseph set up a three-hour glass, and they worked by candlelight and light cast from the fireplace until the sand ran out to the bottom.

On the night of April 24, with the hourglass two-thirds down, Galien handed Joseph the last page of specifications. Joseph sat back in his chair, examined Galien's work, smiled broadly, and tossed his modeling knife across the table.

"Galien, we're finished, and four days early. The drawings and model could not have turned out better. I despair to think of where I might have been, or rather might not have been, without your capable assistance."

"I'm happy to have been at hand."

"You need not come in tomorrow morning, Galien. I have only to prepare for my trip to Bourges and the final presentation to the bishop and other Church officials. But we've hardly had time to speak a friendly word. Join me by the fire for some wine and cake?"

"I'm honored, Joseph."

Joseph added fresh wood to the dying embers and poured goblets of wine. From the right-hand bookcase, he produced a silver-domed cake platter and matching plates. "I guessed we'd be finishing the project today. For a bit of silver, old Nestor baked this yesterday."

Joseph set the platter on the round table, and he and Galien took seats in the chairs before the fire. Galien took a sip of his wine, and then a swallow. "I've never had this variety, Joseph. It's more than fine."

"I only need give the right man a little silver."

Joseph removed the domed platter cover to reveal a large fancy molded cake, crusted on top with honey, raisins, and nuts, crisp golden brown, oozing butter around the bottom edge. He cut a huge hunk for each of them, got up, and returned with a silver-chased ceramic pitcher.

"Almost forgot," he chuckled, and poured viscous clotted cream over the helpings of cake. Galien tasted it and didn't stop. Joseph put a piece on his plate, settled into the other chair, and took a large bite.

"So, where to begin, Galien? You've been a capable assistant."

"I told my father I'd stay at Saint-Amand through the postulant period. In five days, I'll be free to leave."

Joseph raised a bushy eyebrow. "Your thoughts?"

"I'm going home, to give my oath of fealty to Baron Alphonse."

"Galien, you're a fit and able young man, but I can't truly see you as a knight of siege and battle."

"You're keen, Joseph. My family's name and my knowledge of letters and languages will serve to gain me entry into a diplomat's post with a high nobleman." Galien refilled their goblets and waited as Joseph sat back and finished his cake.

"To judge from the way you spoiled Sylvestrus' good looks, you'll be well able to step out onto the battlefield when need be."

Galien didn't blink. "He asked for what I dealt him. And only a week past, I found a scrap of parchment under my breakfast platter in the refectory, with a dagger piercing a heart drawn. When I catch the man who put it there, he'll get the same treatment."

Joseph drew back, shocked. "No, Galien! Go straight to Leo and report it."

"A knight doesn't report such a threat. Rather, he favors sword or dagger."

Joseph rubbed his temples and took a long drink. After a pause, he said, "I suppose I must accept you're a man of the sword, so let us move on."

Galien bowed his head. "In your good time, Joseph."

"Your postulant time and your assignment to me are nearly finished, but I must confess, I've much hoped you were intending to stay at Saint-Amand. I've enough work to last ten years, and had I my way, you'd be here in the studio as my leading assistant."

"Joseph, my course is set. Any thoughts I had toward a life in the Church are over."

"What would you say if I could convince Leo to let you stay on for a time, though you decline to take novice vows? My word carries weight with him."

"I'll think on it, but truly, I can't stay but a few days longer. I've no real place here, and I don't intend to disappoint my father."

"Two more months would be of great help, Galien."

Galien knitted his eyebrows and stroked his chin, then looked at Joseph. "I might be able to spare two months."

Joseph leaned forward. "I have the discretion and funds to hire assistants from outside Saint-Amand, and can pay you one livre per month."

Galien sat back, in deep thought. One livre was twice the salary of an expert draughtsman of long experience. Two livres saved would allow him to purchase some of the knight's gear he yet needed, and become more independent of his father. "If you only need me for two months longer, Father and Baron Alphonse ought to be satisfied. Should they give their approval, I'll be happy to help you."

"Grand!" Joseph said. They raised their goblets in a friendly toast and drank deeply.

JOSEPH SCOTT AMIS

Chapter 15

26 April 1092, the Abbé de Saint-Amand

The studio grew dim after Compline. Galien set his pen down and stretched. Joseph entered the room, filled two cups with sweet herbal tea, and took the other chair. Both sipped at the tea and Joseph said, "I've just been with Leo. He's agreeable to letting you stay here as a layman in service."

"I wrote to my father and sent it with the spirits wagon. He'll send a reply in short time, most likely by horseman. We can be sure of that."

"Leo wants to see you in the morning. Now, it's time for supper."

"If you'd like, I can bring our supper here."

"A grand idea, Galien. We can take it at our leisure and talk." Joseph handed him three silver deniers. "Slip these to Nestor."

A quarter-hour later, Galien and Joseph sat before the studio fireplace with their meal. Galien asked about the studio ceiling, and Joseph described the structure in detail as they ate. Finished, they set their plates aside and sat back with wine.

"Galien, tell me more about yourself. I know you're the third son of the knight Henri de Coudre, but little else save your plans for the future."

Galien gave Joseph a brief history of his life. He touched on his place as the odd man in his family of knights, yet beloved by father and brothers, and recounted the gallant exploits of Henri, Martin, and

Thierré. He said no more of the bloody fight with Sylvestrus or the threatening drawing, nor did he speak of his romance with Lisette.

"And you, Joseph? I know you're an architect of repute and held in high esteem here, but little more."

"I was born and grew up in the city of Reims, and am now thirty-five years. My family has been in the stonecutting and building trades for six generations. I spent my boyhood in the stone yard and on building sites with my father, and was apprenticed to a master stone carver at twelve years. At fourteen, I had learned all he could teach. My father then apprenticed me to the architect Guilliame of Reims, and engaged a cathedral-schooled priest to teach me letters and geometry. I was a busy young fellow for the next seven years."

Joseph paused and lifted the pitcher. "More wine?"

Galien held up a hand. "No. Go on, Joseph."

"After the seven years had passed, Master Guilliame declared me ready to produce my own master's piece. I lacked only a patron, and in due course, my father and Guilliame arranged for one. A parish in the wealthy quarter of the city had amassed considerable silver and wished to spend it on a new rectory and hall. After consulting with Guilliame, the governing board agreed to contract with me as their architect and master builder."

Joseph took another sip of wine. "The new building was finished in two years and didn't exceed the cost estimates by half a livre. It was acclaimed as the best new structure in the city, and the inventiveness of the design was widely admired and predicted to become influential. Guilliame released me from ties to him and had my Article of Mastery drawn up. The Bishop of Reims, the mayor, and the chairmen of the building trade guilds signed it in ceremony. Forthwith, I had full credentials of the architect's profession."

"Surely a lifetime of commissions from the Church and wealthy nobility awaited you, and would have provided a handsome living."

Joseph smiled. "You're wondering why I became a monk."

Galien shrugged and grinned. "Who wouldn't?"

"After the rectory commission had been secured, my father, Master Guilliame, and the parish governing board felt a promising young architect should be married, and married well. I was too busy working to dwell on the matter and complied with their wishes. My bride came of good family and was an attractive and intelligent woman. Though she was most agreeable, we lived together for only a year, and then the Bishop dissolved the marriage for reasons held in privy. It cost her father a bag of silver, but he lost no property."

Joseph took a swallow of brandy and closed his eyes. "When my marriage failed, I felt myself to be in arrears with God and wanted to rest and find peace. I came here and spent some time living in the guest quarters. When I approached Abbot Leo about joining as a brother, he was pleased to have a man of my capabilities, but I wasn't spared the six-month postulant period. However, the monastery life agreed with me and I've stayed on."

"Truly, Joseph, I'm sorry your marriage ended so, but you seem to have lost no opportunities in your profession."

"No, I've only become busier, with more demands on my time. I've decided that God, more often than not, creates artistic men to be lonely drudges and slaves to their work."

They fell silent and gazed at the dying fire. Joseph broke the quiet. "Galien, it's late. You need visit Abbott Leo in the morning. I won't expect you till after the noon meal, and then, I'll need you to gather men and carry the church model and drawings to the loading area. The Bishop of Bourges is sending his personal travel wagon and an armed escort. I'll be leaving two days hence and will return in a week's time. While I'm gone, become familiar with the architectural texts, and see that this studio is straightened up and swept. Also, tell Brother Ignatius I need two more good calligraphers right away, even if he can only spare them for a short time."

Galien rose to leave. "I will. Goodnight, Joseph, and thank you for everything."

"God grant you a restful night, Galien. You've earned it."

Joseph's head nodded to his chest. He drifted off to sleep in his chair, and Galien returned to the postulant quarters.

The next day, Galien ignored the calls to prayers, slept until midmorning, and then visited the vineyard office. Brother Ernoul glared, but didn't speak when Charles left his work. Galien didn't want to risk Joseph's elegant model to rough and inartistic men, and together they borrowed two scribes from Brother Ignatius to assist them in carrying the fragile church model to the storeroom off the loading area.

With the model packed in a stout wooden crate and locked in the storeroom, Galien returned to the studio. He rolled up the precious drawings, placed them into copper tubes with latching tops, then wrapped the tubes in waterproof oilcloth and packed them into an ornate wooden chest with a secure lock.

Joseph, satisfied with the preparation of the models and drawings, gave Galien leave for the day. After Sext and the midday meal, Galien walked to Leo's quarters and requested a short visit with the abbot. Leo waived formality and invited Galien into his office.

Leo reviewed Galien's record. "Galien, you've been here for nearly seven months. Needless to say, your work in all areas has been exceptional. Brother Ignatius gave high praise for your abilities as a calligrapher and artist, and Brother Joseph is very happy with your work and your dedicated attitude."

Galien bowed his head. "Thank you, Father Abbot. I'm grateful to you and Joseph." He chuckled. "Joseph has kept me so busy, I've forgotten my postulant time was over almost a month ago."

"Yes, I've noticed you haven't turned in your habit. In truth, I've yet high hopes that you'll take the next vows and eventually become a full brother. You're a great asset to Saint-Amand."

"I no longer desired the religious life when I arrived, and can't deny events here have turned my heart yet further from it. I'm more than ready to change this habit for my regular clothes."

Leo sighed. "I can't say I'm not disappointed, Galien. You've not found peace of heart or willingness to forgive?"

"I've regained a certain peace, but Sylvestrus faces sure death should he again trouble me."

"That deed will be on your own soul and at your own accountability. Now, as a layman in service here, you'll have a bed in the guest quarters, and I'll only ask you to attend one Mass each day. If you wish to ride out, you can take a horse from the stable."

"That's generous of you, Father Abbot."

"Before he departed, your father asked me to keep your clothes and weapons for you, and left a bag of coins."

"I'd expect no less of my father, God bless and keep him."

"I must warn you, Galien. When you pass beyond the boundary markers of this monastery, you will be under Lord Falcard's jurisdiction. Remain sober and keep your sword and dagger sheathed.

Drunken behavior or an arrest will lead to your expulsion, no matter what Joseph's needs may be."

"You needn't worry, Father Abbot. I'll wait until my time with Joseph is finished to get drunk and cut Sylvestrus' hands and head off."

Leo cleared his throat. "Have you any more questions for me, Galien?"

"Yes. How did Joseph come to have such a studio?"

"You haven't known Joseph long and he's not often given to boasting. He is, beyond doubt, the most gifted and influential architect in this region of France. His reasons for coming to live at Saint-Amand are his own, but his patrons didn't stop seeking him out merely because he became a monk. So Joseph might have a free hand to design and test his visions, a group of rich noblemen and merchants in his home city of Reims provided the funds for the studio and the church renovations. Sir Henri's generous donation went a long way in helping to pay off the last debts."

"I'm happy to see Father's silver used to such good purpose."

"Indeed it was. Brother Honorius will show you to your new quarters, and may God guide your path, Galien. He's with you, believe you or not."

Joseph departed at dawn the next morning in the Bishop of Bourges' own ornate enclosed wagon. The bishop had left nothing to chance for safe transport of the renowned architect and his irreplaceable creations. Galien watched as the procession passed through the gateway, a knight in the lead and six mounted men-at-arms riding beside and behind the wagon, crossbows cocked and swords at close hand.

The gates closed, and Galien returned to the studio to begin the hard work of cleaning up. Dressed in work clothes and boots, he sneezed often as he moved the jumble of heavy, dust-covered items away from the walls to the center of the room. The door knocker thudded, Galien paused pushing a hand-cart bearing stone column capitals, and yelled "Enter!"

Benedict walked into the dust cloud sparkling in the light streaming through the leaded windows, and began to sneeze. Recovered, he walked over to Galien, and they gripped hands. Galien invited him to sit by the fireplace. He cut pieces of Joseph's rich cake, filled a small silver goblet with wine for Benedict, and did likewise for himself.

Benedict took a sip of wine and tasted the cake. "I asked about you on my arrival last night, but my need for sleep took priority over visits to friends. At breakfast, Leo told me of your plans. I'm happy that you're well, but distressed at your decision to leave us."

"As a boy, I yearned to enter the religious life, but shed my last illusions about it here."

"Can you speak of the reasons?"

A dark cloud passed over Galien's eyes. "The day I arrived, we sat in the cloister and you told me things are sometimes not what they seem to be. I found your words to be truth."

Benedict hesitated, eyes downcast. "Yes, I could not help but learn that Sylvestrus caused you trouble."

"He's a marked man for the rest of his wretched life."

"You can't let it pass, with what you've already done to him?"

"I've no intent to seek him out, but should he cross my path with ill purpose, he'll need face my sword."

"To take his life would only stain your own soul, so I'll pray you never see him again. Let's talk of more agreeable matters."

Benedict told of his long stay in Rome. Galien recounted his assignment to the monastery church building, his work with Joseph, and his own plans. After a pleasant hour of conversation, Benedict rose from his chair. "Galien, I must leave now. I don't want to slow your work." Galien walked with Benedict to the door, where they shook hands and promised to soon visit again.

The cloud of dust in the studio had settled. Galien wet a strip of cloth in a table basin and tied it around his mouth and nose. As he set to his tasks, he thought of the dangers yet facing him in the monastery. Surely, Brother Ernoul was in connivance with Sylvestrus, and together they were planning to kill him. He would have to watch his own back and keep his dagger with him at all times.

Chapter 16

18 August 1092, Clermont

Alisende de Coudre attended to her last patient for the day. No treatments had helped the festering sores that ravaged the young woman's body, and she would soon die. Alisende covered her with a clean sheet, spoke kindly to her, and left the convent hospital for the house she shared with Lisette. Once there, Lisette brought her wine. "You're here before nightfall."

"Two patients died after noon and I wasn't further needed, thanks be to God. Another hour in that house of misery and death would have been more than I could bear."

"You've lost the will to continue in hospital work?"

"On the morrow, I'll tell the prioress we'll soon be leaving. Six months here have convinced me God didn't intend for either of us to be nurses, and I want to go home."

8 September 1092, Fortress Mirefleurs

In her room off the great hall balcony, Alisende slept late into the morning. Lisette opened the window to breeze and sunlight, and Alisende stirred and sat up in bed. "I'm happy to be home, but I carry two days of road grime and stink, as well."

Lisette laughed. "I also smell of well-aged game, so I've arranged for a bath. I'll scrub your back and wash your hair."

"After a cup of wine and a little food last night, I could do nothing but fall asleep. Thank you for putting me to bed and seeing to the bath."

"It was my pleasure. I'll have you looking your best for this evening."

+ + +

Darkness was falling outside the open doors to the great hall as Alisende descended the stairs from the balcony. A line of nobles stood waiting to welcome her home and beyond them, the long table was set and decorated for a special occasion. She greeted Baron Alphonse, her father, and Walter d'Avesnes, then came face-to-face with an unfamiliar knight. Martin, standing beside him, said, "Sir Roger de Lyon, my sister, Lady Alisende de Coudre."

Roger bowed his head, took her hand, and kissed it. "The honor is mine, Lady Alisende."

"Are you visiting us, Sir Roger?"

"A long visit, Lady. I've been in the service of Baron Alphonse since spring, and I hope he'll want me to remain in my post."

Alisende smiled at him tightlipped, and said, "I wish you the best of fortune here, Sir Roger," then moved on to greet Thierré and the younger noblemen and women. She felt eyes on her and glanced up at the balcony. Lisette covered a smile and a giggle with a hand. Alisende frowned in return, and turned her attention back to those before her.

At the evening's end, Alisende returned to her room. Lisette stirred, awoke, and said, "Did all go well?"

Alisende began to undress, deep in thought. Lisette got up to put her clothes away. "Say something, Lady. Are you angry with me?"

"Of course not. I've only been thinking. I want us to move back to the estate."

"We moved here at great pains on your father's part, and the estate is now Thierré's. Why this sudden wish to go back there?"

"Wayward knights with a roving eye."

"Whatever your reason, Thierré would be happy for you live there again. I more fear Sir Henri's fury, should you want to undo all he's done on your behalf."

"My father's wrath is nothing to be taken lightly. We're here to stay, and I still don't know what to do with myself."

"You're a wealthy woman now. You can do whatever you like."

Alisende pulled on her nightgown and sat on the edge of her bed, not speaking. Lisette said, "It's the new elder knight, isn't it?"

"Your little smirk from the balcony didn't make meeting him any easier."

Lisette stifled a laugh. "I couldn't help it. You're attracted to him, and he to you."

"I am not attracted to him! I smelled only a rogue and seducer, and intend to keep my distance."

Lisette sighed. "A misfortune I'm only a commoner. I find him more than attractive."

"You're no longer in love with Galien?"

"I'll love him until the moment I die, but must gain resolve to let go of him and become open to new prospects. I yet want children and need find a husband while my youth remains."

Alisende rubbed her temples. "My father is so stubborn about you and Galien, but we need let it rest for now and find something to do. With Galien away, Alphonse and Père Barnard are surely in want of help with their document and account work. Are you interested?"

"Very much so. I'd like to learn something of letters."

"Then I'll teach you what I can. On the morrow, I'll ask Père Barnard if we might help them and work at the table in our room. Here, I'll be well away from any knight who seeks Barnard's counsel and prayers."

5 October 1092, Fortress Mirefleurs.

The late evening moon, high in the clear, cold sky, cast the fortress in stark blue contrast to the grounds, scattered with the fallen leaves of autumn. Thierré de Coudre closed the door to Père Barnard's quarters and walked steadily toward the armory. He thought of Galien and how he had teased his youngest brother about learning to read and write. Now, he only wanted to be able to send Galien a letter written in his own hand. Thierré shook his head and had a laugh at himself.

After a doubtful start in April, his lessons with Père Barnard were now showing promise. He could recite and letter the Latin alphabet and, albeit crudely, write his name and any combination of letters on demand. This evening, Barnard had told him he would be examined a week before Christmas. If he showed sufficient progress, they would begin instruction in written words and phrases, using short verses from the Bible as a guide.

Since his own moment of truth on the night of Roger's arrival at the fortress, Thierré had followed the physicians' instructions to the word, and made a worthy effort to shake old habits. His leg hadn't healed shorter, and he now walked without the stick, with only a slight limp, but the physician yet forbade him to ride any distance farther than Coudre Estate, that at a slow pace. The spells of blurred vision and dizziness had lessened, but they still returned in unpredictable moments, often enough to trouble him. A year after the fight with Baldwin de Betancourt, he felt his future as a fully capable knight still uncertain. Though he had returned to the regular soldiers' schedule as soon as the physician consented, he struggled with the fact that he might be faced with a life as a nobleman farmer and arms trainer.

True to Thierré's expectations, Roger de Lyon had fit easily into life at Fortress Mirefleurs. He got along well with all of the staff at arms, old and young, nobleman and commoner. Modest and friendly in manner, he'd proved to be an approachable and patient resolver of problems. He wore the confidence of a hardened battle veteran, and had secured the deference and loyalty of the men, gained only through genuine attraction to a natural leader. His swift, graceful defeat of Otto Huber had already become a part of fortress lore.

Thierré thought of his own bond with Roger, formed on Roger's first day at the fortress and since grown into close friendship. He again had an inward laugh at himself. Roger's enviable confidence and maturity had fast prompted Thierré to begin to shed the lingering ways of fresh manhood. He had finally found a man to emulate, and their association accomplished that which his father's endless, fuming attempts to discipline his eldest son could not.

24 November 1092, Fortress Mirefleurs

Alisende waited as Lisette laced up the back of her dark crimson evening dress and put final touches to her hair. Lisette stepped back a pace and said, "Lady, I can do no better."

Lisette brought the silver mirror, and Alisende studied herself. "No one but you could do so well, but I should have had this dress altered. It fits my figure too tightly for decency."

"The other young noblewomen will be wearing the same."

"If they want to look like whores, let them. After tonight, take this dress to a seamstress."

Lisette closed the room door. They walked to balcony rail and looked down at the crowd in the great hall. "I hate these things," Alisende said.

"You didn't in the past, if your father and brothers speak truly."

"I do now, but I must fulfill my duty and honor the great knight Crestien de Trielle with my presence."

"Sir Crestien de Trielle is one of your father's and Baron Alphonse's oldest friends and allies. It's your duty, so do as befits you."

"Oh, all right." Alisende walked down the stairs, putting on a smile for the many faces that turned to her. She spotted Martin and quickly joined him. "Get me some wine, Brother." Martin stopped a servant bearing a tray of goblets. Alisende emptied one in a swallow and took another.

"Sister, settle yourself," Martin said. "Old Pierre Bouchard is here, and you might want to hear us talk of the land I'm trying to buy from him. It holds promise of great fortune."

"I'd like to listen, Brother. Will you accompany me to greet Sir Crestien first?"

"At my honor." Martin offered his arm. Alisende reached out to take it, and an elderly noblewoman stumbled into her. The silver goblet flew from Alisende's hand, clattering noisily on the floor, splattering wine. She stooped to retrieve it, tripped, and a strong arm caught her around the waist before she could fall. She found her balance and pushed stray hair away from her eyes. Roger de Lyon stood before her. "Are you all right, Lady Alisende?"

"I think so, Sir Roger. Thank you so much for keeping me from a fall." She glanced to her left. Martin and another nobleman were helping the elderly woman to her seat, a servant mopping up the spilled wine. Alisende looked at Roger and smiled nervously.

"Lady, may I accompany you to the table?" Roger said. She nodded, grateful to leave the awkward scene. They took seats at the baron's table and waited while serving men filled their platters.

Alisende first spoke. "Sir Roger, I know you've become friends with my father and brothers. Please call me Alisende."

"And I'm Roger, if you so please."

"Roger it is."

"Thank you for your kind words, Alisende. Thierré tells me you managed your family's estate for four years and made a success of it. That's most commendable."

"For a woman, do you mean?"

"For anyone. My father held an estate much like your family lands. He died when I was nineteen, and I was only too happy to see my older brother take it. I was grateful to be born a second son, and to ride off as a free young knight."

Alisende crossed her arms, leaning back. "And I suppose you're still a happy and free adventurer?"

"I'm content with my post here at Fortress Mirefleurs. The free riding days ended years ago."

She studied his face and the swordcut scar, frowning. "I see."

Jean Loudon, Thierré, and Martin came to the table and took seats. Alisende turned to Jean and asked after his family. Martin caught Thierré and Roger's attention with talk of his plans to purchase more lands. The wine flowed as they eagerly partook of the good food. After a pleasant hour, Alisende glanced at Martin. "I haven't greeted Sir Crestien yet!"

"Then let's go see him before he retires for the evening." Martin and Alisende rose and bade the others goodnight. Alisende bowed her head to Roger. "Thank you again for helping me, Roger."

Roger rose. "My honor and pleasure, Alisende. I hope we might visit again."

"Perhaps." She took Martin's arm, and they turned toward the noblemen across the room.

Chapter 17

25 November 1092, Fortress Mirefleurs

Roger de Lyon leaned against a stone wall in the armory knights' room, absently cleaning and polishing his weapons and hauberk. Since first meeting Alisende de Coudre, a life undreamed of had entered and stayed in his mind, and he'd tried to push the thoughts away, with no success. The viscount's son with whom she had entered betrothal had paid dearly for his grave offense to her and the Coudre family, but Baldwin de Betancourt had yet left Alisende his own legacy, a fearfully deep distrust of men. He, Roger de Lyon, had his own silver in plenty, and Baron Alphonse would be granting him choice lands, but more than possessions and a title would be needed to gain Alisende's trust and confidence.

The heavy oaken door swung open, banging against the wall. Roger jumped. Jean Loudon burst in. "Roger, there's been a massacre on Route de Voleurs. Alphonse wants us in his quarters, at once."

Roger sheathed his sword and belted it to his waist. "What happened?"

"A band of robbers attacked a large group of pilgrims on the road south of Saint-Julien, half an hour ago. They killed a halfscore or more, and many are wounded."

"Was there no escort?"

"Three of our mounted men-at-arms. The robbers waylaid them with crossbows and took their horses."

They dashed to the inner court, entered the great hall, and took the steps to Alphonse's quarters two at a time. Inside, Père Barnard, Henri, Walter, and Thierré waited. Alphonse addressed them. "We all now know of this tragic atrocity. Walter has dispatched a company to fetch the dead to the fortress and bring the pilgrims yet alive to refuge and hospital here." He stood. "The time has come for the road vermin we've been holding for execution to give up their secrets. Sir Jean Loudon, fetch Otto and Reinhard and have them meet me in the dungeon at once. Interrogation will begin in half an hour."

Roger met Jean at the door to the lower fortress levels and led down torchlit flights of stone steps to the dungeon, three floors beneath the armory. He banged the heavy bronze knocker, and a guard opened the ironbound door. To the right stood a row of six cells enclosed with stout oaken crossbars; to the left, a room walled with rough foundation stones and spanned by hewn beams at the low ceiling, opened before them. Torches set in brackets on the walls and columns cast the room in flickering light and deep shadows. Alphonse leaned against a stout column, arms crossed, glowering. Thierré sat in a chair at a long table.

Roger looked to the center of the room. There stood a heavy wooden table with a naked woman strapped face-up. Reinhard Huber waited at a charcoal brazier set beside the table. He withdrew an iron poker from the coals, held up the pointed end, glowing dull red, and thrust it back. At a rattling noise, Roger glanced to his left. A sweating, naked man with scraggly, dirty hair and beard struggled against hand-manacles riveted to the wall. Otto Huber withdrew iron snips from a brazier, snapped the red-hot blades at the man, and rested them on the coals.

The door creaked open. Père Barnard, Henri, and Walter filed in. The guard threw the heavy steel bolts. Alphonse faced the manacled prisoner, looked him over, and grabbed him by the hair. "I'll allow you one opportunity to answer. Where does your band of robbers keep its nest?"

The man glanced at the two male prisoners behind the cell doors. "I… I don't know, Sire. I'm only a lookout man on the road."

Alphonse studied his heavily-ringed right hand, drew it left, and backhanded the man across the face. "You are a God-cursed liar." He looked at Reinhard and jerked his head at the woman on the table. "Sergeant Huber."

Reinhard pulled the red-hot poker from the coals, walked to the table, and paused, poker above the woman's right breast. Alphonse nodded, and Reinhard slowly lowered the glowing tip to hover half an inch above the nipple. She shrieked like a skinned cat and spat in Reinhard's eye. Coolly professional, he wiped away the saliva and thrust the poker back into the brazier.

Alphonse again backhanded the manacled man. "She's your lover, is she not?" The man gurgled, blood dripping from his chin. Alphonse moved closer. "Answer, damn you!" At the prisoner's vacant look, Alphonse backed away. He looked at Otto and Reinhard. "This pig won't name his she-pig. Therefore, you shall geld both of them."

Reinhard singed the woman's pubic hair with the poker. Otto grabbed the man's scrotum with his left hand and picked up the hot snips with his right. The man wagged his dripping head. "Mercy, Sire! I'll tell you everything."

Alphonse smiled. "That's better." He faced the room. "Père Barnard, take and record this man's testimony. Sir Walter, you and Sirs Henri and Thierré de Coudre will witness. If he hesitates or you sense lies, have the sergeants resume their duties."

Roger noted Alphonse's impressive skill at coercing the needed information by means far short of flesh-rending torture. He glanced at the other knights. The elder men and Thierré waited impassively, but sweat ran down Jean's ashen face. Alphonse turned to Roger and Jean. "Sir Roger, you're to lead the mission to come, and Sir Jean will serve as your second. Roust the company and wait at ready for my summons."

Two hours later, Alphonse stood up at his table and dismissed Roger and Jean. They left the great hall to stand in the cool of the November afternoon. Roger spoke. "Sir Jean, are you prepared to carry out the orders we've been given?"

Jean wiped his brow, nodding slowly, and Roger put a hand on his shoulder. "You know the knight's life is not an easy one, but the morrow's mission will be harder than any battle you've yet fought. Commit to mind that we act for justice and the people we're sworn to protect."

+ + +

As daylight faded, Alisende and Lisette sat exhausted on a low stone wall in the front court, watching Roger and Sergeant Lienart direct the men-at-arms taking the dead pilgrims from a wagon. Roger walked over to them. "Alisende, it's nearly dark. You and Lisette had best go indoors and take a rest."

Alisende rose. "You're right. We're almost dead, ourselves."

"You were both kind to help with the wounded, and your experience in the convent hospital proved invaluable. Lives that might have been lost were saved."

"Thank you, Roger. We've our duty, as you have yours."

Roger returned to the wagons and the two women walked toward the great hall. "Lady, I think you'd do well to take some wine," Lisette said. "And then, I'd like to go to the chapel and pray for the souls now in God's presence."

"We'll both have wine and a bath, and I'll go with you. While you pray for those killed, I'll pray our good baron finally sees he needs to rid our roads of this cursed bandit plague."

26 November, 1092, the Grand Forest, the Barony of Mirefleurs

Roger de Lyon raised a hand. Jean Loudon and the fifteen-man company halted and dismounted quietly. In the dark before dawn and a cold, steady wind, they pulled dark, heavy hooded cloaks close over their light armor and assembled on the snow-blown road.

Roger beckoned to two black-clad men and said, "Kill the road lookouts, now." They slipped ahead with no sound and vanished. He addressed a bound prisoner, the man Alphonse had interrogated in the dungeon. "They'd best be where you said they are. Raise a warning or lead us into a trap, and I'll see you and your woman flayed alive."

The company waited, shivering, until the advance men returned. "Sir Roger, we killed two, and found them at the places he told us." Roger nodded and spoke again to the prisoner. "Now, lead us to the trail." The man stumbled ahead, Roger's sword point to his back. Down the road, he nodded to the right.

The clack of a crossbow startled them, and a man cried out and fell. Shields came up and swords slid from scabbards. Crossbowmen held their weapons at ready. A dark-clad figure darted from the forest's edge and across the road ahead. A long-legged man-at-arms gave chase, but returned emptyhanded. "He climbed over the rocks and ran into the woods, Sir Roger. I couldn't catch him."

"Not to mind," Roger said. "He lost his nerve and now he's saving his own skin." He bent over the fallen man. "Sergeant Lienart, carry him behind the tree line. If he's still alive, tend to him." The battle surgeon and two men-at-arms sprang to obey.

Roger pushed the prisoner ahead, and the company followed in single file onto the forest trail.

"Where are the other lookouts?" Roger asked. The prisoner gave directions, and Roger gestured to the advance men. They drew long daggers, slunk into the dark woods, and returned shortly. "Both dead now, Sir, but there's a guard by a fire in the clearing. The cave entry's well in earshot, so we couldn't risk going in after him."

"Take bows and kill him, and scout the area. We'll move at a slow pace."

Roger waved the company forward. The advance men met them at the edge of a clearing, three yards below the forest trail, ringed with rock outcroppings. An ancient stone chapel lay in ruins at the far side, the slain guard by the fire in the center. Roger tied a gag in the prisoner's mouth, and the company crept down into the clearing. The advance men pointed to a cave. Roger said to Jean in a low voice, "Take six men and wait at ready to enter," and to Reinhard Huber, "Take three men and scout the ruins. Kill anything that attacks."

Roger watched Reinhard and his men enter the crumbling structure, torchlight shivering through gaping windows and between bare roof timbers. The party stepped back into the clearing. With no warning, a dry limb beneath fallen leaves broke with a sharp crack. Light flickered deep in the cave, and Roger turned to Jean. "Go in now, before they can loose bolts." Jean and his men drew their weapons and rushed in.

Muffled sounds of chaos echoed and then all grew silent. Shortly, men and women with hands held above their shoulders walked out into the clearing in pairs, men-at-arms holding swords to their backs. Jean came out last, his right arm around a limping man-at-arms. He helped the man to sit and turned to Roger. "The cave is clear, Sir. We killed two others, and armsman Beuvé took a hard mace blow to a knee." Roger looked at Reinhard. "Nothing in the ruins save refuse, Sir Roger."

Roger gave orders. "Bring the prisoners forward and to their knees. Sergeants Huber, bind their hands." Men-at-arms prodded the eight men and three women to line up side-by-side and kneel. Roger addressed the prisoners. "I ask that your leader identify himself." None spoke, and Roger nodded to Otto Huber. "Find him, Sergeant."

Otto grabbed a woman by the hair and yanked her to her feet. Grinning malevolently, he pulled her close. "Show him, or I'll start by cutting off your nipples." She nodded toward a man, and Reinhard yanked his head back. "This one?" The woman bobbed her head, and Otto lowered her to her knees.

Reinhard dragged the man forward to face Roger. "We've found your store of stolen goods and clothes. Where are the valuables?" The man stayed silent, and Roger hissed, "You've one more chance to answer me. Should you not, I will order our good sergeants to hang you spread-eagled and cut your belly open. We'll still find the valuables, and you'll be left alive for the wolves."

Reinhard cuffed the man. "I'd answer, were I you. Sir Roger de Lyon makes no idle promises."

"They're hidden in the ruins, Sire," the man said.

Roger looked at Jean. "Sir Loudon, take two men and accompany this prisoner and Sergeant Huber there."

The party soon returned, the men-at-arms lugging a strongbox between them. They set it on a tree stump, and Roger turned the key. He ran his hands through eight inches of gold and silver coins, jewelry, and gem-encrusted silver and gold treasures, a prince's fortune. He turned to Jean and Reinhard. "Examine the contents as witnesses."

Roger faced the prisoners. "Sufficient evidence of your crimes has been discovered and witnessed. On authority given me by Alphonse de Rives, Baron of Mirefleurs, I pronounce you guilty of robbery and murder and sentence you to death." He grabbed the man brought from the dungeon by his shirt, pushed him toward the other prisoners, and said to Reinhard, "He's of no more use. Execute him with the rest."

Otto and Reinhard drew falchions and stropped the cutting edges. A prisoner struggled to his feet and started to run, but the long-legged man-at-arms tackled him and forced him to his knees. Roger nodded to Otto and Reinhard. "Sergeants, carry out your duties. The condemned are granted three minutes for prayer." After the count had passed, men-at-arms dragged the prisoners out in pairs, and Otto and Reinhard beheaded them. Roger looked on coolly, but Jean flinched at each gristly chop.

With the executions completed, Roger ordered Reinhard Huber to take the lead, put the robbers' clothes and belongings of no value into the cave and burn it out, and secure the stolen weapons, clothes, and valuables for transport. "I'll send wagons back from the fortress." He looked at the bodies. "Leave them for the wolves. Plant stakes in the ground before the cave and impale the heads thereon."

Roger bade men-at-arms fashion a stretcher and carry the injured armsman Beuvé. Early daylight broke through the leafless trees as Roger and Jean led the stretcher bearers over the forest trail to Lienart. At Roger's inquiry about the bow-shot man, Lienart said, "He's alive, but will die if not brought soon to the fortress."

Roger nodded toward Beuvé. "Look to his knee, also. We're returning now and will send a wagon for them, right away."

The knights walked to their horses. Roger brought out his wine flask, took a short drink, and handed it to Jean. Jean took a long swallow, and they set off at a fast trot. After half a mile, Roger looked at Jean. "You're looking downcast, Sir Jean."

"Those robbers were only poor and desperate people, and we butchered them like animals. I saw none of the justice you spoke of yesterday."

"Jean, when you took your oath, you swore to protect the poor, weak, and defenseless, did you not?"

"I did."

"Think on this. Those men and women chose the greatest share of their victims from the very people you swore to protect. They surely came from the ranks of the poor and defenseless, but they were also robbers and murderers. In doing what we did, you fulfilled your oath and helped ensure that all honest folk, poor and rich, can travel the roads of our barony without fear."

"You speak with certain reason, Roger, but after this, I fear I'm not fit to be a knight. A knight need be hardened to such things, and I can't even bring myself to think of the death that awaits those in the dungeon."

"Jean, rest assured. On my word, you're an exceptional young knight. You only need realize where true justice lies, and accept your part in it."

"Spoken by you, that's indeed encouraging."

Roger nodded. "For those still in the dungeon, Alphonse at first favored the wheel, but Walter, Henri, and I convinced him to take the wiser course of mercy. A swift death by hanging will satisfy the common people and not rouse the sympathy that brutal means well might."

Chapter 18

29 November 1092, Fortress Mirefleurs

A bitter wind gusted on the road before the fortress. The five robbers swayed and twisted beneath the scaffold as the crowd hurried for the shelter of their homes. Roger left the hangmen to their duties and joined Thierré on the path to the fortress gate. He pulled his cloak close. "I'm glad that dirty bit of business is done."

"You can cheer up, Roger. The robbers are gone, the people are happy, and you're about to spend your first Christmas at Fortress Mirefleurs."

"I spent Christmas week last year taking a bridge from a hard-set company of crossbowmen. My men and I were pinned down by ice storms, and it was as cold as Hell must be."

"This year, you'll be more than warm. On the feast day of Saint Stephen, Alphonse holds a reception for the barony's noble families and wealthy commoners, and like friends from neighboring demesnes. The next day, he opens the fortress to everyone, with plenty of food and drink and entertainment. In the evening, Alphonse gives every barony family a big basket of food and wine and a bit of coin, and all of the staff at arms gets an extra reward. A certain knight who's done outstanding service might find Roman gold coins in his gift bag."

"That bests last year."

"I'd say it does. The reception is not to be missed, Roger. The table rivals the king's, and you'll never see so many fetching women in one place."

"I'm interested in but one beautiful woman."

Thierré punched his friend's arm. "The old warhorse is ready to charge, but my sister has grown as cold as his last Christmas."

Roger chuckled. "This old warhorse has never run from a fight."

"You're fighting the shadow of Baldwin de Betancourt now, and he's doing more harm as a cripple than he ever did as a knight."

+ + +

Three young peasant men stood by the road, passing a flask of wine as the hangmen lowered the bodies of the robbers to the ground. When all had been laid in a row, they crossed the road. One stopped at the corpse of a middle-aged man. Otto Huber walked over to him. "Have you one to claim, armsman Jules?"

"No, Sergeant. We're only curious."

"None here worth claiming anyway. We'll leave them out till nightfall, and bury them in the paupers' graveyard at daybreak."

Otto turned back to the scaffold and Jules swore under his breath. "God-cursed bloody hangman. He's bound to rot in Hell."

Jules, Clovis, and Turpén pulled their cloaks close and walked south on Route de Voleurs. Turpén said, "Wasn't that man your uncle, Jules?"

"He was. Henri de Coudre ran him off his plot six years ago, and he had nowhere to go."

"You can't blame Henri de Coudre for everything," Turpén said. "Your uncle was a mean drunkard and nearly beat his wife to death."

"And you're a damned liar. He had one of the best plots on the estate, and old Henri wanted it to farm with his own day men."

"With good enough reason. Your uncle let it lie fallow while he was passed out during the day and out robbing and whoring at night."

Jules grabbed Turpén by the collar and shoved him off the road. "Whose side are you on, dolt? You're starting to talk like a pig-assed nobleman."

"No, I'm only telling what I saw when we were boys. You're a nasty drunk like the rest of your family, and wouldn't know truth if God came down and showed it to you."

20 December 1092, the Abbé de Saint-Amand

Galien hurried across the snow-covered paving to the Saint-Amand church building, and set his portfolio and wooden templates down at the doors. The monastery spirits wagon rolled into the court, Anseau pulled at the reins, and the two big work horses halted.

"Anseau, where are you going? All of the roads are covered in snow and ice."

"A rider came from Fortress Mirefleurs before sundown yesterday. He paid extra coin aplenty to have this load delivered before Christmas. I get to deliver it, but don't get any of the coin."

"My brother can drink half a wagonload by himself. I'm not surprised."

"Sir Thierré de Coudre? I met him there two weeks ago, with the last load. He's a right good fellow, got me a nobleman's supper and took his with me. He wanted to know all I could tell him of you and your work with Brother Joseph."

"You could have let me know sooner."

"You spend all of your time holed up in that nice warm studio, and I've been on the road, nursing my frozen balls. I should have learned letters like you and Charles did."

"It's not too late."

"Galien, I grew up keeping horses and driving wagons on Falcard's estate, and I'll be doing it here till the day I die. Anything you want me to take or tell your brother?"

"Yes, and I have some things to give you for the ride. Let's go up to the studio and get them."

Galien closed the studio door behind them and handed Anseau two sealed pitchers of wine, a halfscore silver deniers, and a small sealed parchment letter. "The wine's from Joseph's stock. With the coin, get yourself and Falcard's men-at-arms a room and supper at a good inn."

"I'm grateful, Galien. I take little wine, but the men will welcome it. To whom shall I give the letter?"

"To Thierré only. It's for a lady."

"Your same lady at home, Galien?"

"It's a hard story for me now, Anseau. I'll tell you one day, when I'm suitably drunk."

They walked out into the cold wind. Anseau climbed onto the wagon and took the reins. "I hope I can make it back by Christmas."

"Don't hurry. The celebrations at the fortress are magnificent, and Thierré will see that you and the men have the best food and quarters. God be with you, my friend."

"And with you, Galien." Anseau flicked the reins, and the wagon creaked toward the gates.

Galien watched Anseau guide the spirits wagon through the gate, and then carried his parcels into the warm church. Glaziers worked at nearby tables, cutting pieces of colored glass to fit into lead frameworks within the new pointed stone windows. Galien and Joseph had finished the final glazing drawings and templates an hour earlier, after a sleepless night of work. Only the completion of the window glazing and a final cleanup of the church interior and grounds remained to ready the building for the Christmas services.

Galien gave the glaziers the templates and drawings, and then appraised the church interior. Joseph's daring design and structural changes had created a spectacular effect. Outdoor light flooded through the multicolored panes into the previously dark nave, and cast shimmering colored patterns onto the new light stone floor flagging.

The new windows drew his eye up thirty feet to tapering points. At first glance, the expanses of glass gave the impression that the side walls floated without support. On second look, daringly slender pilasters bore a groin-vaulted ceiling that reached its peak seventy feet above the church floor. He pulled his cloak close and left the church, pausing at the south side wall. At twenty feet out from each pilaster location, a massive sloped pylon stood forty feet high; from each, a slender stone buttress arced up to join the wall at fifty feet. In that instant, he recognized Joseph's genius. The affable architect-monk had overcome structural problems millennia old in a truly elegant manner, and was now leading the way in new and profound architectural advances.

Galien returned to the studio and noisy snores from Joseph' room, making no attempt to straighten the mess left over from their work. He added logs to the fire and stoked it to a blaze, cut a big piece of Joseph's fresh fig cake, and poured a generous measure of wine. He flopped into a fireside chair and was soon snoring as loudly as Joseph, cake and wine unfinished.

The early afternoon sun woke him to find Joseph in a jolly mood, bustling about the studio. Galien roused himself and together, they put away the books, drawing and modeling supplies, and material samples.

As they brought order to the studio, Galien thought on his time in Joseph's service. He had quickly picked up the skills needed of a capable architect's assistant. On Joseph's return from the church-building presentation in Bourges, he had put Galien to work making tracings: first securing a finished drawing to his table, then placing a thin, translucent sheet of parchment over it, and tracing the drawing with a stylus of hard lead. The light-lined duplicate drawing could then be directly inked, or further revised with the stylus.

The stylus work proved easy, as the lines could be dusted off with a cloth. Inking demanded utmost care in use of the drawing tools: wooden straightedge, triangles, and curves, a steel compass and dividers, and a ruling pen. Inking mistakes could be corrected by carefully scraping the ink away or with paint Joseph had concocted to match the creamy color of the parchment, but parchment cost five times its weight in silver coin, and Joseph's standards were not forgiving.

Joseph's character yet baffled Galien. Though the failure of his marriage would have had little effect on a career of grand commissions from wealthy patrons and the Church, the architect had chosen to retreat into monastic life. As a person of faith and good cheer, he fit well into the life of Saint-Amand, but he also remained a man apart, a privileged recluse completely given to his work. On becoming a full brother, he had taken a vow of poverty and received only an allowance for his professional expenses from the monastery treasury, but he seemed to always have plenty of coin.

In turn, the reputation of the Abbé de Saint-Amand and the monastery treasury benefited from Joseph's presence. To retain his services for a private project such as a new house, a patron made a donation to the monastery. Substantial donations made for Joseph's services, on large projects for the Church and wealthy men, had certainly soothed guilty consciences and purchased remission of sin for avaricious bishops, warmongering barons, and usurious men of commerce.

Their work finished, Joseph poured wine and cut fresh pieces from the cake. Galien added a large log to the fire and pumped the hand-bellows to again bring it to a roar. They sat in the tapestried chairs, eating and drinking in companionable silence.

Emboldened by the wine and friendly mood, Galien broached a question. "Joseph, what happened between you and your wife, for your marriage to end so quickly?"

Joseph downed his wine and cleared his throat. "I've come to trust you in good friendship, and think we can discuss difficult matters. I'm going to tell you something known only to Abbot Leo and myself, and expect you will keep it in confidence."

"You have my word."

"In regard to my wife, I could not adequately fulfill the husbandly duties required to satisfy her physical desires and father the children she wanted above all things." He blushed and looked at his feet. "I have never had a man's usual feelings for women. The physical feelings I have are for men."

Galien, well aware from his years spent in soldiers' barracks that such affairs went on between men, wasn't surprised at Joseph's disclosure. He recalled occasions on which Joseph had asked him to take templates and sketches to artisans at the church building. For these trips into the stone-dust-clouded churchyard, Galien wore outdoor work clothes: tight-fitting braies, a rough linen shirt, and a leather apron. He'd felt Joseph looking at him as he gathered the materials from the studio, but at those times, assumed the architect was studying his physique with a dispassionate artist's eye for a future stone carving, and had given it no further thought.

"Thank you for trusting me, Joseph."

"You needn't worry about me, Galien. I've no intent to turn my affections toward you."

"I wouldn't expect that. I'm only sorry you had to endure an ill-advised marriage."

Joseph smiled, breaking the serious mood. "Dear Clarisse. She's a wonderful woman and bears me no ill will, nor I her. Her father got the worst of it. That fat, greedy Bishop of Reims demanded ten livres of him to annul the marriage without an inquiry, and he paid it. The poor man suffered terribly over his silver, but after all, he, Master Guilliame, and my own father rushed us into marrying."

"And Clarisse?"

"She soon found a suitable husband, the son of a wealthy importer of goods from Constantinople and beyond. They now have two fine children."

"Then your marriage didn't end too badly, except for Clarisse's father." Galien thought with amusement of the coin-grubbing bishop and the drink and mistresses surely bought with the silver.

"I know, but I still feel as though I'm running from ghosts unknown."

"You need to be less serious and not bury yourself so deeply in work."

"Yes, it's Christmas time. For a few days, at least, I'll have no work to do."

JOSEPH SCOTT AMIS

Chapter 19

23 December 1092, the Abbé de Saint-Amand

Galien looked forward to his second Christmas at Saint-Amand. A time of both solemn observance and merry celebration would begin on December 25, and end on the last day of the Feast of Epiphany. At twenty miles from Mont-Brison, the closest large town, the monastery served as the spiritual center for the surrounding countryside, and Christmas of 1092 promised to be a special one. Ranking Church dignitaries, the Duke of Aquitaine, and many other high noblemen had accepted invitations to attend the reconsecration of the church building, and all at Saint-Amand were busy with preparations for the many visitors to come.

Joseph's stunning transformation of the ordinary old church would be at the center of the attention. Abbot Leo wanted to hold the Christmas services in the full light of the new windows, and in a break with the long tradition of late evening, he had rescheduled them for early afternoon on December 25.

Abbot Leo had given the visiting nobles and churchmen priority for indoor quarters. The monks gave up their cells and dormitories and made beds on the floor of the church, and Galien gave up his room in the guest quarters.

Monks set up elegant beds and furniture, laid rugs, and hung tapestries for the duke and his family in Joseph's studio, and Joseph made up a bedroll. He and Galien rolled a velvet cover over the books, materials, and drawings, and with pitchers of wine in hand, set off to join those sleeping on the church floor.

The guests began to arrive on December 24 and streamed in throughout the day. By sundown, more than five hundred visitors were crowded within the walls of the monastery. Men-at-arms wandered among the throngs of peasants, many of whom would drink late into the night. The weather turned colder, with snowfall beginning, and the people camped outdoors built fires in the courtyards. A brother walked among them, inviting the women and children to stay in the church. By late evening, the grand building had grown crowded and noisy; the air pungent with smells of unwashed bodies and pitch-soaked torches burning in brackets set high above the floor. Cold gusts of wind and flurries of snow blew through the doorway as people came and went without ceasing.

Galien and Joseph put down their blankets in a corner of the transept, among the monks and away from the screaming, unruly children. Joseph opened a pitcher, took a drink, and passed it to Galien. Benedict spotted Galien and bedded down beside them. They wrapped up in their blankets and leaned against the cold stone, passing the pitcher. Of custom, Benedict drank little, but on this night he didn't refuse the warming wine. Midnight found the three men soundly asleep, snoring, and oblivious to the commotion that lasted through the night.

Early on Christmas morning, the brothers served breakfast. The crowd of peasants took cheese and loaves of bread from baskets, and lined up for warm ale drawn from casks set up in the courtyards. The churchmen, nobles, and wealthy commoners took seats in the refectory and dined on finer fare.

The Christmas Mass began at an hour past noon. Clouds of fragrant smoke from censers had cleared the air of the previous night's odors. Scores of candles in the chandeliers over the nave brought the soaring new ceiling structure out of darkness; bright daylight filtering through the clear and colored leaded panes in the huge new windows lent an atmosphere of transcendence.

Joseph and Benedict sat among the twoscore brothers on the tall, carved benches in the choir, singing Latin hymns a capella as the duke, his retinue, and noble families filed in and took benches at the front of the nave. Galien took a seat with the younger nobles, and the crowd of common people stood in rows behind their betters.

The hymns increased in pitch and tempo. Two novices swinging billowing censers walked ahead of the procession of Church dignitaries, and two priests walked behind, sprinkling holy water on the people at both sides of the nave.

The singing from the choir faded to silence as the churchmen took high-backed benches flanking the altar. Abbot Leo began to recite the Latin Mass. As his finely honed oratory echoed through the church, Galien glanced toward the front benches and caught his breath. The Count and Countess of Saint-Lille sat but five yards away, among the high nobles.

At the conclusion of the Mass, Abbot Leo announced Bishop Ulrich of Troyes. The bishop praised the redesigned church as a fine and worthy offering to God and recited the Latin liturgy of reconsecration. He blessed all present and thanked Abbot Leo and the brothers for their hospitality. Afterward, the congregants filed out and hurried through the cold wind toward the refectory and the waiting Christmas feast.

The best seats in the refectory, at tables near the fire, were reserved for the nobles and churchmen; the crowds of peasants were admitted in groups and given a half-hour measure to take their meal, collect food remnants, and fill their containers with wine. The monks on serving duty ran frenzied from table to table, but Joseph, seated at the table with Abbot Leo, the Duke and Duchess of Aquitaine, the Bishop of Troyes, and the Count and Countess of Saint-Lille, made for a notable exception. Galien found a seat at a nobles' table a wary distance from Count Bayard, and chatted with the young men and women.

The room emptied as guests departed for their homes well before sundown. The brothers could now take their meal, and Benedict came over to join Galien. A monk brought them wine and a wooden platter of choice leftovers.

"Galien, I'm just beginning to feel better," Benedict said. "I rarely take more than an ounce of wine, and we finished a whole pitcher last night."

"You should leave off some of those prayers and come more often to Joseph's studio. In no time, you'd get used to drinking plenty."

Benedict smiled, shook his head, and took a sip of watered wine. A lively conversation at the nobles' table nearest the fire caught their attention. Of the threescore high nobles and churchmen there earlier, only Joseph, the Count and Countess of Saint-Lille, and the Bishop of Troyes remained with Abbot Leo. Bayard and the bishop watched in rapt fascination as Joseph spoke and gestured intricately, as if he were drawing in the air.

"No doubt Master Joseph is discussing a large new project with the bishop, who wants it, and Count Bayard, who will donate a large sum to finance it," Benedict said.

"Joseph already has a big Church project in Bourges. I fear he'll die from overwork if he takes on another."

"Perhaps so, but Joseph does his work in service to God, with no expectation of reward beyond seeing his creations completed. Die he young or old, God will receive him."

"Don't talk in such a way, Benedict. Joseph is a good friend. I worry about him."

"I know he's your friend, who has been good to you. Be happy he is a man of sincere heart and soul, should God take him from us before what we see as his proper time."

"Benedict, in matters of the spirit, no one gives wiser counsel than you."

"I can only give what I gain from study of scripture and from God through my prayers. None comes by way of my own self only."

Galien looked at the group by the fire. "Count Bayard seems elated at what Joseph is describing. Perhaps he's not so terrible a man."

"Bayard has already sold his soul to the Devil. He believes he can continue in his life of greed and needless warfare and buy his way into Heaven. The Bishop of Troyes is a godly man, but has become infected with the desire to increase his own prestige and power, and encourages Bayard in his delusions. Our good Father Abbot does not speak out in truth, as his position at times forces him to deal with dishonorable men and engage in false diplomacy."

"Benedict, cannot a man like Bayard gain favor with God through donation to works that glorify Him?"

"Never, even if he lives a thousand more lives."

"A thousand lives? Scripture says we live but once."

"Yes, such is said in scripture. Also in scripture, our Lord Jesus Christ states that at the Last Judgment, He will tell many like Bayard that He never knew them, though they did wondrous works in His name."

"Is Joseph not complicit in evil if he builds what Bayard is wishing?"

"Joseph is following his God-appointed path in faith and pure intent, and what he builds will endure to serve God's purpose. Your father followed his path as a knight in the same good faith. Though he killed many men, he did his duty in just service to an honorable lord."

"My father loved his knight's calling, but I've never heard him idly boast of the lives he took. Now, he's an old man who regrets taking young fathers from their wives and children, and can only pray God grants him forgiveness."

"None of us leads the best of lives, Galien, and if your father does rightful penance, God will grant this to him. But some, the powerful oppressors of their fellow men, lead the worst of lives, secure in the false belief that they do God's work, while in truth they dig closer to Hell with each passing day. Such are the likes of Count Bayard. I fear that Bishop Ulrich of Troyes desires a monument as his own legacy and will put his soul in danger, should he ally with so corrupt a man to see it constructed."

Galien turned to his food. In a few short minutes, this extraordinary brother had answered existential questions that intrigued and troubled him, but the monk remained an enigma. A man apart, he followed the rule of Saint Benedict to the minute and continually fingered his prayer beads while near-inaudibly repeating a short prayer to Jesus Christ. On rare occasions, while praying thus, he would drift off, hardly breathing, his eyes closed, a visible effulgence on his face and about his head. Most witnessed this in silent bafflement. Only a few of the brothers at Saint-Amand recognized his immersion in deepest contemplation.

Galien and Benedict finished their meal and walked through the cold late-evening darkness to spend another night on the church floor. Charles put his bedding down next to theirs, and Galien dug a skin of wine from his blankets. Benedict took two sips, fell asleep where he sat, and Galien and Charles covered him up. As they talked and passed the skin, Charles mentioned that Joseph looked unwell as he left the refectory. Galien resolved to look in on him at daybreak, and he and Charles covered up and settled down to sleep.

+ + +

Count Bayard and Countess Rosemonde rested at ease in their room in the monastery guest quarters. Bayard patted his bulging stomach.

"Dearest, I'm afraid I ate and drank too much," he said.

"I knew you'd have a stomachache, but you never listen to me."

"I'll make it up to you. Shall we walk the cloister and talk?"

"I'd love to. It's cold outside, but we're both still dressed. I need only my cloak."

Bayard got up. "Get your cloak, and I'll summon Raymond."

The bodyguard met them outside. Rosemonde took Bayard's arm, drawing him close. They walked in the shelter of the loggia surrounding the cloister, Raymond a discreet distance behind them. The Christmas feast and talk of the new cathedral had put both count and countess in a fine mood.

At a shadowed inside corner, a dark figure slunk from behind a stone column and stood at a wary distance. "A humble servant of God begs a word in confidence with you, mon seigneur."

An intriguing promise of information lurked in the oily, conspiratorial voice. Bayard stopped. "Come forward, where I can see you, and speak."

A hunched man in a brother's habit advanced three paces, into the light of a wall torch. He leered at the elegant countess with an expression both absurdly comical and disturbingly vicious. She wrinkled her aristocrat's nose, threw a frowning glance at Raymond, and stepped well away. Sylvestrus held out his right hand to Bayard, rubbing fingers and thumb together.

Bayard looked down his nose. "Not so fast. What can you tell me?"

"A man you want badly lives at this monastery."

Bayard caught Raymond's eye and jerked his head toward Sylvestrus. The bodyguard pulled a denier from a fat belt purse and tossed it to him. Sylvestrus studied the coin for a moment in the torchlight and looked back at Bayard.

"Mon seigneur, the third son of Henri de Coudre lives within these walls."

"Even God can't help you if you are lying to me. His name and his station here?"

"One question at a time, if it please mon seigneur. I'm old, and my memory is not so good," Sylvestrus cackled, again rubbing his thumb and fingers together.

Bayard looked at Raymond. He tossed Sylvestrus another denier.

Sylvestrus exhaled a steaming cloud of foul breath. "His name is Galien de Coudre, mon seigneur."

"Hmm... that is correct. His station also... out with it!"

Sylvestrus held out his hands, palms up, and looked at him. "Mon seigneur, I am but a poor monk."

Bayard signaled Raymond to give him another coin. He growled at Sylvestrus, "You tell me all, or my man will cut out your tongue."

"Don't do so yet, mon seigneur, before I've told you what you truly want to know."

"Continue."

"He's been here since autumn of 1091, and is assistant to the architect Joseph of Reims."

"Now we're getting somewhere."

"Coudre is no longer a postulant, and now lives in the guest quarters at Joseph's favor. They're sodomites, Sire, and carry on their unholy friendship under the nose of the Abbot."

Bayard raised his chin and smiled. "Ahh. You share priceless knowledge, good brother. What is your name, and where might you be found?"

"Sylvestrus, mon seigneur. Ask for Brother Ernoul at the vineyard office, and no one else, and he'll summon me. But have no doubt that I'll already know you're here."

Bayard stepped back a pace and spoke to Raymond. "Add twoscore deniers to what we have given this good soul."

Sylvestrus fondled the heavy bag of coins. "Mon seigneur, I am at your service forever."

"You'll have much greater rewards later, but that ought to keep you in wine until I need you again. Only be certain to keep your eye on Galien de Coudre, and make sure you're here when I come looking."

Bayard joined his wife. They waited as Raymond glared at Sylvestrus until he slipped away into darkness. As they continued their walk, Rosemonde said, "I can't believe what that horrible man said about Master Joseph. Surely you don't trust him?"

"No more than I would any cutthroat. But he speaks the truth about Joseph, and Galien de Coudre's position strongly implies the same about him. Such friendships in monasteries certainly aren't unheard of."

Rosemonde blushed, hand to her mouth. "Joseph is a sodomite, in truth?"

"My dear, you know I don't undertake matters of consequence with any man before I learn his life story. I made no exception for Joseph, and enough silver reveals the most guarded of secrets."

"But sodomy is a grievous sin. How could you allow a man of that disposition to be associated with the greatest of works for God?"

Bayard stroked his chin, smiling at her. "I pondered that question with much prayer, and God led me to understand that He endows flawed men with wondrous abilities and the opportunities to use them for His own glory. Such ways are of His divine nature and beyond our privilege to question or doubt."

Chapter 20

26 December 1092, the Abbe de Saint-Amand

The next morning, Galien found Joseph ill with a high fever, chills, and chest congestion. Monks came to move out the furnishings set up for the nobles, and Galien bade them leave one bed. Galien slept there and watched after Joseph through the days and nights, feeding him what he could take and giving him sips of warm mulled wine. If the cold turned to hard congestion of the lungs, the only treatments to be had were bleeding, herbed drinks, and hot mustard plasters. Galien thought back to his conversation with Benedict. This illness might well kill Joseph long before overwork could.

26 December 1092, Fortress Mirefleurs

Alisende and Lisette napped and rose at twilight, to ready for the grand reception held by Baron Alphonse on the feast day of St. Stephen. Both washed their faces in the table basin and cleaned their teeth with stiff boar-bristle brushes and soda. Alisende sat before a polished-silver mirror as Lisette braided her long blond hair and arranged it. Hair finished, Lisette helped Alisende with her rich new deep-red evening gown. Alisende selected jewelry from her ivory case and stepped into her shoes. She looked into the silver mirror, touched her bustline, and sighed. "It's sufficient to meet the call of fashion, but I still think it immodest."

"Lady, it's modest for such an occasion, but men would still approach you if it was laced up to your chin."

"I know."

"Will you please be gracious with Sir Roger? He's done a great service for the barony, and to judge from my own words with him, he's truly an honorable knight."

Alisende sighed. "I suppose I will, but he'll only have eyes for my breasts."

Lisette raised an eyebrow, smiling slyly. "The old stallion's blood might get to boiling again."

"I certainly don't want to be the cause for that."

"I think you do, trust me."

Alisende sat on the edge of her bed. "Who's to know? After Baldwin, I don't trust my instincts for men anymore." She picked up a parcel from the bed and handed it to Lisette.

Shortly, Lisette took her turn at the mirror. She clasped her hands, enraptured. "Such a beautiful dress and cap you had made for me!"

Alisende hugged her. "Nothing's too good for either of us."

Lisette wiped a tear from her face, and Alisende smiled. "Don't feel you must hang at my elbow every moment."

"I'd best not sneak any wine, lest I lose sight of some fine nobleman's true intentions."

"I trust you'll manage them."

Lisette followed Alisende down the stair to the great hall, and went to stand with the other ladies' servants-in-waiting. All eyes turned to Alisende, and two young noblemen approached her. She took a goblet from a servant's tray and braved the men's advance. After a few minutes of idle chatter, Alisende excused herself.

She didn't see Jean, Roger, or her brothers, and guessed they were in the armory, sampling some ghastly brew concocted by a foot soldier. She couldn't go to look for them, because the armory was strictly off limits to women, even well-regarded sisters of knights.

Alisende joined a group of wives and daughters of local noblemen, listened to their small talk, and after half an hour of boredom, bade them good evening. At the baron's table before the fireplace, she took a seat and had a serving man fill a platter. She ate in absent minded silence, brushed off young men's attempts at conversation, and talked politely with nobles of her father's age.

She had guessed right at the whereabouts of her men. Martin, Roger, and Jean walked unsteadily into the room, headed toward the food and drink. Behind them, Thierré alone looked sober, and Roger glanced from side to side, as if embarrassed. Alisende waved, and they came to take seats around her.

She looked at them, stifling a laugh with a hand. "What did you find in the armory? Did Otto Mace-man conjure up the Devil's drink and sneak in girls?"

Thierré grinned. "Otto brewed a wicked cauldron of acorn wine, but brought no loose women." The four men gobbled their food.

Pierre Bouchard, an elderly, wealthy grain-merchant, hobbled to the table and leaned on a carved oak walking stick crowned with a wrought-bronze boar-head handle. His long, silver hair flowed over the shoulders of his gold-trimmed, brown velvet gambeson. He flashed a toothless grin.

"Sir Martin, would you join me for a goblet of wine by the fire? We need to talk more of the lands you want to skin me for." Martin greeted him and rose. With "Good Sirs and Lady," Pierre gallantly bowed his head.

A group of nobles from a neighbor demesne entered the hall in a blast of cold air. Thierré glanced at the young women among them, then at Jean, and the two left without a word. Alisende and Roger looked at each other and laughed.

"They have more important things to do than talk to us," Roger said.

"It seems they have."

"Will you accompany me outside? I'd like to walk off some of this food and wine."

Alisende hesitated. "I don't know... I suppose it would be all right."

Roger smiled as he held out a hand to her and they walked to the staircase. In her room, Alisende pulled on a heavy wool overcloak lined with fur and exchanged her evening shoes for a stouter pair. Roger, dressed for the cold, met her at the foot of the stairs and offered her his right arm.

A guard opened a carved entry door, and they stepped out into the still, cold night. Their shoes crunched on the snow-covered paving as they walked toward a fire in the armory yard. A group of men-at-arms sat around the open blaze, drinking, laughing, and telling bawdy stories. At Roger's approach, they quieted and rose to stand respectfully.

The nearest man bowed his head. "Sir Roger."

"I take none of you men are on duty?"

"We are not, Sir."

"Very good. Enjoy your wine, but don't drink too much and feel like Hell at the celebration on the morrow."

"We wouldn't miss it for anything, Sir."

The men went back to their drinking and storytelling. Roger and Alisende stepped away a few paces, into the shadow of a large wagon. Out of sight of the soldiers, they could yet feel the warmth of the fire.

Roger gently took her hands in his. "Alisende, tell me the truth. Is my interest in you misplaced?"

"I… I can't tell you yet, Roger. After the events of last year, I've only wanted to keep to myself."

"With the best of reasons. Had I been here, I would have challenged Baldwin de Betancourt and split his head open."

Alisende smiled at him, touched by his noble words, yet still filled with doubt. "Truly? Baldwin was a formidable opponent. If he nearly killed Thierré, what of you?"

"I've killed five knights in single combat of honor. Any one of them could have taken Baldwin with one hand tied."

Feigning fright, she touched her lips, wide-eyed. "So you're even more fearsome a man than I guessed!"

"To boast of prowess at arms was not my intention. I only want you to understand that my thoughts toward you are of an honorable nature." He reached up, touching her cheek. "You can trust me, Alisende."

"Roger, I've had a difficult time this past year, but I can see you're a man of honor yet in search of a home. Let us agree to friendship for the present."

Roger kissed her hand. "Lady Alisende, my full intent for this evening now stands accomplished." He offered an arm. "Shall we rejoin the company inside?" Alisende took his arm and they walked to the great hall in companionable silence.

With the evening over, Alisende and Lisette lay under thick covers in their cold room. Alisende didn't want to ask Lisette to get up and add more charcoal to the dying fire in the brazier, nor did she wish to do it herself. They talked by the light of the candle on the table between their beds.

"You looked to have become friendlier with Sir Roger this evening," Lisette said.

"You were right. He is a man of honor, but friendship is all he can expect of me."

"Don't keep him at arm's length for too long, lest he get away."

"If that comes to pass, so be it. How did you fare tonight?"

"I spent most of the time chatting with the other ladies' servants. But Lorens Saint-Georges talked to me for a while. He asked me to go riding with him when a warmer day comes along, and I told him I'd keep his invitation in mind."

"Lisette, listen to me. Lorens is a knight now, and should Alphonse give him lands, his sons and daughters would rise to the nobility. This is a man not to be taken lightly, and he's already made the first advance."

A tear ran down Lisette's cheek. "I know, and he's of gentle manner as well, but when I talk with even the most attractive of men, I see only Galien before me."

30 December 1092, the County of Saint-Lille

Count Bayard awoke to his wife's gentle voice: "Why are you so pensive?"

His reverie broken, he only grunted. "Hmm."

"You've hardly spoken since we left Saint-Amand."

Bayard smiled at Countess Rosemonde. "I've much on my mind."

"When you act like that, I feel I've offended you."

Bayard put an arm around his wife and drew her closer. "Dearest, not in thirty years have you once offended me." The barrel-roofed wagon crossed the drawbridge to Chateau Bayard and pulled to a halt in the entry court. The captain of the guard took the countess by the hand as she stepped down onto the pavestones.

She turned to her husband. "Perhaps you ought to take a ride. That seems to help your moods."

"I will. We were only on the road for two hours today, and I slept well last night." Bayard watched Rosemonde walk away with her lady's servant. He shook his head with a smile. At fifty years, with two grown sons, she looked more beautiful and elegant than on the day of their wedding.

+ + +

"Let us ride the road east, toward the Loire. It's been years since I've gone that way."

The knight riding beside Bayard nodded. "At your pleasure, Sire."

They rounded a bend and saw a village a quarter-mile ahead. Though the day was cold and windy, Bayard pulled his woolen hood back, leaving his face and head without cover.

As they rode into the village, people looked at him with surprise and shock, hastily bowing on one knee, saying, "My lord" while looking at the ground. Not one person threw a token before him, cheered his name, or waved smiling. Bayard raised his own right hand with a smile, but no one acknowledged the benevolent gesture. All he could see was fear. Past the village, he nudged his horse to a fast walk and turned to the knight. "Am I such a tyrant, that my people show only fear before me?"

"Sire, I just obey your orders." Bayard's mouth became a thin grim line. Along the road, women quickly drew their children to the side at his approach, and all bowed without looking up.

He glanced at the knight. "Enough of riding. I've affairs in need of attention."

At the chateau, Bayard withdrew into his private chamber and sat in his big chair before the fire. He rang a bell. Shortly, a servant came, bearing a tray with wine and delicacies. Bayard nodded to him and leaned back, drifting into a deep reverie.

What kind of count had he become, that his common people regarded him with only fear, and his noble knights obeyed his orders not only without fair question, but without thought? He recalled the day he'd sworn his oath, thirty-five years past. The young man who had risen with the words freshly spoken, filled with ideals of honor, fair justice, and protection of the weak and helpless, no longer existed. In his place was a spiteful and cruel old man, long given to gain of wealth and lands by any means, delighting in brutal harassment of neighbor demesnes, taking strength from enmity and fear and absolute power.

With a knight's courage, Bayard faced what he had become, and it was more fearful than any enemy he had yet fought in battle, even more so than the fire-breathing dragons of legend. And how would Christ deal with him at the Final Judgment? Bayard knew the answer. His past deeds had put him beyond God's mercy, and not even the building of a great cathedral would save him from the fires and torments of an eternity in Hell.

Chapter 21

31 December, 1092, the Abbé de Saint-Amand

Joseph awoke and sat up in bed at midmorning. His fever had broken and his chest cleared, and he took the thick vegetable stew that Galien brought him with a strong appetite.

"Galien, where have I been?"

"Here only, in your room. You've been very sick for the last five days."

"Yes, you were in my dreams, as were many others. I dreamed the most horrible things."

"You had a high fever, Joseph. It's gone now, and your bad dreams with it."

"I can't lie here any longer. We have work to do. Count Bayard and the countess have pledged five thousand livres to start the foundation work for a new city cathedral in Troyes. The bishop wants me to begin design for the foundations right away and do the drawings for their construction. Then we'll start drawings and a model of the finished building, for the purpose of raising funds."

"Forget Bayard and the bishop and their church for the next few days. Only by God's grace did your lungs not become congested. I'll bring you a lap board and parchment to sketch on, but you are staying in bed. You'll be of no use to anyone if you die now."

"No, I certainly won't be worth anything dead. I'll stay in bed for a day or two, but at least go to Ignatius and secure the services of the two calligraphers."

"What about the church building in Bourges? Do you plan to abandon it, with construction just beginning?"

"Bishop Ulrich is seeking another architect to take it over and supervise the construction. The design is finished, and a competent master can see it to completion. The Cathedral of Troyes is the commission of a lifetime, and we need begin work on it without delay."

"Joseph, sitting in front of me, I see a man who will work himself into an early grave faster than the most foolhardy young knight is killed in battle."

"For a building of such great magnitude and importance, the master architect is bound by contract to that project only. Excepting small commissions, and perhaps houses for a few of the patrons, I will be working on nothing else, possibly for the remainder of my life. The sponsorship and funding through the Church will provide for assistants as I need them."

"That's much less worrisome. At least you won't have such a burden of projects, with each patron demanding your sole attention. But Troyes is so far away."

Joseph looked directly at Galien. "I will be going there to live, in time to begin work on the foundations. The Bishop is providing a house as a studio and living quarters. I want you to come with me to Troyes and stay, until I've found other assistants."

"Joseph, last spring I told you I'd stay for two more months, and now I've stayed eight."

Joseph smiled. "Think of all the coin you've earned in those eight months. And I'll raise your pay by half if you come with me."

Galien threw up his hands. "All right, Joseph. But tell me why Count Bayard isn't seeking to build a cathedral in the County of Saint-Lille."

"The Diocese of Troyes encompasses a wealthy city of commerce and the lands surrounding it, and Countess Rosemonde is a daughter of its oldest and richest noble family. With Bayard and Rosemonde's donation added to the thousands of livres already pledged, clearing of the land and excavation work can begin right away."

"Surely Bayard could spend his silver for his own county. The town of Saint-Lille is the busiest trading port on the Loire for fifty miles each way. Why not build it there?"

"Bayard's peasants are already overtaxed, and his noblemen grumble. Bayard feels that his time is short and wants to be remembered as an important patron of the Church. He knows he might die long before a single spade of earth could be turned for a cathedral in the County of Saint-Lille."

Galien nodded. "Well, that satisfies my curiosity, but I'm still worried for you. Benedict said Bayard is attempting to buy his way into Heaven and eclipse his evil reputation on Earth by funding such an enterprise for the Church. I fear you will lose your own good faith by association with such a wicked man."

"Hold no fears for me. In the matter of the cathedral, I am called to put Bayard aside in my thoughts. I consider my efforts aligned with the will of God, and for His glory only."

"Benedict also said that Ulrich desires earthly glory and, thereby, puts his own soul in peril."

"If such be true, God will be the ultimate arbiter."

Galien sat thinking. With the coin he'd earn in Troyes, he'd have enough to buy a packhorse and trade his old, worn-out hauberk and coif for ones newly made, with enough left over for the many pieces of knight's gear he still needed. He looked at Joseph. "My father hasn't yet complained about me staying longer. He can only be happy to know I'll be able to buy another horse and equipment by myself."

"Then you'll come?"

"I'll write to my father today."

6 January 1093, the Abbé de Saint-Amand

The spirits wagon rolled through the monastery gateway, creaking to a halt. Anseau climbed down from the driver's bench, slapping his hands together in the cold. Galien waved to him from across the entry court and walked over. "We'd almost given you up to the snow and robbers."

"Beside the cold and the ice on the roads, it was a pleasant trip. Falcard's men and I spent a full week at Fortress Mirefleurs."

"I suppose Thierré didn't allow you a sober moment."

"The celebrations were magnificent and your good brother was more than hospitable." Anseau leaned close to Galien and whispered.

"He and a group of men from the armory rode back with us as far as Mont-Brison. A fine night in the fleshpots, it was."

"Anseau, what shall be done with you?"

Anseau winked. "God will light my path in all things. Ah... I've letters for you."

Galien took them, and Anseau returned to his wagon. At his table in the studio, Galien held the first folded parchment up and frowned in curiosity at the unfamiliar hand. He broke the seal and read the note. The lettering was plain and ungainly, and spots of paint indicated many mistakes corrected, but the short message was well-worded and the block-lettered signature unmistakable: THIERRÉ.

Galien read it again, and sat back, happy that Thierré had resumed practice with his sword, but stunned in a greater realization: his obstinate eldest brother was learning to read and write!

After a minute of astonished reflection, he broke the seal on the second parchment and read the letter. He chuckled. Alisende's writing, clumsy next to his own, made a positively elegant contrast to Thierré's unpracticed hand.

24 December 1092, Fortress Mirefleurs

Dearest Galien,

> *I was thrilled beyond words to receive your loving note.*
>
> *Sir Henri hasn't been upset at your staying longer with Master Joseph, but Thierré can hardly wait for you to return home and again join him as his brother-in-arms. He still regrets he mocked your interest in letters and art when you were boys, and wanted you to receive the first note written in his own hand. He labored for hours to finish his letter to satisfaction, and this of no surprise, as he has persevered admirably in his lessons with Père Barnard since last summer.*
>
> *Galien, though it is difficult, I must now reveal my own mind and feelings fully. I don't foresee your father retracting his objections to a marriage between us, and I haven't changed my own objections to marrying*

against his will. My life with your family, and as Alisende's servant and closest friend, has been a blessing without equal, but I yet hold the wish for a husband and children. I must tell you, young men of good position have approached me with honorable intent, and a fitting time has passed since Alain's death. I fully expect I will go to my grave in love with you, but I must move forward and do what is best for myself while youth remains. You must also do the same, and only one of your own station will make a proper bride. Thus situated with fitting mates, we can continue in lifelong friendship.

With Greatest Love,
Lisette

Galien sat with his head in his hands, his heart gnawing with pain, but his mind telling him Lisette had spoken with clear truth. He folded the parchment and returned to his work. After Compline, a serving man from the refectory knocked to deliver their supper plates. Joseph didn't look up from his drawing table.

Galien coughed. "Joseph?"

"Ah, Galien. You broke my concentration, but no matter. My eyes were growing tired."

"Supper's here."

"That was thoughtful of you." Joseph moved aside and held a candle over the floor plan drawing on the table. "What do think?"

"It looks big, but hard to guess how big, at such a small scale."

Joseph pointed with his dividers. "It will measure three hundred feet from the west entry to the farthest end of the choir, and one hundred fifty across the transept. The ceiling vaults will reach one hundred twenty feet at the point of intersection."

Galien folded his arms, frowning doubtfully. "Joseph, such a cathedral has never been built in France. Can it truly be done?"

"Yes. If work continues uninterrupted, it can be finished in forty years."

"Forty years! You'll only need worry about your soul."

"That is true. This one project will keep me employed for my entire life."

They sat at the big work table for their supper. Joseph poured goblets from a pitcher of wine. "What know you of the world outside, Galien?"

"I received letters from home today. My brother's health has improved. He's hoping he can again take up his knight's trade before too long."

"That's good news, indeed. Take the opportunity to go home and visit your family while I'm completing the cathedral design."

"I'm not so sure I want to go home."

"Why not? You deserve it."

"There's a lady dear to me, but I don't want to see her right away."

"A lady, eh? You've much weight on your mind, and I need a respite from this studio. What say we ride out to the Black Crow Inn? Some crisp air might revive us both."

"The air outdoors is more than crisp. It's cursed cold, and the Black Crow is an unsavory dive."

"Galien, I know the place. It's not the best, but the food and drink are excellent."

"I'll be happy to go, but I worry about you. Dress in your warmest, and don't forget your boots and dagger."

"Young man, let me be, and see to your own. I'll meet you in the stable."

Galien returned to his room, belted his sword to his waist, and pulled his heaviest cloak over his shoulders. The guards opened the front gate and Galien and Joseph rode the two miles of snow-covered road to the roadhouse. Inside, they took a high-backed bench against a wall and ordered wine, sharing the dim, grimy common room with only a few hardened drinkers.

They drank their wine and ate fresh bread, butter, and cheese, content to speak but little. Galien stretched his legs out and relaxed, and his thoughts came into focus. Any dreams of marrying Lisette against his father's will needed to be finally forsaken. He would have to remain patient until God saw right to lead him to a fitting noblewoman.

The tavern door opened to a blast of cold wind and snow. A bent, hulking figure in a dirty cloak shuffled past them, and a familiar stink lingered. A pudgy monk followed him at a few paces. Sylvestrus took a seat at a table twenty feet away, motioned Brother Ernoul to sit at another table, and began to converse with two cutthroats who had entered the tavern earlier. Galien thumbed the pommel of his sword as he and Joseph watched them. The other patrons moved to a wary distance.

A cutthroat cursed, banged the table, and got up, long dagger in hand. Sylvestrus pulled his own dagger and backed away from the table, in fighting stance. The cutthroat lunged at him with a waist-level slash. Sylvestrus jumped back nimbly and again took stance. The second cuthttroat circled, grabbed Sylvestrus' forehead with his left hand, and in an instant, thrust a slender dagger up at the juncture of head and spine. Sylvestrus crumpled without a sound, and the cutthroats threw the tavern door open and vanished into the darkness.

Ernoul started, panicked, toward the door. As he trundled by Galien and Joseph, Galien stuck a leg out and tripped him. Ernoul fell flat on his face. Galien jabbed his back with the point of his sword. "Your best crony just got himself killed, and I trust I'll find no more little drawings under my platter."

"N... no, my lord. Have mercy, my lord "

Galien stepped back and let him rise. "Best move your larded ass out in a hurry. You don't want to be here when Lord Falcard's men arrive."

Ernoul looked back at Sylvestrus' body and began to shuffle toward the door. Galien drew his sword back with both hands and swung it, slapping Ernoul hard on the buttocks with a flat side. The fat monk screeched and charged fast through the doorway, and Joseph roared out a laugh.

Chapter 22

8 January 1093, Fortress Mirefleurs

Roger de Lyon rose soon after sunrise and opened his window. A pleasant breeze and bright, early sun in a clear sky foretold a second day of warmer weather. He looked out to the countryside. The snow had melted, and the roads and fields were dry. This fine Saturday wasn't a training day, and the men-at-arms not on guard duty had a free afternoon.

He put on shoes and a robe and walked to the armory. There, he bathed, and the barber trimmed his beard and hair. He returned to his quarters, dressed in his best, and headed to the great hall and the nobles' breakfast. He felt happy. Plans made would come to pass on this day.

Breakfast passed in conversation with Alphonse and Henri, and as Roger bade them a good morning and got up to leave, Alisende and another young noblewoman stepped off the staircase. Saying, "Ladies," he bowed his head.

Alisende glanced at her companion, who nodded and replied, "Sir Roger," and started up the stair. Roger said to Alisende, "I'm looking forward to riding with you today. Jean's to accompany Lady Cecelia, and Lisette has accepted Lorens Saint-Georges' invitation."

"Cecelia and I were speaking of it at the table. She left me to begin dressing."

"Then we'll all meet in the front court at noon. It will be a grand time."

Alisende glanced away, hesitating. "I must regretfully decline, Roger."

Roger frowned, perplexed, and Alisende stared at him until he bowed his head. "As you will, Lady." He turned on his heels and left the great hall for his quarters.

In his room, Roger stripped to his drawers and stretched out on his back. He looked around absently. Though his chest ached as if he'd taken a crossbow bolt, he dozed off.

A rap sounded at the door. Roger awoke and called "Enter!"

Thierré stepped into the room. "I was hoping not to find you here."

"Here I am."

"Alisende backed out before the ride?"

"She did."

"I can't say I'm surprised, but it was still damned rude and stupid of her."

Roger sat up in bed and leaned against the stone wall. He shrugged. "Rude, assuredly. Stupid, perhaps. I'd hoped to take possession of the lands Alphonse has offered me with Alisende as my wife, and expected to win her to my side today, but it didn't come to pass."

Thierré shook his head, frowning. "And I've been hoping that you'll become my brother-in-law."

They sat downcast and silent, and then Roger said, "Are we both too downhearted for an hour of practice?"

"I've nearly forgotten I'm a knight."

"Then let's get into our gear. We need to bring your sword arm back."

+ + +

Men-at-arms stood around in the armory yard as Roger and Thierré recovered their breath and again faced off, steel practice swords and round wooden bucklers in hand. Otto Huber raised a hand, called "Begin!" and the men cheered.

Thierré charged with sword upraised and swung down, but Roger stepped nimbly aside, causing Thierré to lose his balance and stumble. Thierré sprang around quickly, but as he attacked with a low sideswing, Roger caught the wince of pain on his face. Roger deflected the blow with his buckler. Before Thierré could recover, he closed in.

With a fast, deft thrust, and a twist of his blade, he knocked the sword from his tired opponent's hand. Roger picked up Thierré's sword, handed it back, and said, "Five matches are enough for you. Let's have some wine." Thierré nodded agreement, the men clapped and cheered, and the two knights took the stairs back to Roger's room in the armory tower.

Thierré poured cups from a fresh pitcher of wine, then raised his. "Here's to the victor. This beat-up old horse is fit only for pasture."

"Otto called you as victor in one match out of five. I say that's right fair for a man who's hardly picked up a sword in the last year."

"I was all right for the first two matches, but after that, the pain in my leg got worse, and I was seeing in pairs by the time you disarmed me. At this pace, I'll be a greybeard before I'm fit to see battle again."

"Patience. If we practice together steadily, you'll be surprised."

Thierré slumped back in his chair. "I'm a man who's no good anymore, and you're one with a wound to the heart. To Hell with all of it. Let's bathe and dress and ride out to Mont-Brison."

Roger stroked his beard thoughtfully.

"Come on, Roger. Noon is yet an hour away. We'll be in no hurry riding, and we can stay overnight at the inn. The food and wine there are exceptional."

Roger grinned and drank down his cup. "Pour me another one, and I'll take you up on your plan. We both have excuses for God to forgive a Mass missed."

+ + +

Alisende stood at her window, staring out at the Armory tower, empty of mind. The door opened, and Lisette set a bundle on the table. She said, "Lady, Sir Roger and Thierré rode past on my way back from the clothes room. You might catch them if you hurry."

"By the time I can dress to ride and have my horse saddled, they'll be miles up the road. And why would I want to catch Roger? I told him I didn't want to go today, and now he rides off for the brothels with my loose dog of a brother."

"You broke your word to him. Do you expect he'll take a vow of chastity?"

"I expected him to behave as a man of honor, as my father would have."

185

Lisette shook her head slowly and said, under her breath, "You're still a naïve girl."

Alisende drew herself up. "I heard that! I'll have you know, I'm a noblewoman of highest standards. It's naïve of me to expect a common servant girl to understand."

The air hung still and stifling for long seconds. Tears ran down Lisette's face. "Will that be all for this morning, Lady?"

Alisende dropped to her knees, grasped Lisette around the waist, and clung to her. "In the name of God, what have I done? I dismissed Roger like a stableboy and now, surely, have broken the heart of my dearest friend."

Lisette stroked her hair. "You wounded me deeply, but God blesses with the grace to forgive. Come sit on the bed, and I'll get you some wine."

After a cup, Alisende's composure returned. She put her face in her hands. "Lisette, I'm so confused."

"You can no longer let the shadow of Baldwin walk beside you. Fear yet blocks your way back to right mind and happiness."

Alisende sniffled and wiped her eyes. "You speak with the wisdom you've earned. Now, dress for the ride. I'll not add to the harm I've already done and cause you to keep the handsome young Lorens waiting."

12 January 1093, the Abbé de Saint-Amand

Over the first intense weeks of design work on the cathedral, Galien found himself with little to do for Joseph. Elsewhere, the bustling atmosphere of the winery promised a welcome alternative to the oft-somber quiet of the scriptorium, and he found that facility in dire need of a temporary scribe. Over the protests of Brother Ernoul, Brother Ignatius assigned Galien to work there, alongside the jolly Charles.

Charles shook Galien's shoulder. "It's time to quit for the day. I'm hungry."

Galien looked up from his work. "I need to visit with Joseph this evening." He handed Charles a few deniers. "Get a man to make up supper and bring it to Joseph's studio, and buy yourself a pitcher of wine."

"I'll do so, Galien, and thanks. You're not telling him you're leaving, are you?"

"Wait in suspense while you drink that wine." He slapped Charles' back and set off for Joseph's studio.

Ernoul glared at him. "Coudre, you haven't finished that tally I gave you."

Galien winked at the fat monk, grinning with no small hint of malice. "Then summon your friend Sylvestrus from the dead, but I hardly think the Devil will consent."

+ + +

Joseph welcomed him. "I've drawn front and side elevations of the cathedral, and a cross-section as well. Come and look."

At sight of the drawings, Galien caught his breath. The front elevation illustrated twin bell towers, with long, tapering spires rising to a height of over two hundred feet; the side elevation featured rows of huge pointed windows, alternating with tall buttresses. The section view brought the immense scale, and Joseph's structural genius, into tangible reality. The human figures drawn at floor level seemed mere specks within the soaring height of the nave, and the slender arced stone side buttresses defied intuition. Both interior and exterior were decorated with carvings, moldings, and finials in profusion; these yet in fitting proportion to the whole.

"Joseph, if this takes but forty years to build, my amazement will kill me, then and there."

"I'm beginning to feel the same way. Have a drink with me?"

They sat in their chairs before the fireplace and sipped at wine until the refectory man knocked, with their supper. With their plates before them, Galien caught Joseph's eye. "I've made a decision."

Joseph raised an eyebrow. "Your father wants you to come home."

"No. It's fine with him if I follow you to Troyes."

Joseph's good color returned. He topped off their goblets. "Nothing has ever made me happier. What prompted you to decide?"

"Joseph, I must be forthcoming."

"Ahh. Things didn't come to pass for you and your lady."

Galien smiled. "You're keen, Joseph. They didn't, and I'll need leave her be for a time."

"Whatever your circumstances, I thank God you're coming with me."

"Don't think I've forgotten my real profession. I'll be keeping up my practice at sword and horse."

Joseph scratched his head, chuckling. "Galien, you won't need to use that sword on me, but be wary of quarrelsome artisans and masons on the cathedral grounds."

"They'll know not with whom they quarrel."

"I'll pity any man who does. He'll know not how close he comes to losing his ears. Now, is all between us agreeable?"

"Yes. Thank you for your kindness."

"Bask in my kindness while you can. I'll have the larger scale drawings of the final design done in two more weeks. I will need you back here to make tracings for Bishop Ulrich and Count Bayard, while I complete the structural geometry and foundation design. Long before you've finished with them, you'll think me crueler than any Mohametan slave driver."

Chapter 23

23 February 1093, Fortress Mirefleurs

At sundown, Roger knocked on the door to Thierré's room. Thierré opened it and eyed him head to toe. "I've never seen a finer looking nobleman."

"And you. One glance and the ladies will forget your brother's eminent guest."

Thierré laughed. "A thought to savor, but unlikely. A century will pass before our little barony once more sees a guest to equal Archbishop Guy of Vienne."

The two knights crunched across the snow-blown courts to the great hall. Inside, they joined barony nobles and leading commoners, and those of nearby demesnes, in the line to greet the archbishop. Thierré nudged Roger. "I haven't seen our unpleasant neighbors yet."

"Bayard and Gautier? I hardly think Alphonse would invite them."

"Even should he think it proper, his honor forbids. He also knows I'd cut the both of them to pieces."

Roger clapped Thierré's back. "You're not a man to let a sore leg keep him down for long."

The line moved ahead; soon they stood before the archbishop. Roger and Thierré kissed his ring and greeted Alphonse. Martin, next to the archbishop, introduced them. Guy smiled. "Ah, the champion of the field at Vézelay, and the noble knight who nearly went to meet God for his sister's honor."

Thierré looked puzzled. "You know of these things, Your Eminence?"

"Sir Thierré, we men of the Church take our own day's dose of troubles and onerous duty. As a boy, I thought to become a knight, and to talk after supper of the deeds of great men of the sword is a pastime I welcome. I must confess to prayers missed thereby."

The archbishop turned to Roger. "Sir Roger, I was grieved to hear of Lord Chartain's passing. I hope you've found a better welcome here." Roger caught a glimpse of Alisende from the corner of an eye. She was chatting, carefree, with a group of nobles. Since the day of the ride, his own words with her had been few and painfully awkward.

Guy put a hand on his arm. "I'll pray that God direct your fortune." The steward announced supper, and the men and ladies parted for Alphonse and the venerable guest.

The last course of supper over and the tables cleared, Alphonse stood and announced that the honored and reverable Guy of Burgundy, Archbishop of Vienne and son of the late Count William of Burgundy, would speak. Guy, yet a young man and of good looks and affable charm, thanked Alphonse and the elder nobles, complimented all present, and began.

"When I took my post at Vienne, not five years ago, I inherited a cathedral begun forty years past, stuck in a trying hiatus. The quarry that had furnished the stone was three years mined out, and the sole other source of sufficient quality a hundred miles distant by road and river. Only slow progress at exorbitant cost was thus possible, and I despaired to fulfill the Archbishop's task, to again bring this great work to life, with a sustainable plan to continue at a fair cost. Yet God, the Knower and Director of all things, saw fit to answer the prayers of all in our diocese and my own poor ones."

Guy paused, gesturing toward Martin with great courtesy. "One morning, mere days before Christmas past, I received a singular letter. Sir Martin de Coudre, already a knight of renowned valor, informed me of his plans to mine lands that, to his knowledge, bore deposits of great value to our efforts. I replied to him with all haste and shortly, our good architect, Master Richard of Vienne, and I took to the road. We braved two days of snow and ice to meet with Sir Martin and walk his lands. The stone there situated proved to be of highest quality, and the deposits very likely sufficient for many years and many buildings."

He paused for a sip of water and continued, "This evening, I am pleased to announce that our diocese has contracted with Sir Martin de Coudre to be the principal supplier for the stone so sorely needed for our cathedral. May God grant this bring lasting friendship and commerce between our demesnes and great prosperity to the people of the Barony of Mirefleurs."

Guy thanked Alphonse and Martin for their fine hospitality. All rose and applauded, and then began to mingle and converse. Martin joined Thierré and Roger, and needled them. "I trust you two doubters no longer think my boasts idle."

"We stand corrected and convinced, Sir Martin," Roger said.

"I'm pleased. I want to make you and Thierré an offer to invest funds at the inception."

"I think you'll succeed, but I'm guarding of my coin, brother," Thierré said.

Roger stroked his beard. "Hmm. You've my interest, but I'm a poor knight, of little coin."

Martin laughed aloud. "You're not by far a poor knight."

"Truly I'm not, and I've never shied from a risk. But I'll need time to decide what I can do."

Martin looked at Thierré. "You, brother?"

"Where Sir Roger goeth, I follow, but five livres is all I can do."

Martin beamed. "Splendid. I'm pleased to have both of you as investors. And now, if you'll excuse me, I need offer the same opportunity to family and close friends."

"Where there's a denier to be found, you'll find it, Brother," Thierré said.

Roger watched Martin walk toward Jean Loudon and his now-betrothed Lady Cecelia. Lisette and Lorens Saint-Georges stood nearby, in conversation with Alisende. Cecelia would bring a substantial dowry to her coming marriage to Jean, and Alisende could well afford to invest a hundred livres. Lisette and Lorens were of far more modest means, but should they marry, the income from an investment of even two or three livres would make life easier for the young knight and his bride. Roger sighed and took a long drink. He had lands and high position and the promise of more silver in his purse awaiting him, but he was still a man alone.

+ + +

With the evening over and the guests departed, Alisende and Lisette sat in their beds, propped up by pillows. "It was a wonderful evening, and I'm so happy you chose to invest with Martin," Alisende said.

"I need to put the coin and tools I rescued from Alain's brother to best use. Your good brother has promised to return my three livres, should his venture not succeed."

"A noble gesture, but he'll not fail. You already have a fair dowry, and I'll add ten livres more as my gift."

"Lady, you've been generous beyond thought, but I must decline to take what you offer."

"Why would you? I thought you and Lorens were to become betrothed right away."

Lisette pushed her hair back and closed her eyes. "He's asked me to marry him, but I've not yet accepted. I don't know if I will."

"You'll be a fool not to."

"I know, such an opportunity comes rarely to a peasant woman. He's a kind man in all ways, and I'd eagerly share a bed with him and bear his children."

Alisende threw up her hands, perplexed. "He's not Galien, but what other objection could you have?"

"He's not Galien, and that's sufficient."

Alisende grabbed her by the shoulders, shaking her. "Lisette, listen to me! If you truly love and want Galien, Thierré and I will both be behind you. If not, accept Lorens' proposal. You need to make your decision and be ready to stand by it."

27 February 1093, Fortress Mirefleurs

A guard stepped into the elder knights' floor in the armory tower. "You've a visitor waiting, Sir Roger."

"At nearly midnight? Hmm... tell him to come up anyway."

"It's a noble lady, my lord. She wishes to see you."

"And who is she?"

"I... I truly can't say, my lord. But for her eyes, her face is cloaked."

"What are you waiting for, fool? Fetch her wine, and you'd best make haste. I'll be dressed and down shortly."

Roger turned back to Walter and Jean, frowning. The two knights laughed. "Roger, you need to live up to your reputation, be it on or off the battlefield," Walter said.

"You last tall war story had me more than ready for a good night's sleep."

Walter raised his goblet, grinning. "Indeed. I've already sent Henri to bed, and young Jean has a busy day on the morrow. Best we turn in and leave the cat to make his rounds."

Roger hurried down flights of stone steps. On the first floor, he found his visitor, standing with her back to him. "Alisende?"

She turned around. "A good evening to you, Roger."

"What in the name of Holy God could bring you out to talk to me on a cold midnight?"

"I wanted to apologize for my rudeness to you on the day of the ride."

"I accept in all good grace, but it could have waited until the morrow. Is there something else?"

Alisende took a drink of wine and drew a deep breath. "I... I've feelings for you."

Roger half-frowned, stroking his beard. "You've managed to keep them to yourself more than well."

"I know I have, but Baldwin's shadow is now behind me. I've been busy telling Lisette what to do with her own life, and by that, I've come to realize I must again embrace what I thought Baldwin took away."

"If I'm to be included, you'd best embrace it soon."

Alisende put her hands over her face. "You must have another lady by now. Why didn't I listen to Thierré and Lisette months ago?"

"No, I haven't another lady. If your feelings for me are the same as mine for you, we can make up for the time you think lost."

She smiled at him through tears. "Truly, Roger?"

"Yes. Will you take that ride with me on the morrow? I know it's cold, but the table at the new inn in Grand-Forêt is fine, and the entertainment lively."

"That sounds wonderful!"

"Good. I'll have our horses saddled and ready, and meet you in the great hall at an hour before noon."

Alisende clasped his hands. "I'll say goodnight." She put her arms around his neck and pulled him close. When she released him from the long kiss, he bowed his head and said, "You've made your feelings more than clear, Lady."

+ + +

Alisende returned to her room off the great hall, in her elation unconscious of the bitter cold. There, Lisette greeted her with an anxious look. "How... how did it go with Roger?"

Alisende sat on her bed. "Better than I had any right to hope. I've treated the poor man so badly, and he yet loves me."

"You did the right thing, Lady, for the both of you. You'll never find a finer man than Sir Roger."

"How well I know, and how close to I came to ruining all with him. I only hope you're coming around to the best decision for yourself."

"I have, Lady. I'm going to accept Lorens' proposal. Better to marry a truly good man while I have the chance, than become a spinster hoping for Galien."

Alisende sighed. "Yes, I must finally admit my father will never relent." She brightened. "But, think. Lorens is a knight and you hold the most valuable parcel of land in Grand-Forêt. We'll no longer have to keep up all these silly pretenses of rank."

"I'm frightened of moving into a higher station. Everything will change, and nobles by birth will still look down on me."

"Nonsense, girl! Any man or woman who might dare will come to know the hard way that I'm truly Thierré de Coudre's sister."

17 March 1093, Fortress Mirefleurs

Thierré finished reading the letter aloud to Roger. "Your good friend Harald Agnarssen sounds to be a worthy man to represent your past lord at your wedding."

"Harald and I took our oaths side-by-side, and we fought the length and breadth of France together, before we signed on with Lord

Chartain. You Normans make the best of friends and the worst of enemies."

Thierré laughed. "I'm only glad I'm on your side, Roger. What will you do now?"

"First, I accept your invitation for supper at Coudre Manor, but I've much to think of before then."

"What could possibly be worrying you?"

"Alisende told me that she wants to buy Coudre Estate from you, and for me to take lordship."

"Shit, she can have it, and I'll be proud for you take over. I'd much rather have bags of silver than be a cursed farmer."

Roger nodded thoughtfully. "I'm glad you have no objections. Now, the only fight I have is within myself."

20 March 1093, the Abbé de Saint-Amand

"Galien?" Galien looked up at the voice, and saw Anseau standing in the open doorway to Joseph's studio. "Anseau! Once more, God brings you back safely. How was the journey?"

"Nothing more than the usual wine and ale delivery. I've letters for you."

Galien opened the first letter and read. He put a hand to his forehead. "The last I heard of my sister, she didn't want a man near her again, and now she's betrothed! Why didn't you tell me, Anseau?"

"I only wanted you to read of it in her own words."

"Then you're forgiven. Sir Roger de Lyon seems to have ridden in and swept her off her feet overnight. Did you meet him?"

"He's a handsome knight of wide renown, and a kind man as well, Galien. Sir Thierré introduced me to him and your sister, and I conversed long with them. Sir Roger wanted to know all I could tell him of you."

"And Lisette. Did you see her?"

"I did, but have no good news. I saw her in company of a man, a good-looking young knight."

"Yes, I know of him, and I'd best not interfere. She has her own life to lead without me."

21 March 1093, the Abbé de Saint-Amand

Galien's footsteps echoed in the empty studio as he walked through for the last time. Three weeks had passed since Joseph's departure for Troyes. Scribes and illustrators would soon move their desks and supplies in from the crowded scriptorium, and Joseph pass into monastery legend. He closed the door and walked to the front gate of Saint-Amand. Charles and Anseau stood beside two horses from the monastery stable, one with Galien's shield and helmet slung over the saddle.

Anseau embraced Galien. "God be with you, Galien. I'll pray you don't find trouble on the way."

"I'll be fine, Anseau. Thank you again for your open ear. The rich man you met in Mont-Brison paid me half in advance for the swordsman job. I have plenty of coin for the ride, and some left over for my friends." He handed Anseau a small, heavy bag.

"I'm grateful. Your coin will go to God's purposes, Galien."

"I've no doubt. The tavern keeper in Mont-Brison and his girls need give their due to Him, and Abbot Leo already took a halfscore deniers in rent for the horse."

Galien and Charles mounted and rode out the open gateway and onto the road through the vineyards. Half a mile north of Saint-Amand, they turned onto the hard-trodden main road leading northeast through Lord Falcard's estate, toward Troyes.

Charles pointed ahead. "There's Saint-Sebastien, my village." Perched on a high, wooded plateau in the road, the village looked grimly poor, yet not unpleasant. A score of plastered-wattle cottages, wooden outbuildings, and a tiny stone-and-timber church stood scattered among large old oaks that shaded them and softened the atmosphere of squalor and disrepair.

They turned their horses into the village and tied them to a small tree before a cottage. Charles took a large rucksack of food and wine, collected from the monastery kitchen, from his horse's back. He knocked at the weathered plank door. A worn-out looking young woman opened it, and a pubescent girl nursing a baby peeked out from behind her. The woman gasped, said "Mon seigneur," and curtsied to Galien. The girl scurried away and disappeared behind the ragged curtain that divided the dingy, stale-smelling single room.

Galien laughed. "I'm no one's lord, just a friend of Charles."

Charles nodded at the woman. "Roese, you needn't be afraid of Galien. I know him well from Saint-Amand."

The woman retreated into the cottage, and Galien stepped away. "Charles, best I wait outside. Falcard's men-at-arms should be here shortly."

Charles entered the cottage, and Galien sat on a bench beside the door. He drew a parchment letter from his gambeson and, once again, read the neat print.

4 March 1093, Fortress Mirefleurs

My dearest brother Galien,

Brother Anseau has given the news that you are soon to depart for Troyes. I am both happy for you and sad that you will be going so far.

My leg has healed properly, but I remain troubled by pain there. The attacks of blurred vision and dizziness brought on by the blows to my head come much less often, yet return at times most unpredictable. I fear that in heat of battle, such might occur, and I become helpless to fight.

Brother, I suspect God lent me that strength needed to restore honor to Alisende and our family, but in return for my years of prideful sin, has chosen I remain deprived of a full life. If such be His will, I can only accept that dear Baldwin de Betancourt left me not a whole knight. Letters have come to be my greatest solace, and I give thanks to God that He spurred the desire in me to learn. But, should such an adventure as you are to have come my way, I will yet take up arms and ride forth eagerly.

May God guide your every step.
Thierré

Galien smiled. The short letter was an astounding achievement for his eldest brother, a proud, virile knight who had long scorned any thought of books or scholarship. He put it away and looked to a valley beyond the village. At two hours past sunrise, he could see men and women working in the fields. A mile's distance away, the white stone of the Falcard manor house sparkled in the sunlight. Charles came out with bread and cheese, a pitcher of water, and cups.

"My father is in the fields beyond the manor and won't be back until night. Let's eat something before Falcard's men arrive."

"The woman in the cottage seemed frightened," Galien said.

"My sister saw that you're a nobleman."

"And so? She had no reason to fear me."

"Lord Falcard and his sons and nephews take their pick of the women on this estate, and you're a nobleman, like them. It shows all over you, even in plain riding clothes."

"My father never behaved in such a way with the peasant women on our lands, or let the farmers' families go hungry."

"Falcard takes the same share of our crops in good harvests and bad. He and his sons use women as they see fit and drag the young men out to fight and die in their feuds. Your father sounds to be a man of honor."

"Before my brother Martin took Count Bayard prisoner, for nobility, we were poor. Our lives and fortunes went hand in hand with the peasants on our lands. It would have been unthinkable to treat them as Falcard does his people, and I can't see my father acting differently had we been rich."

"Perhaps not, Galien, but love can be blind."

Two men-at-arms with Falcard's colors on their shields rode into the village, halting before Galien and Charles. Galien stood up, and one man dismounted. "You're the swordsman who's to ride with us?"

"I'm Galien de Coudre, and at your service, sergeant."

"Oh, pardon me, Sir. You're a knight."

Charles looked at Galien and smiled, palms up.

"I'm no knight, sergeant; only a man with a ready blade. A rich trader hired me to ride beside his daughter."

The sergeant nodded. "We'd best be going. The travel party is waiting for us at the inn, three miles east."

"My gear's in my saddlebags. I'll put it on when we get there."

Galien and Charles gripped hands and then embraced. Galien gave him a leather bag holding a score of deniers. "I'll write after I've settled in."

Galien mounted his horse and followed the sergeant onto the road. He looked forward eagerly to the new adventure, feeling but little apprehension. He was leaving home once again, this time for a far-away city. And Sylvestrus was gone, forever in Hell.

JOSEPH SCOTT AMIS

Chapter 24

22 March 1093, Coudre Manor

At two hours past noon, with midday supper over, Henri fell into a doze on the bench before the great room fire. Roger and Alisende stood beside Thierré at the window, looking at the meadow beyond the house.

"I've never seen finer lands," Roger said.

"I can't believe that you're soon to be my brother, and haven't ridden them."

"You spend most of your days and nights at the fortress. I've only been here at the house a few times."

"Then we'll get our horses saddled and take a ride, Roger," Thierré said, nudging him with a wink. "Let's get out of here before Martin can bore us with his plans."

Martin looked up from his quarry diagrams. "I heard that, brother Thierré. Roger and Alisende listen when I speak of the work upcoming, but you always slither past me."

Alisende patted Thierré's cheek. "You've silver in the quarry like the rest of us, so be a good boy and look at the plans. I'll take Roger for a ride myself."

Thierré returned a sheepish grin and said, "Alisende's right, Roger. I need to learn how Martin schemes to squander my coin."

Alisende and Roger mounted in the front court. Alisende led onto the meadow. "We'll ride to the nearest village, and then take the path that runs through the farmlands." They followed the winding trail through the thick forest beyond the meadow and into Saint-Julien. The people outside greeted Alisende with a nod and "Lady," but shied from Roger.

"Lady, your subjects respect you, but they seemed a bit timid at the sight of me."

Alisende laughed. "They suspect you're to be the next lord, and are wondering what kind of tyrant you might be."

Roger turned at a movement. Two young men, passing a pitcher back and forth, walked from behind a building corner, spotted them, and darted into a side lane, out of sight. Roger looked at Alisende.

"Jules and Clovis," she offered. "They're lazy drunkards and rant on about how they hate noblemen, but do enough odd jobs to pay their own way, and manage to show up for training days."

"I've seen them at the fortress. A slovenly pair. How did Henri deal with them?"

"They're not criminals, or rabble-rousers of any matter. My father put them in the dungeon once or twice, but never found reason to have them flogged. He usually tried his best to ignore them."

They turned their horses onto the farm path and, after half a mile, paused at a high crest. In the distance, they could see Coudre Manor. Alisende led them on a trail between the cultivated fields, to the meadow. She looked at Roger. "I've a flask of wine in my saddlebag. Care to share with me?"

"Of course."

They dismounted, and Alisende spread a cloth on the grass. They sipped at the wine and Alisende said, "You've seen the estate now. What do you think?"

"It's the finest holding in the barony."

She kissed him on the cheek. "It was given to the Coudre family as a freehold when this barony was founded, and the family still owns all of it. Speak the word, and you'll be the new lord."

"Thierré is already lord of your family's holdings, and Alphonse has offered me the best choice of his lands. I'd rather us begin on what I've earned."

"Roger, Thierré never wanted Coudre Estate. He'd much rather sell it to me. I want to raise our children on the same lands where I grew up."

"Hmm. Then Coudre Estate will remain in your family?"

"It will, Roger. I want to pass it on to Galien after our children are grown, and then we can build a house on your lands."

Roger played his last weak hand. "To take lordship of your family lands when I have my own wouldn't be honorable."

"You men are all so silly about your honor! Thierré would have lost none, had he left Alphonse to carry out Baldwin's sentence, and you and my father stand as the knights most honored in this barony. To become lord of Coudre Estate is but your fair due, and you can rent out the lands Alphonse gives you."

Roger took a sip of wine and stroked his beard. "You speak with wisdom and good sense."

"If only men could speak to each other with good sense before drawing their swords."

+ + +

Faint sounds coming from the window woke Henri from his doze. He rose, looked out to the meadow, and saw Roger and Alisende leading their horses, hand in hand, smiling and laughing as lovers. At twenty yards from the house, they paused for a long minute, kissing deeply.

"All of you, come now and look," Henri said. Martin, Thierré, and Lisette got up from the table and crowded next to him, to watch the couple break away from their kiss and walk their horses around the corner of the house.

Lisette opened the front door for them. Alisende brought Roger to stand before the family, kissed his cheek, and said, "I want to present the next lord of Coudre Estate!"

Henri rose first and embraced Roger, and after congratulations and toasts had been made, Thierré put an arm around his friend's shoulder. "Welcome back to the farmer's life, good Roger. My cozy little knight's cell at the fortress has never looked better."

23 March 1093, on the road to Troyes

By late morning, Galien was riding easily beside his employer's daughter; at sixteen years, a lovely, self-assured noblewoman. They'd met at the inn the day before, and since, she'd told him of the sights and towns along the unfamiliar road. At a pause, Galien said, "Pernelle, I'd like to hear more of Troyes."

"It's a fine and busy city. Noblemen who've taken to commerce have homes there. I think you'll find it a place to your own purposes and much to your liking."

Galien chuckled. "That's encouraging for this loose-footed nobleman."

"My father is also of independent mind. After he took his oath, he followed the knight's profession for two or three years, and then forsook it to take up another."

"Might I ask how came your father to leave the knight's life for commerce?"

"He saw early that opportunity was to be had beyond bloody feuds over lands and a few livres. At my birth sixteen years ago, he was scarcely past thirty years and already among the wealthiest men in Troyes."

"My brother left the knight's life at twenty-one years, but his riches came with one sword stroke."

"Martin de Coudre's valor and the wealth he gained are legend, and my father says he's soon to be much richer. Surely, he offered you an investment in his quarry?"

"He did, and I asked my father to invest three livres of my saved coin at home."

"You were wise to do so, Galien." Pernelle glanced at the sky. "The sun is high, and a good inn only a mile ahead." With a fetching smile, she put a hand on his. "My father and I will be honored to have you join us at the table."

26 March 1093, Troyes

As the sun moved low, the travel party rode through the wide city gateway. Galien sat in his saddle, amazed at the throngs of people of all descriptions, streets and buildings like he'd never seen before. Pernelle threw up her arms. "Home, at long last!" She turned to Galien. "But I'd almost rather continue our ride."

"As would I, Lady, but Master Joseph has first claim."

"My family and home and table have the same on me. And after those, my own sweet bed." Pernelle pointed to a street lined with large, impressive town houses, faced with costly materials: cut stone with carven embellishments, or carefully crafted timber and plaster. "The house the diocese provides for Master Joseph is just ahead, and my father's is but a short walk distant. You can both expect a supper invitation within a week's time. There, you'll meet the leading men of our city, and I'll get to see you again."

The party stopped before a town house with a dressed stone façade. Pernelle said, "You're home, Galien."

Galien bowed his head. "Lady Pernelle, I accept your invitation with honor, and do so on behalf of Master Joseph. Please excuse me now, that I might say goodbye to your good father and our other companions."

Pernelle glanced toward her father, ahead of them, talking to others in the party. She leaned over and kissed Galien on the cheek. "I'm so happy that you're here, dear Galien."

Galien sat on his horse, watching the party ride away. He'd not expected such a welcome to a new city, and Pernelle, a noblewoman of wealth to befit a duchess, had been a pleasant companion over the six-day ride from Falcard's lands, but her chatter of noble friends and her father's wealth and holdings had often grown tiresome. Yet, from the beginning of the ride, she'd made no effort to hide that she liked him very much, and her supper invitation and kiss at parting confirmed that her intentions strayed far past friendship.

The townhouse door opened, and Joseph stepped onto the street. "Galien, my dear boy! God heard my prayers and brought you to me safely." Galien dismounted and embraced Joseph embraced. Taking his bags from the horse's back, he walked the tired animal to the stableman at the side gate, and followed Joseph into the house.

28 March 1093, Fortress Mirefleurs

After supper, Alphonse bade Roger come with him. They held torches as they walked down the stone steps to the fortress treasury, two floors below ground level. Alphonse unlocked two steel-bound doors, and they entered a stone-walled room. Alphonse put a key into a strongbox lock and said, "Choose one piece for Alisende, whatever you'd like. I'll leave you alone, and Père Bernard will come down and lock the doors."

Roger opened Alphonse's own jewelry chest, filled with treasures, and ran his hands over the items, first picking up a silver-and-gold reliquary cross, then a bronze Viking sword-pommel with runic inscriptions inlaid in silver.

A gleam caught his eye: a wrought-gold ring, laced with old Frankish designs, holding a large, flawless emerald. Surely, the ring had belonged to a great noblewoman or even a queen, been taken by a Viking or Mohametan raider, and passed on through generations of the long-dead pillager's descendants. Roger studied it in the torchlight, slipped it into his belt purse, and returned to Alphonse's quarters with the key. Alphonse said only, "I know you chose well, Roger."

8 April 1093, Fortress Mirefleurs

The warm sun of late afternoon greeted the guests in the great hall as they drifted into the court. Roger and Alisende rose from their seats and climbed the stair to their rooms. The emerald ring on Alisende's right hand gleamed in the candlelight as she changed her bride's dress for riding clothes and a light cloak. She met Roger on the balcony and took his arm. Together, they descended the stair and walked through the hall doorway to meet their escort.

Roger helped Alisende onto her horse and mounted his own. Martin and Roger's brother Vincent, in full battle dress and on warhorses, took position in front of them; Thierré, Harald Agnarssen, and Jean Loudon fell in behind. Men-at-arms held up steel-headed lances, and the five knights planted the butts into leather sockets, raising the ashen shafts fully upright. Banners bearing the colors of the Barony of Mirefleurs, the Coudre family, and the Lyon family, flapped in the wind.

The crowd assembled in the court cheered and waved, and Thierré raised his left hand to signal advance. The party moved slowly down the trail from the fortress and turned onto the road to Coudre Estate as the sun moved lower and the warm wind turned to a cool breeze.

20 May 1093, Fortress Mirefleurs

In the fading light of the cool spring evening, the Abbé de Saint-Amand spirits wagon lumbered around the last turn on the trail to the

Fortress. The portcullis creaked up, and the draft horses pulled the wagon into the front court. A team of men-at-arms began to unload the casks and barrels of wine and ale. Anseau climbed down from the driver's bench.

A knock sounded at the door to Thierré's room. He opened it. "Anseau! Good to see you again."

"And likewise you, Sir Thierré. Galien was well and in high spirits on the day he left for Troyes, and I bring his letter to you."

"I'll read it now. You know the way to quarters and food, but you always have my invitation to take supper in the great hall."

"Sir, in truth, I'm only a poor monk and a small skinny peasant. I'll be more at ease taking supper in the armory hall with the men-at-arms who rode beside my wagon."

"Do what pleases you, but should you change your mind, you'll be welcome." Anseau left and Thierré lit a candle. He broke open the letter, written in Galien's elegant, practiced hand.

25 April 1093, Troyes

> *God's Blessings, my brother Thierré.*

> *I cannot but first commend you on learning to read and write. The letters you've sent, penned in your own hand, have been a source of both surprise and great pleasure for me. I was happy to read of your continued improvement in health, and must share my optimism for you. Thierré de Coudre is a man of strongest resolve and will, one day soon, don his hauberk and helm and ride forth at the head of his men!*

> *I deeply regret I missed Alisende's wedding and haven't yet met Roger. You are all so close to my heart, and I think of each of you every day. Give my loving best wishes to Father. I am happy to know grandchildren wait close in the future for him, and that we brothers will become uncles. Coudre Estate was a good place to grow up for all of us, and I'm pleased that Roger and Alisende will raise their children on the family lands.*

In His wisdom, God has chosen to take me far away on a great adventure. I pray He will grant me safety on the roads until I return to be with my dear family again. Be assured, I will keep up regular practice at arms and horse, and will be ready for you when I come home.

Of my time in Troyes, I'll write you a longer letter, by way of Anseau at Saint-Amand. Foremost, continue your own efforts in reading and letters.

With the greatest love,
Galien

Thierré read the letter without difficulty, before he opened his armoire to begin dressing for supper. A knock sounded, and he called "Come!"

Anseau stepped into the room, a cup of wine in his hand. "Sir Thierré, I'd take you up on the supper invitation."

"Ah! A taste of wine and you become the charming fellow you are. One of Père Barnard's habits ought not to fit you too badly."

"I'll need to have a bath, lest it be ruined."

Thierré sniffed and chuckled. "Long days on the road do make a man stink. Wash down and return quickly. Alphonse takes his seat at sunset."

Talk at the baron's table was lively, Henri and Alphonse with a noble guest, and the younger chatting among themselves. Thierré sat quiet. He glanced at Anseau and smiled to himself. The monk sat talking with Roger and Alisende, holding his wine like a nobleman. Lorens Saint-Georges was telling Jean Loudon and Lady Cecilia of the plans for his upcoming marriage to Lisette. Jean and Cecilia listened closely, but Lisette seemed to be far away, lost in her own thoughts.

Thierré heard Alphonse's deep laugh. The baron's health had grown much poorer; his face grey, as if death shadowed him; his legs swollen and crisscrossed with bulging blue veins. At the least exertion beyond speaking, his breath turned to short gasps, and he could walk only a few steps before needing assistance. Thierré thanked God Alphonse had appointed Henri to the post of first advisor. With no heir apparent, Alphonse had a pressing need for a permanent successor, and

Père Barnard and Thierré's father were not permitting the baron to neglect his last affairs.

+ + +

With the evening over, Lisette climbed the stairs to the room that Alisende had shared with her. Now she had it to herself, and would stay until her marriage to Lorens. She took off her evening clothes, put on a day dress and cap, and left the room. At the gate to the armory court, she spoke to the guard. "I'd like to speak with Anseau, the monk."

"Lady, you know women aren't allowed to enter, and besides, most are sleeping now."

Lisette handed him a denier. "I'd be pleased if you'd bring him to me."

The guard bowed his head. "As you will, Lady. I'll fetch him in short time."

In a few minutes, Anseau stepped through the open gateway. "Walk with me, Brother Anseau?" Lisette said.

"I'm honored. You're no longer in the service of Lady Alisende?"

"No longer. Père Barnard offered me a fair wage to stay here and assist him with his work, and Lady Alisende has hired a new head servant for Coudre Manor."

"I hope no ill feelings have come between you."

Lisette laughed. "None in the least. We'll always be as close as sisters."

"I understand you're to be married to the young man you sat with at supper. Living here, you're near to him."

"I suppose."

They took seats on a stone bench. Anseau glanced at Lisette, noticing her pale demeanor. He put a hand on hers. "Lady, if you'll permit, I must say, all does not seem well with you."

Lisette bit her fist. "You see rightly, dear Anseau."

"You surely asked to see me with a purpose. How might I help you?"

Lisette took a sealed parchment letter from her bodice and handed it to him, following with a small bag holding coins. "See that Galien gets this letter in the shortest of time. I'll be in your debt for life." She stood. "I need to go now and let you return to your sleep."

209

+ + +

Henri de Coudre bade his supper companions a good night. In his room, he donned his nightshirt, poured a cup of wine, and sat, deep in thought. The guest of honor for the evening at Alphonse's table, a nobleman from the north of France, had brought wonderful news from Troyes. Galien had been keeping company with the daughter of one of the richest men in that city, a knight of distinguished family as well as a great man of commerce, and rumors of a betrothal were swirling.

Though Galien would still take his oath and gain his knighthood, Pernelle's father favored his work with Joseph of Reims. Architecture was a commoner's profession, but for Henri's own son to complete the building of the greatest cathedral in western Christendom would yet be an honor without compare for the Coudre family. With marriage to Pernelle, Galien would far surpass all of the Coudres in wealth, even Martin.

Henri couldn't be happier. He'd have no more worries about Galien and Lisette. Alphonse had heard the brave Lorens Saint-Georges' oath of fealty, and had decided to grant him lands. Lisette would soon become the wife of a landed knight, and what more could she want?

Chapter 25

10 June 1093, Troyes

Galien and Pernelle strolled, arm-in-arm, through the crowd of richly dressed guests in the great hall of the palatial Troyes townhouse. Galien caught a glimpse of Joseph in best evening form, in finely-tailored clothes, with only a crucifix at his chest as a sign of his monastic status, the center of attention in a group of wealthy cathedral patrons and high-ranking churchmen.

A large man grinned widely at them, and Pernelle whispered, "That's Ludovico Santovini. Together, he and my father have grown as rich as kings."

They walked over to greet him. "Signor Ludovico Santovini, please meet my friend, Galien de Coudre," Pernelle said.

The two men bowed heads and shook hands. Pernelle continued. "Galien, Signor Santovini is one of my father's dearest friends, and often his partner in business ventures."

Ludovico beamed. "And Sir Galien is no less than Master Joseph's noble and talented assistant." His big, abundantly bearded face, notable bulk, and deep baritone voice suggested endless good humor and generosity; his sharp black eyes, a business man of wiliest nature.

Pernelle glanced away, waved across the room, and exclaimed, "Oh, Count Hugh's daughters would visit with me!" Without a word to Ludovico and Galien, she hurried away.

The two men shrugged, and Galien frowned. "I suppose comparing the cost of her attire with the daughters of the Count of Troyes is more important than we are."

"Give it no mind, Sir Galien. She's just being a woman. Now, what do you think of my home?"

Galien looked up. Eighteen feet above the floor, set with stone and tiles in intricate patterns, huge smooth beams, decorated with painted motifs and carved moldings, spanned thirty feet. "It's quite impressive in structure, Signor Santovini, and the design is pleasing in all aspects."

"It is so, but Master Joseph's work has rendered it old-fashioned. I built this house only five years past, and now need have him build me another, in keeping with the new style."

"I'll tell him so," Galien promised, "and you'll be our first commission, outside the cathedral."

Ludovico slapped Galien's back with a huge, ringed hand. "That would be splendid, Sir Galien." He lowered his voice. "I only wish I could have you in my employ. Bad eyesight forced my account keeper and lead scribe of twenty-five years to accept my pension two years past, and since then, the business so good here has forced me to hire fools. All the best men are taken and held fast with silver."

Galien nodded graciously. "You honor me, Signor. But you'd not find me the man you need, as my talents are in drawing and illustration."

Ludovico laughed. "Whatever your talents be, I'd not try to lure you from Master Joseph."

Galien stroked his chin, in thought. "Signor Santovini, I do know a young man who'd meet your needs in the best ways. His character is beyond question."

"I'd like to hear more of him, but two investors stand by anxious to hear of my plans for their silver. Can you visit with me on the morrow?"

"I think Master Joseph will loose me from my chains for two hours."

"Excellent. Come here at noon and share my table. Now, I must ask my leave of you."

"To give such is my honor."

Ludovico put a hand on Galien's shoulder. "Lady Pernelle's father speaks only the best words of you. A simpleton could see how much she likes you, and she's of the nobility, as you are."

"I'm happy to hear her father's good opinion of my poor self, and I couldn't have wished for a better companion than Lady Pernelle."

"Then you both please the other. Hold fast to her, Galien. Marry Pernelle, and you'll be a happy nobleman and the richest architect in France."

Ludovico took his leave. A servant exchanged Galien's near-empty wine goblet for one brimming. He half-emptied it, thinking. With no doubt, a marriage to Pernelle would raise him to great wealth and fame and please his father beyond measure, but he might also be entering a cage of gold, and he be a man who could well come to think that he had forsaken his own soul.

13 June 1093, Troyes

Midafternoon came, and Galien hurried to pick up the twine and marking chalk for Joseph. He walked from the townhouse through the crowds to the cathedral grounds. At the guardhouse, Thorvid the Fat, the guard on duty and one of the more civil of those disagreeable men, greeted him with a gap-toothed smile, a polite bow of the head, and "Sir Galien." Galien nodded in return and entered the fenced grounds.

The plan of the church, now clearly revealed by the mighty stone buttress footings visible above the ground, nearly exceeded in area the entire town of Grand-Forêt. He spotted Joseph and the surveyor, Master Begue, at the choir end of the cathedral, four hundred feet away. On the building site, Joseph's authority surpassed even Bishop Ulrich of Troyes, and with the architect's mighty bulk in a distinctive rich robe, wearing a feathered red velvet cap, holding a six-foot ivory-inlaid oaken measuring staff as the symbol of his office, he could not be mistaken.

Galien joined Joseph and Begue and the master mason. They worked for an hour to finish measuring and staking the wall foundations at the choir. Joseph mopped sweat from his forehead and said, "Galien, what say we leave early? The Cat and Rooster is serving roast duck and asparagus tonight, and I'd be there for first pick. We'll get a bath at the barber's stall."

"An agreeable thought, Joseph. Let's go."

The sun was low in the sky as Joseph and Galien opened the doors to the neighborhood inn. They entered the cool, comfortable common room and took seats at their usual table. The serving girl on duty walked over. Joseph put an arm around her waist and said, "Dear Claire. You know what to bring for me and Sir Galien."

She smiled at both of them. "I do, Master Joseph. I'll bring your wine right away, and then pick the two biggest ducks for you good men."

"Two ducks for me," Joseph said.

"As you wish, Master Joseph."

Claire walked away, and Galien looked at his master sternly. "Joseph, how many times must I tell you that you need shed weight? You'll end up like Baron Alphonse."

Claire brought the wine, and Galien poured their goblets. Joseph took a sip and smiled. "My dear Galien, another matter concerns me. I'd hear of your meeting with Ludovico. Is he trying to take you from me?"

"Assuredly not, but should he offer me three times your pay, I'd not leave you."

"I'm relieved to hear that, but I'd still like to know of what you spoke."

"Pernelle introduced me to Ludovico during the gathering at his house, and he told me of the troubles he's had finding a reliable account keeper and scribe. I thought right away of Charles Falcard, and we talked of him at noon table. I'm to write to Charles and bid him come here."

Joseph looked thoughtful. "Charles is fast and neat at letters and good at figures. He's gained much experience in the Saint-Amand vineyard office. Do you think he'd leave there?"

"I'd bet that he would for the right coin. He's not due to take final vows for another year."

"Well, he'll be welcome at our house. Twoscore deniers will make his journey the easier, and I'll be happy to provide them."

"Joseph, you're the most generous of men."

Joseph slapped his forehead. "Perhaps generous, but certainly forgetful. A letter for you came to the house yesterday. The writing isn't familiar, but it bears your family's seal. I put it in my bedside drawer for safekeeping."

"It's likely from Thierré."

"No, I know Thierré's hand. I'll fetch it for you when we get home."

+ + +

Joseph took the letter from his table. Galien glanced at the writing on the outside, in Alisende's hand. He broke the seal quickly and read.

20 May 1093, Fortress Mirefleurs

My Dearest Galien,

> *Through Thierré and your father I've been kept abreast of the outstanding success you've found, both with Master Joseph and in the business and social life of Troyes. Though this holds no surprise for me, I must yet congratulate you.*

> *Galien, since I last wrote to you, I've made a decision that will set the course for the remainder of my life. You must already know that Lorens Saint-Georges, a good and kind young knight, proposed marriage to me in February. I held off my answer until mid-March, and at that time accepted his proposal. We are to be married mid-August.*

> *I know you have been keeping close company with a young noblewoman. Please understand that though I do not wish to disrupt what must be growing between you, I cannot be at peace until I know your plans and your true and final feelings toward me.*

> *Dear Galien, God has again blessed me with great fortune in this honorable offer of marriage, but I must tell you that should you still want me as your wife, I am willing to forsake all of it.*

> *However, I will not go against your father's wishes. Only upon Sir Henri's full consent and blessings and*

those of Baron Alphonse will I enter into betrothal with
you.

   Know that whatever be your plans, I will embrace
my own future with good cheer and determination, and
will always love you and hold the best of wishes for
you. I ask only you favor me with a reply in a short
time.

With my greatest love,
Lisette

Galien let out a long, slow breath and carefully folded the letter. "Dear Joseph, I have never more needed your wise advice and counsel."

30 June 1093, Fortress Mirefleurs

In Henri's quarters, Thierré read Galien's letter aloud. Henri's face turned darker with each line. Thierré looked up. "That's all of it, Father."

Henri slammed his fist onto the table. "Blast that spoiled brat! He's had more opportunities than any man could dream, and he wants to just throw it all away. I'm going to disown him."

"Father, calm your mind and think. Galien's never given a care for riches. He didn't question the place in the Church you planned for him until you'd taught him to wield a sword."

Henri poured a cup of wine and emptied it in one draught. Good color returned to his face. "And I was happy when he chose knighthood over the Church. But I'll not allow him to marry a peasant and keep our name. If he disobeys me to marry Lisette, I will disown him. He can stay in Troyes with Joseph of Reims and do work befitting his new station."

"Father, architecture is a profession of prestige and honor, which only few men of highest ability are allowed to enter. You and Mother were married in the church on the Mount of Saint Michael, remember?"

Henri's mind drifted back to that sweet day. "Of course I remember! Think you I'm becoming too old and forgetful?"

"No, Father, I only wanted to tell you that the architect who designed and built it was a nobleman."

"That can only be one of your tall tales, Thierré."

"Father, his name was William, and he was a son of a Count Robert of Volpiano, in the north of Italy. The Duke of Normandy had him build the lower structures and the church where you married Mother."

Henri scratched his head and scowled. "Hmmph... I'll find that out for myself, and you'd better not be lying to me."

"Why would I lie? Joseph of Reims most desires that Galien succeed him and finish the cathedral. Wouldn't you have Galien lend our noble name to the greatest testament to Christ's faith to ever be built in France?"

"Hmm... such would be a service to God and an honor that would endure until the Last Judgment."

"It would so, Father. And another thing. Lisette is no poor peasant. Rather, she's a woman of means. She holds the land in Grand-Forêt where her father's mill stood and has property and coin of a worth of twenty-five livres at the fortress treasury. She also invested three livres in Martin's quarry."

"Yes, I knew she was not near destitution, but if you're not lying to me, her means are much greater than I realized, and would make a dowry. Who told you?"

"Alisende, and you know she's no liar."

"Your sister is certainly no liar, and you've given me much to think about," Henri said, looking darkly pensive. He slapped his hand on the table. "Now, pour me another cup of wine and get out of here."

JOSEPH SCOTT AMIS

Chapter 26

5 July 1093, Troyes

Galien leaned back in his chair at Joseph's work table. Before him lay tallies for the next wagonloads of stones for the foundation buttresses at the cathedral. After two years as Joseph's assistant, Galien had decided that, although he loved design and drawing, the creation of elaborate details, and seeing those things become real before him, he ardently disliked the tedium of the endless everyday tasks that were the lot of the architect.

This discovery, added to constant dealings with dull, contentious craftsmen far beneath him in the social order, forced him to question the prospect of staying with Joseph and finishing the cathedral after his master's death. Indeed, the prospect of returning home to take up a diplomat's post was seeming mightily appealing.

He picked up the finished tallies and his measuring staff, and with his distinctively embroidered red velvet cap on his head, closed the town house door, and stepped out into the street. Making his way through the crowds, he approached the entry to Pernelle's father's grand stone town house. There, the guards on duty, who had always called him "Sir Galien" with the utmost courtesy and respect, only glared down their noses as he passed.

Galien glared back, but his stomach churned. Just days before, those same guards had thrown him out into the street, on the order of Pernelle herself, after he told her of his intention to marry Lisette. What a scene it had been: she had flown into a rage, the likes of which only women were capable, throwing her goblet of wine in his face, pummeling and slapping him with both hands, before calling the household guards to remove him from her presence. He had known Pernelle would be terribly disappointed, perhaps even troubled at heart, but she was not a lady with whom he could have fallen in love; in temperament, the two of them could hardly be more apart. In hard truth, he, a nobleman, had chosen a commoner over her, more than a noblewoman of her station and ambition could bear.

He sighed and continued to walk toward the cathedral grounds, deep in thought. If his father and Baron Alphonse chose not to give permission for his marriage to Lisette, and they married against those wishes, Galien was sure Henri would disown him. He, Galien de Coudre, had again let his heart lead him, this time placing his future beyond his own power to influence or change.

9 July 1093, Coudre Manor

Lisette and Alisende rode into the front court of Coudre Manor. The stableman took their horses, and head servant Dagobert greeted them at the front door. In the big second-floor chamber, they lay down on the bed to rest in the cooler air. "Thank you so much for coming all the way to the fortress to ride here with me," Lisette said.

"I'd do anything for you, dear sister, especially today."

After a few minutes, they heard sounds from the open window. Lisette glanced out to the front court. Henri and Martin de Coudre had arrived. She looked at herself in the silver mirror, pushed back stray hair, and said a prayer. Her fate would be decided very shortly.

They left the room and walked down the staircase. Henri waited in the great room. He motioned for Alisende and Lisette to sit on the high-backed bench. "Lisette, my son Galien has again proposed marriage to you, and has informed me of the same."

"Yes, Sire."

"You'd be breaking off your betrothal to a young man of great promise, and Galien has chosen not to pursue marriage to a wealthy noblewoman. I can only conclude you must truly love each other."

Lisette nodded. "We do, Sire."

Henri stroked his chin, looked out the window, and mused. "I foolishly assumed that Baldwin de Betancourt shared his father's high character, but my grave mistake in this matter only invited disaster. In the end, I could only leave Alisende's heart to heal, and the choice of husband her own."

Thierré scowled and jerked a thumb at Roger. "And look what she dragged along."

Roger thumped his dagger. "I'll see you outside, barnrat."

"Stop the horseplay, both of you," Henri said.

Thierré grinned at Lisette. "Roger came here a beat-up old knight, and my father treats him like a child with the rest of us. Do you truly want that for yourself?"

"Nothing would make me happier."

Henri frowned. "Lisette, you know well of the objections I've had to the particular friendship between you and Galien."

"Yes, Sire."

"Though Galien puts off his oath, he's well enough established with Master Joseph to take a wife, and the dowry you would bring is adequate. I have come to see no one suits him better than you, and that together you have sufficient means for the beginnings of a successful marriage."

Lisette felt her heart pounding. "S... Sire, am I hearing you truly?"

Henri winked and smiled. "Your ears aren't lying. Now, listen again. I'll give Galien one year to complete what Master Joseph requires of him, and then he will obey my wishes. He will come home and take his oath, and I will arrange for him to enter the diplomatic service of a high nobleman. Do you understand what will be required of you as his wife?"

Lisette looked him in the eye, not blinking. "I do, Sire."

"Good, and there is another thing. As your wedding gift from the Coudre family, I, Martin, Roger, and Thierré have agreed to finance the rebuilding of your father's mill, and to let it out to the best man we can find. With the rental, the lord's share of the earnings, and the profits from your and Galien's investments in the quarry, you'll be well enough situated to live as should a noble couple in diplomatic service."

Lisette gasped, "Sir Henri, you're far too generous!"

Henri, looking slightly embarrassed, said, "Let us move on. Thierré has advised me that Galien's great responsibilities with Master

Joseph will not allow him the time to come home, and your father has passed, God rest his soul. Who then will give your hand in marriage?"

"Master Joseph has agreed to stand as my father."

Henri beamed. "Master Joseph honors all of us. I no longer have any objections to a marriage between you and Galien. You both have my approval and blessings, and those of Baron Alphonse."

Lisette put her hands to her mouth. She could only dab at her eyes and wipe tears from her cheeks. Alisende hugged her. "Welcome to the Coudre family, dear sister."

"We need to address another matter," Henri said. "Lisette, you will need a proper escort for your journey to Troyes."

"I can manage the journey myself, Sir Henri."

Henri looked at her sharply. "Lisette, you are soon to be a noblewoman, and you can quit the 'Sire' and 'Sir Henri'. "'Father' is now most fitting."

"Hear, hear!" Thierré said. He looked to Paul and Lucie. "Fetch the best wine from the cellar, and join the rest of us for a goblet."

Martin cast his eyes at Henri and grinned slyly at Thierré. "You'd best ask Father first, Brother. You do remember the last time you crossed him."

Thierré waved off the warning. "Let him flog me. I'm too happy to feel pain."

Henri laughed. "There'll be no floggings today. We've still a serious matter at hand."

"You've no need for worry, Father. Lisette already has two knights to escort her."

"I've heard nothing of this, Thierré."

"I spoke to Alphonse after he gave his consent for Lisette, and you'd left his quarters. He's given me two months leave from duty and three men-at-arms, so I might escort her to Troyes and stand with Galien at their marriage. Roger told me he and Alisende wish to go, also."

Henri looked at his son-in-law. "Roger?"

Before Roger could speak, Alisende took his arm and said, "Father, Roger will have an enclosed wagon built for Lisette and me, to ride as noblewomen should."

Roger grinned sheepishly, and Henri grumbled, "I should have been told first. Thierré, you're not yet fit for such a journey."

"I've already told Galien I planned to be there if you gave your approval, and I'm sorry it had to be a surprise for you. The ride will help me to regain my fitness."

"It's all right, Son. You've done what befits a family of our rank, and the time of year couldn't be better for a long ride. I can't help but agree, it will be good for all of you."

"What have I done to merit such blessings?" Lisette said.

Alisende grasped her shoulders. "You've only been your good self."

31 July 1093, Troyes

Galien studied Charles as they finished their late supper at the Cat and Rooster. In the twenty months since they'd met at Saint-Amand, his homely peasant friend had become a young man of notable good looks. He'd grown taller, and the fat of youth had disappeared. His stylish new clothes showed off broad shoulders and a flat stomach; a well-groomed short beard hid the scars of bad skin on his cheeks. A waxed moustache and the dagger at his belt lent him a rakish air.

"We'd best go home, Charles," Galien said. "I've a long, hard day waiting on the morrow."

Charles leaned back, clasping his hands behind his neck. "Well, I don't. Ludovico's leaving on a day's journey, and he bade me take my leisure. I'm going to order a pitcher of good wine and drink it."

Galien got up. "You deserve it, but don't drink too much and be sick on your free day."

After Galien left, Charles sat content, thinking of all that had come to pass since Galien's letter, just short of six weeks ago. The serving girl Claire stepped to the table.

"What more would you like, Sire?"

He ordered the wine, and Claire brought it with a platter of cheese. "You've become a regular supper companion of Master Joseph and Sir Galien, but I must apologize; I don't yet know your name."

Charles smiled at her. "Sit with me and share some wine, and I'll tell you."

Claire glanced around. The hour was late, the public room nearly empty. She sat, and Charles poured two cups. "Charles Falcard. I'm not a nobleman like my dear friend Galien de Coudre, so you needn't call me 'Sire'."

"All right, Charles it is."

"And yours? I've only seen you from across the room."

"It's Claire. To keep company with men so important, I thought you must surely be a nobleman."

"No, I'm only a poor plowboy and monastery runaway. I came here but a few weeks past to seek my fortune."

"You look to have done well enough already."

"I spent my first two weeks of earnings with Signor Santovini to buy the clothes I'm wearing, and Galien lent me the dagger."

"Ludovico Santovini? He's an important man. What do you do for him?"

"I'm his scribe and account keeper, on a month's trial. I've high hopes he'll ask me to stay."

Claire leaned closer. "Oh, you're a man of letters."

Charles heard real interest in her voice and it showed in her eyes. He studied her face: oval and framed with dark hair, features regular and well-drawn. He couldn't fail to notice her well-rounded bustline.

"Only by God's grace did I gain the opportunity to learn," he said.

"Claire! Where are you?"

She turned to the voice and called, "I'm coming, Father," but added, "Will I see you again soon, Charles?"

"Certainly, Claire. Your father's come to walk you home?"

"No, he's half-owner here. More patrons must have come in."

"I'd pay for my wine."

She smiled, not taking her eyes off of him. "There's no need. Welcome to Troyes."

+ + +

25 August 1093, Troyes

Tears came to Thierré's eyes as Lisette slid the gold ring onto Galien's finger. Bishop Ulrich of Troyes draped the surplice around their clasped hands and pronounced them man and wife. The new-wed couple kissed as long as was proper and turned to walk down the aisle to the open doors. Thierré stepped forward to embrace Master Joseph, and together, they followed the couple into the paved court in front of the chapel of the old Troyes cathedral.

The wedding guests gathered in the waning daylight. Before Galien could help Lisette into the waiting barrel-roofed wagon, Alisende held her in a long embrace. Charles and Claire stood arm in arm, Ludovico Santovini and his wife beside them. Claire squeezed Charles' arm, whispering, "You're next." A tear ran down Joseph's face and into his beard as he stood silently next to Bishop Ulrich. Thierré and Roger mounted their waiting horses and rode forward to lead the procession to the wedding feast.

Iron-shod hooves clattered on the cobbled lanes along the route to Joseph's town house, where the driver drew the horses pulling the wagon to a halt. Thierré gave his hand to Lisette as she stepped down, and then he and Roger took position facing each other. They put their hands on their sword hilts and waited as Galien and Lisette walked between them and through the doorway to the sound of the guests' cheering.

+ + +

One candle burned in the second-floor bedchamber. A cool, late-evening breeze blew in through the windows opened to the back courtyard. Lisette kissed Galien's cheek. "I'll expect you to make love to me like you just did every night."

"Best watch your words, lest you find me too eager for you."

Lisette giggled. "Could you speak to Alain, he'd say you can't be too eager for me."

"I'll be at full ready to rise to your challenge."

She giggled again and said, "Can I get you some wine, husband?"

Galien sat up against the headboard, crossed his arms, and looked down his nose, frowning. "Such is your wifely duty now, but I'll permit you to share with me."

Lisette made a face and stuck her tongue out at him. She got up from the bed, pulled on a light dressing gown, and returned shortly with a pitcher and two silver cups. They drank, and Lisette said, "Tell me truly. Had I married Lorens, would you have married Pernelle?"

Galien drained his cup. "In truth, I thought you lost and entertained the thought of asking Pernelle's father for her hand in marriage, but I knew it likely would not have been a happy match. Then, a voice spoke and bade me wait a while longer, and after came your letter."

"So you decided to forsake a beautiful and pleasing noblewoman whose father is nearly as rich as a duke?"

"Lisette, she is beautiful and rich, but hardly pleasing to me. In short time, I was sitting at the desk in this room, writing the letter that came to you."

"Still, I can't believe you gave up all that wealth and power to marry me."

"Christ asked, 'What profits a man, should he gain the whole world yet lose his own immortal soul?' Had I chosen Pernelle only for her wealth, knowing you waited for me, I would have been betraying both of you and selling my own soul to the Devil."

Galien stroked her hair as she shed a few tears, then she brightened and said, "Alisende always made life good for me. After having her as an example, I think I can be a noblewoman now."

Galien looked at her slyly, raising an eyebrow. "Proper noblewomen overlook their husbands' indiscretions."

She grabbed him by the hair. "Noble or not, should you stray, before I'm done with you, you and your lover will swear the souls of Thierré and Gautier of Saint-Lille have come to live in this one small woman."

Galien held up his hands, grinning. "I wouldn't want to face that, and bow humbled at your forewarning."

Chapter 27

6 October 1093, Fortress Mirefleurs

With a deft move of his right foot, Thierré snagged Roger's heel. Roger stumbled. Thierré bashed Roger's buckler hard with his own, and then thrust the blunt tip of his steel practice sword into the right side of his opponent's chest.

Roger raised his sword and shield high. "I yield, good Sir!"

Thierré slapped him on the back, and they sat on a stone bench, mopping the sweat from their faces. A man-at-arms brought them a skin of water.

Otto Huber called Thierré the victor. The men standing around clapped and cheered. Henri and Walter d'Avesnes walked over to the two knights, and Walter said, "Sir Thierré, two victories in four matches with Sir Roger tell me you're fit to return to full duty."

Thierré and Roger stood. Walter glanced at Roger and Henri. Both men nodded. Walter looked at Thierré. "Ready to take lead of the Saint-Lille border patrols again?"

Thierré said, "Yes, Sir Walter!" and then flashed his wicked grin. "Gautier can once more start counting the days he has left to live."

18 November 1093, the town of Grand-Forêt

Thierré led his patrol down the path from Fortress Mirefleurs, to join Roger at the main road. He signaled advance, and the mounted men followed the two knights toward the road to Grand-Forêt. At the crossroads, a peasant boy ran toward them, halted before Thierré and

Roger, and doubled over, out of breath. He gasped and pointed toward Grand-Forêt. "Sires, Gautier of Saint-Lille and five armed horsemen are drinking in the tavern."

Thierré looked at Roger, waved forward, and took off at a gallop. The eleven-man company rode hard to keep up, the boy trotting after them. Thierré signaled the party to halt at the edge of the town and turned to Jean Loudon. "Follow us, halt on signal, and hold for orders."

Roger and Thierré rode side by side into Grand-Forêt. The road, usually busy at noon, was deserted. At the side of the tavern, a stableboy stood watch beside six warhorses nosing in the feed troughs. Roger scowled and put his hand to his sword hilt, and the boy scampered out of sight, around the back corner.

Thierré reddened in fury. He turned to Roger and said, "I'm going to haul *Sir* Gautier out by his balls."

Roger grabbed Thierré's shoulder. "No, your temper has the best of you. I'll go. Get the men into position."

Thierré, now a little calmer, nodded in assent. Roger dismounted and put his helmet in the crook of his left arm. He entered the tavern and paused in the warm, dimly lit common room, to find Gautier and five armed men sitting at a trestle table, pouring cups of wine from a large pitcher. Roger walked over to them and said, politely, "Sir Thierré de Coudre would speak to Sir Gautier, outside."

Gautier fixed a cold stare on Roger. "If Coudre wants to speak to the Count of Saint-Lille, he can come in and do so."

Roger ignored the taunt. "Sir Gautier, might I remind you that you and your men are in violation of boundary law and subject to immediate arrest?"

Gautier got up and faced Roger. He stood six feet tall and lean, with large hands and long limbs, a man with a formidable swordsman's build, not unlike Thierré. In features, he strongly resembled his father, but his hair was dark reddish-brown and his skin olive.

"I haven't seen you before. Are you Thierré's new saddle boy?"

Again, Roger didn't flinch. "Sir Gautier, who I am does not matter. What does is that you are in trespass, as are your men, and Thierré de Coudre is the ranking knight with jurisdiction over this area of the Barony of Mirefleurs. I advise you to speak with him, as I requested."

An aristocratic knight at the table said, with authority, "Gautier, go and talk to Thierré, and show him respect." He appeared older than Gautier and wore the mail and sword of a wealthy, high-ranking nobleman.

Gautier downed his cup of wine and spat to his side, onto the floor. He picked up his helmet from the table, put it on, and sneered at Roger. "Take me to him, saddle boy." Roger followed Gautier out the door and, at three yards from Thierré, ordered him to halt.

Thierré stood alone in the road before the tavern, helmet in his left hand. The point of his sword rested on the ground before him, his right hand draped over the pommel. The eight barony horsemen and Jean Loudon waited across the road.

Thierré spoke. "Gautier, you and your men are to leave the tavern without delay and get on your horses." He looked at Roger. "Sir Roger de Lyon and our men will escort you to the border markers. Once across, you are not to trespass onto this barony's lands again."

"You escort us personally, or we don't leave. Didn't your seigneur teach you manners? A knight escorts a count. He doesn't send his saddle boy."

At the insults, Thierré's face turned white; his eyes, a paler, icier blue. He put on his helmet and laid the blade of his sword on his right shoulder. Roger held up four fingers and pointed to the tavern. Four mounted men-at-arms crossed the road and pulled up behind Gautier, cutting him off from the tavern door and his men.

"First, *Sir* Gautier, you are no count," Thierré said. "Second, you are the one who plainly knows nothing of proper conduct. An honorable knight does not insult or demean another of his rank."

Gautier laughed nastily. "You're not speaking to another retainer, boy. I will succeed my father as Count of Saint-Lille, and when I do, you'll wish he was back."

Thierré spoke again, in a low voice. "Gautier, I've made you an offer to leave the Barony of Mirefleurs with only a warning. It is now withdrawn. Unbuckle your sword belt and helmet and drop them in front of you."

For a second, Gautier didn't move. His right hand darted to his sword hilt. Thierré lifted his own sword from his shoulder and pointed it at Gautier. "Or I can butcher you where you stand. Your men will be arrested and confined to the dungeon at Fortress Mirefleurs, then interrogated and executed or held for ransom. Alphonse's disposition isn't patient of late."

Thierré suddenly winced at a sharp flash of pain in his head. The scene before him blurred. He swayed but kept his feet, standing fast.

Gautier sneered, grinning wide. "You look like Baldwin de Betancourt took more than his fair measure of your hide, Thierré. Were I you, I'd retire to my lands, right now."

Recovered, Thierré stepped forward, his sword point to Gautier's chest. "If you want a fight to the death, you have it. But kill you me or I you, Sirs Roger de Lyon and Jean Loudon stand ordered to hang your men from that oak tree to strangle, and then cut your own guts out. Their corpses will be left hanging till they rot, and what's left of you, dead or alive, will be fed to pigs."

Gautier glanced around at the barony men. He had no choice but to drop his sword belt and helmet.

Thierré turned to Roger and said, "Sir Roger, honor me and bind Sir Gautier's hands," and then called across the road to Jean, "Sir Jean, take your men and bring Sir Gautier's out. Should they resist, give no quarter." Jean saluted and nodded to his four horsemen. They dismounted, drew their swords, and followed him into the inn.

Thierré winked at Roger. Roger drew his dagger, walked to the horse bearing Gautier's shield, and cut a rein off the bridle. He returned to Gautier and said, "Hold them out." Gautier, eyes glittering black hate, spat again and complied.

Roger bound Gautier as the five men came out of the tavern, Jean and his men-at-arms behind. Thierré addressed them. "Your leader, Sir Gautier of Saint-Lille, and the rest of you are in violation of a boundary agreement sealed by the Duke of Aquitaine and Count Bayard of Saint-Lille. I declare each of you guilty of criminal trespass. By law, you should be arrested and confined to the dungeon at Fortress Mirefluers, but I have chosen to let you go free, upon payment of a fine for your foolish and unlawful action, which will be forfeiture of your weapons and horses. If you are again apprehended in the Barony of Mirefleurs, you will be executed on the spot, without trial."

Gautier and his men looked at each other with expressions of shock and hesitated. Thierré said, "Drop your weapons and helmets in front of you, now! Any man who pulls a dagger loses the hand that drew it."

Gautier's men dropped their equipment, and Thierré gave orders. "Line up single file behind Sir Gautier. Sirs Roger and Jean, take two men, escort the prisoners to the border double time, and return here. Wine and food for all are on me, and we'll divide up these fine horses and weapons." He looked at Gautier's horse and smiled at the costly stallion's humiliated former owner.

Roger mounted his horse. To Gautier and his men, he said, "You heard Sir Thierré. Move and be quick about it." On foot, they trotted off on the path to the border crossing, a half-mile away, with the four horsemen riding beside them. The aristocratic knight who had advised Gautier to speak with Thierré caught Roger's eye. He nodded with a slight smile, and Roger returned the nod.

At the stone border markers, Roger got off his horse and faced Gautier. "You're on your own now, but we're going to sit here on our horses and watch until you're well gone. Consider yourself lucky Thierré de Coudre's saddle boy was on hand to keep him from killing you."

Gautier glared at Roger as the Devil might a soul newly arrived in Hell. "I'll be back to take your cods and feed them to my hunting dogs." This declaration made, he turned and led his men in a weary trudge into the County of Saint-Lille.

5 February 1094, Fortress Mirefleurs

Thierré got up from the table in Père Barnard's quarters, rubbed his eyes, and looked out the window into the cold night. He had at last finished his lessons, and Barnard had presented him with a key to the same fortress bookroom where Galien had spent many hours.

Thierré took a decanter of wine from Barnard's work table, poured a large goblet, and sat back. He admired his own neat, crisp calligraphy, nearly as happy as the day that he was sworn a knight. Though now most often a modest drinker, he drained the goblet, poured another, and once again read his letter to Galien.

5 February 1094, Fortress Mirefleurs

My dear brother Galien,

I must beg your apology for the delay in writing to you. Père Barnard is an exacting teacher and insisted I take full charge of my own progress, after I had mastered the basic elements. He would only review what I wrote and leave it to me to do over properly. This letter required a week of evenings to draft, and then copy, to a neat standard of penmanship!

The greatest news is that Alisende is now sure she is three months expecting; thus, her first child, and Roger's, will be born in July. If a boy, they will name him Henri, after Father, as Roger's older brother has already named his first son after their own. If a girl, they will name her Gabriele, in honor of our mother.

They are happy in the old house. Roger had glass set in lead put into the great room windows. With the light and the tapestries they have hung, the dark old room looks cheerful. I think a visit to Martin's rich home put this into Alisende's mind to do.

Father is still acting as Baron Alphonse's first advisor. Alphonse has much lessened his drinking and eating of flesh. He is not nearly as heavy now, and can once again breathe without gasping, but he is most weak, being unable to walk at all without assistance. He feels his days are soon to end and will need a successor shortly. In this regard, Father has begun a search for Alphonse's lost brother.

Martin's account keeper has reviewed the quarry finances, and his report was a good one, showing a fair profit realized after but one season. The Archbishop of Vienne has been more than pleased with the stone supplied, as well as Martin's close attention. Thus, a reputation has begun to grow, and Martin has received inquiries from new customers. Of course, he intends to take as much business as comes and has asked Roger to work beside him. Alisende is again ably managing the estate, allowing Roger to devote his time to the quarry, and with the large investment that Roger made, he will become Martin's full partner in a short time. Lisette will be happy to hear her land in Grand-Forêt has been readied for new construction upon it. Roger has engaged a capable builder, and the rebuilding of the mill will begin within the next week.

Alisende is more than pleased with all of this. Since she and Roger married, she has made no secret of her wish that he end his soldiering days. Now that they are to be parents, with surely many more children to come, she looks to be getting him under her thumb, and isn't this what all women want?

Roger has been reassigned to the safer patrol routes for his duty days, and he is most deserving, as, last November, he skillfully handled a dangerous confrontation at Grand-Forêt, in which Gautier of Saint-Lille and his henchmen were bloodlessly rendered impotent and sent back across the border in humiliation. The barony has thus gained the military advantage in the Saint-Lille border areas, but I've no doubt Bayard has taken his measure of Gautier's hide, and when we next encounter him, he will be meaner and more ready to fight than ever.

The family is prospering, healthy, and happy, but I still feel heavy-hearted at times, and long to leave here for unknown and faraway places. The grand ride to Troyes and my stay there did nothing but fan the flames of that longing. Of the great occasions in my life, only the taking of the knight's oath ranks with the day I stood beside you as you were married. I was pleased to be able to tell Father and Martin about your wedding day and happiness with Lisette, the great cathedral and your high role in its construction, and of the kindness and generosity Master Joseph of Reims has shown to you and Lisette, and extended to all of us in fullest measure.

Write as often as you are able, Galien. I can now ably read anything you send, and look forward to this with the greatest of eagerness. Please extend my

*continuing love to our dearest Lisette, and my fondest
and most respectful regards to Master Joseph.*

May God keep all of you.
Thierré

Thierré finished his goblet, wrapped the parchment sheets in velvet, and put them in the polished wood lock box on Barnard's table. In a warm glow of wine, he wandered out onto the balcony and came upon the bookroom door. Deliberately, he returned to Barnard's quarters, picked up a candlestick, walked back to the bookroom, and opened it with his key. Inside the room, he took three volumes from the table. After another goblet of wine in Barnard's room, he set off in a pleasant haze, books in hand, toward his own quarters.

6 February 1094, Fortress Mirefleurs

"Anseau," Thierré called. He crossed the torchlit court to the wagon, loaded with empty casks and barrels, and held out a heavy, impressive-looking sealed parchment packet. "This is for Galien."

"Sir Thierré, Galien's an important man now. I'm nearly afraid to take such a letter to him."

Thierré smiled. "Anseau, there's no gold in it. His older brother has only learned to read and write, and has much news for him." He put a small green leather bag on the wagon seat. "You've never failed me before. Take this for yourself."

Anseau took the letter and tucked the bag of coins into his waist purse. "God bless you for your generosity, Sir Thierré. I'll make sure that Galien gets it, on my life and faith."

"Thank you, Brother Anseau. Go with God and have a safe journey."

Thierré turned toward the armory. Anseau reined his team of draft horses through the open gateway and onto the path down the low hill to the main road. He halted in the breaking dawn, bounced the bag of coins in his hand, and smiled, his thoughts on the girl at the tavern in Mont-Brison.

Chapter 28

26 April 1094, Troyes

Lady Lisette de Coudre woke and felt Galien's side of the bed. Faint dawn had only begun to light the room, and he was already up and gone. Work on the cathedral began well before daylight, six days a week, and Galien and Joseph joined the workmen that crowded the Cat and Rooster Inn for the daily early breakfast. She rolled over and went back to sleep. Life with two architects had brought its own share of work, yet also new comforts.

She got up at midmorning, washed and dressed in their chamber, and stepped down the wide stone staircase to the ground floor. Lisette loved the spacious townhouse the Diocese of Troyes provided for its renowned architect. She and Galien slept and had their private life on the second floor, and Joseph lived in the spacious master's quarters on the street floor. From there, he seldom needed to pull his bulk up the staircase and could come and go in discreet privacy.

In the kitchen, she opened the window shutter to the well-planted and trimmed-back courtyard and sat in the cool morning light and breeze as she took her breakfast. Finished, she put final touches to her hair and cap, picked up a basket, and pulled open the massive oaken front door. In the fifteen-foot cobbled lane between the rows of stone-faced and timber-and-plaster town houses, she joined the well-dressed neighborhood folk and moved with them toward the city square and market place, only a short walk north.

She purchased bread, cheese, meat, and fruit for Galien and Joseph's lunch, browsed in stalls and shops, and chatted with a neighbor woman on the walk back to the town house. The water delivery man came at late morning, and the washwoman picked up the soiled clothes. Lunch basket in hand, Lisette again set off north.

At the city square, she crossed to the route to the cathedral grounds. The foul odors from a detour through the poorest section of the city were sufficient to alert a blind man at fifty yards away. The narrow, crooked lane, well patrolled by city guardsmen by day, teemed with beggars and grimy children. Lisette kept a hand over her mouth and nose, her eyes straight ahead, and her pace aggressive. To hand a beggar a coin would invite swarms of others, and the crowds of children, innocent and wretched in demeanor, harbored those at watch for a pocket to pick or purse to cut. Any thief caught by the guardsmen had little chance of escaping the hangman's noose, but for these unfortunates, the hunger of the moment was far more compelling than the fear of death.

The unpleasant route abruptly discharged onto the broad, open cathedral grounds. Lisette joined the queue of women waiting to pass the guardhouse and share the noonday meal with their men. Wives of humbler men offered her their places, but she politely declined and waited her turn. After eight months of marriage, she felt comfortable in her station as a noblewoman, but still often bemused by it.

At the guardhouse, Thorvid the Fat greeted her with a smile, a bow of the head, and "A good day to you, Lady Lisette." She walked to the row of old trees at the western edge of the grounds, found a shady spot, and spread a blanket over the grass. She spotted Joseph, Galien, and the surveyor, Master Begue, at the choir end of the cathedral, five hundred feet away. Joseph and Galien tipped their caps in polite leave of Master Begue, and Galien waved to her.

Galien kissed Lisette and sat next to her on the blanket; Joseph eased his bulk onto a bench. Each drained a flask of fresh water from Lisette's basket, and they ate eagerly. With appetites eased, Joseph said, "Galien, while you were checking the footing levels with Master Begue, I visited with Ulrich in his quarters."

"I wondered where you'd wandered. You usually don't let a half-inch mistake get by."

"You know what to look for as well as I do. This was a matter of greatest importance."

Lisette gave Joseph her full attention, and Galien shrugged. "So tell us."

"A month ago, I told Ulrich, and notified Leo at Saint-Amand by letter, that I intended to leave the monastic order. All has been confirmed now. I'm no longer a monk."

Lisette dropped her piece of cheese mid-bite. "Joseph, you're only teasing us."

"No, dear Lisette, I'm not, and want to calm any unease you and Galien might be feeling."

"This is sudden, Joseph, but I can't say I'm surprised," Galien said.

"Soon after we came here last year, Galien, I began to realize I wanted my own life back, but knew I needed prove my worth to Ulrich and Bayard and the other wealthy donors. It seems I succeeded, for Ulrich's heart nearly failed on my first telling him. He declared he would go to any length to keep me as architect for the cathedral."

Galien smiled. "I am happy he didn't drop dead on the spot."

Joseph raised an eyebrow. "Yes, that would have been unfortunate, but he lived through it. In the weeks since, all of the powers behind this project have come to agreement. I am to keep my position for life, at a salary I can't yet grasp, and lifetime occupancy of the house we live in. I very much want for you to stay and gain your own qualifications as an architect, and see the cathedral to completion after I'm gone."

"Joseph, you know Lisette and I will be returning home after the foundations and crypt are finished."

Joseph sighed. "I can still try my best to keep you." He mused, "Count Bayard grumbled mightily at my having you here at all."

"Bayard can rot in Hell. Honorable men despise him, and Lady Lisette and I have no plans for a friendly visit to the County of Saint-Lille in our future."

"Do tell us how you feel, Sir Galien," Joseph said, and they all laughed. Master Begue waved from the far end of the cathedral. Joseph nodded. "Go and see what he needs, Galien."

The cathedral workmen were finishing the noon meal, their wives packing baskets to leave. Joseph pulled himself to his feet with his staff. "No need to have supper ready tonight, Lisette. I've already ordered for us at the Cat and Rooster."

Lisette put a hand on his arm. "Joseph, I'd rather Galien stay here and work with you. I'm happy in Troyes, and not looking forward to going home as a noblewoman."

"Galien must follow his father's wishes. I'm afraid that leaves you and me no say in the matter."

8 July 1094, Troyes

Galien took a chair at his desk and broke the wax seal on the folded parchment packet, just delivered. The open windows facing the houses across the street let pleasant morning light into the bedchamber, and he had no need of fire or candle to read.

Lisette leaned back in her armchair. "Alisende and I have exchanged four letters since I've been here, and Thierré has only now written to you again."

"We're busy men with enemies to fight and a cathedral to build, and you and my sister are noblewomen of leisure. You've plenty of free time to trade gossip by letter."

"I beg your pardon. The jobs of running this house and keeping the accounts and seeing that you and Joseph are fed well and dressed properly for work have proven no change from my duties at Coudre Manor. You may call me a noblewoman, but I'm still a servant."

"You make a point I can't argue."

She smiled. "I'm only joking. What woman could have two more appreciative men? Read on."

Galien unfolded the parchment and read aloud.

25 June 1094, Fortress Mirefleurs

Dearest Galien,

With this letter, I have no ill or alarming news to convey. Rather, I wish to express the family's continuing best wishes to you and Lisette, and to bring you abreast of events at home.

For a period after your marriage, Father was quite fretful, thinking you and Lisette easy targets for the mischief of Count Bayard. He has since come to realize that in your position, Bayard will not dare make a threat against either of you. He is at peace in mind and now talks most often of the grandchildren that Lisette will give him.

In your last letter, you lavished praise on this thick-headed knight becoming a lettered man, and now comes my turn to express pride in a brother's success. The monastery was, in many ways, alike to the shelter of home for you. In leaving there, and taking the woman of your love and choice to wife, you truly became your own man, and Lisette has her well-deserved place as a full member of our family and a noblewoman. Knowing Lisette to be audience to this letter, I must now make my claim to your first son as my own charge, to be trained at arms and horse under my direction and Roger's.

.Alisende has had no problems with carrying their child. The expectation of the birth next month has brought the family close again, and we all meet at the manor for a large feast after Sunday Mass. Dagobert has proven his worth in the kitchen with his wonderful dishes. Though Lucie's health is frail, she and Paul still faithfully serve the family, but they only take light duty now.

I'm glad that Alisende and Lisette wish to bear large families, as I grow more rooted in my bachelorhood, and Martin is much too occupied with commerce to seek a wife. Several of us from the fortress make the ride to Mont-Brison once or twice a month, to sample the good wine so abundant there, but Martin always declines. He seems to be only interested in making his wealth grow and acquiring more lands.

The quarry has gained many more customers, and Martin and Roger have been busy excavating the entire extent of the land Martin purchased from Bouchard. Martin has also purchased the tract adjoining the quarry, and paid much more dearly than for Bouchard's land. Aside from the wealth it has begun to bring to our family, the quarry is fast proving a blessing for the entire barony. All of us in the family who invested will be due to receive our first dividends in late autumn.

The mill is now nearing completion, and a fine piece of work it is! Father and Roger heard inquiries from a number of possible tenants, finally selecting an experienced miller, who, along with his wife and two grown sons, came from south of Le Puy in search of a fresh opportunity. They are a nice, hard-working family, and we're confident that the mill will be at full production in short time.

Walter d'Avesnes retired to his lands on the first day of June, and Alphonse promoted Sir Jean Loudon to marshal of the barony's forces. Roger was next in line, but with marriage, lordship of the estate, and the quarry, he is only serving with Father as an advisor. Had I not been injured so gravely, I would have been next after Roger, but I have no regrets, being only thankful I was able to return to full duty shortly after returning from Troyes.

Though my injuries still trouble me, I am more settled at heart, and my newly-found ability to read plays a large part in this. You will be pleased to know I have taken some books from the storeroom here at the fortress and am slowly finding my way through them. In the course of my readings, I often consult Père Barnard, a learned and kindly man who has become a good friend. I am ashamed that in years past I derided him as a befuddled old priest.

The Saint-Lille border has been calm since the confrontation with Gautier last November, so much that Alisende does not object to Roger again riding patrols with me two days a month. We greatly enjoy each other's company, and as long as I don't try to lure him to drink all night, Alisende is content.

Father is well and active. He has worked hard to assist Alphonse, but dislikes the details of governance. Alphonse's health is poor but steady, and he plans to announce his plans for succession shortly, before he passes away.

I cannot forget Master Joseph. Please convey my fond and respectful regards to him.

As always, I have passed too much time in writing, but must reveal my own anxiety before closing. Life has been peaceful here at home, so much so that I cannot help but worry this might portend of great change and calamity.

Your loving brother,
Thierré

Galien looked up. "This letter is worthy of a schooled monk. Thierré couldn't begin to spell 'cat' three years ago."

"You share the same blood. Though you were more inclined to the scholar's life, your talent for arms showed early on. Thierré surely had like aptitude for letters."

"If he thought so, he kept it well to himself. He declared letters to be only for monks and the effeminate, and did nothing but bully me about my scholar's ways."

"And you're now the closest of brothers."

"We decided to quit hating each other and became brothers-in-arms."

"I love Thierré as you do. I'll be honored to have our first son train at arms under his guidance. My own father and mother would have been so proud to see their grandson become a knight, and to know all their years of hard work at the mill didn't go in vain."

Galien sat on the edge of her chair, taking her hands. "Dearest Lisette, I've no doubt they're watching from God's kingdom as we speak."

Chapter 29

26 October 1094, north of Grand-Forêt

"Sir Roger!" The knight riding to Roger's left grabbed his shoulder. Roger signaled the patrol to halt inside the shadows of the forest edge. He looked where the knight pointed. Three men with falcons on their wrists stood in the middle of a farmer's field, a hundred yards away. A flock of quail rose from trampled crops, and they loosed their birds.

"That can only be one man," Roger said. "Sir Clement, dismount and lead three men with crossbows on foot to flank their rear, then close in and put them under arrest. If they draw swords, loose bolts without warning. We'll ride fast to your aid, should you have trouble."

"Yes, Sir." Clement de Sens dismounted and led the crossbowmen in a swift crouch between rows of grain. Roger signaled "hold" to the two mounted men-at-arms behind him. He smiled as the freshly-sworn Clement and the bowmen took the trespassing falconers by surprise. The offenders dropped their sword belts at the point of the crossbows, and Roger rode ahead at a walk. The men-at-arms followed him in single file, halting at the scene of the arrest. Gautier of Saint-Lille glared at Roger. "You again!"

Roger smiled. "Yes, and once more, I've you and your cronies by the balls."

Gautier spat and looked at his companions. He sneered at Roger. "It seems you do, and I must accord you proper respect. What's your name, again?"

"Roger de Lyon. I'll trust you're not stupid enough to forget it a second time."

Gautier put his left hand to his waist and bowed with a wide flourish of the right. "Do pardon my insolence, good Sir. I knew not that I speak to the man who tamed Thierré's sister."

"Shut up and take that damned smirk off of your face, Gautier. I've the authority to order you and your friends executed, here and now."

Gautier quieted and Roger continued, "Be thankful once more that Thierré's saddle boy is present to show you mercy. You'd already be missing your head if he were leading this patrol."

Clement snickered. "Sir Roger, I rather think old Bayard would thank us for doing what he'd like to do."

"I suspect you speak truth, Sir Clement, but today, my disposition leans to mercy. Sir Gautier and his companions will pay reparation to our farmers for the crops they've trampled and be allowed to depart."

Roger stared at Gautier. "Sir Gautier, you and your companions will pay twenty deniers each in reparation."

Gautier took the coins from his belt purse and tossed them before Roger's horse. "That's threescore times the worth of your filthy farmers' crops."

"My mood is changing for the worse, Gautier. Pick up those coins and hand them to me."

Gautier gave the coins to Roger with a hateful stare, and his companions followed suit without protest. Roger drew his sword, pointing it toward the border. "Now, lead your horses over. We'll toss your swords to you after you've passed twenty yards."

"What about my bird? My prized hunter has yet to return."

"You're out of luck. Young Sir Clement yet lacks a good bird. Yours will be his reward for his craft and courage."

"Lyon, today I swear before Holy God, I'm going to kill you."

"Be careful what you swear, Gautier. Every man who has spoken that oath to me lies rotted in his grave."

6 November 1094, Fortress Mirefleurs

Shortly after dawn, a guard admitted Henri de Coudre to Baron Alphonse's quarters. Alphonse, awakened from his doze, painfully drew himself up to a sitting position. "Henri… did you find them?"

Henri took the chair at the baron's bedside and poured him a cup of watered wine. After a drink, Alphonse said, impatiently, "Speak, man! Are you going to tell me or not?"

"Sire, I bring tidings both sad and happy. As we've long suspected, your brother passed five years ago and his wife two years after, but their daughter is alive and well, and has not married."

Alphonse came alert, suddenly looking much better. "God rest my brother and his wife, yet we need also give thanks to Him. Is she beautiful and pleasing? Did she consider the proposal?"

"She is all you could want in a baroness, Sire. And, knowing the man you would have as your successor by his wide reputation, she readily consented." With this, Henri opened a portfolio and showed Alphonse signed and sealed documents.

Alphonse looked briefly at the parchment pages, then sank into the pillows at his back. "Henri, all I wanted will be accomplished, and now I can die at peace."

Henri chuckled, and said, "You can't die just yet, old friend."

"No, indeed, I can't. I want the betrothal proclaimed shortly, and to have all accomplished before the first day in December. The announcement will be made a week hence, at noon in the great hall. All in our barony are to be invited and freed from their duties. Go first and see the patrols get the word out, then prepare the great hall for a crowd and a feast. Spend the all the coin you need for food and drink aplenty and organize guard and serving staff."

"All shall be as you wish, Sire, and I'd best catch the patrols before they leave. Martin is here and will come to sit with you in my place."

13 November 1094, Fortress Mirefleurs

Henri de Coudre surveyed the great hall from the dais erected at the wall facing the doors to the court outside. All was in order, with colorful banners newly hung from the great beams above; Baron Alphonse and the barony's leading noblemen seated in carven chairs. The tables at the floor had been moved to the walls, and bore a sumptuous feast. He signaled the guards, and they pulled the heavy oaken doors open.

Cold wind and snow gusted through the doorway. The people waiting outside crowded into the hall until it was packed inside and out, and the doors could not be closed. They gave the weather no mind as a young noblewoman climbed the steps to the dais, and Martin de Coudre rose and came to stand beside her. Henri raised his hands to quiet restive voices, then helped Alphonse to his feet and held his arm.

Alphonse looked askance at Henri. "Sir Henri, I would stand without assistance." He nodded to Martin and the lady beside him, and again spoke, his words halting, coming between gasping breaths. "The good people of our barony have long known that my health be failing, and I have come to realize my time to meet God comes shortly. In this matter, I will announce my successor, but first will present the sole remaining person of my blood and heiress to all I possess, my late brother's daughter, the Lady Sybille de Rives."

Sybille, tall and elegantly slender, with flawless white complexion and shimmering pale-blonde hair, dipped her head and smiled at the barony people. As the crowd began to cheer and clap, Alphonse raised a hand for silence. Taking a deep breath, he said, "I announce the betrothal of Lady Sybille to Sir Martin de Coudre. By their marriage, Sir Martin will take my place as Baron of Mirefleurs. May our lands grow richer and our people prosper in peace, in the many years of Baron Martin's just and able leadership to come."

Sybille took Martin's arm and smiled at him, and the joy in the hall could not be contained. Thunderous cheering and clapping erupted, with shouts of "Baron Martin!" and "Baroness Sybille!" Men raised weapons and containers of wine and ale, calling for toast after toast and clashing swords together; women threw flowers and tokens to land at the couple's feet.

Alphonse, exhausted from his efforts, began to sway. Henri helped him back to his chair, then turned to the crowd, his left hand raised. After the hall had grown quiet, he said, "The marriage will take place two weeks hence, in the fortress chapel. The Bishop of Le Puy will bless us with his presence, and will join Sir Martin and Lady Sybille in the sacred bond of Holy Matrimony."

Henri waited as the crowd again voiced applause, and raised his hand. "Our dear Baron Alphonse wishes to declare that on the day of the marriage, his worldly affairs will end, and Sir Martin and Lady Sybille will assume the titles and duties of Baron and Baroness of

Mirefleurs. I will continue in my present position as first advisor, and pray to Holy God that Baron Martin de Coudre will yet listen to me."

The crowd of nobles and commoners laughed at Henri's aside, and again let loose with cheers and toasts. Alphonse sipped at a goblet, tasted the food, and bade Henri and Barnard escort him to his quarters.

+ + +

A heavy snowfall had begun at midafternoon, and Henri advised all to return home. From their seat on a low wall in entry court, Jules, Clovis, and Milon watched the barony people file out through the fortress gateway.

Jules took a long, gurgling swig from a pitcher of ale and wiped his mouth with a dirty sleeve. "I hate that dog's ass Martin de Coudre worse than any damned nobleman. Now he's to be our mighty baron and have all of Alphonse's lands and silver, and old Henri is his first advisor. The Coudres finally have this barony as their own kingdom."

Clovis spat and grabbed the pitcher. "Henri bought that shit Galien his big job on that cathedral with Alphonse's silver, and now Galien's slut from Grand-Forêt is prancing around Troyes like a noblewoman. I still haven't forgotten the day Martin and Galien poured out our ale, to their own God-cursed amusement."

"That's only one of the times they've made fools of us. Thierré still makes us shovel out horse shit when we should be riding patrols. The Devil take the whole Coudre family to rot in Hell."

Jules swayed in his seat, took another long swallow, and looked at Milon. "What's wrong… did Thierré have Otto Huber cut your tongue out?"

"No, simpleton. I just don't care to join you dolts in your curses."

"Well, no surprise in that. Your family has been kissing the Coudres' asses for a hundred years," Clovis said, and in a mocking tone, "You can keep on kissing for a hundred more, but you'll still never get to be a knight."

Milon reddened. "No one in my family kisses anyone's ass. We're honorable people who've worked hard to earn our place and lands."

"Pig shit. Etien was only lucky to be with Martin the day he got Bayard. If I'd kissed up like he did, I might be sitting on coin and a holding."

Milon stood, hand on his sword hilt. "You insult my father, and you fight your way through me first."

Jules nudged Clovis and handed him the pitcher. "Calm down, fool. Etien's a better swordsman than any rich boy knight at the fortress. Don't piss his son off enough to draw on you."

Milon sat and took a drink. "You're thinking with your head instead of your cock for a change, and I'll tell you the truth. You're both lazy drunkards and a disgrace to your excuses for families. Try working a few honest weeks and showing up washed, with your gear in order, for the next couple of patrol days. You might find things begin to look different."

"That's easy enough for you," Jules said. "But those blasted Coudres have it in for Clovis and me and always will. Better to work for a little silver when we need to and have our cocks hard and ready when Lutisse is in the mood to put out."

Clovis roared out a laugh, nearly vomiting.

Milon shot them a disgusted look. "I've known you two all of my life and still call you friends, but you're headed for more trouble than I, or anyone else, can fix. You'll have no one to blame but yourselves when Otto Huber puts the nooses around your necks."

He climbed onto his horse, reined him toward the gate, and left his disgruntled companions to their wine. Clovis and Jules were drunken fools, but of one thing they'd spoken truly. Very likely, he'd never be given a chance to become a knight.

Chapter 30

7 April 1095, Fortress Mirefleurs

As Thierré and Jean Loudon waited on their horses outside the fortress gate, Thierré spotted Roger riding north on Route de Voleurs. "He's here on time. Ready to go?"

"I'm always ready for hunting," Jean said. "What few beasts and birds might await this time of year, let them come." Jean scratched his falcon's hooded head and looked to his bow and quiver of arrows.

Thierré patted his steel-headed boar spear, grinning, and they nudged their horses down the trail. The three knights set off toward the south and turned east at the first crossroads, toward open meadows and forest pathways.

"I'm happy to see you good men again. It's been a while," Roger said.

"You've been a slave in that quarry since Martin became baron. Jean and I've been about our regular duties."

"Slaves don't get paid in silver by the bagful. How goes it at the border?"

Thierré shrugged. "Trade in Grand-Forêt has picked up with the nice weather. Jean's assigned more men to the patrols, and all's quiet and peaceful."

"No disputes between you and Martin?"

"Why should there be? I don't give a dead rat for his and Father's load of work, and Sybille gets all of Martin's attention anyway. In any event, I've my own coin in plenty now and don't intend to stay around here forever."

"That reminds me," Roger said, "The priest in charge of the archbishop's silver passed on some news of interest when I delivered stone to Vienne two weeks ago. Pope Urban held chair over a Church meeting at Piacenza in early March. Thousands came, of all stations."

"Piacenza? That's a good ways south into Italy."

"Word travels fast in the Church."

"So it does," Thierré said. "What is the news, then?"

"The Emperor of the Greeks is worried about the Turks that sent the Greek armies packing in 1071 and took most of their territory south of the Black Sea. He sent diplomats to ask the pope to gather a thousand knights from France and send them to Constantinople to make a show of force."

"To scare the Turks out of crossing the waters and invading?"

"Yes. His Holiness was concerned and told them that he'd think on it, but made no promises."

Thierré grunted. "Let the Greeks fight their own battles. With Bayard and Gautier but three miles away, I'm busy enough."

Jean whistled, pointing to a flock of game birds flying low over a meadow. The knights loosed the ties on their falcons' hoods and rode at a fast canter toward the prey.

26 October 1095, Grand-Forêt

At cold nightfall, Thierré called the patrol men to a halt before the Grand-Forêt tavern and dismissed them. He turned to Roger. "Will Alisende allow you a drink with her loose brother?"

"She'll have no suspicions. It's too late to make it to Mont-Brison."

The knights handed off their horses to the stableboy. In the public room, they took a table near the fire, and the serving girl on duty came to take their order. "I've not seen you before." Thierré said. "Are you newly hired here?"

"Yes, my lord."

"Your name?"

"Jenise, my lord."

"Jenise, I'm Thierré de Coudre, and with me, Sir Roger de Lyon. We're regulars on patrol in this district."

Jenise curtsied and smiled. "I'm pleased to serve you, my lords."

"And we to meet you."

She took their order and walked away. Roger said, "You didn't flirt with her. I'm impressed by your newfound self-control."

"I must tell you the truth. What Baldwin dealt has weakened me, and this afternoon in cold winds and sleet only made the pain in my leg worse. Tonight, a roll with a girl is the last thing on my mind."

Jenise brought their order. Thierré took a long drink of his wine. "I must say, this does make the leg feel a bit better."

A man in a long cloak approached the table, the deep hood shadowing his face. "Sirs, might I have a word?"

Thierré looked up. "When I speak to a man, I prefer to see him." The man pulled back his hood and unfastened the cloak to reveal distinguished features and expensive dress. Only a dagger hung at his belt.

Thierré leaned back and stared at him. "Should we know you? If you're one of Gautier's men, you have a count of ten to get on your horse and ride fast to that border. This wine is good, and I'd rather have another goblet than trouble to take off your head."

Roger topped off Thierré's goblet and said, "Go easily, Brother. I recognize this knight and believe he is here in friendship. Join us for some wine, Sir?"

"I will, and thank you, Sir Roger. Sir Thierré, your caution is to be admired."

Thierré nodded and the tension broke. Roger waved to Jenise, who brought a fresh pitcher of wine and set out a goblet for the stranger.

He took a drink before he spoke. "My name is Renauld d'Evreux. I'm the only son of Olivier d'Evreux, Count Bayard's brother. Gautier is my first cousin and seven years my junior."

Thierré exhaled slowly. "How do you know Sir Roger and me?"

"When Sir Roger came into this tavern the day you and your men surprised Gautier's patrol and took our horses and weapons, he showed admirable diplomacy and restraint in his attempts to reason with Gautier."

Thierré took a drink, licked his lips, and smiled broadly. "That was indeed a good day for our company. Please tell Sir Gautier that his prized stallion is getting the best of care in my stable. Your own horse found an excellent home with one of our younger knights."

Renauld laughed, in good spirit, at Thierré's painful jab. "It was not a good day for any of us, least of all, Gautier. My uncle let him molder in the dungeon for a month and then laid two dozen lashes on him before the assembled knights. Gautier stayed in hospital for two weeks, and was then broken to stable hand for another month."

"I would have given him eight dozen, cut his ears and nose off, and sold what was left to a Mohametan slaver," Thierré pronounced. "Now, Sir Renauld, what is your business here and with us?"

"On that day, I saw Sir Roger as a man I could trust, and signaled him good intentions to the best of my ability. Now that I appear to have the confidence of you both, I'll tell you why."

Renauld paused, and Thierré nodded. "Go on."

"The County of Saint-Lille is rotting from within, and the rot deepens quickly. Many noblemen are sorely displeased with Bayard's cruelty and greed and unceasing dishonorable conduct, yet his family and loyalists who he has made rich and powerful beyond their wildest dreams continue to support him. Our peasants have suffered grievously, first from poor crops, and after, when Bayard neglected to take measures of relief. He lavishes silver on a grand building for the Church, in a city far from our own county, and lets the people struggle."

Renauld looked to Thierré and Roger in turn. "In short, a nobles' revolt fast brews in Saint-Lille, but no leader has come forward, and no unity exists. Right now, fear and distrust rule."

Roger said, "I'm hardly surprised. The news you bring is naught but good for us, yet we can do little, save guard our borders and protect our interests."

"Alphonse was wise to make Sir Thierré's brother his successor," Renauld said.

Thierré spoke. "He could have chosen no better man than Martin. We've able leaders and a strong force of knights and men behind them, and thanks be to that fool Gautier, the border is secured. I think only an event yet unforeseen will create the conditions needed for the overthrow of Bayard and his loyalists."

"As do I," Renauld said. "I approached you only hoping to begin friendly and discreet discussion. You have my word, no person in the County of Saint-Lille, save my father, will know of this meeting."

"Very well, Sir Renauld. We buy your story and welcome further talk. Our enmity has been going on for more than half a century. For the few civil words exchanged in that time, the County of Saint-Lille might as well be India to us, and the time for a change has come."

"I'm pleased, Sir Thierré, as my father will be."

"Now, some rules," Thierré said. "All meetings between us are to take place on our home ground. You are to come alone, dressed and armed only as you are tonight. What person can we all trust?"

"Rixende, the daughter of this inn's owner. She is fully loyal to your barony and has my trust. Say Renauld to her, and you can rest certain I will appear at the time you wish."

"Agreed. Messages from both sides will be sent through Rixende. Sir Roger, have you anything else?"

"For now, this should stay only between the two of us, and either can meet Sir Renauld alone, if need be."

The three knights nodded in agreement. Renauld pulled the cloak over his shoulders and fastened it. "We are understood, good Sirs. I'm grateful to you for hearing me out."

Thierré held up a hand. "Before you leave, I've another question. Why were you in Gautier's company at our previous encounter?"

"Gautier's father asked me to ride with his patrols and keep him out of trouble, and I had succeeded until that day. At a hundred yards from the border, he set his horse to a gallop and signaled his men to follow. They couldn't disobey his orders, and I had no choice but to follow and try to keep him in line."

"That's the truth, Thierré," Roger said. "Sir Renauld ordered Gautier to come out front and speak to you before a tense situation could turn deadly."

"All right, Sir Renauld. We'll extend our trust to you. But don't forget that either of us can take a man's head off in an eyeblink."

Renauld reddened at Thierré's last jab, but said calmly, "You won't find that necessary, Sir Thierré." He turned smartly and left the tavern by the back door.

Wine and food finished, Thierré and Roger mounted up and rode in wind and sleet toward the fortress.

"Well?" Roger said.

"He's not lying, and it's all on our terms. He doesn't know our minds any more than before he approached us."

"We made our position of strength clear."

"We did, and though Gautier's had his teeth filed, we still know the trouble the bastard is capable of starting. I'll tell Jean we need more men for the regular patrols."

"You know Rixende, and I don't, Thierré. I can only assume you consider her worthy of our trust."

"I've known her since I began riding patrols and had a few good rolls in her bed. I don't doubt she and Renauld are lovers now."

Roger shook his head. "Thierré, when are you going to settle down?"

"When a woman who can tame me comes along, but I doubt such a lady lives."

"Perhaps not. Baldwin de Betancourt knocked you around some, but you're still a most unruly beast."

They turned at the junction to Route de Voleurs. Thierré reined his horse to a halt at the path to the fortress gate.

"Goodnight, Roger. I know better than to ask you up for more wine. With young Henri here, and you out at the border late in cold and sleet, Alisende's no doubt tearing her hair out or looking for a war axe to take to you."

Roger laughed. "The second possibility is the more likely. It's time to get home, and in a hurry." He waved goodbye and rode off at a gallop down Route de Voleurs.

Chapter 31

1 November 1095, Fortress Mirefleurs

Henri de Coudre sat at Alphonse's bedside, watching him as he took his morning meal. At forty-eight years, the former Baron of Mirefleurs was but a haggard, greenish-skinned shadow of the robust, energetic man of but five years past. Servants took away the remnants of the breakfast and Henri stayed with Alphonse.

Alphonse spoke. "What news do you have for me this morning, Henri?"

"High churchmen from all of France are to come for a conference at the cathedral in Clermont, three weeks hence. His Holiness Pope Urban will hold chair at the meetings, and then the Holy Father will make a public address, in a meadow outside the town walls. He has asked that noblemen and men-at-arms of all stations come and hear him."

"That's certainly not ordinary news. Will he speak of the Mohametan Turks that threaten the Greeks and harass Christian pilgrims in the Holy Land?"

"I think that is his purpose."

"Then I will go."

Henri rubbed his temples. "The journey by wagon will take nearly two days each way. I'd worry terribly for you."

"I have never before been in the presence of a pope, and I'll attend. I don't care if it kills me."

"To see the Holy Father and hear his words will be a blessing without equal for all of us. I shouldn't discourage you."

"I can live through a two-day ride in a decent wagon. If I don't, at least my last journey will have had a godly purpose. If there's a man who needs such, it is me."

"Consider it done, old friend. I'll make all the arrangements."

26 November 1095, Clermont

At Thierré's signal, the barony party halted with the line of mounted travelers. A hundred yards ahead, guards directed groups, in turn, onto a path to the grounds beyond the main road. He turned to Martin. "We've a wait."

"I'm sore in the ass and ready to walk for a while."

They dismounted and led their horses to the edge of the road. The shoulder sloped gently down to a broad meadow, golden with late autumn. A mile away, the church and guard towers of Clermont rose above the ground mists of early morning. Henri, Roger, and Jean joined them.

Thierré watched the line of people, horses, and wagons stream to the center of the meadow. Canopied and bannered tents already stood in orderly rows, and as noblemen's wagons arrived, men jumped off and began, without delay, to add to the small city. He chuckled when he noticed that while the nobles were forced to wait their turn to be directed by guards to suitable places for their flamboyant tents, commoners and poor peasants, not so burdened by possessions, ignored the guards and climbed off the main road to freely choose places for their own haphazard camps.

"Best we look in on Alphonse," Thierré said.

Martin nodded. They walked to the enclosed wagon that had carried the ailing old baron for the two-day journey over rough roads. Inside the well-appointed conveyance, Alphonse was sitting up in his bed, taking light food and wine. He looked at his successor with good-humored contempt. "I told you I'm not going to die until I've seen the pope. Do something useful."

"We only wanted to tell you we've arrived at Clermont, Sire," Martin said.

"You've told me. Go and send Henri here. I'd share breakfast with him."

Thierré shut the carriage door behind them. A whistle sounded. He looked toward the road cutoff, and the guard beckoning with an upraised hand.

"It's our turn. Let's move ahead."

They mounted and nudged their horses to a slow walk. "Alphonse barked at us, but he still looks like he's been to Hell," Martin said.

"If he makes it through the morrow, I'll be the first to credit the pope with a miracle."

As the sun moved low, the pleasant late autumn afternoon turned damp and cold. Thierré, Martin, Jean, and Roger put on cloaks and strolled about the grounds in search of wine and conversation. Though rumors of a renewed Turkish threat to the Empire of the Greeks and atrocities against Christian pilgrims enroute to and from Jerusalem, had fast spread throughout France after the Piacenza meeting in March, the barony contingent came across no knight or nobleman who could state with certainty whether Pope Urban had called attention to these matters during the previous days of Church conferences in Clermont. After an evening of talk and drinks, they returned to the barony tents, drowsy with wine and food, but little wiser to the pope's intentions.

In the matter of sleeping quarters, the young Baron of Mirefleurs and his three leading noblemen deferred to their elders. In the luxuriously furnished central tent, they bade Alphonse, Père Barnard, and the other elder noblemen goodnight and God's blessings, then took their bedrolls into the austere soldiers' tent and bundled up for the cold night.

27 November 1095, Clermont

Thierré, Martin, and Roger stepped out at midmorning and walked the thirty-foot aisle of grass that separated the rows of noblemen's tents and led to the raised dais from which the pope would speak.

Thirty yards from the barony tents, the banners of the County of Saint-Lille proclaimed the presence of Count Bayard and his sons. Thierré glared and clenched his teeth. Martin put a hand on his brother's sword arm and shook his head.

Thierré took an exaggerated bow. "Have no cause for unease, my liege. Any murder you require will be carried out with the utmost discretion."

"I don't want anyone murdered, dolt. All I ask is that you stay well clear of Gautier. This is a holy occasion, and I'll not have our barony's reputation stained by your bad temper."

Roger nudged Thierré, pointing to tables set up for men-at-arms. "Food."

Martin smiled. "The surest way to calm a restless beast is to fill his stomach. Let's have this one well stuffed before he can go on a rampage."

They took seats at a long trestle table and heaped the soldiers' breakfast onto wooden platters. Thierré ate and sipped small ale, watching fascinated as workmen erected canopies of ornate cloth, lugged heavy carved chairs, and set up a throne, canopied with rich red cloth embroidered with silver and gold, for the pope.

Sated with the solid food, Martin, Thierré, and Roger returned to the tent. Martin glanced at Thierré. "Feeling all right, Brother?"

"If Gautier comes near me, I'll kiss him."

Roger laughed. "I think he's calmed enough to let out of his cage."

Thierré belted on his sword and Martin paled. "Just keep your hands off of that."

+ + +

As the hour of the pope's address drew nearer, a warmer wind blew in and drove away the bone-chilling damp. In the crisp late morning air, beneath a cloudless sky, Thierré didn't need his cloak. When the sun had risen to its highest point, the Bishop of Clermont's guardsmen rode between the rows of tents, calling, "All gather, for His Holiness the Pope is soon to speak."

Thierré joined the barony men in the crowd, moving toward the dais. He and Martin helped Alphonse to the high-backed benches set up for frail nobles and clergy, then returned to stand with their fellows. Humbler folk took places where they pleased, and their betters made no objection.

The pope's procession approached on the path leading from the gates of Clermont and turned to halt before the dais. There, distinctively uniformed guards took places beside the door to an ornate barrel-roofed carriage, and Pope Urban II stepped out.

A fit man of fifty-four years, he waved off assistance, took his seat on the canopied throne, and pulled back his gold-trimmed hood to reveal strong features and close-cropped grey hair. A bishop placed the domed crown of the papacy on his head.

Urban rose and made the sign of the cross with his right hand. All present kneeled as the pope raised his eyes to Heaven and said the Pater Noster, then stood as he lifted both hands to shoulder height, palms upward. He turned to the bishop and grimaced. The richly robed cleric stepped forward, took the heavy crown, and replaced it with a mitre covered with embroidered cloth-of-gold.

The pope took his place at the lectern at the front of the dais, warming to the audience with a self-deprecating anecdote. His style of speech was pleasing and disarming, yet powerful, and could be heard by all. He surveyed the crowd, giving extra scrutiny to the high noblemen who stood in the first ranks, and began his address. "Most beloved brethren, I, Urban, who by the permission of God am Chief Bishop and Prelate over the whole world, would extend our own welcome and blessings to all of you."

Applause and cheers followed. The pope raised a hand for quiet. "Oh, race of Franks, race beloved and chosen by God, set apart from all other nations by the situation of your country, as well as by your Catholic faith and the honor which you render to the Holy Church, to you our discourse is addressed. For you, our exhortations are intended, but we would first speak a divine admonition to you."

The noblemen glanced at each other, nodding agreement, looking satisfied with themselves. Urban swept a rigid forefinger over them and spoke sharply. "Think that I praise the rulers who stand here before me? I am told you are so weak in your exercise of justice that those who would have safety on the roads of your provinces fall victim to robbers by day and night, and your knights and men-at-arms are but servants of your own avarice, warring with your neighbors. Therefore, I reenact the Truce of God, proclaimed long ago by our Holy Fathers, but for as long a time, shamefully cast into disregard. I exhort and demand of each of you that you keep the truce in your demesnes. If any man would be led by his greed and arrogance to break the truce, by the authority of God, he shall face the penalty of excommunication."

The high noblemen, who had but a few moments earlier looked at their fellows in complacency, now cast around with fearful faces, knowing the pope had seen into their hearts. A muttered discussion ensued among them, and before too long a time had passed, the greatest among them, a mighty count, knelt before the dais and said, "Your Holiness, we give thanks to God you have seen fit to reveal our grievous shortcomings. We would make repentance and a faithful promise that all injustice in our demesnes will be brought to rightness before God, and the truce kept, on penalty of our souls."

Urban looked at him sternly. "Do as you now promise, and by God's grace, your mistakes will be forgiven."

After Urban had heard and made judgment on other matters of faith and law, he again took the lectern. "Now that you have heard our words of correction and made firm promises to keep peace among yourselves, I have also come to warn you of the gravest danger to all of Christendom."

The crowd grew hushed, with full attention focused on the pope. "The same Mohametan Turks who wrested vast territories from the Empire of the Greeks twenty-four years past again show signs of warlike intent toward our Christian brothers in the East, and at this very moment, pose a direct threat to the ancient and holy city of Constantinople. The Emperor Alexios has requested I call upon the arms-bearing men of France to join in a mission of utmost consequence that will, at the least, thwart these pagan Turks in any scheme to make a westward invasion, and at the greatest, drive them out of the Christian lands they now occupy."

Thierré, drowsy after the heavy breakfast, came to full attention. The pope's words had struck a loud note in his warrior's mind.

Urban's voice rose. "These Turks have killed and captured many Christians, and have destroyed churches and devastated the Empire of the Greeks. If this be permitted to continue, the faithful of God will be much more widely attacked by them, and their first objective will be to take Constantinople. Such a conquest would provide them a firm base from which to invade and conquer the lands that lie westward, such as yours, in our own France. All Christian nations might well be reduced, and the eleven hundred years of progress made by Christ's faith destroyed."

The wind gusted cold and hard. Urban turned to the churchmen in his retinue. The crowd again grew restive, murmuring in nervous excitement. Thierré looked around. Count Bayard stood immersed in Urban's words, his younger son, Evrard, beside him at respectful attention. Gautier's expression evidenced only boredom and cynical disdain.

Urban, warmed by a cup of wine, plunged into greater detail. "The caliphs of the Turks can hardly be called men. Indeed, they are demons of the blackest heart. Those many Christians who dwell within the cities and lands ruled by their armies of mindless fiends inhabit a living Hell on Earth. Though I can hardly voice the atrocities and injustices inflicted on innocent Christian pilgrims, who seek only to visit the birthplace and lands of our Lord, I must do so. The Turks are masters of the cruelest tortures; of certainty, the servants of Hell have no greater skill. With swords, they split the bellies of peaceful Christian men, children, and women with child, in search of gold and jewels. They violate Christian men with circumcision and pour the blood thereof on altars and into baptismal fonts."

As the Pope continued to speak of Mohametan atrocities, Thierré's stomach clenched in anger and tears clouded his eyes. He glanced at those standing near to him. Tears streamed down battle-scarred faces, and hardened men of all ranks wept openly or cursed under their breath. Though Urban spoke aloud to all present, he also spoke inwardly and privately to Thierré de Coudre.

Urban paused for a long minute, appraising his audience with a hard, piercing gaze, then slammed a fist on the lectern. He voiced his next words with great force. "Noblemen and knights of France, though you call yourselves Christians, by your warring without cease, and murder of innocents beyond count in your greed for lands and treasure, you have placed your souls in utmost peril. But you may yet find redemption, by way of the very prowess you so gravely misuse."

Noblemen shifted uncomfortably, and Urban again slammed the lectern. "Let those who have been robbers in the guise of knights now truly become knights. Let those who have been fighting against their brothers and relatives now fight in a proper way against the infidels. The time has come for you, who have been wearing your very selves out in body and soul, to draw together as brothers-in-arms and in Christ. Be you thus united, you will reclaim Christian lands long lost, and if God so wills, drive the enemies of Christ from the most sacred place in Christendom, the blessed city of Jerusalem."

Urban drew breath and stretched out his arms. "I challenge every capable man of the sword, knight or foot soldier, to give his life to this holy mission. Die you on the way, whether by land or sea, or in battle with the pagans, by the power of God with which I am invested, you shall gain remission of all sin and the keys to the eternal Kingdom of God. Any person who wishes to take vows and enter Christ's army, step forward and do so."

The audience stood astounded and silent. Urban urged them. "Willing Christians, do not hesitate. The time grows shorter, and those who would go ought not put off the journey, but need rent their lands and collect the funds for their expenses. As soon as winter is over and spring comes, let them be ready to eagerly set out on the way, with God as their guide. Such is His own will."

Urban blessed them once more and returned to his chair. A richly robed bishop doffed his miter and knelt before the pontiff, bowing his head with hands together, in an attitude of prayer. The pope put his hands on the bishop's head, speaking quietly. He made the sign of the cross and the bishop stood.

The bishop took the lectern and spoke. "I am Adhémar, Bishop of Le Puy, and I have taken a vow to do as His Holiness Pope Urban has directed. His Holiness has asked me to represent him for the remainder of this meeting, freely giving the same vow to all who would take it. Those who would join Christ's army now, step forward and receive the keys to the Kingdom of Heaven. God wills it!"

The crowd caught up the cry, thundering "God Wills It! God Wills It!"

Fully half of the noblemen and knights, and a great number of men-at-arms and common people, crowded to the dais. Women asked to take the vow alongside their men, and at more than one thousand, the number of volunteers far exceeded expectations. The scores of Church officials who had shared the dais with the pope waded into the crowd and began to hear the vow of each person, individually. High churchmen took the cloaks off of their shoulders, giving them to monks and women, telling them to cut the rich cloth into as many small crosses as could be made.

Thierré's own will, and an infinitely greater one, pulled him forward. He fell to his knees before the dais. As Bishop Adhémar spoke the vow to him, he repeated: "I vow to henceforth fight as a soldier of Christ unto death or safe return, to worship at the Holy Sepulcher, and to wear the cross in full view until my vow be fulfilled."

Adhémar pinned a cross to the right shoulder of his gambeson, put both hands on his head, and said, "Hold firmly to the vow you have taken, and your sins will all be forgiven. Go now, join your brother knights in Christ's army, and sin no more."

Adhémar moved to the next man, and Thierré rose to his feet. Count Bayard knelt in the grass, enraptured; his younger son, Evrard, knelt beside him. Gautier stood in place, arms crossed, dark and surly expression unchanged. He caught Thierré's eye and sneered. More volunteers patiently waited to take their vows, and, after all were sworn, a cleric stepped to the lectern and announced, "All kneel for His Holiness."

The pope took the lectern. "You are now soldiers of Christ and sworn to his service only. Go and prepare for the duty with which God has charged you." Again, Urban said the Pater Noster with the greatest of devotion, and then raised his palms upward in a magnanimous gesture of blessing. The volunteers rose in unison and, to a man, turned to watch him step off the dais, toward his waiting carriage.

Thierré cast his eyes on the barony party. The young knight Guy Robard, Robert of Coudre Estate, three men-at-arms, and elder knight Walter d'Avesnes had also taken the vow.

Guy Robard joined Thierré to support Alphonse for the walk back to the barony tents and lead him to his bed. All of the men who could fit into Alphonse's tent gathered around the dying man.

Alphonse looked at Martin and said, breath rasping, "Baron Martin de Coudre, sit next to me."

"Yes, Sire." Martin picked up a stool and set it at the head of Alphonse's bed.

"Martin, I will not live to see the morning, and I would tell you my wishes for burial."

Martin motioned for Henri, Walter, and Père Barnard to come close and witness. "Continue, Sire Alphonse," he said.

"My body is to be buried in the chapel yard at Fortress Mirefleurs, next to my wife and son. The burial Mass will be said by Père Barnard, and you and Sybille, your father, and Walter, alone, are to attend. The marker is to be inscribed only with my name and years of birth and death, and the words *Operibus Anteire*."

"Your wishes are our law, Sire," Martin said. "Can you tell me the meaning of the phrase to be inscribed?"

"What I have done my whole life, speak with actions rather than words."

Martin's gripped Alphonse's forearm. "Your actions have been our examples to follow, Sire. I can think of no better words with which to honor you."

Alphonse raised himself on an elbow, his pain of body apparent. "I chose well in you, Martin."

Henri lowered the dying lord's head to the pillows. With a breath approaching a gasp, Alphonse said, "All save Walter, Henri, and Barnard, leave me."

+ + +

The sky dimmed with coming evening, and the cooks had boar stew, bread, and cheese ready. The barony men ate with few words, and sipped at their ale as the wind blew colder. After an hour, the two elder knights and Barnard walked out of Alphonse's tent.

"He has passed. God rest his soul," Barnard announced.

"God rest his soul," each man repeated, in his own time. A swordsman took a flute from his satchel and began to play a slow, haunting tune. The men around the fires raised cups and joined voices, in remembrance of the just baron who had long led them with honor.

Chapter 32

28 November 1095, Clermont

By midmorning, the noblemen's camps had broken. Mounted men and wagons moved out of the meadow and onto the main road in slow procession. Henri, Roger, Thierré, and Martin walked at ease beside the wagon bearing Alphonse's body as the caravan inched along.

They halted in their tracks as a group of men stepped from between wagons ahead. Count Bayard and his brother, Olivier, walked toward them and stopped at twenty paces; Gautier, Evrard, and a knight stood behind them. Martin put his hand on Thierré's sword arm.

Bayard stepped forward to face Henri, and said, "Please accept our sympathies, Henri. God has surely taken Alphonse's soul to eternal rest."

"That's very kind of you, Bayard. In turn, accept our sincere thanks."

Henri and Bayard bowed their heads in polite parting. Henri held up his hand to signal a continued halt as Roger, Martin, and Thierré exchanged amazed glances. Bayard and Olivier turned in front of a wagon and stepped out of sight.

Gautier, Evrard, and the knight halted at forty paces. The knight bent to inspect a cracked wagon wheel. Gautier turned around and raised a hand. "Thierré! Now that we're on good terms, I can give you news of your brother Galien."

"God save us all," Martin said, tightening his grip on Thierré's sword arm.

Gautier grinned wide. "Joseph of Reims is a sodomite, and I've reliable word that your brother serves as his catamite."

Thierré tore away from Martin, hand on his sword hilt. Roger held an arm in front of him, but he pushed past and stepped toward Gautier. "Gautier, every time you speak, more shit drops from your dog's ass of a mouth."

Gautier's grin grew broader. "I haven't told you all. Ulrich married Galien to that common whore for the sake of Joseph's reputation."

Thierré's face turned pale white, and Gautier said, beaming, "Your little piss of a brother is Joseph's favorite bitch."

Steel sang as Thierré drew his sword from the scabbard. "Gautier, you've a count of three to get on your knees and beg your apology, but don't hurry. I've been waiting for years to cut your legs out from under you."

Gautier dropped his grin, drew his own sword, and took stance. He pointed the blade at Thierré, saying, "Here's your chance, Coudre. But I'll only take your hands and cods, and not kill you."

In one motion, Thierré raised his blade high, stepped forward, and swung down. Steel clanged as Gautier deflected the blow, but the force staggered him. Thierré drew his sword right for a lethal sideswing, and Roger grabbed his wrist with a crushing grip. "Both of you stand down, now!"

Evrard and the knight caught Gautier by the arms and held him back. Gautier glared at Roger. "You're out of line, saddle boy."

Roger stepped forward and said, "No man speaks of my family in such a foul manner, least of all you, Gautier."

Gautier tore loose from his captors, swiftly pulling his dagger from his belt. Faster than Gautier could make another move, Roger slammed a right fist into his stomach, grabbed him by the hair, and threw him to the ground. Gautier rolled over, slashing wildly with the dagger, and Roger kicked him hard in the ribs. He drew his sword and put the point to Gautier's throat. "Give thanks to God I didn't use this on you, Gautier. You'd be looking the Devil in the face at this very moment."

Evrard and the knight pulled Gautier to his feet. He pointed a rigid finger at Roger and spat, "From this day on, you're a walking corpse, Lyon."

Bayard and Olivier hurried back at the commotion. Bayard addressed his eldest son. "Sir Gautier, clean yourself up and get in line. You've turned this holy occasion into a cursed disgrace." Bayard stared Gautier down until he turned away, and then approached Henri. "Sir Henri, I would apologize."

Henri bowed his head in acceptance, and said, "I think it best we leave two hours apart and take separate routes."

Bayard nodded slowly, mouth clenched in a thin, grim line. "Only God could help us if our parties were to meet on the open road."

"You leave first and take the northern road. We can make it to the inn on the southern route before sundown."

"Agreed," Bayard said. He walked back to Gautier, stood before him for a moment, and turned away, shaking his head in mighty disgust.

+ + +

The sun reached its highest point in the cold blue sky. Bayard turned around and motioned his sons to ride at each side of him. "Gautier, I trust your temper has cooled enough for civil conversation?"

Gautier didn't look at his father. "Yes, Sire."

"You made fools of all of us."

"I did, Sire."

"I'm glad you realize that, and you'd best give thanks to God that you're still alive." Gautier reddened but didn't reply. Bayard slapped the back of his head. "You don't remember Roger de Lyon's name from Vézelay? What kind of simpleton are you?"

"Father, you supplied wine and food and women for the young knights who proved themselves. Thierré and I were too drunk and... busy to remember much of anything."

Bayard chuckled and nodded. "Point well made, Son. You and Thierré were brothers-in-arms for that one day, and all of you earned your honors and your good time with your courage and blood."

"So, what's the problem with Roger de Lyon? All I know is he married Thierré's sister."

"A very big problem. Confront him again, and you'll find yourself speaking your next words in Hell."

"He's a man of reputation?"

"I'll tell you firsthand, Roger de Lyon is the Devil's own swordsman. After Peter de Villiers made his breakout charge at

Vézelay, Roger's horse fell to a lance, but that didn't faze him a whit. He kept fighting on foot, with a sword in his right hand and an axe in his left, and killed nearly every man in twoscore feet around him. After the battle was over, he hailed a peasant, and gave him a bagful of silver for his donkey and cart. Then, he stripped the men he'd killed of their best weapons and gear, and piled it in. He also took a wealthy knight yet alive and held him for a weighty ransom. That was the beginning of the fortune he's gained since."

Gautier turned pale. "Shit."

"Just don't make the same mistake again, and be thankful Thierré has as bad a temper as you do. If Roger had drawn on you instead, he'd have killed you with the first stroke."

Bayard took a package of bread and cheese and a sealed pitcher of wine from his saddlebag and passed them to his sons. They rode companionably, talking of lighter subjects as they ate and drank. Finished with the respite, Bayard again became serious. "Now that Evrard and I have made vows that will take us away for years, I've come to important decisions."

Gautier and Evrard awaited their father's next words in silence.

"On our arrival home, immediate affairs will require a halfscore days of me. After those are completed, I'm going to make a fast ride to Troyes for a visit to the cathedral. I plan to be gone for no more than three weeks. While I'm away, Viscount Odo will govern in my place. Understood?"

The brothers glanced at each other, nodding approval. "Understood, Father," Evrard said.

"Now, let us speak of the holy expedition. Evrard, you are my second son, but are worthy of an inheritance to match your brother's. If God wills we gain lands in the East, you will have holdings and riches there."

"That's kind and generous of you, Father."

Bayard looked at Gautier. "You will not join any expeditions or campaigns, but remain at home until, by God's grace, Evrard and I return. Viscount Odo will take the duties of count in my absence. You are to obey him, assist him in governance, and stay out of trouble."

Gautier ground his teeth. "Father, you dishonor me. As your eldest son and heir, I should have those duties."

TO SHINE WITH HONOR

"You should indeed, but your foolish actions at Grand-Forêt three years ago, and your unforgivable repeat of those actions this morning, have cost you that privilege. One act of misbehavior while we're away will cost you the office of Count of Saint-Lille, and it will go to your brother."

Gautier rode on, teeth clenched and reins gripped tight, as Bayard continued. "Don't even think to disobey me and join an expedition for the East. If you do so and come home alive, you'll be lucky to inherit a broken-down horse and saddle." Gautier scowled and galloped ahead, cursing.

Bayard turned to Evrard. "Son, I meant what I said to Gautier. I'm praying he'll quiet down and mature while we're away, but if that doesn't come to pass, you will succeed me as Count of Saint-Lille."

Evrard cast a questioning glance. "Father, you'd truly deny your first son his patrimony?"

"The needs of our county come first, and I'm still enough in my right mind to have planned ahead. The Duke of Aquitaine has agreed that if Gautier proves unfit, you are to have my office."

"Beatrice's father paid you a heavy dowry to gain an alliance and make her a future countess. He'd be more than angry."

Bayard nodded thoughtfully, pulled the silver stopper from his rich leather wine skin, took a swig, and handed it to Evrard. "He's a good friend, and I owe him a debt of honor, but if I'm dead, he'll be your problem."

+ + +

The barony party left the Clermont grounds at noon, a safe two hours behind and five miles away from the Saint-Lille delegation. Martin, Roger, and Thierré rode abreast at the head of the line.

"Brother, I knew you were gone the moment the pope made his call," Martin said to Thierré.

Thierré's face took on a lustre Martin had never seen before. "I've waited years unknowing for that call, and could not deny it when it came, by God's own Grace. Though my wounds are still troublesome, I need embrace my knight's duties in full measure, and give my life and sword to the greatest cause of our time."

269

Martin looked askance at his brother, chuckling. "The sinner most prolific has now become a saint, but we more humble souls need keep our homelands safe and ready for his return."

"Martin, I've long needed another man equal to you at the quarry," Roger said.

"The quarry is all yours, Roger. Begin to search without delay, and hire the best man at the salary he wants. We're certain to lose more men to the pope's expedition, and Jean and I will need act fast to recruit replacements. Gautier is waiting like a hungry wolf for Bayard and Evrard to depart."

"Evrard's the one decent man of the three, and a pity he took the cross with Bayard," Thierré said. "No telling what that horse's ass Gautier will stir up without his father to watch him."

"Thierré, your temper is a fair match for Gautier's," Martin observed. "You put on quite a display of it this morning."

Thierré drew his sword and thumbed a razor-sharp edge. "I couldn't stand there and listen to his filthy insults."

Martin shook his head, exasperated. "Put that damned thing away! You need to forget Gautier and save up your bad disposition for the hordes of Turks you'll be fighting."

Thierré sheathed the sword with a thunk. "I can't forget. Why would he say such things about Galien and Lisette and Master Joseph?"

Roger took two bulging skins of wine from his saddle bag. He pulled the stopper from one and tossed the other to Thierré. "Other than a wish to provoke you to attack him, none of us can begin to guess. Take Martin's advice, and let us worry about Gautier. You've plenty of work ahead."

After a few long swigs, Thierré grumbled, "I suppose I have, but knowing the bastard is still on the loose is worse than a bout of the bloody flux."

Martin changed the subject. "You both saw the knight kneeling beside Evrard? He took the cross also."

Roger shrugged. "I did. Is he anyone important?"

"He's Olivier d'Evreux, Bayard's younger brother and Renauld's father."

Thierré guffawed. "He looked a sight more agreeable than his pig of a brother. Hard to believe they had the same mother."

"I think Olivier's in on Renauld's plan to rid Saint-Lille of Bayard," Martin said. "In going to the East, Olivier will leave Renauld to oversee his holdings and men, and a door open to us."

"Wants to do in his own brother, eh?" Roger said.

"Renauld will tell us, soon enough."

"I'm not so sure I want to leave home now. Things are getting too interesting," Thierré quipped.

"I don't think you'll be leaving anytime soon. As yet, the expedition has no leaders or organization. What we saw yesterday may have been the beginning and the end."

+ + +

Waning daylight was turning to cold, dark evening when Thierré woke from his doze. He looked at Martin. "Where are we stopping for the night?"

Martin pointed to lights ahead. "That's the same town where we stayed on the way to Clermont. The inn was more than decent."

Thierré brightened. "It was, indeed. Good food and wine, soft beds, and comely whores in the public room."

Martin needled him. "Thierré, you've joined the ranks of God's saints, remember? You must forsake your ways of habit, I fear."

"I took a vow to fight for God's cause, but He knows a man like me can't live like a monk."

Chapter 33

9 February 1096, Fortress Mirefleurs

At the distant sounds of voices and a crowd's hubbub, Baron Martin de Coudre looked up from the quarry diagrams on his table. Roger de Lyon got up and stepped through the open doorway to the balcony off Martin's quarters. At midday, the sun shone in a cloudless sky; the air unseasonably warm. Roger returned. "It appears Peter the Hermit has arrived, and a fair part of the barony has come out to greet him."

Martin sighed. "Best we join them." He rang his bell, and the guard on duty opened the door. "Yes, my lord?"

"See that our horses are saddled and ready." The guard hurried away.

Martin and Roger walked to the armory court, mounted their waiting horses, and rode through the open fortress gateway. There, they halted for a look at the crowd, and Martin led the way down the hill. On Route de Voleurs, the people parted for their baron and his leading nobleman.

Martin looked around him. Perhaps two hundred men, women, and children of all stations milled about the road, conversing excitedly. They turned as one to the hill, as a donkey bearing a small man climbed a few yards and halted. The man dismounted, faced the people, and slowly swept his eyes over them.

Martin studied him: short and thin, wearing only a soiled, worn monk's habit, carrying a pilgrim's staff with a small earthenware water jug tied at the end. His bare feet were black with dirt, long reddish hair and beard unkempt and unruly. Despite his marked appearance of wretched poverty, his bright, dark eyes demanded full attention.

He looked over the people before him, and said, "I am Peter. On behalf of God and the Holy Father, I have come to speak to you this day and, with all humility, beg you hear my words."

"Speak! Speak!"

Peter raised his arms high, and the crowd hushed. His next words came forth rich with power. "The Kingdom of God is at hand, and the time comes shortly!"

He paused and raised his face to Heaven, again swept his eyes over the audience, and spoke slowly and intimately, "As I speak to you this moment, the hordes of mindless Mohametan fiends so close to Christendom wait for Satan's orders, and innocent Christians are dying the cruelest of deaths at their hands. On the day holy Jerusalem is liberated from these devils, Christ will return to judge the world, but that day will only come by the resolve and blood of Christian warriors. I beseech all who would take up Christ's charge to join in His mighty army. Take the vow the Holy Father has freely offered, be marked with the cross, and gain remission of sin and life eternal! Die you in the holy fight that lies ahead, or live to see Jerusalem liberated, our Lord awaits to open the gates of Heaven for all who hold faithful to their vow."

Martin and Roger sat on their horses, watching and listening as Peter continued his exhortations, looking at each other in amazement at the small man's powers of speech and persuasion. At last, Peter raised his arms, opened his hands wide to Heaven, and cried out loudly, "Come forward! Be not afraid! Come forward! Know that God wills it!"

The crowd caught up the cry, "God Wills It! God Wills It!" A score or more came forward and knelt before Peter. In a scene akin to Clermont, Peter began to give the vow to each. Two monks traveling with him pinned felt crosses to the right shoulders of the volunteers' garments. When all had been sworn and pinned, Peter bade them stand and face the crowd. He embraced each in turn, raised his arms, and spoke in mighty exultation. "Before you stand new saints, freed of sin and earthly obligation and prepared to take their place beside our Lord

Jesus Christ and the Holy Father to destroy the servants of Satan! God Wills It!"

The crowd cheered again and slowly began to drift away. The volunteers stayed with Peter's entourage, listening as he gave teachings. Martin glanced at Roger. They turned their horses onto the path up to the fortress. Otto Huber, who had also watched Peter speak, walked a score of feet ahead, and they reined up beside him.

"You listened, Sergeant Huber?" Martin said.

"I did, Sire. The cause is holy and of great import, but those who choose to follow that madman are fools."

Martin grinned. "Otto, you've not hesitated to speak your mind in all the years I've known you."

"Sire, that mad monk and his band of ragged pilgrims have not one tested leader among them. Given such a lack, they'll march only to certain death; there is no chance they will gain sight of Jerusalem."

"You're right, Sergeant Huber," Roger said. "We just lost three more men-at-arms and can't afford to lose them, or any who might follow. Every man we have stands in awe of your prowess, and you've great influence. Do your best to keep them of sensible mind."

"I will, Sir Roger, but that Peter could charm a wild boar to put on mail and take up a sword."

"Or better, turn Gautier into a toad," Thierré said.

Otto chuckled. "Sir Thierré, I've no worries you can deal handily with Gautier. I only hope we've seen the last of Peter."

Martin and Roger reined their horses up the trail and dismounted in the armory yard. They took seats on a low wall. "Roger, it's good you spoke to Huber as you did," Martin said. "Do the same with the knights and men-at-arms and the men at the quarry, and I'll call a meeting for the farmers and the leaders from all of our villages. We're bleeding people from the barony's every vein to Peter and his ilk. It's beginning to show in produce and revenue, to say nothing of our strength at arms."

After he and Martin parted, Roger went straight to the armory. In the arming room, he found retainer Thomas Bergier. The pious middle-aged widower, who had entered service to Baron Alphonse four years earlier, was taking weapons and equipment from his storage place.

"Thomas, you're leaving us?"

The loyal knight nodded. "I am, Roger."

"You were in the crowd watching Peter, but you didn't come forward."

"I needed but a short time to think and pray. I'll ride south today and catch up with Peter's party."

"Think on it longer. Thierré would be happy to have you riding under his banner."

"Thierré and I talked about it after Clermont, and I'd thought to join him, but Peter's people have the greater want. They know nothing of warfare and sorely need experienced knights."

"That's selfless of you and a credit to our calling."

"After hearing the Holy Father at Clermont and Peter today, I know I only want to use the gifts God gave me in service of my brothers and sisters in Christ."

"I'll not try to dissuade you. Have you told Jean you're leaving?"

"I have. He discharged me with honor and gave me my pay due."

Roger took a heavy bag of coins from his belt purse and handed it to him. Thomas bowed his head. "You're too generous, Roger. But I'm only a poor knight and accept your gift with gratitude."

"Is there anything else I can do for you?"

"My second son watches over the family lands, between Clermont and Limoges. I need send word to him."

"Thierré will pen a letter for you and make certain he gets it. You only need ask."

"Thank you, Roger. My years here have been good ones."

"You'll be missed, Sir Thomas. Go with God, and if He wills you return, your place here will once again be yours to take."

26 May 1096, Fortress Mirefleurs

A man-at-arms entered the arming room. "My lord, the baron has asked to see you, in his quarters."

Thierré didn't look up from the weapons before him. "He'll have to wait a short while."

"I'll let him know, my lord."

Thierré set his sword on the work table, scrubbed his begrimed hands in a table basin, and picked a falchion from his newly polished collection of weapons and armor. He held up the blade to catch the light and thumbed the sharp edge. Satisfied with the morning's work, he set it down and went to meet Martin.

"Come in, Brother."

Thierré took a chair in Martin's quarters and poured a goblet from the wine flagon.

"Have you heard the latest news?" Martin said. Thierré shrugged.

"The mob that gathered at Cologne left for the East on the twentieth. Peter the Hermit ignored Pope Urban's last plea and bade them march ahead. None of the knights riding with them could convince Peter to bide his time."

"Twenty thousand poor and gullible people," Thierré said. "They'll come to no good end."

"I can't help but agree with you. How go your own plans?"

"Raymond of Saint-Gilles is beginning to gather an army of southern French. I've been thinking to join with him."

Martin stroked his beard. "As will Bayard and Evrard, I expect."

"Old Bayard seems to have become more peaceful. I still scratch my head when I think on his courtesy to Father after Alphonse died, and he's made no trouble since."

"No doubt he's appointed Gautier to the post of head troublemaker, while he puts on a face of reform for the expedition."

"I've had to put Gautier and his insults to rest. Don't stop watching your own back."

Martin stared out the open balcony doors. "Jean has proven his worth as marshal. He has my full confidence."

"I noticed some new faces, last training day."

"Jean's recruited fresh men-at-arms, but we've lost knights and I'm hard put to find replacements."

"Perhaps it's time to raise the best men-at-arms to knighthood," Thierré said. "You and Jean and Roger can continue to search for noblemen."

"I thought of that, but like with women, I'm awfully choosy."

"And you proved wise to forsake them until Sybille came along, brother Martin. I've had another thought. Clovis and Jules didn't take the cross, like I hoped they would. Why not sentence them to it, next time the patrol arrests them for making mischief?"

"Tempting, but I've vowed to uphold the highest standards of justice. For those two, it would be a death sentence. They're but shiftless drunks, not criminals."

Thierré leaned back, grinning. "That's why you need men of no scruples. Give me the word, and they'll vanish into the forest for good."

Martin shook his head. "I've no more doubt the expedition is the best place for you. The Turks won't have a chance." He took a heavy green bag and a document from his desk and set them before Thierré. "I tried to get you to invest more in the quarry, but you've done well, nevertheless."

Thierré read the document and hefted the bag of coins. "I knew you and Roger were getting rich, but I didn't expect my paltry five livres to turn into thirty."

"I thought this to be the best time for you to take your profits. Business has begun to slow. Your share might only be worth half that in a month."

"God bless you, brother. Other than the ten livres I gave Galien and Lisette when they were married, I still have all of the silver Alisende paid me for Coudre Estate, and she continues to pay the balance out of her earnings from the quarry. With this added, I'll be able to gather a company under my banner that a son of Count Raymond would be hard put to match."

31 May 1096, the County of Saint-Lille

Evrard of Saint-Lille turned to his second knight. "You take over for the rest of the afternoon. I need to visit with my brother." The knight bowed his head and waved the patrol men forward. Evrard reined his horse onto the lane leading to Gautier's country house. In the front court, a stableman took his horse. He stepped onto the porch and sounded the wrought-bronze door knocker. Gautier's wife Beatrice greeted him.

She laughed. "You needn't have come dressed for battle. Gautier's in a fine mood today."

"I left my patrol early. Father told me he took supper with Gautier last night, and I'd hear of it before my own turn with the old man."

Their five-year-old son ran out through a doorway with a wooden sword in hand and took stance. Evrard smiled. "Here's a fearsome young knight with a deadly blade at ready."

"Father's going to teach me how to fight, Uncle Evrard!"

The boy hugged Evrard around his right leg. Evrard tousled his hair. "Learn well from your father, and you'll be the toughest knight in France."

Beatrice put a hand on the boy's shoulder. "Bayard, go to the back court and practice there for a while. Uncle Evrard needs to visit with your father."

The boy ran off, and Evrard entered Gautier's private chamber. Gautier rested at ease in a heavy chair, feet propped up. "Brother! Come in and have a drink."

"I intend to."

Evrard sat and Gautier handed him a goblet of wine. "I had supper with Father last night and he told me of all of his plans for the future."

"To judge from your mood, his plans must be good ones."

"After my fight with Thierré and Roger de Lyon at Clermont, I was certain he intended to disinherit me, but he reassured me that I am yet his heir."

Evrard raised an eyebrow. "You're willing to serve under Odo?"

Gautier grinned widely. "More than willing. I promised Father I'll keep my peace."

"I trust you'll forget your pet quarrel with Roger de Lyon."

"That dog's cock has dishonored me too many times, but my patrimony is more important than the satisfaction of killing him. I'll let him be."

Evrard rose to leave and put a hand on his brother's shoulder. "Learn to rein in that bad temper. It might get you killed the next time."

Gautier nodded sagely. "I'm afraid you're right, Brother. When I take office, I'll want you as my viscount, before any other. You and Beatrice are the only souls who'll be able to keep me in line."

+ + +

At sunset, Evrard knocked at the door to his father's quarters, and Bayard welcomed his second son. They sat by the open window in the cool evening breeze, sipping fine old monastery wine. Shortly, a servant announced supper. They took places at the table, and reminisced on past hunting seasons and Christmas festivities, to be sorely missed over the coming expedition.

Bayard paused, growing serious. "Evrard, we're soon to leave for a long campaign, and our ages suggest you have the better chance of coming home alive. Last night, I spoke to Gautier in regard to my final wishes, and will now do the same with you. You recall the discussion we had as we rode home from Clermont?"

Evrard smiled. "You were never more yourself, Father. How could I forget?"

"I meant what I said then, and last night, I told him one fist fight will cost him his patrimony." Bayard looked his youngest son in the eye. "You'd best prepare yourself to become Count of Saint-Lille."

Evrard nodded in perceptive agreement, and Bayard continued. "If you and I both die in the course of the campaign, Viscount Odo will have the duties of count until he judges Gautier fit to take the office, or until his son Bayard comes of age. Your cousin Renauld will take the post of viscount, and the duties of count, should Odo die before his time."

"I think you've planned well, Father."

Bayard frowned. "I feel my years, and much remorse for a life fallen short of the ideal for a knight and just ruler. I pray to God I find release from my burdens in the holy expedition to come, and die at peace with Him in distant lands, if that be my destiny. Should I return home, I want only to pass the years that remain to me unburdened, in the company of your mother and our grandchildren."

"Then Gautier or I will become count on our return from the Holy Land?"

"That is my intention, and I truly don't expect Gautier will hold to the restraints I've put upon him. With this in mind, you can begin right away to lay the foundations for your own success."

Evrard put down his goblet, giving full attention to his father's words.

Bayard continued. "Before we leave, I want, above all, to begin to erase the dishonor that stains our family name. Last night, I told Gautier I've come to my own peace with the Coudre family, and have forsworn any vows I've made to harm them."

"The last time I heard you speak of them, you swore to kill Henri de Coudre and his sons. I was surprised at your friendly overture to Henri after Alphonse's death."

"I wanted that overture to signal a change of intent on our part, and your fool of a brother ruined it. Evrard, before the coming expedition, I want to make the first moves toward a new peace and friendship between our county and the Barony of Mirefleurs, and before I pass away, to see a conclusive end to our enmity."

"Those are honorable steps on your part, Father, and you've my full approval and support. What can I do to help you?"

"I'll soon be sending you as my emissary to Martin de Coudre. In your meetings with him, you'll make our position clear, pledge a truce for the duration of the expedition, and present our ideas for open borders, free trade, and a military alliance."

"I'm honored you would ask me, Father; yet, I have misgivings."

"Tell me."

"Gautier's capable of undoing all you want to accomplish. Confinement at Odo's fortress for the duration of the campaign might be the best measure."

"I know, but he's my first son, and I've tested his manhood enough. Odo will keep him on a short chain, and I can only thank God for our dear Beatrice. She can calm Gautier down more surely than ten knights set upon him."

Evrard chuckled. "How well I remember Gautier's consternation when he learned you'd chosen a lady ten years his senior to be his bride. Now, he swears he can't live without her."

"I'll gladly take the credit for that wise choice, Son. Now, have you left any concerns unspoken?"

"Father, I pray all of your decisions will prove right, but I can't say I have no doubts."

"Evrard, we'll soon speak again of the future. I'll consider any doubts you have with the most serious of mind, and act on them if reason proves it necessary. For tonight, I'm ready for another platter of beef and more of this wine."

JOSEPH SCOTT AMIS

Chapter 34

21 June 1096, Fortress Mirefleurs

Père Barnard read the last lines of the treaty agreement aloud and looked to the noblemen seated at the great hall table. "Might I answer any questions?"

Martin turned to Thierré. "You've read and all is in order, Sir Thierré?"

"All looks to be in order, Sire, and Count Bayard's seal and signature are properly affixed to the documents."

"Very good," Martin said. He nodded to Evrard of Saint-Lille and Viscount Odo. "Sirs, the documents need only our seals and signatures, and we'll have an agreement."

+ + +

Martin and Evrard walked together to Evrard and Odo's horses, waiting flanked by two Saint-Lille knights. The baron and the count's son gripped hands. "I'm grateful to you and your father for seeking to open a door long closed between us," Martin said.

"The Holy Father deserves the first praise, Martin. At Clermont, my father finally came to face his time might well be short. He wants to be remembered as a man who once brought war, but spent his last years repentant, as one who sought to bring peace."

"With God's blessings, we can look forward to a new era of friendship and prosperity shared between our demesnes. I'll pray He protect you and your father and bring you home safely, Evrard."

"Thank you for your prayers. Great responsibility will await me, should He grant my return."

30 June 1096, Grand-Forêt

A latch clicked open and hinges squeaked. Martin turned his head.

"Here's our last man, and not a moment late. Take a seat, Sir Renauld."

Renauld shut the door to the back room at the Grand-Forêt inn and took a seat at the table with Martin, Roger, and Jean. "What have you to tell us, Renauld?" Martin said.

"You know Gautier is to succeed as Count of Saint-Lille, even if Bayard should return from the pope's expedition."

"Yes."

"However, Viscount Odo will have full authority while Bayard and Evrard are away, and Bayard put Gautier under the strictest of conditions. He fully expects Gautier will break them, and Evrard succeed him as count."

Martin stroked his beard. "Hmm. Evrard said nothing of this during our meeting, save a hint when I bade him goodbye."

"You know Bayard's passion for secrecy, and I need tell you another thing."

"Please do, Sir Renauld."

"Bayard hinted to me and Odo that Gautier might have an accident, then smiled and winked."

Martin chuckled. "And the crafty old horse's ass claims he's repentant." He looked at Roger. "You wouldn't grieve overly much if a wild boar got the best of Gautier?"

Roger smiled. "I can't say I would, but a planned accident doesn't smack of repentance."

"Sirs," Renauld said, "I believe Bayard has truly become repentant, as do my father and Odo, but he's also a practical man who cares deeply for the future of our county. I can assure you, we can all look forward to peace between us for the duration of the expedition, and a firm alliance when it's over."

Martin frowned. "And what of the noblemen's revolt?"

"If Odo keeps the peace and abides by the treaty, any reasons for a revolt will fall away. But we won't cease watching and waiting for a moment."

"We're confident as well, Sir Renauld, but with Gautier yet free, I think we need to continue our meetings."

"I'll agree to that readily. His capacity for mischief knows no bounds."

+ + +

The serving girl Jenise crouched in her hiding place behind the back room wall, until the men departed at nightfall. Sir Gautier would be furious to learn what she had heard, but delighted to have the information, and, should God will, pay her handsomely for it. She straightened her clothes and hair, slipped into the back hall, and said goodnight to Rixende, before beginning the walk to her father's house, across the border in the County of Saint-Lille.

1 July 1096, Grand-Forêt

Michel awoke to loud rapping. Though his head throbbed from the previous night of drinking, he pulled himself up from the floor, took a long pull on his wine-flask, and straightened his clothes. He opened the armory shop door, to find the last man he wanted to see standing before him. "Uncle François!"

The heavy, well-dressed peasant stepped into the dirty, disorderly room, his jowly cheeks turning red as he looked around in silence. He opened a portfolio and handed a document to Michel. Michel stared at the parchment. "I can't read it."

"My loan to you is now in arrears, and this business has passed to my ownership. If you doubt me, I'll have the priest come and read it aloud."

Michel stammered, "D... do you mean to throw me out?"

"I have the lawful right to do so."

"That damned whore stole my coin. It's not my fault."

François glared. "I should slap you for those curses. Lisette is a good young woman who deserves all of the fortune she's gained. She took nothing from you, and any blame for the failure of this shop rests squarely on your shoulders."

Michel looked at the floor, and François continued. "I'm going to give you one more chance, and only because your father was my dearest brother. I will return one month from today. If you have this shop in order and open for business, I'll grant you terms for one year. Should you succeed in restoring the business to good reputation and fair profit in that time, we can discuss the terms for you to regain full ownership."

"Th… that's generous of you, Uncle. But I have no coin."

François handed him a weighty leather bag. "This is the last of my generosity you'll see." He sniffed the air. "When did you last wash? You stink of wine, as well."

At a loss for words, Michel gulped.

François opened the door. "I'll take my leave now."

Michel followed him onto the cobbled lane. François looked long and hard at the peeling blue paint on the door and the crooked, dirty sign. "This is a mighty shame for our family to bear. You'd best set down that wine pitcher and busy yourself." He shook his head and walked away.

Michel poured the contents of the leather bag onto the front room table, counted seven livres in gold and silver coins, and grinned drolly. His ill-tempered uncle had given him a more than fair amount with which to start afresh; indeed, nearly a small fortune. He took another long drink of wine, picked up a broom, and hummed a tune as he began to sweep the floor.

20 August 1096, Troyes

Joseph and Galien stood thirty feet apart, pointed steel tips on their measuring staffs held firmly against the top of the foundation wall, between two buttress footings. The master stonemason tied a cord around Galien's staff at the three-foot mark and walked to Joseph's location. He looped the cord around Joseph's staff, pulled it taut and tied it, and adjusted it to the same height. Joseph nodded, and the mason unhooked a sighting level from his leather tool apron. He bent to one knee and began to adjust the instrument.

"Master Joseph!" A priest from Bishop Ulrich's staff hurried to the architect.

"Can it wait, Father? We've an important sighting to take. The masons are to begin setting stones today, and I'd not delay them."

"I'm afraid it can't. His Eminence would see you and Sir Galien in his greeting room, right away."

Joseph asked the mason, "Can you give your men another task until we return?"

"Certainly, Master Joseph. They can begin sorting the stones in need of final cuts for your inspection."

"Good. Should we not return today, that will keep them busy and increase our ready inventory."

Joseph and Galien entered the bishop's quarters. Ulrich's face was grim. "Friends, I have no good news to share. Rather, I received a letter from Count Bayard this morning. He's suspended his next donation of a thousand livres, and any further funding, until he returns from the pope's expedition or his successor takes office as Count of Saint-Lille."

"What of the other largest donors?" Joseph said.

"Jaquelin d'Arcy's funds and Count Hugh's didn't arrive when promised, and I've had no word from either. Ludovico Santovini delivered his pledge, but it will sustain work for only a few weeks. I don't think we'll see more coin from any of them, and the regular flow of smaller donations has diminished to a quarter."

Joseph stroked his beard. "We've lost men already. Most of them have been laborers, but the pope's expedition is on the minds of all."

Ulrich got up from his desk, clasped hands behind his back, and turned, looking at the fresco of Christ and the Saints on the plastered wall. He took a deep breath and faced Joseph and Galien. "I'm now compelled to make decisions that will affect all involved with the cathedral. With a lack of funding from Count Bayard and the other donors, the work cannot continue long. What advice have you, Master Joseph?"

"We need to finish the crypt and seal it to the weather. Finishing the wall foundations at the choir will prevent the buttress footings there from shifting, and we must continue to lay foundations between the nave and transept buttress footings for as long as feasible. There is no good purpose in setting dressed wall stones at the choir."

"Very well. Inform the men. Busy them as you see fit to accomplish those tasks, but don't let anyone sit idle. If masters and journeymen find the tasks required beneath them, they are free to leave without censure."

"Yes, Your Eminence. What of Galien and myself?"

"I can pay your salaries only until the work we speak of is accomplished. I'm afraid you must seek other commissions to occupy you until we can again begin work on the cathedral."

"That might be years, Joseph," Galien said.

"I've enough requests for small work to keep busy here for a good year," the architect said. "Should I receive a large commission elsewhere, I'll be forced to leave Troyes."

Ulrich nodded. "Provision has been made for that possibility, Joseph. Your contract with the diocese is to be amended to give you first right of refusal when work on our cathedral can again commence."

+ + +

After supper at the inn, Joseph, Galien, and Lisette returned to the town house. Joseph said goodnight and went to bed. Galien and Lisette changed into their nightclothes, poured wine, and sat close together on the high-backed bench in their chamber. Galien stared through the open window facing the street, and Lisette squeezed his arm. "What now, dearest love?"

He kissed her forehead. "We needn't worry Joseph will lack for work. Most likely not a cathedral before this coming war is finished, but rich men still wait to hand him their silver."

"Then why are you so pensive? You hardly said a word at supper."

"It's Thierré's letter, the one that came last week."

"You read it and put it away without telling me what he wrote."

"You know the barony's lost Thierré and other knights to the pope's expedition. Martin is in dire need and asks that we come home right away. He wants to make me a knight in short time and have me take my place as a leading nobleman."

"We've stayed here far longer than the year your father gave you, and he hasn't become impatient."

Galien smiled. "He's a grandfather now. I think he's forgotten we exist."

"Joseph still holds out hope you'll decide to stay with him and become an architect. His heart will break when you tell him we're truly leaving."

"I'm loath to tell him, but he'll understand the reasons. What are your thoughts about going home?"

"I must confess… I've many doubts and fears."

Galien leaned back, crossing his arms. "Tell me all of them."

"To return home a noblewoman will be difficult at first, but it's something I must face eventually. And though your family has accepted me as your wife, I nurture the fear they might abandon me, should you die early."

"You're Father's daughter now, and a noblewoman, as much as Roger is a nobleman and his son. Our children will take their places as his grandchildren beside those of my sister and brothers."

"Your words are reassuring."

"Be assured beyond a doubt. Father loves you as his own, and any man who might dare question your place will need face him, Roger, and me. I wouldn't want to be in such a man's shoes, far less when Thierré returns."

"And Martin?"

"Though his feelings toward our marriage might have been unsure, he still loves you. His need for our presence, and his knight's honor, far outweigh his stubbornness."

"I'll fear for you when you become a knight."

"Only God knows what will come to pass. I might as easily be killed in an accident at the cathedral. Is there anything else?"

"With the mill to be under our charge, we'll need visit Grand-Forêt often, and I yet fear Michel."

Galien raised an eyebrow, grinning. "Then my first task will need be find an excuse to have him hanged."

"Galien! A Christian doesn't plan such things!"

"It's the warrior's burden, Lisette. A knight is bound by his oath to take lives if the cause be just, and can only pray God will accept his penance. Why do you think so many knights and men-at-arms gladly answered the pope's call?"

Lisette rubbed her temples, sighing. She took a drink. "Galien, I must tell you the truth. I've hoped you were planning to stay with

Joseph, and we would build our life here, but I took on the responsibilities of a noblewoman with our marriage."

Galien put an arm around her shoulders and pulled her close. "The pope's expedition has already taken so many of our countrymen away, and surely more will follow. I can only do what my mind and heart tell me best."

"And what do they tell you now?"

"We've still much work left to do to close down the cathedral grounds. I won't leave Joseph before it's finished."

Lisette kissed his cheek. "Galien, I'd expect no less. After all, you're a son of Henri de Coudre."

Thanks for reading!

If you enjoyed the book, please consider leaving a review wherever you purchased it.

Author's Note

To Shine with Honor began as a story of three Holy Land pilgrims compelled by circumstance to take up arms and participate in the events that led the First Crusaders to their successful siege of Jerusalem in July of 1099. However, the family of Henri de Coudre took on a life of its own in the first few pages, and what was intended to be a single volume evolved into a nine-hundred-page first manuscript of a three-volume tale that spans nearly thirty-five years in France and the Middle East; before, during, and after the First Crusade.

The fictional story is set in a framework of historical places and events constructed with careful reference to the works of leading historians and scholars of the present time, as well as medieval accounts, but as a fiction writer, I've also taken my fair share of literary license.

The settings of the Barony of Mirefluers and the County of Saint-Lille and all locations within them are fictional, as are the characters. These domains would be geographically located southeast of the present city of Clemont-Ferrand and west of the Loire River; in the late 11th century, within the Duchy of Aquitaine.

Saint Amand was a Frankish missionary bishop who lived in the sixth and seventh centuries and is a patron saint of wine and beer makers. The Abbé de Saint-Amand of *To Shine with Honor* is entirely fictional; named after the historical saint for the reason that its principal products are wine and ale. This location also serves as the setting for the greatest liberty with history taken in *To Shine with*

Honor, the account of the fictional architect Joseph of Reims and his role as the originator of "Gothic" architecture. The historical precedent for the great Gothic cathedrals of Europe is the reconstruction of the Abbey Church of Saint Denis located north of medieval Paris, under the patronage of the visionary Abbot Suger. This work began in 1135 and was completed in 1144; unfortunately, the name of the architect who worked closely with Abbot Suger to bring this magnificent church to completion has been lost.

In the creation of the characters of Joseph of Reims and his patron Abbot Leo, and the reconstruction of the church at the Abbé de Saint-Amand, I have adapted this historical account, transplanted it into the late eleventh century, and relocated it geographically.

The present Cathedral of Troyes was begun ca. 1200, after the previous Romanesque structure was destroyed by fire in 1188, making this a plausible location for the beginnings of a fictional Gothic cathedral in the late 11th century. The present Cathedral of Vienne was begun in 1052, was under construction at the time of the story, and is proximate enough to the fictional Barony of Mirefleurs for story purposes. Bishop Ulrich of Troyes is a fictional character; Archbishop Guy of Vienne, a historical person.

The fictional version of the address given by Pope Urban II at Clermont on November 27, 1095, was constructed using both present and medieval sources, principally the accounts of Fulcher of Chartres and Robert the Monk. Similarly, the scene with Peter the Hermit is a composite construct drawn from present and medieval sources.

The silver denier was the only currency minted in 11th century France, but due to a scarcity of precious metals, a variety of coinage could serve as legal tender. The livre, equal to a pound weight in silver, was the basic unit for accounting purposes, with 12 silver deniers equaling one sou; 20 sous/240 deniers, one livre. To avoid confusion, the livre and the denier are the only units of currency used in *To Shine with Honor*; for story purposes, one livre equals $1000 US, and one denier, about $4, "rules of thumb" suggested in a reference source. By this calculation, the amount of ransom paid for Count Bayard would be a large fortune today, but roughly equal in livres to the gross annual income of a similar nobleman of the times.

Knights play a prominent role in *To Shine with Honor*, and for the story context of the late 11th and early 12th centuries, their status and roles require clarification. By the late 11th century, the "sworn" or "dubbed" status of knighthood was in the process of adoption by the elite warrior class; the familiar trappings of chivalry, elaborate heraldry and costume, and knighthood reserved in law for men of noble birth were yet in the future. At the time of the story, an exceptional warrior not of noble birth could made a knight, and though this was a first step into the world of nobility, it did not automatically make him a nobleman. In the feudal system, nobility was the province of long-term landholders; the lands given as a fief by a superior lord. If the newly-made knight had the fortune of lands granted, and/or married well, his children and further descendants would come into nobility by process of assimilation.

An "ordinary" knight or adolescent nobleman would be addressed with the prefix "Sir" by social inferiors; among his peers and superiors, as a formal or casual honorific; "ordinary" noblewomen were addressed as "Lady" at any age. Knights in paid long-term service to a lord were usually called "retainers" or "household knights"; those employed for relatively short-term military service, "mercenaries."

"Father" as a title and address for priests of the Latin Church was not in use at the time of the story, but as it is familiar and often a term of endearment as well as reverence in present times, I have taken the liberty of using it.

Similarly, the use of the terms "architect" and "architecture" instead of "master builder" and simply "building" will strike some readers as historically inaccurate, as the former are considered to have come into wide use centuries after the events in *To Shine with Honor*. This is deliberate on my part, to emphasize the role as that of master designer and engineer as well as supervising master of actual building works. And lastly, to give honor due to my former profession and its part in inspiring the creation of Joseph of Reims and his grand cathedral.

JOSEPH SCOTT AMIS

Select Bibliography

Asbridge, Thomas, *The First Crusade - A New History,* Cambridge University Press, 2000

Asbridge, Thomas, *The Crusades - The Authoritative History of the War for the Holy Land,*
Harper Collins, 2010

Boswell, John, *Christianity, Social Tolerance, and Homosexuality - Gay People in Western Europe from the Beginning of the Christian Era to the Fourteenth Century*, University of Chicago Press, 2011

Carroll, Warren H., *The Building of Christendom*, Christendom College Press, 1987

Dass, Nirmal, *The Deeds of the Franks and Other Jerusalem-Bound Pilgrims*, Rowman & Littlefield, 2011

de Charny, Geoffroi, *A Knight's Own Book of Chivalry,* University of Pennsylvania Press, 2005

Fletcher, Banister, Sir, *A History of Architecture,* Nineteenth Edition, Butterworths, 1987

France, John, *Victory In The East - A military history of the First Crusade*, Cambridge University Press, 1994

Frankopan, Peter, *The First Crusade - The Call from the East*, Belknap Harvard, 2012

Gravett, Christopher, & Nicolle, David, *The Normans,* Osprey Publishing, 2006

Icher, Francois, *Building the Great Cathedrals,* Harry N. Abrams, not dated

Madden, Thomas, *The New Concise History of the Crusades,* Rowman & Littlefield, 2006

McGlynn, Sean, *By Sword and Fire - Cruelty and Atrocity in Medieval Warfare*, Phoenix, 2008

Neilson, George, *Trial by Combat from Before the Middle Ages to 1819 A.D.*, G.A. Jackson, 1909

Nicolle, David, *The Great Islamic Conquests,* Osprey Publishing, 2009

Oakeshott, R. Ewart, *The Sword in the Age of Chivalry,* Lutterworth Press, 1966

Oakeshott, R. Ewart, *Records of the Medieval Sword,* Boydell Press, 1991

Oldenbourg, Zoe, *The Crusades,* Pantheon Books, 1966

O'Shea, Stephen, *Sea of Faith - Islam and Christianity in the Medieval Mediterranean World*, Profile Books, 2006

Peters, Edward, *The First Crusade - The Chronicle of Fulcher of Chartres and Other Source Materials*, University of Pennsylvania Press, 1971

Riley-Smith, Jonathan, *What Were the Crusades? Fourth Edition,* Ignatius Press, 2009

Riley-Smith, Jonathan, *The First Crusaders, 1095-1131,* Cambridge University Press, 1997

Riley-Smith, Jonathan, *The Crusades, Christianity, and Islam,* Columbia University Press, 2011

Stark, Rodney, *God's Battalions - The Case for the Crusades*, HarperOne, 2010

Acknowledgments

I would like to give special thanks to those who have helped bring *To Shine with Honor* to reality:

Jennifer Sawyer Fisher, principal editor, and Mari Christie; editor, book and cover designer.

Rachel Moreno; map artist.

Randolph McKee, John S. Brown, and Clyde Phillips; steadfast readers throughout the project.

Vanessa Greatorex, Dr. Andrew Latham, and Deanna Proach; scholars, authors, historical editors, and critics.

Pim Wiersinga; author, teacher, and true man of letters, whose example has provided that great and intangible quality of inspiration.

J Stephen Roberts and Rand Lee Brown II; colleagues in Real Crusades History.

Dr. Helena Schrader; scholar, author, historical editor, and critic, who took time from her busy diplomat's schedule to give a last-minute critique and work with me to improve *To Shine with Honor* greatly.

Last, but certainly not least, my wife, Gayle, who has put up with a husband lost in the Middle Ages for the nearly eight years from first sentence to publication.

About the Author

Joseph Scott Amis retired from a thirty-year professional and business career in 2004. He has since devoted his time to medieval and Crusades studies, and writing of historical fiction. Scott is also a writer and managing editor at Real Crusades History. A native Texan, he lives in Dallas.

https://www.facebook.com/JSA.Literary/

About Real Crusades History

Real Crusades History is a historical society, focused on exploring the true story of the Crusades and dispelling the unfortunate myths surrounding them and medieval Christendom.

Real Crusades History Links:

http://www.RealCrusadesHistory.com
https://www.facebook.com/RealCrusadesHistory
https://www.facebook.com/groups/RealCrusadesHistory

Coming Soon

To Shine with Honor, Book Two: *A Trail of Blood*

Young nobleman Galien de Coudre finds his wits, skill at arms, and faith in God and himself tested to the extreme as he enters a dark forest of tragedy that rips his family asunder, and rides into blood-splattered battle in a war between ruthless barons vying for domination of his home lands in France.

As Galien clashes swords with fearsome enemies, his beloved elder brother Thierré de Coudre crosses a great river a thousand miles away, into parched and inhospitable lands occupied by hordes of fanatical and formidable warriors bent on annihilation of the Christian infidels. Thierré, taken to drugs to ease his longstanding pains of body, by prowess in battle yet earns renown and gains a friend and mentor in a powerful Norman aristocrat.

Will the devils striving to take Galien's soul drive him to destruction or to seek redemption in the far-flung Holy Land? Find out in the next exciting volume, To Shine with Honor: A Trail of Blood

To Shine with Honor, Book Three: *The Holy Land*

His demons vanquished and his loving, high-spirited wife at his side, Galien de Coudre embarks on a perilous journey by sea to the Holy Land, there to reunite with his brother Thierré and have his skill at arms and endurance tried to limits undreamed of in the bitter

struggle with Islamic forces for possession of the ancient and sacred city of Antioch.

In simmer of 1099, nearly four years after Pope Urban II made his historic call to arms, Galien finds himself before the mighty walls of Jerusalem, the city of Christ Himself, among the surviving corps of hardened fighting men resolved to capture the Holy Places for Christendom in a last desperate effort of which the fruits are certain: victory or death.

Will Galien finally have his life of peaceful scholarship, dreamt of as a young boy, in the new Kingdom of Jerusalem, or will he be compelled to once more take up his sword and journey long distances over land and sea to fight battles that will shape the lives of his descendants for the century to come? Find out in the final volume, To Shine with Honor: The Holy Land.

www.ingramcontent.com/pod-product-compliance
Lightning Source LLC
Chambersburg PA
CBHW021206250626

47155CB00008B/2703